Rest Beyond the River

H. L. Chandler

A Wings ePress, Inc.
Adventure Novel

Wings ePress, Inc.

Edited by: Jeanne Smith
Copy Edited by: Heather O'Connor
Executive Editor: Jeanne Smith
Cover Artist: Trisha FitzGerald-Jung

All rights reserved

Wings ePress Books
www.wingsepress.com

Copyright © 2019 by Louise Chandler Guffy
ISBN-13: 978-1-61309-626-0
ISBN-10: 1-61309-626-7

Published In the United States Of America

Wings ePress Inc.
3000 N. Rock Road
Newton, KS 67114

Dedication

To fiction readers who love to imagine 'what if?' Thanks for spending time with this story.

* * *

One

East of Flagstaff, Arizona on Interstate 40, Micah Jordan Hanson stopped for gas. He had come over one hundred and ten miles since he'd buried the old man in Peach Springs. Well, not exactly Peach Springs—Taylor had insisted his bones should rest in Nelson Cemetery. The slab of wood used for a headstone simply read *Taylor*. Micah never called the old man by any other name. As Micah fueled the 1979, faded-red Ford pickup, he shook his head in wonder over the last couple of days. He'd been hitchhiking out of Barstow when the old man stopped for him.

Micah had been headed to the only place he considered home, a piece of ground in the mountains outside Falls Creek, a little town west of Asheville, North Carolina. All these years later, the cabin on the twenty acres was probably near to falling down, but it didn't matter since he was the only one to live there. Knowing Jena and Jordan wouldn't be there with him, he closed his eyes against the hard knot of pain in his chest.

If he'd known why Taylor had picked him up, he might not have taken the ride. In the past few months, he had had his fill of death.

He'd be glad to die if he hadn't promised Jena that no matter how bad things became he'd fight to live. His beautiful Jena, only thirty years old. She and their five-year-old son crushed almost beyond recognition by an eighteen-wheeler with faulty brakes. Jordan died right away; Jena lingered for a little over a week, during which time Micah discovered he didn't know himself at all. He'd thought he was level-headed, always planning ahead, confident, making sure he and his small family were secure, a sensible man. Then he found he was none of those things.

One Friday afternoon at the end of February, while he worked in their little sandwich stand on the beach in Venice, California, a call came about the accident. Now, more than three months later, he was still stunned, in a mental fog, and so filled with pain he was amazed he could function at all. Nothing seemed real because his real life ended when Jena's did.

They had been married ten years. A simple ceremony, only a few friends attended the small church wedding. They neither one had close family, which was one of the things that drew them together. They planned to have a family, eventually a house, but first a business of their own, a make or break adventure. They had sky-high hopes, and were eager to work hard to achieve this goal. They rented space in an old hotel fronting the boardwalk; the building was broken up into apartments above and storefronts below. The unit they leased had one bedroom, a living room, bath, and kitchen above their commercial space. They named it Sandwich Heaven. It was his heaven, too. Five years ago another part of their dream came true—Jena was pregnant with Jordan—still she worked beside him until the day they went to the hospital.

As a little burble of gasoline sounded at the top of the pickup's tank, Micah quickly released the pump handle and dislodged the nozzle. Damn, he'd almost over-filled the gas tank, a good example of his mental condition. It made him doubt he'd make it to the cabin nestled in a mountain cove. He didn't question why he headed there... it was instinct; his granddad had lived there and left the property to Micah five years ago. Growing up, he had spent summers with his granddad. Those months in the green mountains, catching tadpoles in a dark, shallow woodland pond and sitting on the front porch in the cool of the evening, were the most peaceful times he had ever known. While his ten years with Jena had been the most exciting, the years he had felt completely alive. Now, regardless of his promise to Jena to live, he felt dead.

Micah screwed the gas cap in place, wiped his hands on the sides of his jeans, and went into the station to pay. He used cash. He still had credit cards, but they were too much a part of his past; he didn't plan to use them in the future either. What with the insurance companies in a tangle, it would probably take years to settle, and the mess with the landlord over giving up the lease on the business and the small apartment, the legal situation was enormous. Micah had found an attorney, and had turned the problems over to him. Next, he'd gone to the bank and drawn out their savings, a little over ten thousand dollars, filled a small backpack, and started walking east. The wreck had demolished their car and he had no desire to buy another; he left everything behind.

Crossing part of California to reach the beginning of Interstate 40 was something of a blur— there had been a taxi and a bus mixed in with some walking. When he had reached the junction of Highway 15 and Interstate 40, he had begun the trek in earnest. He had put one foot in front of the other; the heat of the pavement had come through the soles of his desert boots, while the band of his boonie hat soaked the sweat from his brow. It felt right to be walking. Maybe he could walk forever. He figured mileage, giving his battered brain something to do as his eyes squinted into the heat-waved distance. Barstow to Needles, one hundred forty-three miles. Walking twelve hours a day, maybe longer in the cool of the night, averaging a couple of miles an hour, twenty-four to thirty miles a day, at best it could take almost five days. Something in the back of his mind, left over from when he was a competent functioning person, said his journey was folly.

Now he was driving. The old man had insisted, and Micah hadn't felt like arguing, which was probably why he'd gotten into the old Ford pickup, that along with the small voice that warned against such a long walk.

He'd been standing beside the one-mile marker east of Barstow thinking about putting out his thumb, but before he could, Taylor pulled to the verge and motioned him over.

The pickup was a faded red; Micah judged it was near thirty years old, but as it idled on the roadside, the F-150 engine sounded okay. He hitched up his backpack and walked to the driver's side. The old man was rail-thin, bones with parchment skin stretched over them, his lips narrow and dry. The only life was in his burning blue eyes, like a butane flame. The first thing he said was, "You in any hurry to get where you're going?"

Micah shook his head. "No."

"Then get in."

Micah hurried around the front grille and opened the passenger side door. Both windows were down about nine inches to let in some air, but raised enough to shield from blowing road grit. He hadn't really expected the air conditioning to be working, and as if reading his mind Taylor said, "Bought it new back in seventy-nine. Engine is good; just didn't have the money for keeping up the extras."

Micah nodded. The way he felt, hell wouldn't be too hot for him, like a punishment for being alive when the two most important people in the world were not. He put his backpack between his feet on the floorboard. Behind him in the truck bed, a tan tarpaulin covered a load of some kind. The old man didn't say what and Micah didn't ask. Taylor pulled back onto I-40 and introduced himself.

"Name is Taylor. You?"

"Micah Hanson."

"Going far?"

"North Carolina."

"That is a far piece. Not in a hurry, though?"

"No reason to be."

They traveled on in silence for almost two hours. The great Mojave Desert stretched out to the north, miles and miles of hot sand, rocks, stubby bushes, and low gray hills in the distance. Taylor stopped for gasoline in Needles. Micah took advantage of the stop to use the restroom, and wash his face. As he walked back to the truck, a slight breeze cooled him through his sweat-soaked cotton shirt. He found Taylor inside at the cash register; he offered to pay for the gas but Taylor just shook his head. Instead, Micah bought a couple cans of ice-cold Coke. They stood in the shade of the station's over-hanging roof and drank them. Taylor turned his head away, but Micah saw him take some sort of pill with the drink. He tossed his can in a nearby trash barrel and Micah followed suit. When they reached the pickup, Taylor leaned against the bed, struggling for breath. Micah hurried to him.

"You okay?"

Taylor nodded, grimaced, making lines tighten around his bright blue eyes.

"Yeah. But how about you drive for a while?"

"Sure, sure. Glad to."

Micah took Taylor's arm and helped him into the passenger seat. He didn't like the old man's pasty color or the sweat running down the sides of his face. He quickly climbed into the driver's seat and Taylor handed him the keys. He put the truck in drive and carefully got back onto the highway. He kept glancing at Taylor.

"We're near town. Maybe you should see a doctor."

Taylor clenched his jaw and shook his head as he leaned back against the seat.

"If you do as I ask it'll be a big favor for me," Taylor said.

Keeping his eyes on the road, Micah raised an eyebrow; he wondered what price he'd be paying for this ride. Still, he could always stop, get out, and start walking again. He looked at Taylor.

"What is it you want, old man?"

Taylor didn't answer, so Micah drove on. They crossed the long flat bridge over the Colorado River near Topock. It was mid-afternoon. Micah didn't mind driving all night if the old man wanted to. Along about evening they'd need to find something to eat; however, from the looks of Taylor, he must live on air. Micah didn't have an appetite either. He hadn't kept track of his weight, but he'd tightened his belt several notches and his jeans were baggy in the seat. Neither the weight loss nor the long trip across the country meant much because his destination seemed as empty as what he'd left behind.

Interstate 40 turned north. Micah figured Kingman was maybe forty-two miles ahead, and they should probably stop there. He didn't even know where Taylor was going. He hadn't asked. It was another symptom of his scattered, numb, brain-dead condition. He nudged Taylor with his elbow.

"You awake?"

Taylor grunted.

"You didn't tell me where you're going. Kingman is up ahead."

"Kingman," Taylor muttered. "Yeah. Sixty-six takes off north near Kingman. Take that."

"Why?" he asked the old man.

Taylor coughed and straightened up a bit.

"I'm headed for Peach Springs. Hope you don't mind going out of your way. Sixty-six will hook up with forty around Seligman. You can head on east from there. I reckon forty will take you clear through to Carolina."

The old man slumped back, looking more tired than he had before; the speech seemed to wind him. Micah wondered why Peach Springs and how he'd hitch a ride from there to Seligman; maybe a bus ran on the Highway 66 spur, or Amtrak. Seems he remembered something about a scenic train route. It really didn't matter...he was still headed east, even with the detour off the interstate. At the turn, Micah took Route 66.

As the highway bent toward the east, the sun behind them put long, purple-blue shadows beneath the highway signs and the clumps of brittle bushes. The distant mountains developed dark skirts with sunlit tops, and the pickup's shadow ran down the pavement in front of them. Even the air seemed to take on a faint shade of blue, the landscape softer at the end of another day. Micah wore a wristwatch, but he rarely looked at it...without a purpose or responsibility, daylight or dark kept time close enough for him.

In a short while, they pulled into what was left of Peach Springs: a closed filling station with old glass-top pumps, and a few rundown stores. The best-looking building was a motel with an Indian motif as this section of old Route 66 ran through a small corner of the Hualapai Reservation. If tourists wanted to spend the night, the lodge seemed the only option. Micah slowed the truck. If Taylor didn't say something soon, they'd be on the other side of Peach Springs.

Taylor roused himself and pointed a shaky hand toward a side road. The remains of a long roofless whitewashed building stood on the corner. When Micah turned onto the dirt road, the gravel crunched and the dust flew. He rolled up his window and slowed to about fifteen miles an hour.

"How far?" he asked.

"Up there, just round the foot of that rise."

The road made a bend to the right and once around the curve there was a doublewide trailer parked at the back of a dried-out patch of ground. A sagging electric line ran from a tall pole to the end of the trailer. Off to the side was a shiny blue two-door sedan, a marvel in the dusty country. There was a carport beside the trailer, but the car sat in the open. Taylor thumped his fist on his thigh.

"Stop. Stop. This is it."

Micah pulled onto the wide area, bumping over a couple of rough spots. He stopped, turned off the engine, and looked at Taylor.

"Where are we?"

"Charlie Redman. He knows I'm coming." Taylor clawed at the door handle. "Help me out."

Micah jumped out and ran around to the old man's door. From the look of him, he'd not make it to the trailer on his own. Sure enough, his knees buckled. Micah put an arm around his middle and Taylor leaned against him. They started a slow shuffle toward the door. Micah wondered if he should yell or should have honked the horn...if he let go of Taylor to knock, the old man would probably fall.

When they were a few feet from the cinder block front steps, the door opened. A man nearly as old as Taylor, but in better shape, hurried toward them. He was shorter than Micah's six-feet, and on the plump side. He had black hair, obviously a dye job, but it went with his brown skin and brown eyes above a wide, thick nose. His face was round like his body; he wore a red, green, and blue striped shirt hanging loose over khaki pants.

Charlie Redman held out his arms to Taylor.

"You made it."

Redman took over Micah's job of supporting the old man and the two wobbled, staggered, and stumbled up the steps and through the door. Not knowing what else to do, Micah followed them into a front room filled with furniture: two sofas, one green and one brown, three blue recliners, several end tables, and a big screen television. Part of a kitchen was visible down a short hallway. Charlie led Taylor to the green sofa. Taylor fell more than sat and Charlie took his ankles and raised his legs to help him lie down. He grabbed a pillow from one of the recliners and tucked it behind Taylor's head.

Micah stood near a venetian blind-covered window, his hat in his hand, and felt invisible. He didn't think there was anyone else in the house; it seemed quiet and empty save for the three of them. From the look of the place, Charlie was a bachelor. If a woman were about, she'd surely have opened a window to freshen the place up a bit. Taylor raised his hand and pointed toward Micah.

"He helped me."

Charlie seemed to take notice of him for the first time. He looked toward Micah and said, "You're welcome to sit a while."

Micah took the recliner nearest the window.

"Thanks. Guess this is as far as Taylor is going. What's the chance of a bus or some other transportation from here to Flagstaff?"

Taylor motioned Charlie closer. "I need some water." He patted his shirt pocket. "And my pill."

"Right away, you bet."

Charlie rushed to the kitchen and came back with a large purple plastic tumbler. He took something from Taylor's pocket, helped him sit up, and held the drink to his lips. When he'd finished, Taylor seemed out of breath, but spoke again to Charlie.

"Out in the truck, the glove box, truck title. Get it."

Charlie nodded and started for the door. Micah beat him to it.

"Let me go. He seems to need you to stay with him."

"Yes. He does."

Micah found the truck title along with the original manual; it looked in as good condition as the Ford. He quickly jogged back across the gray/tan sandy dirt to the front door. It was much cooler in the trailer; he'd been so intent on watching the two men he hadn't noticed before. He handed the pickup's title to Taylor; the old man took it and laid it on his chest, his hand covering it. He moistened his lips and almost smiled.

"Charlie, I want Micah to have the truck. Better him than a chop shop. Help me sign it over."

"Sure. I'll get a pen."

Charlie hurried from the room and Micah frowned down at Taylor.

"What do you think you're doing? I don't want to buy your truck."

"Not buy. Give. Charlie don't need it. It's a good truck. You'll keep it up. It'll get you there."

Micah started to argue, but Taylor clenched his eyes, bared his teeth and a moan escaped from between them. "I'm dying," he gasped. "Casket is in the truck bed. Charlie knows what to do."

Charlie came back into the room with a ballpoint pen in hand.

"Yes, I do. We talked about this. Help me get him up so he can sign his name."

Micah blinked in confusion.

"You talked about giving me the pickup?"

"No." Charlie smiled, making his round face seem merry. "No, about helping Taylor to his final resting place."

"Oh."

Micah couldn't think of a worse resting place; he doubted anyone could turn the hard, dry ground to make a grave. There sure wouldn't be any green sod to cover the mound. It startled him to know the casket had been in the truck all this time. Another symbol of death, it seemed it was all around him. He slumped down onto the recliner and watched the two old men.

Charlie put a tray on Taylor's lap and helped guide his hand to sign the title. Charlie filled in the date and laid another piece of paper on the tray, which Taylor also signed. Exhausted, he fell over and Charlie quickly removed everything and helped him stretch out on the sofa. Taylor closed his eyes; a raspy breath slipped from his lips. If it were not for the shaky rise and fall of his rib cage, he would have looked dead already.

Outside, the sun was fast setting, leaving the hot land to slowly cool. The trailer grew almost dark and Charlie turned on the lamps on the two end tables. Micah didn't know what to do. He didn't want to invite himself to stay. Maybe he could get a room at the Indian motel on the highway. He stood.

"You want me to help you bring in Taylor's things from the truck? I didn't see a bag for him. Maybe it's in the truck bed along with the casket."

Taylor didn't move; he seemed asleep. Charlie went to the door and motioned Micah to follow him. They stepped out into the approaching night, and Charlie gently closed the door. When they reached the pickup, Charlie went about unfastening the ties holding down the tarp, and Micah hurried to help him. When they removed and folded the covering, Micah stared at the long wooden box with an American flag and a sprig of some kind of flower carved on the lid. Stuck down beside it in the bed stood a slab of the same wood with the word *Taylor* chiseled in the center. Charlie picked it up.

"Guess he got too tired to carve his whole name."

Micah started to ask what it was, but Charlie said, "Help me get the casket out. We can put it in the carport."

Sitting beside the grave marker and casket, there was a battered suitcase. Micah couldn't imagine what was in it, surely not clothes. Taylor wasn't going to need them unless he wanted to be buried in them. Micah wondered if when his time came, his mind would be clear enough to arrange his final resting place. Probably not. More than likely, he'd drop over in the cabin, or out in the woods somewhere. If he ever reached the cabin and if it should happen that way, it was fine with him.

He and Charlie struggled with the casket and finally got it positioned, along with the grave marker, and they stretched the tarp over them; it would keep most of the dust off. Although considering where the box would end, a little dust shouldn't hurt. Charlie picked up the suitcase.

"You got a satchel?" he asked.

"Just a backpack. It's in the cab. Suppose I better be going. It isn't far back to the motel. It didn't look busy."

Charlie frowned.

"You stay here. You can go in the morning. I'm not much of a cook, but I got some frozen pizza." He opened the door. "Come on."

"Okay. I'll get my backpack."

Inside, Taylor was asleep so they were quiet. Charlie took Micah into the kitchen where a small table and two straight-backed chairs stood in the middle of the room. Micah sat while Charlie went about arranging a meal, and he talked as he worked.

"Me and Taylor was born in this town, when it was a town. Out on road nineteen there was a big limestone quarry. Most men worked for the cement company." Charlie laughed. "Truth, it wasn't much of a town. Taylor and me went to school together and we joined the army together. Been friends all these years. Haven't seen each other much, both had families to take care of, got in touch more once we was both alone."

Charlie put the pizza into the oven, opened a couple cans of Coke, and sat at the table.

"I don't know who'll see to my burying. Have a son, but he's far away."

"Should we wake Taylor? He hasn't eaten anything I know of."

Charlie shook his head and took a drink of his Coke.

"I appreciate you letting me stay the night," Micah said.

"Think nothing of it. You'll be driving on down the road in the morning."

"I don't feel right about Taylor giving me the truck. You could sell it to help pay for the funeral. Or keep it yourself."

"I don't need it any more than Taylor does. I may last a bit longer; I'm a few months younger than him, but I got all I need."

Micah didn't want to ask the men their ages; however, he guessed they must be close to ninety. Charlie didn't show age like Taylor, but he wasn't sick.

They ate the pizza, and watched some news on television. Afterward, Charlie gave Micah a sheet and a pillow and pointed him to the brown sofa where Micah, more than falling asleep, felt as if he passed out.

Morning came quickly. Around six o'clock, Charlie gently shook Micah's shoulder.

"You awake?"

Micah blinked, sat up, and rubbed his hand across the whisker-stubble on his face.

"Yeah."

"Taylor is gone."

Micah swung his stocking-covered feet to the floor. "Where?"

"Slipped away around two-thirty."

Micah felt stupid. "Oh."

He and Charlie had bacon, eggs, and a second cup of coffee. Micah thought they should hurry.

"No rush now," Charlie said. "Taylor's beyond caring. I'd appreciate it if you'd give me a hand before you leave. We'll get him buried, and you can be on your way. If I'd thought Taylor was going so soon, we could have left the casket in the truck."

Micah helped clean and dress the body and put it in the casket. Taylor had lined the inside with foam and covered it with a striped sheet. Micah couldn't believe he was in the middle of the desert burying a man he'd met yesterday. They used the truck to transport the casket with Taylor's remains to his last resting place.

The cemetery was on a slight rise covered with gravel, sand, and some larger rocks. The place was unattended and only a few of the scattered graves had markers. One wooden cross leaned to the side, an arm touching the ground. If it weren't for a couple of tall uprights of rough wood holding a crosspiece with the cemetery name, and a few strands of barbed wire around one side, the whole site could blend into the landscape. A more desolate place Micah had never seen. How Taylor could rest easy here was a puzzle; still, a few years beneath the hot dry earth might mummify him for all eternity.

Charlie Redman had brought two shovels and ropes to lower the casket, also a big red cooler with iced water. He had thought of everything. The digging was hard dusty work; the nearest shade was at the foot of the distant mountains. A short, narrow-leafed mesquite tree beside the fence made a mockery of any sort of shade. As noon drew near, Micah began to worry about Charlie. He told him to sit in the pickup; both doors open he might catch a breeze. With sweat running down his face and his arms shaking, he agreed to rest. Micah zoned out as he dug and the hole became deeper and longer. This was insane; he'd be here digging for years. His hat started to drip with sweat, even the crown was wet. He wanted to take off his shirt, but feared a wicked sunburn. Just keep digging. Like walking, but instead of one foot before the other, it was shovelful after shovelful over his shoulder. Hot as blazes, wet as sop, his eyes burning from the salt, Micah dug, his muscles burned and his back ached. He'd dig to China if it kept him from thinking.

A pebble struck his shoulder. He turned and looked up. Charlie stood at the sloped end of the narrow trench; he was a wavy blur against a hard blue sky. Micah blinked the sweat out of his eyes. Charlie stuck out his hand.

"Climb on out of there. You one crazy fellow."

Micah grabbed the offered hand and let Charlie pull him up the slope. Charlie handed him a big plastic tumbler and he filled his mouth and drank; even the water was warm. With his thirst quenched, he looked at Charlie who laughed.

"Ice water not so good in a hot body. Might crack your radiator." He almost chuckled. "After you rest you can have something cooler."

All Micah could do was nod.

The pickup seat was hot but there was a small breeze and they were out of the direct sun. In the distance, a dried, loose bundle of sagebrush became a tumbleweed and skittered across the barren landscape. The land looked as dead as Taylor. Micah wiped his face with his shirtsleeve and frowned. They couldn't just plant Taylor out here; it could be against the law. What was he thinking to go along with these two crazy old men? He took another drink of water and handed the tumbler back to Charlie who asked, "More?"

Micah shook his head. "Listen, I've been thinking. Don't we need a death certificate, permission to bury someone? How do you know he's dead? There's got to be paperwork, even out here."

Charlie patted Micah's shoulder. "Don't worry. It's all taken care of. You must have noticed Taylor taking pills. He's had the help of a friendly doctor. A good guy from the old days. By the time he went to the doctor, it was too late. Taylor was done with living anyway. The doc helped him with enough pills to keep the pain down to a roar, and he'll file a death certificate when I give him a call."

"Still, it doesn't seem right."

Charlie held up his hand. "I know. Not by the rulebook, but who's to know? They sure as hell can't hold Taylor accountable. Me? I'll probably be out of reach before anyone notices. And you? Who besides me and Taylor know you're here?"

Micah squeezed his eyes shut and shook his head. The world was getting crazier and crazier.

"Wait. What about the pickup? I can't drive off under these conditions. I admit it would help me get where I'm going, but is it legal?"

"All taken care of. The other paper Taylor signed was a bill of sale. All you need to do is sign it. I signed as a witness to the sale. It along with the title will let you register the truck when you get settled."

"No, no. I can't buy a car from a dead man."

Charlie heaved a sigh. "You *are* one crazy fellow. Nobody knows when you and Taylor got here. I dated the title and sale a week ago. You paid one dollar and other considerations. Between us, the consideration was you driving him here. No one is going to question it."

Micah took the plastic tumbler and held it under the spout of the big water cooler. He filled it, drank the whole thing, and wondered if he'd fallen into some alien universe. Charlie got out of the truck and motioned Micah to follow.

They lugged the casket to the side of the grave. The wind had already blown some of the dirt back into the hole. They arranged the ropes under the wooden box and lowered it to the bottom of the trench. Micah's heart pounded. This was nothing like the burial of his family, but it hurt almost beyond bearing because there was nothing to soften it, no music, no flowers, or a canopy over the gravesite. This was death in the raw. The end of life. No matter how long a person lived, this was the result. How could people go on, knowing life meant no more than this? If the world had a king, he would die the same as Taylor...death made life pointless. Either humans lived under a cloud of denial or they were insane. Micah wondered which one he was.

He and Charlie each took a shovel and started filling the hole; they moved slowly... no need to hurry. As they neared the end, Micah dropped his shovel and retrieved the grave marker from the truck bed. They placed it, filled in around it, and finally gathered large rocks to place at the base to keep it upright. Over time, the wood would weather and decay. In years to come, Taylor's grave would look like the other unmarked mounds; there'd be nothing to show he lived this life. Micah must have spoken aloud.

"Sure there is," Charlie said. "He had a daughter. She had two sons. They have children."

"Where are they now?"

Charlie shrugged. "The daughter passed away. The son-in-law remarried."

"Maybe we should say something over his grave."

"You can if you feel like it. Me and Taylor said what needed to be said around midnight last night."

Micah took off his hat and looked down at the mound of rocks and grit at his feet. All he could come up with was, "Good bye, and thanks for the ride."

Charlie picked up the rope and one of the shovels.

"We're finished. Don't look sad, he's in a better place. Left this world of toil and trouble and went to his reward. We're just cleaning up after him."

Micah kept quiet. If Charlie felt better thinking that, more power to him.

Back at the trailer, Micah parked the pickup beside Charlie's car. He didn't know if he should stay for a while or move on. It still felt strange to take the Ford; yet, it would be stupid to turn it down. The two old men seemed to think they had made it legal, and even in his confusion Micah thought it was. He'd go to the department of motor vehicles in North Carolina to register the truck. If stopped on the way, the transfer papers should be enough, and if they weren't it didn't matter. After losing the only ones who made his life worth living, nothing worse could happen to him.

"You're welcome to stay the night," Charlie offered.

"I better go on. I won't ever get over Taylor giving me his truck. And thank you for the night's sleep and the meals."

"Come on in. I'll get the truck's papers. Stay a while if you want, but it isn't far to Flagstaff. Even driving slow you should make it in a couple of hours."

Micah followed him into the trailer and smiled.

"It will probably take that long. Taylor didn't want me driving over fifty or sixty. He took good care of the engine."

Charlie nodded as he handed Micah the documents, all signed by William Taylor. He'd had a first name after all, but he was still just Taylor to Micah. They went back outside and Charlie stood on his cinder block steps and waved as Micah drove away. The dust billowed behind him, finally hiding Charlie Redman.

Two

Twilight fell over the Arizona desert as Micah drove east toward Winslow. Charlie had been right; he'd reached Flagstaff in less than two hours. The Ford was humming along. When he'd stopped for gas outside Flagstaff he'd checked the oil and other fluids. He admired Taylor's faithful maintenance of the truck. Air conditioning would be nice, but he could do without it, even in the humid Smoky Mountain summers. Micah was inclined to keep the pickup as a sort of tribute to Taylor; there should be something to show the man passed this way. A new paint job and the old Ford F-150 might be a showpiece. The interior wasn't bad, but even it could stand some restoration. Micah ran his hand around the rim of the steering wheel.

His encounter with the two old men was a puzzling experience. It left him with the feeling there were no strangers in this world, and when the need arose, most people could work together. Yet, the strife and anger among races and nations portrayed on television put the lie to his reasoning.

East of Winslow, the traffic grew thin with fewer big trucks, but each one a grim reminder of his loss. Past Holbrook, the evening traffic increased. While the sun sank below the western horizon, the brown and amber land turned to lavender. Minutes later, the wind started blowing; the gusts came fast and strong. For a bit Micah wished there was a data plan on his phone; internet would be helpful. Instead, he tried the pickup's radio. Amazingly it worked. Micah moved up and down the dial seeking a news or weather report. He found mostly static. The wind increased along with the radio's irritating crackle and screech, so Micah turned it off. Sheets of dust swept across the interstate, a sand storm in the making.

On the westbound lanes of the highway, a Winnebago motor home swayed in the wind. Micah rolled up both windows and closed the small rear window slider; he put the headlight beams on high and drove on through the gathering darkness. He'd hoped to have an hour of twilight left, but the storm was whipping up enough grit to hasten the night. If they didn't shut down the interstate because of the storm, Micah intended to tough it out, keep going with hopes of driving out the other side. He'd checked the mileage from Flagstaff to Gallup and with the old truck steady on sixty it should take around three hours. The vague idea was to reach Gallup and see how he felt… to stay the night or drive on was a toss-up.

About fifteen miles east of Holbrook, tiny bits of sand pinged against the metal doors and hood. The truck's surface was already in sad shape; maybe the scouring sand would save removing the old paint if he decided to refinish it. With each passing minute, the storm grew stronger, to the point the headlights didn't penetrate more than a few yards into the darkness. Micah hadn't been feeling much other than dismay and sorrow; now anger simmered. All he wanted was to get out of this dry deserted land and to his refuge in the green mountains. He needed healing, not sandblasting in this dark sweltering heat, and what if the engine clogged? Maybe he should pull over and wait it out.

Before he could decide, headlights blazed through the murky night…something was coming toward him from the left. The minute the plunging car became visible, Micah instinctively pressed on the gas and the Ford shot ahead into the dark. He misjudged the highway and plowed into the raised sandy verge on the right. Behind him, a car had jumped the divider. It landed on the eastbound pavement. Directly behind it, a huge tractor-trailer twisted and tumbled; the screech and groan of tortured metal was loud over the howl and whistle of the wind. The truck cab stopped short of ramming the car as the wreck piled higher.

Breathing hard, Micah leaned forward across the steering wheel; it took a second before he had sense enough to kill the engine. He was shaking, trembling from head to foot as the wind howled and horns began to honk. He grabbed his phone, punched in 911, and his voice shook as he reported the accident. The operator assured him help was on the way. This section of Interstate 40 was about to be shut down because of the dust storm; he was to stay where he was. With the sand swirling in the darkness, he wasn't sure what he could do other than sit in the truck and wait. In the rearview mirror, he saw the headlights of the wrecked auto shining toward the south. He thought the first one was a small car, and the one behind it a huge truck and trailer. He saw something flickering, like a small flame.

Micah opened his backpack and took out a pair of sunglasses; insane in the dark, but he needed to protect his eyes. He grabbed a spare shirt and tied it around his head, wrapping most of his head and shoulders. It took all his strength to push the pickup's door open. Outside, he staggered against the strong wind to reach the pileup; he could barely breathe, and the blowing sand pelted him. His mind swirled like the desert wind, while multiple sirens wailed in the distance. A pause in the wind cleared Micah's vision; it appeared the big rig had run upon the car, probably not seeing it in the storm, and thrown it across the median. The back of the semi was still partly in the westbound lanes; traffic backed up behind the two-vehicle wreck, making a string of blurry headlights stretching in either direction.

When he reached the small car, the trunk was smashed forward nearly to the back seat; he peered through the cracked side window. A young man was slumped over the steering wheel, the windshield shattered. Beside him, the passenger airbag had deployed. Micah hurried to the other side of the car...an airbag hid her face, but from the screams and waving arms it appeared the passenger was a young woman.

Micah tugged at the passenger door, it came open, and the young woman kicked and clawed against the airbag. Micah thrust his arms into the car and crammed the airbag down into the floor. As the young woman screamed and fought to be free of the seatbelt, Micah tried to help her and she looked up at him with frantic, wide blue eyes.

"Help him, help him," she yelled.

Micah nodded and reached to take the girl's arm.

"Are you hurt?"

She said no, but blood was running down the side of her face. Micah wasn't sure what to do; moving injured people wasn't smart. The wind picked up a bit and hurled sand into the car.

"Help is on the way; sit tight."

Micah looked around, searching for the flickering flames he'd seen. If there was fire, these people needed to get out. He shut the door and made his way toward the big truck's cab. The driver was halfway out, holding onto a bar near the door, while his feet rested on the step. Micah reached him and leaned in close.

"Are you okay?"

The driver looked dazed but nodded. Micah pointed to the worrisome flickering light.

"Is there fire?"

The driver lowered his feet to the ground and kept his head down to protect it from the wind.

"No," he shouted. "I set flares."

Micah left him sitting on the truck's lower step and struggled across the highway divider to see what was happening to the westbound traffic. In the limited visibility, he saw several cars backed up; the first three or four had bumped into the ones in front of them. Micah went to the back of the big rig where the driver had set three flares. He took one and headed down the line of cars. At the end, he placed the flare about ten feet from the last car. If the wind let it stay, it might warn on-coming traffic. When he returned to the truck, the driver was on his CB radio. Micah left him and went back to the small car where the couple remained inside. The wind had abated to the extent Micah could walk without leaning forward; his mouth was dry and even with glasses grit scratched his eyes. He opened the back door and squeezed into the car. The girl turned to look at him.

"He won't wake up." Her voice cracked.

"Help is on the way; the sirens are louder. Can't you hear them?"

She nodded, but the panic on her face said she hardly knew what she was saying.

Micah understood the feeling. He still wanted to get the couple out of the car, as it didn't seem safe for them to stay there. Time stretched out; the sound of police and ambulance went on forever, never reaching the injured drivers. Distant headlights came from the west. Micah couldn't sit and wait; he told the girl to stay calm and climbed out of their car.

Outside, several men from the line of backed-up cars had clustered around the truck. Micah walked to the driver.

"Do you have any more flares?"

The driver gave Micah a pouch of three flares. Micah and two of the men went along the eastbound lanes, waving the flares to alert the oncoming traffic. As one of the men stood waving a flare, the first car slowed and stopped. Micah and the other man placed their flares along the highway at ten- and twenty-foot intervals. It was just in time, as two more cars neared the accident site. A tall black man got out of the first car and asked what was wrong, and Micah left the three men to deal with the eastbound traffic. With more headlights blazing and the wind slacking, visibility was better at the crash site. With luck, there would be no fatalities, although several of the men gathered around the big truck spoke of banged heads and bruised knees. Two had deployed air bags.

At last, two police cars arrived along with an ambulance, and the uniformed men quickly took control of the area. When the ambulance pulled to a stop, Micah rushed to one of the paramedics; he pointed to the car and told him about the young man, then followed him to the car. The medic checked the girl, helped her to stand, and took her place in the car to check on the young man. The wind was still blowing, but not as fierce. Micah led the girl toward the back of the ambulance where two attendants were assessing the truck driver. With the arrival of official help, the scene turned active, and Micah decided there was nothing more he could do. As one of the medics dressed a cut on the girl's head, he started to leave.

"Don't go," she called.

Micah turned back.

"Please, I don't know what is wrong with Kyle. Can you find out for me?"

Micah nodded and trudged back to the car; it was a black Toyota. The medic was still inside the car with a man Micah now knew as Kyle. Micah climbed into the back seat.

"Is he going to be okay?"

The paramedic turned toward Micah.

"Maybe. Hope so. Need to get his neck stabilized. You know him?"

"No. The girl with him asked me to check on him."

Kyle still wasn't conscious, but Micah didn't see any blood.

"Is he breathing?"

The medic nodded. "We'll need to get the driver's door open to get him out. Can you stay here and watch him for a bit?"

"Sure. What should I do if he wakes up?"

"Nothing other than keep him still and calm. I'll be right back."

Suddenly the night seemed foreign. Shafts of yellow from headlights pierced the dark, red and blue lights from police cars and ambulance whirled and blinked, turning the area into a carnival; only the hurdy-gurdy music was missing. The surreal scene was a dark replay of what had ruined his life. Micah leaned forward from the back seat and studied Kyle. He looked to be in his twenties with soft brown hair, probably brown eyes; the side of his face toward Micah was smooth with even features. He and the girl, they were probably a couple, maybe married. Micah leaned closer, searching Kyle's left hand for a ring, and found the band of gold. Micah hoped, with all his heart, Kyle was not seriously injured.

Mercifully, the storm calmed a bit more. Micah unwound the shirt from his head and folded it in his lap. Shortly, a wrecker was on the scene, and at the direction of the police, the first order was to get Kyle out of the car. When the medic returned and got into the car beside Kyle, Micah got out. Looking around the busy area, he didn't see any more he could do, so he started toward Taylor's pickup. He still had trouble thinking of it as his own. As he passed the ambulance, the girl came toward him, a white bandage on her forehead. Her blonde hair hung limp and damp around her thin, drawn face.

"Sir," she called, waving. "Wait a minute, can you?"

Micah stopped and waited for her. She was wearing jeans and a blue cotton blouse. When she reached him, she held out her hand.

"I'm Myra. Kyle is my husband; thanks for staying with him. The medic told me he'll have to go to a hospital in Holbrook. We live in Downey, California. We have been visiting family and were on our way home." Myra put a shaky hand to her forehead. "I don't know what to do. I want to stay with Kyle, but what about our car, and our things in it?"

Micah looked around; another police car was on the scene, and a second tow truck had arrived. It appeared they were making headway, removing Kyle from the car and onto a nearby stretcher. Myra pointed toward her car.

"I don't know if they can get him out. They can, can't they? They told me to stay back. Do you think he's okay?"

She seemed to be ready to fly apart. Micah shrugged.

"I don't know his condition; the medic said he's breathing and they've put a brace on his neck."

Myra's hand covered her mouth, stifling a sob, and then she lowered her head and cried, great gasps shaking her whole body. Micah's heart beat faster and he wanted to run, but he couldn't leave her like this.

"Look, I'll stay with you. Come on, they have him on the stretcher."

Myra clutched his arm and started toward the advancing stretcher, where an IV bottle hung above Kyle and a medic was on either side of the gurney. When Myra reached Kyle, she leaned forward, repeating his name, and kept pace as they hurried to the back of the ambulance. Inside were two women, one with a bandaged arm, the truck driver, and three small crying children; there didn't seem room for Kyle. However, they loaded the stretcher and the ambulance was ready to leave. Myra looked from the ambulance to Micah, back and forth.

"I need to go with Kyle. But there's no room and what about our stuff?"

She was wringing her hands, and Micah knew he had no choice.

"Come on. I'll help you."

As the ambulance, siren wailing, took off, Micah pulled Myra toward her car, while she kept looking back at the departing ambulance. One of the wreckers had pulled the car farther away from the cab of the truck, while the police were busy speaking with drivers of the long line of cars near the accident. The last thing Micah wanted to do was give some kind of statement. Instead, he cornered the wrecker's driver, and pointed to Myra.

"This is the car's owner. Her husband will be in a hospital in Holbrook. She can give you their information. Will you let her get their belongings out?"

The wrecker driver was agreeable, so Myra unloaded two suitcases, a large box, and found her purse under the front seat. With all the baggage sitting at her feet, she dug through a billfold and provided the wrecker with the information he needed. With the injured cleared away, the police began moving some traffic along, and the wreckers starting towing the damaged vehicles away. The wind had lessened; now it only whipped clothes and hair around, leaving most of the sand on the ground.

Micah led Myra to Taylor's pickup.

He put Myra's baggage in the pickup bed, threw his backpack in after it, and helped Myra into the truck. As talkative as she'd been before, now she was quiet, pale, and silent in the dark. It was well after midnight and Micah thought they were about fifteen or twenty miles east of Holbrook. He started the truck, made a left turn, and drove carefully across the median. The truck bumped and bounced, but made it to the westbound lanes where the traffic was starting to move as a patrolman waved the cars forward. Micah slowly passed by the rear of the semi, then picked up speed, heading in the wrong direction for him. No question of making Gallup this night.

Still, he couldn't have driven away without trying to help. Maybe one of the tow truck drivers could have given Myra a lift, or perhaps the police would have, but too late to think of that now. He regretted making the offer; he should have driven on the minute he saw what was happening. Even driving slowly through all the dust, he could have been nearly a hundred miles closer to Gallup. Now, it was possibly fifteen miles west to Holbrook, the same fifteen miles to get back to where he'd been nearly two hours earlier. If such delays continued, it might be fall or winter before he reached North Carolina! As the lights of Holbrook appeared, Myra placed a tentative hand on his arm.

"Do you know where they took Kyle?"

"No. Don't worry, we'll find it."

"I am so grateful to you. I don't know what I'll do while Kyle is in the hospital. I don't even know if he's okay. I should have crowded into the ambulance. What shall I do? We were visiting in Little Rock."

"Arkansas?" Of course it was; he didn't know of any other Little Rock.

"Yes. I have a cousin there; I can call her." Myra picked up her purse and rummaged through it. "I have a cell phone in here someplace. What time is it? I wonder if Crystal will be awake."

Micah silently drove on. He didn't know the answer to her questions; he had plenty of questions about his own life. Myra retrieved her phone but just held it in her lap, put her head down and softly cried.

Micah drove faster.

~ * ~

Very early the next morning, the far horizon turned pink and the dark night brightened to a grayish blue. The day dawned cool and dry, the rocky landscape fresh and innocent of the previous night's tantrum. Micah sat in a booth drinking coffee. Across from him, Myra, her face washed clean of any makeup, looked younger than she had at the site of the wreck. She still seemed shaken, but she could smile. She had replaced the small bandage on her forehead with a Band-Aid.

"How can we ever thank you? I don't know what I would have done."

"That's okay."

"But this has surely taken you out of your way and delayed you. Is someone waiting for you?"

Micah shook his head and pushed away the dirty plate, empty of two eggs and bacon. He'd eaten because it was the sensible thing, he was too tired to argue, and Myra had insisted on buying him breakfast.

When he'd delivered Myra to the hospital, he meant to leave Holbrook for a second time, reaching Gallup by morning. Instead, here he sat in a cafe staring out a grimy window feeling as empty as he had when Taylor picked him up outside Barstow. Myra smiled at him.

"You haven't said where you're going. Guess it is none of my business. Just you are so much help, like an angel when we needed one. Your truck wasn't damaged, which is a miracle in itself."

Micah managed a half smile, and nodded.

"I was lucky to get out of the way."

"Well, whatever it was, I'll not forget how you helped. If you're going as far as Little Rock I want you to be sure and call my cousin, Crystal, if you need anything at all."

Micah had the piece of motel notepaper with Crystal's phone number tucked in his shirt pocket. He couldn't imagine any circumstances in which he'd call her, yet it had seemed rude to refuse to take the information. He was glad Kyle was not badly injured: a couple of cracked ribs, possible concussion, and a badly bruised shoulder. The doctor was going to release him later today. Since his air bag had failed to inflate, he and Myra would probably have months of dealings with the automaker.

When they'd arrived at the hospital, Myra had begged Micah to go in with her, and again, he couldn't refuse. They had been there almost two hours and, after Myra spoke with the doctor and sat by Kyle's bedside, Micah had tried to say goodbye. Kyle had been conscious enough to offer his thanks. When he had started out the door into the hospital hallway, Myra had followed him and asked for one more favor. Could he drop her off at a motel on his way out of town?

A Best Western was close by with available rooms. Again, Micah saw his way clear to leave, but not until he had carried the two suitcases and the big box into the motel room for Myra. She had thanked him and said their last name was Clayton, and he'd be welcome in their home anytime he was in California. Micah filed it away under useless information; California was the last place he expected to revisit. He had his attorney's name, address, and phone number; he'd use long distance to handle any unsettled business in California. The attorney was charging a hefty fee...let him earn it.

With Myra checked into the motel, a helpful desk clerk had arranged for a rental car, which she could pick up around eight in the morning. Micah saw it coming: she'd need transportation to the rental agency; surely, there'd be no need of him afterward. However, he did catch a break...the agency was going to deliver the car. He had lost hours of travel time, and it was almost morning. Micah was all set to be on his way, except he hadn't had the energy to refuse having breakfast with her.

"I insist," she had said. "Just let me freshen up and we can find a place to eat."

He had to admit the food helped.

The waitress refilled their coffee and Micah started to pick up the check. Myra shook her head and grabbed it.

"I told you, this is the very least we can do. Drop me at the motel and you can be on your way. I'll pray for you, Micah. I hope you have a good trip and get wherever you are going safely."

Micah's eyes grew damp and he ducked his head. He was tired and stressed out; life had hit him hard these past months. Adrift in an alien world, his only anchor the cabin in the mountain cove, he felt vulnerable, but once across the Mississippi he'd be okay. When he could trust his expression, he looked up and smiled.

"Thank you. It was good to have company for breakfast, better yet to have them pay."

They both laughed. Myra took her purse, scooted across the booth seat, and stood. Micah followed her.

The pickup was parked nose-in to the diner, and while they ate, three other cars had arrived. The sun rose fast and it cast a golden glow over the town, turning adobe bricks a bright amber; already the air felt hot and dry. There was still a lot of desert to cross before reaching some cooler areas. Myra took her place in the pickup and he drove back to the motel. As if she knew he'd not appreciate a long goodbye, Myra patted his arm and opened the door.

"You be careful. And thanks again."

Micah watched as she stepped to the motel door, turned, waved once, and unlocked the door. He waved back, put the Ford into reverse and backed into the parking lot, made a sharp turn and headed for Interstate 40.

Myra had said they would release Kyle that evening; they'd stay at the motel one night, possibly longer depending upon how Kyle felt and the condition of their wrecked Toyota. The Claytons should be okay, and Micah was glad.

He thought about stopping in Gallup to find a bed; however, he'd probably keep driving. He was too numb to be tired. Besides, with Gallup only around one hundred miles away, it would be too early to stop; maybe he'd rest in Albuquerque. A warm breeze blew through the pickup's window, ruffling his light brown hair and fluttering his shirt. If he made good time, he could reach Tucumcari by late afternoon...it felt like a plan. He could drive another seven or eight hours; he'd get there around four or five, find a motel and hope he could sleep!

Before leaving Holbrook, Micah had filled the gas tank, and headed east driving the same fifteen or twenty miles he'd driven before. The stretch of Interstate 40 didn't look any better traveling it a third time, and this time the sun was blazing straight into his eyes. He took out the sunglasses, tried to wipe the dust off the lenses, and put them on. They weren't much help. By noon, he was past Gallup, New Mexico and well on the way to Albuquerque. He watched the traffic closely; he'd had enough of wrecks. The big trucks pounded along, making him grateful for the divided highway; he rarely passed any vehicle, and sometimes hung back to ride in a space empty of traffic. The whoosh of road noise and the hot wind beat about his head and he squinted into the bright day.

He reached Albuquerque around two-thirty, where he stopped to eat and fill the pickup's tank. Standing beside a gas pump, he stretched his legs and arched his aching back. He should find a motel and get some rest; there was no hurry, and no one was expecting him, no one in the whole world. Some people might consider this freedom, but to Micah it was like being inside a gigantic empty bubble. Nothing in there and no way to get out.

As he shut the truck's door and settled onto the worn driver's seat, the journey to reach the cabin drove him; it was his only goal and if he didn't complete it he might as well be dead. True, no one was waiting for him in North Carolina, or anywhere else; still it was the only place he could imagine going. If he gave any thought to what he'd do when he arrived, it was to park the truck, go inside, and make it livable; any plans beyond those were lost in a pale blue haze. For now, his reality was mile after mile of road, and day after day of travel, alone and struggling to adjust.

Three

When Micah reach Tucumcari he was past caring about anything other than food and sleep, and it was possible sleep felt more important. He hadn't slept since leaving Charlie Redman's trailer. He stopped at a Best Western, parked the truck, and opened the door to the cool, dark room. He dropped his backpack on the long bench beside the television, staggered to the bed and fell across it. He managed to remove his boots before straightening out and resting his head on one of the puffed-up white pillows.

He hadn't checked the time when he entered the motel room, but when he awoke at six the next morning, he guessed he'd slept twelve hours. His eyes were dry and gritty as the desert sand storm. It hurt to blink, and his clothes were stiff. He rolled off the bed, hobbled to the air conditioning controls, and turned it down to seventy. In the bathroom, standing over the stool, he managed to empty a bladder holding surprisingly little liquid; he needed to drink more. He pictured Jena's blue eyes narrowing and her soft lips pursed as they always did when scolding him. "Okay, sweetheart. I'll remember." He didn't realize he'd spoken aloud until the sob that followed startled him.

He knew from experience, this was a crucial moment. If he didn't get busy, he'd break down. The second sob tightened his throat, choking him, and salty tears made his eyes burn. Micah clenched his teeth until they felt near to cracking and tore off his sweat-stained shirt. Completely stripped, he stepped into the bathtub, turned on the shower, and stood under the spray until he'd regained some control. Micah had cried at the funeral, it was like death claiming him; no one could live through such pain. Afterward, he'd done his best not to cry.

Once showered, he managed to shave. The face staring back was thin, the jawbone square and prominent. The brown eyes were blank, with no light behind them; the gold flecks had died out. With his face dry, he pulled on a tee shirt hiding an upper body stripped of fat; the muscles of his arms, chest, and abdomen stood out well defined. Three months of no California beach time and already the tan was fading. He didn't plan ever to see another ocean. It would remind him of time with Jordan, playing ball and taking the boy out on a boogie board. He didn't need those memories, not if he kept his promise to Jena, because such thoughts would surely kill him.

The morning news on television helped distract him. More terrorist attacks, thank God not in this country...this time. He was patriotic; he loved his country, and would fight to defend it. While married, he never thought of re-enlisting. He was busy with day-to-day survival, like millions of Americans, trying to live a decent life. Now, at forty, he was too old even with a credit for the six years he'd served, and his heart wasn't in it.

He had a change of clothes in the backpack, wrinkled but acceptable. He crammed the dirty underwear and jeans into a paper laundry bag. When he started to stuff his shirt into the laundry, he found the note with the number of Myra's cousin. Out of habit, he added the number to his cell phone's contacts before throwing the note in the trash. He'd have to do a wash sometime, but for now, Walmart could supply clean clothes. The mountain cabin had an enclosed back porch with a washroom; he remembered an old wringer type washer, an antique, and it would be a match for the

Ford pickup. A corner of his mouth lifted in a half smile. He started to turn off the television when a report came on about the unusual earthquakes in Oklahoma. The strangeness caught his attention.

Living in California, earthquakes were part of everyday life; they were a concern, but life didn't offer complete safety to anyone. When tornados ripped across the Midwest destroying mile-wide swaths of a town, the threat of a *someday* earthquake didn't seem bad. Now Oklahoma was in double trouble: earthquakes, and tornados. It was a short report. This being New Mexico they had local news of more importance. However, they gave a fair amount of time to the fact Oklahoma, in recent years, was experiencing an average of up to three quakes a day. Some so mild only a seismograph could detect them, others strong enough to shake dishes, and a few bad enough to damage foundations. The largest to date was a magnitude 5.8 near Pawnee. Micah paused and sat on the edge of the unmade bed, the remote in his hand.

He listened a minute longer. His next stop was Oklahoma City; maybe he'd pass on through and stay in Fort Smith instead. However, Arkansas wasn't out of the quake picture either. Some fault lines running east/west through the Ouachita Mountains linked Arkansas to Oklahoma's tremors. Micah frowned; the San Andreas Fault was well known and studied, everyone knew about how earth plates slid slowly past each other and when enough tension built, they shifted in a sharp jerk. Earthquakes in the middle of the country seemed strange; it was supposed to be far more stable.

The announcer looked into the camera as he read his report. A study had determined the swarms had increased in size and frequency because of wastewater injections along with fracking, the practice of pumping water into cracks in the shale rock to force out the oil. This was oil country. The quake danger wasn't only to commercial and residential property; a great pipeline carrying hundreds of thousands of gallons of oil could be at risk. Starting in Oklahoma's Cushing Oil Hub, the line runs under farmland, rivers, forest, past Fort Smith and, after tunneling beneath the Mississippi River, reaches Memphis.

Micah's stomach rumbled and he clicked off the television. None of it mattered to him. If Californians had learned to live with Mother Nature's tantrums so could everyone else. The news didn't bother him. All he cared about was accomplishing his goal by crossing the Big Muddy and reaching the Smoky Mountains. The earthquake report was interesting, but Japan and places along the Ring of Fire with all the volcanoes and earthquakes were undoubtedly in more danger than some location solidly in the center of this country. He looked around the motel room checking for anything he might have left out of the backpack. He felt almost rested; at least as much as he had in the last three months.

It was strange, no matter how many hours he slept, he awoke feeling about the same; it was a hard to define sensation. His body had gained strength from the rest, but the underlying weariness remained. He had had one session of grief counseling two weeks after putting his family into the ground. The counselor was an older woman, a motherly type, and she had given him a list of instructions about how to deal with the stages of grief. Well, he sure wasn't into *denial.* Nothing was more real than Jena and Jordan's death. The image constantly burned in his memory, and there was no expectation of it growing dim.

The counselor, Nina Sims, had urged him to keep on with his normal life. Take a bit of time to grieve, open the sandwich stand, keep Sandwich Heaven the success it was. Didn't he think Jena would want him to? He had wanted to hit Mrs. Sims; instead, he had shoved his hands into his pockets. It was the dumbest advice he'd ever heard. He couldn't wait to get away. He would have left sooner except for the legal entanglements. The only bit of relief he had found was when he had put the backpack over his shoulder and started walking. He couldn't outrun the pain, but he could pick where to endure it.

He never spoke with Mrs. Sims again. However, to be fair to her, literature the funeral home gave and most of the booklets did advise against making big changes soon after a loss. That might be okay for some, but not for him.

New Mexico's morning sky stretched high, wide, and hard blue above a brown and tan landscape. He checked out of the motel, found a decent cafe where the breakfast was hearty enough to last all day, and left Tucumcari heading east to Oklahoma City. The big rigs and small passenger cars whizzed past, doing well over seventy. He and the Ford poked along at sixty. Once in a while the radio picked up a signal clear enough to provide a bit of music, but it was mostly static. In the distance, rocky outcroppings formed a high, dark gray ridge between the brown foreground and the blue sky. Micah studied the countryside and marveled how anyone on a horse had managed to cross it. An even greater mystery was what made them want to; still, the lure of buffalo hides and gold was the answer.

As heat shimmered on the distant pavement, Micah let his mind wander. Jordan had been a happy, smart little boy. Micah pictured him as a successful adult; he could have been anything he wanted. Jordan gave meaning to his parents' lives; he justified Micah's existence. The morning sun glared through the windshield, and the faithful Ford rolled east at a steady pace. When Micah drifted, lost in thought, the wind through the open window kept him alert. The countryside flattened out even more, no distant hills to break up the horizon. The engine noise from passing traffic was almost like the surge of breaking sea waves; the heat and the monotonous scenery, along with the emptiness inside Micah, seemed to suspend time.

By midmorning, he was near Amarillo, Texas. He would have made it sooner were it not for drifting along, sometimes dropping back to fifty miles an hour. Another four or five hours should get him to Oklahoma City; too early to stop for the night, still the heat made him tired. However, mid-June wasn't August and the wind did cool him a bit. He hated to admit to emotional or mental fatigue, but since there wasn't a rush, an early stop in Oklahoma City seemed sensible. It would give him time to do a load of laundry, buy a couple changes of clothes at a Walmart, and let the Ford rest, maybe even find a Jiffy Lube; the old pickup deserved it. It was a plan, the only one other than getting to the cabin.

Interstate 40, mostly following old Route 66, ran east and west across the country like a worn-out hallway carpet down the middle of a house. Traffic in both directions was intent upon getting somewhere. Drivers in a hurry, not paying much attention to the roadway except to curse the sections under repair, and those needing it. Small wonder both coasts considered this fly-over country. Yet Micah had chosen not to fly. It would have made the transition too fast; he needed time to adjust. Walking and hitchhiking would have been fast enough, but Taylor had intervened. Now Micah felt a connection to the old Ford pickup and through it to Taylor. For some reason he couldn't understand, the two were like a huge rock in the middle of a raging river. The current had swept him up onto this rock and he didn't feel like turning loose. The miles disappeared beneath the truck's tires and Micah leaned over the steering wheel doing his best to think of nothing but the road ahead.

He wasn't hungry but the pickup needed fuel several times before reaching the day's destination. With the sun past its zenith, the afternoon driving was easier, no glare on the windshield. Farther into Oklahoma, the landscape changed. It was still flat, but greener and across the wide fields, trees surrounded ranch homes. Creeks and ponds came into view, and several pickups passed towing motor boats indicating a nearby lake, but not much in the way of a real river. Not like the gushing streams and deep green rivers in the Carolinas. The mountain hideaway pulled at him.

Near the city, the noise, fumes, and heat increased, along with the tractor-trailer traffic and non-commercial vehicles, none of which decreased their speed. It was a strain keeping up and at the same time following I-40 through the interchanges. Once he took a wrong turn and had to get back on the highway. Industrial sites lined the interstate; the oil business was evident with lots of pipeline companies. When he saw a motel, Micah was more than ready to take the exit. It wasn't a chain motel but there was a fair looking restaurant and a Burger King nearby, along with a gas station. He parked outside the motel office, climbed from the pickup, and was shocked at how his legs shook.

The motel lobby was clean, but the furnishings looked cheap. The young man behind the desk was efficient and had Micah checked in and out the door quickly. Micah found his room near the back of the 'L' shaped structure and parked in the lot. He lifted his backpack and bag of laundry out of the truck and headed for the room. He was pleased his room reflected the lobby, clean and inexpensive. In the breezeway between the two sections there were soft drink machines, an ice bin, and a laundry room. He thought about doing laundry and finding a place to eat; remembering the Burger King he decided to do both.

Climbing back into the pickup took an effort, but the thought of a big hamburger, fries, and a shake encouraged him. He'd pick up his meal, return to the motel to eat while doing a load of laundry and recharging his cell phone. Tomorrow, before heading for Fort Smith, he'd see about getting the truck serviced and hit a Walmart for a few items.

By the time he folded the clean laundry and put it in the backpack, Micah was almost asleep on his feet. After a quick shower he fell into bed. He awoke around three in the morning, turned off the television, drank a glass of water, and passed out again. When sunlight slanted through the gap in the drapes, Micah opened his eyes. He stretched, rolled over, and swung his legs out of bed. It was nine in the morning; there was no hurry, yet he hadn't planned to sleep this long. He dressed and was out the door in twenty minutes.

He slipped the door card into his front pocket and headed for the pickup. Checkout time was noon, and he'd have breakfast before removing his things from the room. The overcast day was warm with a mild wind. The motel was on a paved dead end just off a main street running beneath the interstate; the underpass made an easy on and off. The restaurant was a few blocks from the motel. Micah stood in the parking lot near where he'd left the truck.

He looked in both directions and frowned. Several yards away, a white Chevy stood beside a brown van, and to his left was a blue pickup with a camper top over the bed. He walked down the middle of the lot, looking to either side. A couple of cars were standing in front of motel doors, and a few were parked nose in to a privacy fence. The fence was on the other side of the narrow lot opposite his room. That was where he'd parked, the truck's front bumper against the fence; he was sure of it. He was not functioning normally, hadn't since his family died, but he wasn't this far gone. He knew where he'd parked the damn truck!

He started jogging along the long arm of the motel, turned the back corner, and searched the area on the short backside. Most everyone had checked out, making it an easy search. When he returned to the other section of the motel, a family of four was loading up the brown van and the white Chevy was gone. There was no way he had missed finding his pickup; maybe someone mistakenly towed it away. Charlie would not have reported the pickup stolen; he would have no reason to do so. Micah's heart pounded. He wanted to sit down on the curb and cry. How could he have lost Taylor's truck? A wave of sickness swept over him.

As baffled as he was, he couldn't just stand there. He hurried to the motel office. When he opened the door a waft of cold air carried the smell of fresh coffee. The older lady behind the desk smiled.

"May I help you?"

Micah gripped the edge of the counter.

"I'm Mr. Hanson. My truck. It is gone. Could it have been towed away by mistake?"

The gray-haired woman blinked behind her large glasses; her pale pink lips parted to form a round surprise.

"Towed? I doubt it. Was it in need of repair?"

Micah's stomach churned and his chest tightened.

"No. I parked there last night. There was nothing wrong. Check my registration on the computer."

"Well, yes," she said as she clicked away on a keyboard. "Micah Hanson?"

Micah nodded, his throat dry, and his underarms wet.

"Ah, yes, there we are. I don't understand. You can't find your car?"

"Right. Where is the fellow who checked me in last night? Maybe he knows something."

She cocked her head and pursed her lips.

"Let me think, here; I'll check the schedule." More clicking on the keyboard. "Ah, yes, Jamiel. He wouldn't be here until five."

"Can we call him at home?"

"I doubt he took your car."

"Look, please call the police for me. I need to get some help here."

A flash of alarm lit the blue eyes behind the glasses. "The police?"

"Yes. Never mind. I'll call them myself."

Micah walked around the corner of the desk to the sitting area. He sat, took out his cell phone, and started to dial 911. He hesitated. The Ford was still in Taylor's name; he had the bill of sale, and the title, but it might look suspicious since the transaction had taken place in Arizona. He didn't have Charlie Redman's phone number. He could probably find it, or the police could. He lowered his head and stared at the phone in his hand.

"Would you like a cup of coffee?"

He looked up at the clerk, who was holding a paper cup of coffee. It seemed easier to take it than to refuse. When he thanked her and took the cup, she smiled.

"I am so sorry. Someone took my son's car last year. They finally found it, but it was pretty torn up."

Micah nodded and took a sip of the coffee. It was actually good. Obviously, he wasn't going to get much help from the motel staff. He needed to think. He stood and finished the coffee in one long gulp, crushed the cup, and tossed it into a wastebasket. The clock above the complimentary breakfast bar read half past ten. He had the room until noon. When he left the lobby and walked along the empty parking lot to his room, he was more lost and lonely than ever. It was like having someone pound away at a broken rib. His injuries were almost bearable; this blow might put him under.

In the darkened room, he drew open the drapes; the housekeeping cart was a couple of doors away. He sat on the edge of the unmade bed and tried to think. He could call the police, make a report, fill out papers, and answer questions. He would need to stay in town until they found the truck, or until he gave up hope. Even with the reasonable rate at the motel he couldn't afford it for many weeks, or months. He didn't have insurance on the truck so he couldn't make a claim.

He'd lost everything else; he could let this go. He had his backpack, all his personal belongings; the interstate was close by, just start walking east. The walking part wasn't hard, and once away from the towns and cities, the police weren't a big concern, although it was always an ordeal when a patrol car pulled up, just to check. He had been stopped west of Barstow, California. The patrolman was a reasonable type. Micah had explained, showed his driver's license, gave his attorney's phone number, and the whole process only took half an hour. The officer thought he was crazy to attempt the long walk, but he didn't arrest him. He could start walking again, pack up, and get on down the road, leaving Taylor's truck behind.

Outside, the cleaning cart pulled up to the window. A young, dark-haired woman looked in, shrugged, and spread her hands. Micah stood and opened the door. She had a good smile, and looked nice in her plain blue uniform.

"Do you want the room cleaned?" Her Oklahoma accent made the sentence draw out longer than necessary.

Micah didn't know how to answer. "Can you come back later?"

She smiled and her dark eyes crinkled at the corners. "Don't know if you are coming or going, huh?"

Micah nodded. "You may be right."

She started to push the cart on to the next room. "Give a whistle; I'll be on this side for another hour at least."

Micah stepped out onto the sidewalk behind her. "Wait."

She turned with raised eyebrows. "Yes?"

"Someone stole my old red Ford pickup last night. Does this happen much around here?"

"You mean in the city or this motel in particular?"

"Both, I guess. What are the police like?"

She threw her head back and laughed. "Just like they are everywhere. Some nice, some jerks. Why, you not partial to police?"

"No reason to avoid them. I'm passing through. How hard would they work to find an old pickup?"

The nametag on her blouse said, *Norma.* She looked like a decent person, but he doubted she'd be any help.

Norma tilted her head to one side.

"How old a pickup is it? Maybe you should wonder why someone would steal an old car. You sure you didn't just misplace it?"

"Not unless I'm losing my mind."

Norma turned to open the next door, but stopped and looked over her shoulder. "You just let me know if you want the room cleaned, okay?"

Micah nodded and went back into his room. He slumped down in the armchair, put his boots up on the square coffee table, and stared at the blank television screen. He tried to form a plan. He could call the police, stick around for a few days and hope they'd find the truck, or cut his losses and move on. Nothing seemed to click; both ideas seemed wrong. Yet, he couldn't sit there forever, or maybe he could. Rent the motel room while he looked for a cheap apartment, find a job in Oklahoma City, and end his trek here. The plan seemed as near to death as his promise to Jena would allow. Micah sat staring at his hands, twisting the gold band on his ring finger round and round.

When he looked up it was a few minutes past noon. The morning gone, wasted. He'd never been this indecisive. He left the room and hurried to the motel office. The clerk smiled.

"Did you find your car?"

Micah shook his head.

"Are you here to check out? It is past noon, you know. Under the circumstances, maybe we can overlook it. You missed our complimentary breakfast. But I think there is still orange juice, and a few bran muffins."

She was trying to be nice, doing what she could to help. Most people were kind. He hadn't met any real bad people, except for the thief who took the truck. Anger replaced the shock and worry; if he could find the scum who took Taylor's truck, he'd beat him senseless. Micah's heart pounded and heat rose in his chest, while his muscles tightened. A fury was building and it surprised him. He hadn't felt this ready to half kill anyone in all the years he'd been married. When his family died, there'd been no boiling anger; the sorrow and grief were too overwhelming. Besides, the driver of the semi had died, too, all of them struck down by a mechanical failure. Micah had never been angry at Fate, God, or any unseen force. Life was what it was... you dealt with it, at least he had until now, but the loss of the truck was too much.

"Are you okay? Mr. Hanson?"

"What? Oh, yes, sure. Can you help me arrange a rental car?"

Her face lit up. "Why, of course. How about Enterprise? They will bring the car right over."

"Fine. Thanks."

The overhead flood light above the desk turned her gray hair a sparkling silver as she bent over the keyboard and started typing. He wasn't hungry but it would probably be a while before the rental car showed up. He should take advantage of the muffins and juice the clerk had mentioned. He ended up drinking two glasses of juice and eating three muffins. He finished with a cup of coffee. When he went back to the desk, the clerk smiled at him.

"A car will be here shortly. They have a daily rate, a weekly, and something longer. They will drive you to their office where you can make the arrangements. Now, will you be checking out?"

"No. Here, let me pay for another night."

Micah took out his billfold. Since he wasn't using a credit card, the night clerk had asked for payment in advance, and the day lady was satisfied with the same arrangement.

"And tell the maids to never mind about cleaning the room. I didn't mess it up much."

When she asked about more towels or soap, he declined. Besides, he'd just as soon not have anyone in and out of the room while he was gone. He kept the biggest part of his money hidden at the bottom of the backpack, along with some personal papers. He returned to the room and took his seat beside the window. As he waited for the rental to arrive, he focused on what the maid, Norma, had said. Why would anyone steal an old truck when the lot had new pickups and cars available, and why did he care this much about losing an old vehicle? That answer came easy. It was Taylor's truck. The old man had taken excellent care of it, except for the exterior paint, and he'd put it into Micah's care. He didn't want it junked or cut up for parts. From the first, Micah had felt an obligation; Taylor gave him transportation to finish his journey, in return, he was to take care of and respect Taylor's last possession.

The question of who would want the old truck took more thought. A stupid teenager, thinking no one would care if he took such an old truck, and it could end up abandoned or wrecked after a joyride. The police would find it, and if it were a total wreck, it would end up as junk. Micah doubted he'd want to spend much to have it repaired. Sorry, Taylor, Micah thought.

Lost in thought, Micah suddenly shocked himself by wondering why he'd asked for a rental car; he was losing it for sure. Maybe wanting to go on down the road motivated it; still he had paid for another night. Neither one a well-thought-out action; however, they both pointed to staying around at least another day. Instinct was a tricky thing.

The sound of a car horn made Micah look up. A compact Nissan was idling in front of the room. Micah rose, went out the door, it locked behind him, and he climbed in beside a chubby young man. As the desk clerk had said, they drove to the Enterprise office. Micah gave them sufficient information to convince them he wasn't stealing the car, or using it for nefarious activities, and after parting with more cash, he drove away.

Back in the motel room, he found the phone book and started searching for auto parts, junk yards, and antique parts dealers. If a teen didn't take the truck, someone restoring a 1997 Ford F-150 or someone selling parts to such a person might want it. Micah found the motel's stationery and a ballpoint pen to copy addresses and locations. If an individual restoring his own old Ford had taken it, there wasn't much hope. It would be in a neighborhood or on a farm, somewhere Micah could never find. It was hard to imagine a guy with enough patience and care to restore an auto, to be a thief.

However, if by a stroke of good luck it ended up at a parts dealer, maybe there was hope.

Micah found four possibilities, each located in distant parts of the city, two in small adjoining towns, the closest an area called Yukon. He vaguely remembered seeing its exit sign. With the addresses on paper, he put them into his cell phone. The phone was finally useful for something other than keeping in touch with his attorney. He only had voice service, but before leaving when he still had internet, he'd downloaded a free map application. He hadn't expected to need it; however, it could help now. Micah wasn't into technology. He could keep books on a computer, do internet searches, use the cell phone, but otherwise he didn't have much use for it. With the North Carolina destination in mind, he hadn't brought the laptop along. He doubted there would be service to his back-woods cabin. There used to be electricity, and water came from a well; he really didn't need more. He could do without television; he didn't want to hear what disasters were overtaking the world. If trouble came through the mountains into his little cove, he'd deal with it.

The Nissan was like riding in a kiddy car after the Ford pickup, and the traffic was more intimidating, but he arrived at the first location without a mishap. He'd picked the closest, hoping to get a feel for the area before heading clear across the city. The auto parts building was in an industrial area. There was a pipeline company on one side, and some type of manufacturing on the other. Cars and pickups stood in the diagonal parking in front of the businesses. He parked near the parts store and went inside. A tall man behind the counter asked if he could help. Micah waved him off and walked up and down the aisles. There were two other men doing the same. The labeled shelves, stacked high, held a confusion of parts; the place looked as if it carried parts for any make of car. Micah thanked the man at the counter and went back to his rental. If the Ford was already salvage, he'd never find it. He had just wanted to see the inside of the parts store.

Before getting into the car, he walked along in front of the pipeline building. All the buildings were metal, some of them large as any barn, with smaller front offices. From the looks of this street, the metal building business was booming. There was a vacant lot next to the pipeline company. Micah stepped out into the weeds and continued walking. Chain link fencing divided the lots behind each building; stacks of different gauge pipes formed huge pyramids held in place by chains. Micah moved on to the back of the fence where it bordered an empty field. Someone might stop him, but he continued. When he reached the rear of the auto parts store, there was the same arrangement, and this chain link enclosure held wrecked cars.

There were all makes and models. Some trucks, some vans, most were half stripped, others waiting to be worked on. None of them looked in as good condition as Taylor's Ford. From his position, Micah could see down the three rows where there were maybe ten autos per row. Micah took time to study each vehicle. The truck was not there. Either it wasn't there yet, or it was at one of the other three dealers. Maybe it was too early to be at any of them. However, it might not show up at all. Micah retraced his steps along the back of the business to the rental car.

He wasn't exactly disappointed; he didn't expect much, and maybe this effort was to soothe his conscience. Before leaving town, he'd report it to the police. It would be an entangled mess, showing them the paperwork he had on the Ford, and telling how he had come to own it. They'd probably never find Taylor's truck, but he would have done all he could to recover it. He was still hesitant to involve the police because it could reveal the situation surrounding Taylor's death and burial. His anger returned and he drove on toward the second auto parts location. He'd decide about the police later, after checking these stores. One down, three to go.

The second store was much the same as the first. It was on a dirt road with not much traffic, a large metal building with an enclosed lot behind it, and Micah hesitated to linger. There was no reason to go inside the building this time. He hated losing the truck, but if it were already a pile of parts, that was the end of it; nothing more he could do. There was a large mailbox at the side of the road with Antique Auto Parts painted on the side; behind the building was a gravel parking area. He kept driving; at the end of the block there was a cross street. Micah turned to the left, made another left, and was soon driving along the back of the parts store's lot. On the right-hand side of the street was a trailer park, its center road paved, in contrast to the city's dirt street.

Micah stopped the car and studied the lot. It didn't take long; there were ten cars, not a pickup in the bunch. He stepped on the gas pedal, and roared away, raising a cloud of red dust. When he reached a busy main street, he headed back to the motel, where he used the cell phone's map to locate the third store, another shop on the edge of town. Evidently, these businesses needed room, an area to store vehicles, a large building with a breakdown shop in the rear, and retail in the front. He set the phone on the passenger seat and took off, a heavy weariness sweeping over him, a weakness in his arms and legs. Useless, what a waste of time.

It took forty-five minutes to reach the third location. Micah's mouth was dry and his vision blurred from squinting into the afternoon sun. He should have taken his sunglasses, but he'd forgotten them. Nothing about him seemed to be operating properly. If he didn't get to his mountain cabin soon, he wondered if grief could kill, not that he cared. Still, the theft angered him; he'd like to get his hands on the bastard who took the truck. What kind of human thought they had a right to someone else's property? It was hard to imagine what went on in a thief's mind; had to have no self-respect.

Arnold's Auto Parts was on a two-lane highway. A big, gated, self-storage was to one side and an empty lot on the other, maybe as much as an acre. A large bar and restaurant built of logs with a high-pitched roof stood on the corner; the smell of barbeque filled the air. There were only two cars parked in front, still early for dinner. Above the railed front entrance the sign read, Silver Saddle. They probably did all their business at night. Micah's stomach rolled and his mouth grew moist. His body had used up the three muffins and was running on what little stored fat he had left. Forgetting to eat was becoming a habit. He didn't want to think about himself; when he did, he came close to admitting he was a total wreck. Maybe Nina

Sims and all those booklets were right, he should have stayed in familiar surroundings and worked through his loss. Still, no sense thinking about it because he could not do it.

Run, run, and run. If he were lucky he might outrun the pain. He'd hide somewhere it couldn't find him; being a coward didn't matter, he wasn't hurting anyone. Not like crooks who stole things and caused others untold aggravation. He would never meet up with his crook, and it was a good thing because under the pain and grief something volcanic bubbled. If the world would let him alone, not mess with him, he could keep it tamped down.

Micah drove the Nissan slowly past the parts store. There were two pickups diagonally parked in front of it. At the corner, he pulled into a convenience store, turned around, and cruised back past the store. At the front of the big empty lot next door, he pulled to the curb and stopped. If questioned he'd say he was lost and checking directions. However, the few men on the street didn't seem to notice him. From his location, one side of the fenced lot was visible. The chance of Taylor's truck being there was nil to nothing, but he'd set this task and if he left without looking, it would bother him. Not caring if anyone became suspicious, he climbed out of the air-conditioned car into a hot, dry day.

Crossing in front of the car, he stepped over the curb and headed through the field alongside the auto parts building. Green shoots were growing up through last year's dead yellow stalks, along with a few briars and stick tights, which clung to his pant legs. Looking straight ahead, Micah marched through the level lot toward the back of the building, trying to seem as if he belonged there. Chain link about eight feet high lined the sides of the enclosure, while across the back was a six-foot-tall wooden privacy fence. Micah stood studying the graveled storage lot. There could be as many as twenty-five vehicles, many in broken down rusted condition, others almost new, but obviously wrecked. He hated seeing wrecked autos; too many memories. Kyle and Myra came to mind and he wondered how they were doing. He also remembered Myra saying she'd pray for him; he almost laughed, but didn't. He appreciated her caring.

He walked farther along the fence, trying to sort through the vehicles in the lot. When he finished here, there was one more place to check. It was close to four, the afternoon almost gone. The next shop was in the northwest part of town, directly north of where he was now. He should easily reach it in thirty minutes, if he didn't get lost. As he walked along checking what looked like a junkyard, he was anxious to finish this task. It would ease his sense of responsibility. Soon as he searched the last location, he could return the rental car. Still, it might be wise to keep the rental and turn it in at Fort Smith, or Little Rock. Driving would make up for the time he'd spent with Taylor, the Claytons, and now this wild goose chase. Then he could resume the trip with his original intent of trudging along day after day, the mindless activity giving him time to heal. He'd decide later how to proceed, for now there were junk cars to inspect.

When he reached the corner where the wooden privacy fence started, he walked along behind it, heading toward the other section of chain link. As he tromped over the weeds, he glanced through the narrow gaps between the wide boards. Near the far corner, a flash of red caught his eye; he slid to a stop, and stared through the crack in the fence. His heart pounded; he could hardly catch a breath. It was Taylor's truck!

For a minute, he stood still, too shocked to think, but quickly snapped out of it as he tried to decide what to do. He could go inside to confront the man and demand his pickup back, maybe accuse him of receiving stolen goods. Or call the police, have them come and help him retrieve it. Micah put his hand to his head and closed his eyes, as different plans raced through his mind. The title and bill of sale were at the motel in his backpack. If he involved anyone in the recovery he'd need to prove the truck was his. He continued to look at the faded red Ford F-150, and then he moved along the wooden fence trying to see the front or the back bumper. He was sure this was the old red Ford. Even the paint was faded in the right pattern; a California license plate would clinch it.

When he reached the corner where the chain link started again, he saw the front bumper and the California plate. They hadn't done anything to the pickup, probably hadn't had time, and because it was out of sight they thought it was safe. If the thief had a forged title, the shop owner could think he'd made a legitimate purchase, and the police could question the title Micah had. Charlie could swear it was good, but reaching him would take time. Micah doubted the business owner was interested in waiting for Micah to prove ownership.

A vacant acre stretched behind the business before connecting with another street holding a strip center; the low red brick building housed a variety of businesses. From a distance, he could see rooftop signs for Custom Cabinets, Jiffy Plumbing, and Bruner Electrics; other enterprises had names and services too small to read, painted on doors and windows.

The afternoon sun slanted through the collection of wrecked vehicles, making them sparkle and gleam. He ran back to get a better view of the Ford, and yes, it was true. He wasn't mistaken. He turned and ran to the street and climbed into the rental car, sat gripping the steering wheel, his heart racing, while a barrage of plans pounded at him. The cell phone was in his hand to call the police, but he did not, for all the reasons he'd not called them before. He could go inside, explain what had happened, and maybe even offer to pay for the Ford, but he was too stubborn for that. He would not pay for something stolen from him. The hot interior of the Nissan threatened to cook his already bubbling brain. Micah turned the key, started the engine, put the car in gear, and slowly drove away.

When he passed the log restaurant, he drove faster. A plan was forming. He'd seen a Walmart near the interstate; it would be the first stop. Next, Enterprise Rentals, he'd not need the Nissan since he had found his pickup. Someone from the rental agency could drop him back at the motel. It was part of their service; in Micah's opinion, a good part.

Four

Sitting in the Walmart parking lot, Micah grew calm. A plan was in place, maybe not a good plan, but it was a quick solution. He wasn't in the mood to hang around Oklahoma City, and he was tired of life messing with him. He'd parked far from the store's entrance, using the long walk to construct a shopping list; the lot was too full to find a close space anyway. The sun beat down, bringing sweat to his brow. When he stepped inside a wave of icy air chilled him. As usual, the store was crowded. Jena didn't like shopping in a Walmart; she searched out local providers and bought online. Micah thought she'd understand this time.

He grabbed a cart, started for the luggage section, and quickly picked out a large black duffel bag. A fifteen-inch pry bar easily fit inside, as did the two-gallon, red gasoline can. The bolt and wire cutters, claw hammer, along with a flashlight, completed his purchases. All things he'd need at the cabin, necessary everyday items. Standing in a relatively short checkout line, he wondered what he was forgetting. Oh yeah, a change of clothes and new underwear. He raised an eyebrow. If this plan went wrong, new clothes didn't matter, the state would provide them.

The next stop was a Shell station near the motel. The rental car company would charge more if they had to refill the tank; besides, the little red can had to be full in case the Ford was thirsty. A Burger King supplied Micah's fuel. He parked in front of the motel room and lugged all his purchases inside. He called Enterprise and requested they pick up their car. He decided to wait until after returning the car to have dinner. He'd reheat the hamburger and fries in the microwave.

As he sat beside the window and waited, Micah considered the plan. A tiny voice, probably the same one who had advised against walking nearly two thousand five hundred miles, warned against this action. It might as well have remained silent. The Ford deserved to be rescued. In less than thirty minutes, a guy from Enterprise knocked on the door and the driver who'd dropped him sped away. One more trip to the rental office and a return to the motel completed Micah's transaction. He could have kept the rental, but he couldn't drive two vehicles! He turned on the television, nuked his sandwich, making the bun a bit tough, and settled down to eat. Going over his plan for the evening kept him from tasting his food. He had paid for another night in the motel, but he didn't think he'd stay until morning. Once he picked up his backpack and loaded the Ford with the recent purchases, he'd head east as fast as possible.

That evening the motel started to fill up, even though it was still daylight. Micah watched as travelers' lugged baggage out of cars, SUVs, and trucks. Several young children, set free from the confines of a car, ran along in front of the rooms, yelling as they went. The sight sent a bolt of sadness straight to Micah's heart, but he almost smiled anyway. Twilight softened the scene, making the warm evening bearable. The traffic visible from the motel slowed, people already home or having dinner in a restaurant. While a few blocks away, the big trucks on Interstate 40 kept on whizzing past. Around eight, Micah packed the big black duffel bag, phoned for a Yellow Cab, and stepped outside to wait. He hoped it would be fully dark by the time he reached Arnold's Auto Parts.

The taxi arrived in about ten minutes, Micah plopped the big duffel bag onto the floorboard of the backseat and climbed in after it. The driver didn't give the bag a second look. "Where to?" he asked.

"You know a restaurant called Silver Saddle?"

The driver looked up into the rearview mirror.

"Yes, I know the one. Rustic log building?"

"That's the place."

Micah settled back. The ride would take at least thirty minutes unless the driver knew a faster route. After paying for a second night in the motel along with the afternoon's purchases, car rental, and now the cab ride, retrieving the Ford was expensive. Farther from the main highways, the night grew darker, but it still wasn't dark enough to suit him. When they reached the more industrial area, the businesses all looked closed. Still, someone could be working late. The plate glass windows glowed a faint blue with inside nightlights. Buildings with enclosed areas behind them had tall yard lights illuminating the lot. If Arnold's Auto Parts was the same, the flashlight was a waste of money for this job.

The taxi pulled up in front of the Silver Saddle. As Micah paid, the driver asked, "You want me to pick you up later?"

Micah shook his head, opened the door, and pulled the bag out behind him.

"Thanks, I'll call if I need a lift."

The driver nodded and took off.

Micah stood with the bag at his feet. The sound of loud country music spilled out into the warm night, along with the tantalizing smell of sweet hickory smoke. The restaurant's location made sense; there were no neighbors to complain. The parking area was full, with more pickups parked along the building's side. Other cars arrived and found parking near a closed plumbing business. Either the nighttime activity would be a cover for what Micah had planned, or it meant more potential witnesses. Security cameras were a bigger concern than Silver Saddle's customers; they seemed intent on good food, loud music, and drinks.

He picked up the duffel and headed into the darkness of the large vacant lot. A tow truck stood in the weeds beside the auto parts store. Micah was sure it had not been there earlier. He had supposed the thief had hotwired the truck; still, no one would question the towing of an old truck. Maybe the parts store owner made a mistake and towed the wrong pickup. Yeah, right. Micah wasn't in the mood to be charitable. He continued along the chain link to the back where it joined the tall wooden fence.

The storefront businesses on the street behind the auto parts appeared closed and quiet. A few of the front windows showed a faint light. The night still seemed too bright, but it wasn't going to get any darker. In the distance, a dog barked and Micah froze. There was no answering bark nearby; still it didn't mean some big, silent hound wasn't patrolling Arnold's back lot. Micah started moving. The longer he stood there, the greater the risk.

He unzipped the bag and took out the pry bar. He placed the edge between two fence slats and put the bar to good use. Nails screeched and a long spear of wood broke off one slat. In minutes, four of the boards were on the ground; Micah could enter the enclosed lot. So far, he wasn't trespassing, just damaging property. He'd hoped to take down enough of the back fence to drive out, but he hadn't thought to bring a saw to dismantle the three rails. Wondering how crazy he'd become, Micah bent over, stepped across the bottom rail and into the back lot. He stood still and listened. No alarm sounded and no pit bull came to ravage him.

He was about six feet from Taylor's Ford. When he reached the pickup, he walked completely around it. The tires looked okay; he gently opened the driver's side door. When the dome light came on, he quickly turned it off. His heart was pounding and his hand trembled. If he didn't get moving, he'd lose his nerve. His legs seemed to have turned to lead. Since the wooden fence was out, he'd need to find a way through the chain link. He managed to start walking. The Ford was facing east, the side away from the restaurant on the corner. Micah reached through the opening in the wooden fence and pulled the duffel bag through into the lot. He removed the wire and bolt cutters and headed for the metal fence. He hadn't noticed a gate when he'd been there that afternoon, but there had to be one.

Micah walked the entire length of the fence to the back corner of the metal building. There was no gate; he hurried across the back of the building to the other chain fence. Sweat ran down the side of his face; the night was warm, but this was a nervous sweat. The opposite fence was also gateless. Puzzled, Micah went back to the east fence. The Ford faced the fence, and with vehicles on either side, there wasn't room to turn it around, or to back it out. He started at the corner where the chain link met the wooden fence. The metal fence posts looked about ten feet apart; taking out one section would have to be enough. However, the top rail would have to come down. Maybe he could drive over the tension wire at the bottom. This meant he'd probably be driving over the downed section of fence as well, but he could do it.

The top rail was the problem. He didn't have a heavy screwdriver to loosen the bolts; maybe the bolt cutter would work. He ran his hand along the top rail of the first section and stopped in surprise when he saw the second ten-foot section didn't have a top rail. No gate, just a section easily detached. He almost laughed aloud. The second section had a heavy metal rod forced through the fabric of the overlapping links attaching it to the first, but there was nothing high enough to stand on to pull the rod out. He ran back to the Ford, took the gasoline can out of the duffel, poured the two gallons into the tank, threw everything back into the duffel, and climbed into the pickup.

He slipped the key into the ignition, and holding his breath, turned it over. The engine sounded as loud as a locomotive. With the gearshift in low, he inched forward until the hood was touching the fence. He shut down the truck, got out, and climbed to the hood. From there he managed to grab the rod and work it up through the links of the fence. He was doing this in a dream; someone should have stopped him by now. In a minute, he'd hear the wail of a siren. The rod came up out of the fence and the section fell halfway over. Micah threw the rod aside, climbed off the truck, and scrambled to the half-folded fence. With his mind spinning, he grabbed the unconnected side of the fence and pulled it around toward the third section.

This opened up a ten-foot pathway for the truck. Micah was so nervous he couldn't swallow. He quickly checked to make sure all the tools and the gas can were in the duffel which he slung into the pickup bed. Inside the cab, he restarted the truck, put it in gear, and carefully drove between the metal fence posts. He thought about reattaching the section of fence, but decided against it. The distance between Arnold's Auto Parts and the sprawling self-storage compound was about the same as to the street with the small strip mall. Turning right would take him back to the street in front of the parts store and past the big restaurant with all the people coming and going. To the left it was darker and across the vacant back acre lay a silent street.

Being cautious, Micah turned left. He worried about ruining a tire. Even though the ground seemed level, it could be hiding plenty of junk beneath the tall grass. He leaned over the steering wheel and stared ahead. Earlier he had wished for more darkness, now he wished for less. The Ford bumped and lurched, but finally the front tires jumped up onto solid pavement. The noise from the restaurant/bar was still loud, but distant. There were no streetlights and the closed storefronts cast a pale bluish glow into the night. The street was empty of traffic, but Micah kept the headlights off anyway. His heart had stopped hammering and he could breathe a bit deeper.

At the next north/south cross street, Micah turned on the headlights. He took a left toward the interstate. It took two more turns to reach the nearest on-ramp. He accelerated to keep up with the lighter nighttime traffic, except for the big rigs which never stopped rolling. The oncoming vehicles' headlights made a river of white, while those before him were a stream of crimson in the night. When he reached the exit for the motel, he thought maybe he'd gotten away with stealing his own pickup. A harsh laugh scraped the back of his throat.

As he pulled into the motel parking lot, he was startled to find the space in front of his room empty. A stroke of good luck. If possible, he'd chain the pickup to the support column holding up the second-floor walkway. There was no way of knowing who had taken the truck. It could be someone working around the motel and if they saw it, they might take it again out of pure spite. He stepped down from the cab, took the duffel out of the truck bed, and went into the room. The drapes were as he'd left them. He opened a narrow space so the truck's chrome bumper remained visible. He rearranged his backpack, checked the envelope holding the truck title, bill of sale, and the hidden compartment with his money. He had entrusted most other important documents to the attorney in Los Angeles.

Micah's throat was dry and the realization of what he had done made him tremble. He went to the motel sink, unwrapped a glass, filled it with water, and drank it straight down. He filled it again and did the same. He looked into the mirror and barely recognized the thin face reflected there. Any minute there could be a knock on the motel door. The self-storage units next to Arnold's Auto Parts undoubtedly had security cameras; most businesses did. He went to the bed, fell back onto the mattress, and stared at the white ceiling. He tried to imagine explaining what he had done. He could offer to pay for the damaged fence as it couldn't be much.

He closed his eyes and put the back of his arm over them. Maybe he'd sleep, find escape in unconsciousness. However, his thoughts refused to stop, and it made him dizzy. He sat up and turned on the television. Clicking through the stations was worse than the endless tape running in his mind. *No rest for the wicked.* After long hours of work in the sandwich shop, Jena used to say that. She'd laugh, tired but happy, and pull him up the back stairs behind her. Maybe he'd done something wrong this night, but it wasn't wicked. Unable to rest, Micah set about preparing to leave.

With both bags repacked, he went back to the pickup. He walked completely around it checking for damage. It seemed okay, but there was no time to service the truck as planned. It suddenly occurred to him the thief might have removed the vehicle identification number and replaced it with a false one to fool the parts storeowner. He checked the door and found a metal information plate; by some miracle, it appeared original. He'd compare it with the title later. Besides, the identification number should also be somewhere else on the under carriage.

Micah loaded the bags into the cab, locked the truck, and walked to the motel office. He would like to take a shower and rest a while, maybe even get something more to eat, but he couldn't wait to put hundreds of miles between him and Oklahoma City. There was a different clerk from the one the night before. This was an older man.

"Where is the young guy who was here last night?" It didn't matter, but Micah had wanted to ask if he'd seen someone take the truck.

"Quit. Sudden like, left me with a double shift. What can I do for you?"

Micah placed the door card on the counter. "Checking out."

"Anything wrong?"

"No. Just want to get a real early start."

The clerk looked at the round clock on the wall near the sitting area. It was half past two. The clerk raised his eyebrows,

"That you will," he said.

The hour startled Micah; he'd stayed in the room longer than he realized.

Back at the truck, Micah sat with his hands draped over the steering wheel and thought of the soft bed and warm shower on the other side of the door. Maybe he should have stayed. All the adrenaline had drained away, leaving weariness. He felt like crying; instead, he clenched his eyes and shook his head. Fort Smith beckoned. Driving sixty and with a few stops, it shouldn't take more than three and a half hours. In another three hours after that, he might be past Little Rock and on the way to Memphis, which was across the river! The thought brought a surge of energy. He was almost there, and from Tennessee, it was all downhill.

Micah cranked up the Ford, backed away from the curb, and headed toward the street. Better driving at night anyway, a bit less traffic. He was bone tired. The expression took on real meaning, for his bones actually seemed to ache. The service road's next intersection with a main highway also had an interstate on-ramp. As he drove up the incline and watched for a break to merge onto I-40 east, he frowned. There were more people driving this time of night than he had expected. There were too many people everywhere! He looked forward to the solitude of the cabin. He kept rolling ahead ready to speed into the widest gap. Suddenly the truck jerked sideways. It seemed to lift upward at the same time.

Hit something! Micah jerked his head from side to side to see what had happened. Instantly, the pickup lurched forward. He still had his foot on the gas pedal and there was a break in traffic so he shot into the slow lane and drove on. Ahead of him, a big semi had pulled onto the verge. He moved to the left to give it plenty of room. He checked the rearview mirror and both side mirrors looking for a pile up or cars stopping back at the on-ramp. Traffic seemed slower, but none had stopped. If he'd hit something...or someone...he had to go back. The headlights lit a green information sign but he passed before he could read it. Looking for the next exit, he slowed to fifty and wondered if he'd ever get away from this city.

In about a mile, there was a sign and he slowed to take the exit. At the crossroad the yellow and red of a Conoco Station was on the right. With streetlights, neon from restaurants and filling stations, the night was brighter. He pulled in, parked, got out, and went inside. The man there was talking on a telephone. He held up his index finger to signal that he'd be with Micah in a minute. Micah couldn't help overhearing the man's conversation.

"You okay?" There was a pause. "Sure as hell did."

Micah tried to step away and look out the front window.

"Did you call Jerry to see if they're all right?" The man sounded concerned.

Micah hoped the guy wasn't having as bad a night as he was.

"Well good. A couple of broken dishes ain't the end of the world. Bye, talk at you later."

The station attendant hung up the phone, and turned toward Micah.

"Sorry about that. Now what can I do for you?"

"I'm not sure. I think I hit something at the on-ramp the exit before this one. I couldn't turn or stop to find out. I thought that could cause more trouble."

The man frowned. He looked to be around thirty years old, a pleasant face with expressive brown eyes. When on the phone, concern had filled them, now they were warm with welcome.

"Wow. Too bad. I'll call and see if there are any reports."

He seemed to have the police on speed dial. However, given Micah's last day, maybe everyone in Oklahoma City did. While he listened and waited, he regretted stopping. What if the auto parts dealer got to work before the police sorted this out? Maybe he should run right now. The station attendant hung up and smiled.

"Nope. No report of anything in this area. If you had hit something, another driver would probably have called it in, don't you think? Might have been a dog that crawled off into the bushes."

Micah hated to think that. He'd never had a dog, but he wasn't cruel either.

"I hope that didn't happen. It could have been something in the road, a piece of tire rubber. Sorry to have bothered you. Guess I'll go on."

"What did it feel like?"

"What do you mean?"

"Maybe a shaking, or like the ground shifted."

"The truck sort of gave a lurch, almost like a stumble."

The man scratched his jaw and twisted his mouth to one side.

"You know we just had a tremor. Shook dishes out of the cabinet at my house. Right here the Pepsi machine near danced across the floor. A fellow out at one of the pumps said it almost knocked him off his feet. Made him stumble, like you said it felt in your pickup."

"A tremor, like an earthquake?"

"Yep. Getting them fairly regular. Nothing to be worried over, though. Not like those people in California living on the edge. Naw, this is just ground settling. Lots of drilling been going on for a long time. Nothing like a big fault line, nothing like that."

"Thanks for telling me. Maybe that is what I felt. I hope it was. Hey, not that I wish any great ground shaking, but a little tremor is better than hitting something." Micah went to the door, opened it, and turned to say goodbye. "Thanks, again."

The attendant raised his hand in farewell.

"No problem. Safe driving now."

Micah pulled to the verge of the highway, waited for a break in the light traffic, turned left, and took the next right onto the ramp heading east. Back on the interstate things seemed normal, with cars whizzing past. He knew they were probably irritated that he wasn't going over seventy as they were, but until he knew the old truck better, he'd not push it. It had lasted this long in Taylor's care, no reason to make changes now. When driving in a vacant space, the headlights made a yellow tunnel through the darkness. Occasionally, the roar and glare of a semi gained on him, and hurling past, it almost pulled the Ford in its wake. It felt as if the world had narrowed down to a long black road that would never end.

The radio picked up a local station and there was a short report of the minor earthquake. Micah was still a bit concerned, yet it hadn't felt like a straightforward bump, like running over something. It was a kind of lift and jerk to one side, it had happened fast. He'd been watching the road. He was convinced he would have seen something as large as a person, unless they were already lying on the road. Micah shook his head. This line of thought was not helpful. Traffic accidents were something he badly needed to put out of mind.

The past was past…like all the empty miles behind, nothing could change it. Every hour, every day, put distance between Micah and his old life. The past grew dim, a gray mist hiding the happy days it hurt too much to remember. He had fought to build this foggy barrier, yet flashes of those days stabbed through the haze like shafts of golden sunlight. Painful bolts of bright memories that could bring him to his knees in sorrow. Micah clenched his jaw and glared into the fast fading night. At times, he lost track of where he was going, suspended between past and future, living in an ever present 'now' with no purpose.

About ninety miles east of Oklahoma City, Micah stopped at Henryetta for gas at a Shell station. There had been less traffic after getting out of the Oklahoma City area, and he'd made good time. It was still dark, but a feeling in the air signaled dawn's approach. He walked around a bit, bought a couple bottles of spring water, and got back on the road. Later when he spotted a rest area, he took the exit. There wasn't much in the way of facilities, just some picnic tables, but it was dark enough for the trees to hide a bathroom break. Four big trucks stood on the siding, dark and silent, the drivers probably sleeping. Micah considered stopping to sleep, but he wasn't sleepy, wasn't hungry either; his only urge was to cover more miles. The quicker the better.

Beyond Henryetta, the land started a slight roll, with low hills and black trees etched against the dark skyline. There were more creeks and ponds, and the moon put a silver slick on the water at a river crossing. By five in the morning, he was west of Fort Smith. Even allowing for stops he could be somewhere east of Little Rock before nine o'clock, and Little Rock was halfway to Memphis. His excitement grew. He was going to make it, and he had gotten away with taking the truck. He hit the steering wheel with the palm of his hand. A spark of hope flickered. He could do something to fight back after an injury; he didn't have to take everything life dumped on him without retaliating.

He stared into the distance. The divided interstate stretched toward the brightening horizon as the night faded into a predawn gray. Thirty minutes later, with the sun rising, a light breeze picked up and the smell of dew-damp fields washed through the open window. It cooled his face and he realized how warm he was. He touched his forehead where the skin felt hot and dry. It went along with the mental confusion of being both angry and sad. Instinct had demanded recovery of the pickup; it kept him from being a total victim. Still, there was no way to fight against the loss of Jena and Jordan. Grief cut too deep. It felt as if someone had peeled away a two-inch-wide strip of muscle deep inside his chest, from neck to belly. On the surface the skin looked the same, but underneath oozed the bloody wound. It was still raw, and he wondered if it would ever heal.

Traffic picked up. Exhaust from the large trucks mingled with a rising dampness, creating a light form of smog. The noise level also increased. He cringed and rolled the window up. The sounds and smells made it feel as if a band were tightening around his forehead. Micah frowned, trying to relieve the pressure. He could not afford sickness, yet his back ached and his neck was stiff. He might need to take a rest, but it was really too early to stop. He swallowed and his throat hurt, probably only dry. He hadn't had anything to drink for several hours, and no food since the hamburger last night. The rising sun sent a pink-tinged, golden light into the sky where it backlit a bank of billowing white clouds while Micah's thoughts drifted, concentration lost. Memories, ideas, and plans whirled in a mix that made grabbing one of them impossible.

The Ford slowed and a car honked as it sped by on the left, the tractor-trailer rig he'd been following disappeared into the distance. Nearing Fort Smith, he didn't see any place to pull off the interstate, but past Van Buren a rest stop materialized. He took the exit and relief settled over him. It was a large area atop a low ridge, and like other stops, in full use by trucks, cars, and vans. Micah pulled into a parking space and turned off the truck. The sun was rising above hills to the east, casting long shadows beneath the cedar trees. Micah sat looking at the rest stop facilities, gathering the energy to walk the short distance. He felt disoriented and sat staring at the rolling hills beyond the rest stop. It was a nice view, with lots of green stretching into the distance.

As he sat trying to gather his thoughts and strength, this trip felt wrong. Running clear across the country to a broken-down cabin which could well be gone seemed crazy. Harry Miller, his attorney, had tried to talk him out of it. Harry had stared at him with those strange gray eyes that very nearly matched his gray hair, and said, "Call me, Micah. I may need to consult you concerning some of these arrangements." Micah had promised to call Harry every few days.

He wasn't sure how many days it had been since he had talked with Harry; probably it was before he met Taylor. He tried to count backward, but couldn't. He didn't think it had been over a week. He realized he was not doing at all well, mentally or physically. He might not make Little Rock after all. At least not today. That little voice spoke in the back of his mind telling him to turn around, head back the way he'd come, can't outrun yourself, it said. He shook his head trying to rattle the words and make them stop. The only thing he was sure of at that minute was that he badly needed to piss. He welcomed such a solid impulse, it was something that took no thought.

He opened the pickup door and swung his legs out, putting his feet on the pavement. He stayed seated while gaining his balance. Others at the rest stop went about their business, going to the brick facility, or having a snack at one of the outdoor tables. Seeing them unwrap sandwiches and take the top off a thermos sent a powerful signal. He was hungry! Micah, urged on by his bladder, locked the truck and hurried along the sidewalk. Afterward, he went back to the truck and found the remaining bottle of water. Walking around had helped, drinking did too. Of course, he would go on, maybe not in such a rush. This wasn't a race. It made no difference what date he arrived in North Carolina. When he'd planned to walk, it would have taken well over two months, even if he'd been able to walk twelve hours a day, which he doubted he could have done. His vague plan was to arrive there before winter. There was no reason to hurry; a day and night to recuperate sounded reasonable.

The interstate ran to the north of Fort Smith, but there were small towns where he could stop. He'd find a nice motel, a good restaurant, and they must have a Walmart…they covered the country like a rash. He needed to buy new underwear, extra jeans and shirts, perhaps a cooler to start carrying drinks and food. Couldn't afford to get this run down. Might even pick up some things he'd need at the cabin, or need even more if the cabin was not standing. Camping things, maybe a couple of five-gallon gas cans. Gas stations could be some distance from the cabin. Also, now was a good time to service the Ford. He might even inquire about some anti-theft devices! Mapping out the day and the coming night helped. Nothing beat having a plan.

Not far from the rest stop, Micah came to a service area with a Love's Travel Stop. He filled up the truck, found some coffee for himself, and headed on east. He had been told there was a Walmart not far ahead in Clarksville; it wasn't a surprise, he had expected to come upon one shortly. As the morning brightened, so did Micah. He didn't understand his bouts of confusion and doubt. He knew it had a great deal to do with his sudden loss, for he'd never been this way. It was akin to being ill, something from which to recover. Jena had been the wise one, always knowing how to react and adjust. He was more of a steady type, okay so long as he had a plan.

Clarksville turned out to be exactly the right place. There was a Best Western motel where he hoped they would take an early check-in. Micah smiled politely and explained how tired he was. Fortune also smiled, as they had an empty room. Even more, it was a room on the first floor near the office with safe parking for the Ford. Not that he expected to lose it again, but his sense of security was on shaky ground. After dragging the duffel bag and backpack into the room, he fell across the bed and passed out.

He awoke at two in the afternoon. He sat up, looked around the room, and for a second wondered how he'd gotten there. His mind cleared. He felt better. Six hours of rest had worked a miracle. A shower and clean clothes completed the restoration. By the end of the day, Micah had finished what he'd set out to do. He'd bought the clothes and supplies, and on impulse added a sleeping bag and a large tarp. The cabin might not have a bed, and it could have a leak in the roof. With so many purchases to protect, buying a cover for the pickup's bed seemed in order. It took an hour's driving time, plus an hour for purchase and installation, but it was well worth the effort. That evening, the old truck sitting in front of the motel room looked good with its new black bed cover. Before, he had thought of it as Taylor's truck. Now, Micah had some pride of ownership. It renewed his resolve to get a paint job for the pickup. He'd probably keep it red, as the color seemed to suit it.

Later, Micah found a sit-down restaurant, where he had chicken fried steak with mashed potatoes, gravy, and a side of green beans. The apple cobbler with a scoop of ice cream was a fitting finish. Back at the motel he turned off the television at nine, went to sleep, and awoke at six to take full advantage of the motel's complimentary breakfast. By seven-thirty Micah and the Ford were ready to resume their journey.

As they rolled along I-40 east, the old radio picked up a few clear stations. There wasn't much new on the morning reports, a couple of local auto accidents and a convenience store robbery. On the national front, North Korea was threatening destruction again. Micah switched to a music station until the static made it irritating. He drove on into a morning filled with traffic, people hurrying to work, going about their lives, never knowing what disaster could be awaiting them. Micah shoved the pessimistic thought away. It wasn't healthy.

Interstate 40 pavement was a mixed bag. From California to Arkansas, Micah had traveled sections that were in relatively good repair; others were a challenge to dodge potholes. Some holes were big enough to swallow a whole tire. Usually the right-hand lane was like a washboard due to the heavy truck traffic. Micah didn't drive fast enough to take advantage of the smoother left lane. Instead, he watched for the rough spots and guided the old Ford through them. East of Little Rock the traffic grew heavier, the westbound lanes especially crowded. When the two sections of the divided highway were close enough to watch I-40 west, Micah frowned, puzzled by the flow of cars and trucks that were almost crawling along.

Maybe an accident back west, he thought. Something had happened to block traffic. Yet, he'd come from that direction and hadn't seen anything. It might have happened after he had passed by. He turned on the radio to catch any news of the holdup on I-40. Static made it difficult, but a weather report came through. *A thirty percent chance of showers and thunderstorms. Partly sunny, with a high near eighty-two. East-southeast wind around five miles per hour.* More static. Micah reached to turn the radio off when a special report started. *At eight this morning a massive explosion destroyed a section of the Hernando de Soto Bridge.* The crackling reception cut out the rest of the report. Traffic on the westbound lanes continued to increase, then the trucks and cars heading east started piling up in front of Micah.

Beyond Forrest City, traffic slowed to less than forty miles an hour. Micah had to tap the brake pedal constantly. He tried to look ahead, but the tanker truck in front and the semi to the left made it impossible. As the line moved along it was clear that traffic across the Mississippi on this particular bridge was either extremely slow or nonexistent. The speed of the westbound traffic increased to near normal, while Micah's progress continued to slow. He wasn't in a hurry, but this development disturbed him. A destroyed bridge meant a change in his route. Inching along, he thought about other bridges across the river. Maybe they were funneling traffic onto Interstate 55 to cross the river there. If so, they'd divert him at that intersection.

There were other bridges, one to the south at Helena, Arkansas, or Caruthersville, Missouri to the north. Either one would do. Still, if he could get across at Memphis it was shorter than driving north or south, even with the delay. He tried the radio again, hoping to find more news about the bridge. Maybe it was still passable, only slow.

He tried to be patient, no need to be upset, nothing gained by stewing over something he could not control. Yet, he found his fingers drumming on the steering wheel and his jaw clenched. If it hadn't been for the dust storm and the stolen truck, he would have been across the river by now. This damaged bridge would not have affected him. He didn't regret taking time to help Myra and Kyle, he could not have done otherwise, but it felt as if something was conspiring against his reaching North Carolina. As the vehicles in front of him moved faster, he smiled. Now they were getting somewhere, he could accept a temporary setback.

At the next exit, patrol cars parked on either side stopped each car as it came even with them. They gave directions and hurriedly waved the car or truck on, indicating the road ahead. It appeared they were not stopping traffic, only directing it. Micah eagerly slowed to a stop opposite the state trooper's white car. Before Micah could ask a question, the trooper said, "The interstate ahead is closed. You must take one of the next two exits. Please move on."

The trooper gave an impatient wave, allowing for no questions. Micah stepped on the gas and moved on toward the next exit. The first exit was to some state highway going north, but wanting to stay on an interstate, he took the second exit, 277. He soon realized that it put him on Interstate 55 also heading north. The blocked south access canceled the use of the I-55 Bridge. Frustration set in and Micah found a turnoff that took him onto a service road that looped under I-55 and headed back south. From there he took the first exit that put him heading west on I-40. He started looking for a gas station, preferably one near a fast food restaurant. He was more than ready for a rest stop and some information about the road east.

The land in the Mississippi basin was as flat and featureless as the southwest desert. At least some areas in the desert had distant mountains and ridges to break the skyline. Here, distant trees were the only relief. Micah shook his head. He couldn't believe a further delay was making him backtrack, again! It was past noon and if things had gone as expected he would have been across the river in Memphis by now. He had left Clarksville at seven-thirty. He should have covered the approximately two hundred forty miles in four hours, even at his pace. He grew a bit calmer when he realized the rerouting hadn't cost much more than an hour. He could handle that. About forty minutes later, he was back at Forrest City and behind schedule by almost two hours. However, he was past caring.

Forrest City looked like a nice place, well stocked with all the required franchise operations. Micah chose a Taco Bell where the burritos were filling and tasted good. In the booth behind him, two middle-aged men in overalls were having lunch and talking about some land purchase. When he finished eating, Micah stopped by their table.

"Sorry to bother you, but do either of you know why the Memphis river crossing is closed?"

Both men were round-faced, one with gray hair, and upon closer inspection, one was much younger than the other. Could be father and son. The younger one spoke.

"The big bridge was blown up. They don't know if it was an accident or on purpose. Took the whole middle out. Closed both directions. Five minutes later an oil tanker jumped the divider on the Old Bridge and took out a bunch of cars. They don't know if the two are related."

Micah was stunned. He had to get a better radio. The older man looked up at him.

"You traveling through?"

"Yes, on my way to North Carolina. But not having much luck taking interstate forty."

The older man picked up a paper napkin, wiped his mouth, and invited Micah to sit down.

"Thanks," he said, "but I need to move on. I'd like to be across the river before evening."

The younger man nodded.

"You might try crossing at Helena, about an hour from here. Maybe another hour and a half to get back on forty up around Memphis."

Micah nodded and thanked them for the information. Outside he went back toward the interstate where he found an Exxon station. As he filled the truck's tank, it occurred to him that having extra gasoline was a good idea. He opened the pickup bed and took out both five-gallon cans along with the two-gallon container he'd first bought. Gasoline for an emergency was a comforting thought, as was deciding to fill the cooler he'd purchased. At a nearby grocery, he picked up bottled water and some fresh fruit, along with a box of granola bars as a tribute to Jena. She had tried to educate him, but unless it tasted like a candy bar, he wasn't interested. Beef jerky, chips, and peanuts should hold him in an emergency, such as not locating a McDonald's.

Micah stopped in a strip mall parking lot and took out his cell phone. Hardly worth carrying it since he had no one to call. Yet, the map application was handy for directions. It appeared Highway 1 straight south, hooking up with forty-nine, should get him to Helena. Even though he had stopped for lunch, gasoline, and a bit of shopping, he could still be in Memphis and back on I-40 by around five. He put the phone on the seat beside him and suddenly bent over, clutching the steering wheel. The pain hit him hard; he felt hollowed out, stripped of flesh and blood. A great void surrounded him, an emptiness so deep and wide it astonished him. He gasped, choking on a sob. His eyes remained dry, the grief too severe for tears.

He closed his eyes, leaned back in the seat, and waited for the attack to pass. Jena had made him promise to live. He wondered if she'd have insisted if she had known how hard it was. He'd heard that time was the healer, but it was hard to imagine a time when he'd be free of grief. It struck without warning, leaving him shaken and with an overwhelming sense of hopelessness. A great longing for what he could never again have. He wanted to grow stronger. He'd left California because healing there with too many reminders seemed impossible. Although, so far, distance wasn't helping. Maybe time *was* the answer.

As he recovered, he sat looking at the strip center with its grocery store, Subway shop, and nail salon. He had never suffered from depression, he had been happy. Not laughing-all-the-time happy, but rather a quiet peaceful joy. Problems were challenges to solve, and if done successfully, a source of happiness.

"Take good care of yourself. Promise me," Jena had said with her last breath. He didn't realize he was crying until tears dripped off his chin.

He threw his head back, took a deep breath, and wiped his face. This wasn't taking 'good care of himself.' A deep weariness washed over him. Micah was tired. If he closed his eyes, he'd instantly sleep. There was no reason to push on in this condition. If he were physically ill he'd make allowances. There were several nearby motels. He was anxious to move on, but another afternoon and night wouldn't make any difference. An early start tomorrow seemed right. He'd watch the news and perhaps the I-55 Bridge would reopen. They usually cleared wrecks within a matter of hours. He felt sure that tomorrow at least one Memphis bridge would be open.

Five

Micah awoke the next morning at five. He felt physically better and resolved to gain control of his emotions. Everyone knew the adjustment period was difficult, millions of people went through it, support groups and counselors spent untold hours helping survivors cope. This blow did not kill, and if handled properly it would strengthen. As he shaved, Micah spoke into the steam-fogged mirror. "Get a grip. You are stronger than this. Don't shame Jena!"

He grabbed his shirt from a hanger, put it on, and reached for his jeans, hopping into them as he went for his socks and boots near the armchair. As he finished dressing, he turned on the television hoping for information on the bridge closings. This motel offered a free breakfast, no need to bother making coffee in the room. If he couldn't find out about the Memphis bridges by the time he finished eating, he'd head south on Route 1 and that would be okay. Might be more interesting than the interstate, anyway.

After listing to television news for several minutes, he gave up and headed outside. A few other motel guests were also early risers. His room was on the first level halfway to the front office. His long strides took him past three doors, but when he started to take the next step, his boot came down in mid-air. The sidewalk had buckled, dropping several inches, and Micah fell forward. He landed on his hands and knees onto shaking concrete. He tried to rise, but fell again. Several feet ahead, the sidewalk cracked.

Screams pierced the air but they seemed dim and far away. Half-standing, arms outstretched for balance, he saw the pickup dance like water on a hot grill as it shimmied sideways into an empty parking space. The instant Micah understood what was happening, he started to move from under the second story walkway. He scrambled out into the asphalt parking lot. There was noise, a deep lingering boom like a vibrating thump on a giant drum. With no thought for his action, Micah headed for the pickup. Another man was struggling to get his car door open, while a woman with two small children was herding them back into the motel. Micah yelled at her.

"Don't. Get out of there. It can fall on you."

She either didn't hear, or didn't understand.

As suddenly as it started, the quake stopped. Everyone froze, looking around, waiting. When the ground moves it does more than bring down buildings, it shakes confidence in everything. Micah leaned on the pickup bed and waited. He thought he'd left this sort of problem behind. As he waited for any aftershocks, people started moving about, and the next tremor was too slight to notice unless you expected it. The motel looked okay except for a small crack that zigzagged from the foundation to the top floor. The sidewalk had several cracks, but the parking lot fared better, asphalt being more flexible than the rigid concrete.

As minutes passed, people recovered, motel doors opened and guests, some in nightclothes, came outside. They looked stunned, and started asking questions. Everyone agreed it must have been an earthquake. They also expressed amazement that it should happen in this location. Micah crossed the lot to his room where he carefully entered to check for damage. His bag was on the table beside the television where he had left it, the room's ceiling appeared undamaged. However, the wall beside the front window had a long crack, probably corresponding with the break in the outside wall. The window glass was unbroken. The motel might be unfit for guests until a thorough inspection and repair; still, it didn't seem too bad.

The bathroom appeared fine. Water still ran from the faucets and the stool flushed. Micah sat on the edge of the unmade bed and struggled to regain his earlier calm. He thought of all the obstacles and delays in the past days. It was hard to deny the suspicion that fate or something didn't want him to reach North Carolina. He dismissed the thought as fanciful. What possible difference could it make where he lived? He was like a wood chip floating on a wind-tossed sea, washed back and forth, touching things, but never connecting. Trying to make sense of life, or find a pattern in it was useless. His stomach rumbled. He was hungry, that was something anyone could understand, something reasonable, and solid. He stood and headed out the door to inquire about the free breakfast.

Others had decided upon the same course. The lobby and eating area were packed. A woman behind the coffee counter was busy cleaning up spills and refilling the coffee maker. People helped themselves to the array of breakfast items still on the counter. They even picked up individual boxes of cereal from the floor and poured the contents into a bowl. No one seemed fussy after such a frightening experience. Micah took a cup of coffee and managed to fill a paper plate with several strips of bacon and two bran muffins. He squeezed into a seat behind a corner table, and while he ate, he listened to the chatter filling the room. An earthquake was exciting.

The motel manager didn't seem to know what to do. If the building was damaged, the guests couldn't stay, although none of them seemed eager to leave without more information. Micah intended to leave as soon as he'd had enough to eat. He needed to find out about the I-55 Bridge. In his judgment, that was the one more likely to be open. Even a multi-car wreck was easier to clear than repairing the bridge carrying I-40 traffic. From last night's reports, the **Hernando de Soto Bridge** could take months to repair. They still didn't know what had caused the huge explosion right in the middle of the big 'M' shaped span.

If the Memphis-Arkansas Bridge didn't open soon, that left the Frisco Bridge and the Harahan, one a railway the other with two rail lines and a pedestrian bridge, neither any good to him. The lobby's large television, tuned to a news station, was hanging on the wall above a sofa. When a report about the earthquake started, the crowd grew silent. As with most emergencies and disasters, it took time for the complete story to emerge. Arkansas had suffered little damage, as the quake was mild. The man sitting at the table with Micah shook his head and raised an eyebrow.

"Didn't seem all that mild to me."

"The motel is still standing, guess it could have been worse," Micah offered.

The man agreed.

A lady still in hair curlers hushed them and peered at the television, as an old man near the sofa turned up the sound. There wasn't any information about the bridge. Micah expected as much since an earthquake was more exciting. When a 'breaking news' report appeared, he stopped a muffin halfway to his mouth, hoping they were finally getting around to the bridge. Damage to the east was worse than first suspected. Geologists were still studying the event and had no detailed explanation for the mild tremors that had hit the entire length of the Mississippi River. Minnesota had flooding because the river's limestone bluffs had crumbled into the river, blocking the flow and backing up tributaries.

Micah gulped the last of his lukewarm coffee, crumpled the cup, and pitched it into a trashcan at the end of the food bar. He didn't need to hear any more news. The bridge at Helena was closer than the one near Caruthersville, and he wanted to get across the river before anything else happened. Both vehicle-carrying Memphis bridges would not reopen until repaired, and he didn't want to wait. At any minute, he expected a swarm of locusts, or some other delay. Behind him, the lady with curlers in her hair had a young, red-haired boy by the arm, pushing past Micah as they headed for the door.

"Come on, Andy. We need to find your dad and get out of here."

Micah stood aside and held the door open for her. She nodded her thanks.

"We're heading back to Tucson. There's nothing across that river we need to see!"

He followed them into the parking lot and started toward his room. He had already packed, only needing to load the pickup. Activity had increased. Nearly all the motel's guests seemed in a rush to leave. It brought a tiny smile to Micah's lips. People in this part of the country were unaccustomed to the ground shaking. They reacted like a disturbed hill of ants. He loaded the pickup bed, fastened the cover, and stepped up into the cab. There was a line of cars at the motel exit waiting to turn out onto the main street. Micah intended to take Main Street south as it turned into Highway 1. From there it was a straight shot to Highway 49, and he'd be in Helena in no time. A couple of the drivers were impatient, they honked as if that would get them out of the lot faster. Micah frowned and leaned forward to see the main street. It seemed too busy. There shouldn't be this much traffic in a town of under fifteen thousand. The tremor must have brought people out to see the damage.

As he edged into traffic, the going was faster because most everyone was turning north back toward I-40. Micah was satisfied with his choice. He didn't want to be stuck on the interstate again. He'd drive south clear to the crossing at Greenville, if he had to. The extra cans of gasoline and the snacks in the cooler were comforting. No one would believe the obstacles on this trip. Helping Taylor had actually felt good. It had taken his mind off things, although he could have done without the other delays.

At the edge of town, on the right stood a Citgo station. The pickup's gas gauge was a hair off full. Micah quickly pulled in behind two cars and waited his turn at the pumps. Not knowing where the next station might be, there was no sense taking chances, especially off the interstate. People standing at the pumps talked to one another, smiling and laughing over the excitement. When his turn came, he went into the station to arrange to pay cash. Three men were standing near the door talking about the earthquake. Micah listened.

"Knew it was coming..." said an old black man, "...told my kids they shouldn't live in a big city. Not safe if trouble comes."

After paying, and as Micah put money back into his billfold, he stepped closer to the men.

"What big city is that?"

"Why, St. Louis. Thank the good Lord they were out of there when it happened." He turned back to his friends. "Rolen had a vacation and he took Cassie and the kids to the Jersey shore."

Micah's curiosity overcame his hesitance. Maybe they weren't talking about the quake.

"What happened in St. Louis?"

"Flooded. The Missouri backed up and spilled out across the whole city. They say it has something to do with what's going on up and down the big river. Slides blocking things."

"Have you heard anything about the crossing at Helena?"

The old man shook his head.

"Not directly. But nobody is getting across at Memphis."

"Yes, I thought not. The explosion on the one bridge and the wreck on the other."

"That's not all. Both those bridges have near collapsed. Those things you said might have weakened them but the earthquake finished the job. I hear they closed the train tracks and walking bridge, too. No getting across near Memphis, lest you want to swim." The old man chuckled.

The television news had mentioned flooding in Minnesota where riverbanks had crumbled. Geologists were quick to point out that the Minnesota area was not earthquake prone, although, there was a known fault line and over the years, several minor quakes had occurred. Micah's heart beat faster and worry tinged his thoughts. If the river flooded that far north, and with St. Louis under water, something big must be happening. He went back to the truck and pumped four gallons of gasoline into the tank. So far, the pickup had averaged around ten or eleven miles per gallon. This would get him forty miles or more down the road. It was good that he had stopped, because now the line for gasoline reached to the curb.

He felt a great kinship with the woman in the curlers; it *was* time to get out of here. However, he appreciated the irony of heading east toward the problem, rather than west away from it. Still, he wasn't willing to give up. The Memphis bridges shouldn't have collapsed with this minor shake. It was more than probable that the earlier damage had weakened them. All the other bridges across the Mississippi should still be standing. Their great expanses of steel girders and pilings of reinforced concrete would have survived this light quake. From his experiences in California, the shaking he'd felt at the motel was no more than a magnitude 3.5, 4 at the most. In retrospect, it had lasted only seconds. The crack in the motel wall and broken sidewalk spoke more of faulty construction since a minor shake damaged it. On the west coast, a tremor this minor would not have made the news. They reported tremors in Oklahoma and Arkansas not for their size but for their uniqueness. Earthquakes should not occur in the middle of large, stable earth plates.

Traffic was light south of town. It was mid-morning, and a much later start than Micah had wanted. On either side of Highway 1, vast green fields stretched toward the east and the west. The few houses stood far back from the road and several miles apart. The people living in them probably felt little shaking, and if they were outside they might not have noticed at all. A seamless blue sky soared miles above the emerald floodplain, a distant line of trees the only mark on the horizon. Space here seemed even greater than that of the western deserts. The lack of hills or rocky outcropping gave the impression of a land without boundaries. Micah was anxious to reach Highway 49 and turn east, but not in such a rush as the jacked-up blue Chevy truck that came up fast behind him. It honked, and roared past on giant tires. Micah shrugged. The driver was either going to a fire or just a speed freak.

Other vehicles, mostly pickups, heading north flashed by in the other lane. Maybe they had heard about the earthquake and were going into town to see the damage. If so, they'd be disappointed. There hadn't been much; most of the town looked normal. Maybe a few items fell off store shelves, but probably not even that. Micah was looking forward to crossing the Mississippi. It had been years since he'd seen the river. He remembered it as an inspiring sight.

Hard to imagine it started out in the north as a narrow stream, but it gained volume and speed as the Ohio River and the Missouri River poured into it. It deserved its reputation as big and mighty. In places, it was miles across. It supplied water and transportation, and it connected the big cities. It was one of the country's great features, like the Rocky Mountains or the Great Lakes.

Micah recalled the conversation back at the gas station, the old man telling about the flood in St. Louis caused by the Missouri River backup. He'd like to know more about that. He wondered if the same thing might happen in Cairo, where the Ohio joined the Mississippi. If he weren't in a hurry, he'd stop and inquire. Instead, he turned on the radio. Music, weather, and a talk show were all that came in clearly. He turned it off, no real need for news. He was going to find a bridge and cross the river before anything else happened! It was encouraging when the highway divided with two lanes in each direction; no need to worry about those who wanted to go around him. However, the relief didn't last any longer than did the divided highway.

Near Highway 79, the line of trees to the east caught Micah's attention. They were moving! In the next instant, the field rolled toward him like an ocean wave. He didn't have time to slow the pickup before the two-lane pavement buckled and split. He fought the steering wheel, at the same time taking his foot off the gas and slowly pressing the brake. It all seemed in slow motion, but he knew the destruction was happening in split seconds. There was noise almost like the ringing of a deep-throated bell, along with the sound of wood cracking apart. Micah took his foot off the brake and twisted the wheel to the right, dodging a section of broken pavement. He wasn't sure what to do. The ground continued to shake and roll almost like a dog flinging water out of its wet coat.

His instinct was to *run*, get out of the area as fast as possible. This was the second tremor of the day. From all indication, it was stronger than the first. Yet, in the open countryside, with pavement the only manmade feature, it was hard to judge the strength of the quake. Several cars and a large delivery van going north passed by in the opposite lane. They swerved and curved around crumbling pavement the same as Micah did. The two-lane highway was woefully narrow for the fast, erratic driving. Glimpses of the other drivers showed faces as terrified as Micah felt. He wished the divided highway hadn't ended. He wasn't familiar with the country but when a paved road leading west presented itself, he intended to take it. This earthquake seemed centered near the Mississippi River. He had heard of the dormant fault near New Madrid, Missouri. He didn't know how far north of Memphis that was, but he was southwest of Memphis by at least forty miles. Maybe this was another fault, something related to the rumbles coming out of Oklahoma.

Micah cut into the northbound lane to avoid a portion of asphalt that had fallen away into the ditch. The earth's shaking had subsided, but Micah's hadn't. He gripped the steering wheel and wanted nothing more than to get to solid ground. Ahead in his lane, a car was in the ditch almost on its side. A young woman and two small children were standing beside it. Micah slowed and stopped several yards from them. The children were girls, one not more than six, the other half that old. They were clinging to the woman, probably their mother. She raised her arm to wave at him. For the minute, there was no traffic in either direction. He parked as near the edge of the pavement as was safe and climbed out of the pickup.

The young woman was thin. She was wearing a sleeveless summer dress, and her long red hair was tied back with a ribbon. The two small girls were dressed the same as their mother. She raised her arm, a purse dangling from her shoulder, and called out to Micah.

"Can you help us?" She pointed to the car. "Can you pull us out of the ditch?"

All three of them seemed rooted to the spot, afraid to move. Micah came forward, walked around the car, and shook his head. The ditch was almost four feet deep and twice that wide. His pickup could not pull it up the incline and back onto the road, even if he had rope or a chain. The three of them were lucky they had been able to get out.

"Sorry. You need a wrecker. Where are you going? I can give you a lift."

She took one tentative step toward him, the girls still clinging to her side.

"We were going to visit my mother. She lives in Greenfield, just a few miles down the road."

As she spoke, a light tremor made the road quiver. The small girls screamed and their mother turned a shade paler.

"You have everything you need out of the car?"

She nodded.

"Come, I'll help you."

The four of them hurried to the pickup. Micah helped the mother onto the bench seat, and handed up one child after the other. As he ran around the front of the pickup, a truck coming from the south whizzed past. Once behind the steering wheel, he wondered if he was going the wrong way. The cars going north all seemed in a rush. He turned to the young woman.

"I'm Micah Hanson. On my way to North Carolina, but this earthquake is slowing me down."

He tried to laugh, but it didn't sound cheerful. Still, the young woman smiled, while the children regarded him with huge round blue eyes.

"I'm Tracy Greer. This is Alice..." She indicated the older girl. "...the baby is Carrie. We live in Forrest City. We felt the quake this morning, but it didn't do anything to our house. My husband went on to work. I called my mother and she was okay, but she was scared. Guess I should have stayed home."

Micah glanced at her as she pressed her lips together as if to cut off her babbling. He quickly turned his gaze back to the road, watching for damage.

"How much farther is Greenfield?"

"Not far. My mom is alone. She stayed in the house after Dad died. I told her she's welcome to come live with us."

The ground gave a sharp jerk to the right. Micah pressed on the gas, no reason other than the urge to out-run the danger. The two little girls were silent, too scared to do more than press tighter to their mother who wrapped her arms around them. Micah wanted to comfort them, but he didn't know what to say. Tracy raised her hand and pointed toward a green sign indicating a mile to Greenfield.

"There," Tracy said. "We are almost to the turn-off. It's the first road to the right after the Sonic. You could let us off at the corner. It's just a couple of blocks after that."

"No, that's okay. A couple of blocks aren't that far out of my way."

On the outskirts of town they passed by a low metal building. The large sign near the road indicated it was an auto repair. The building seemed okay but the sign was hanging sideways from a leaning pole. The gravel parking lot had a wide crack and the front wheel of a Honda hung over it; the other three wheels were on solid ground. As they came into town, more damage was evident. Although, this didn't seem to stop people from being out on the streets. The traffic lights were working, but it made Micah nervous to sit waiting for the light to change. He couldn't say why, but he felt safer when moving. Near the main crossroads of town stood a three-story building with flowerbeds and a fountain out front. Tracy gasped.

"That's City Hall; what's left of it."

Micah slowed the pickup. The building was red brick and the southwest corner from top to bottom had crumbled. People were gathered around, some of them digging through the rubble. An ambulance stood at the curb, but if anyone was hurt, they were still inside. Tracy shook her head.

"A tornado came through town last spring and that building didn't get a scratch."

A distant siren sounded and Micah drove on. Nearly every building showed some sign of damage. There were cracks in the pavement. One side street had a broken water main spewing a four-foot-high gusher. Tracy trembled, and the children remained quiet as fawns hiding from a predator. Micah spotted the Sonic a block ahead. Tracy didn't speak, but she pointed at the street beyond.

Micah turned onto a street that had businesses for the first block and became residential after that. People were out checking their houses, finding cracked foundations and damaged carports. In the next block, Tracy nearly bounced up and down on the pickup's seat.

"Look, that's my mom."

A heavyset woman with bright blonde hair was at the bottom of the front steps struggling to set a huge flowerpot back onto the porch. Micah swung into the driveway and before he could completely stop, Tracy had the door open. She stood Alice out onto the ground, climbed after her, and turned to grab Carrie. The woman had let the big flowerpot topple and rushed toward her granddaughter. She picked up Alice and, hugging her, swung the child around. In a minute grandmother, mother, and children were embracing. The house didn't look badly damaged, yet on closer inspection the garage door did seem to be hanging crooked with a large crack in the top header.

Tracy quickly explained to her mother how Micah had helped them and that her car was back along the road in a ditch. She introduced her mother as Barbara Meeks. They urged Micah to come in and have a cold drink. They wanted to thank him. He was tempted, but felt the urge to move on. Tracy smiled.

"I understand. If you don't live here, who'd want to stay around!"

Micah stood with one foot on the ground, the other on the edge of the pickup's doorframe.

"I'd stay if you need help with anything."

"It's okay, I know people here, and I'll call Gary. He'll be mad about the car, but that's just too bad!"

Holding Carrie, Barbara said, "If people have earthquake insurance I expect there will be a lot of claims. Are you sure you won't come in? It's almost lunch time."

"No, I better go. I wanted to try the bridge at Helena. Have you heard anything?"

Barbara bounced Carrie on her ample hip as she shook her head.

"I doubt you'll have much luck there. The television said there's flooding all along the river, clear down to Greenville. Besides that, they claim bridges have to be inspected before normal traffic can start up. You could stay here till we find out something."

"Thanks, but if the road is blocked, I'll go to the Gulf if I need to."

They all laughed as Micah swung into the truck and settled behind the steering wheel.

"Are you sure you'll be okay?"

Tracy nodded.

"Yes. The river has flooded before. If we have trouble here, Mom can come stay with us. What we fear is heavy rains. They cause creeks to rise, giving us some bad flooding. I expect this flooding is only some sloshing around because of the earthquake."

Micah believed that Tracy and her family could cope with the situation. As he drove away he looked in the rearview mirror and saw the little group waving. There had been some friendly people along this route. Not all of them had anything to be happy or friendly about, which made him consider his own character. If crisis revealed character, what did his running away reveal? The question scarcely touched his mind before it vanished. Resettling at the cabin was the thing to do! He refused to question it. Taylor had given him transportation, that should be some type of proof.

He was halfway to the highway that turned east toward Helena; should a problem arise he'd turn around and find another way. After two quakes that had produced minor damage in the area, Micah was aware of the slightest tremble. He watched for problems with the pavement. Most of the damage was to the sides of the road, where the built-up bank formed a verge. In places, it had melted away, leaving the pavement with no foundation. It was more comforting to see the broken and fallen away asphalt than to wonder if there was a void beneath it. With this in mind, he drove as close to the middle line as possible, edging over when meeting oncoming traffic. He also watched the eastern fields for further sign of disturbance. The trees were not shaking, but the water level in the ditch seemed higher.

Any number of things could account for the rising water—the quake could have changed the course of the big river, crumbling banks might dam streams, or sections of land dropped letting the water accumulate. Tracy was right about the flooding. Heavy rain was a greater danger. There was only so much water in the river, but thinking of all the tributaries feeding it gave him pause. For his purpose he worried more about the integrity of the bridges, and if the authorities might restrict crossings. He suspected they'd play it safe and close a bridge even if he'd be willing to drive over it. South of Greenfield the trees grew closer to the highway. They were overgrown with kudzu forming green banks, almost like small hills in the flat land. Some of the ditches held patches of white Queen Anne's Lace.

On the outskirts of Helena, his shoulders relaxed and he realized how tense he'd been. With the river minutes away, he only needed to find out if traffic was crossing the bridge. There didn't seem to be any disruption. Vehicles were moving along in both directions. With his practice of buying gasoline whenever available, he watched for a gas station; if there was a restaurant nearby, even better. With his goal in sight, he was relieved enough to be hungry. There didn't seem to be any earthquake damage and his hopes for an intact bridge increased. Still, with some of the buildings it was hard to say whether the quake or age had caused their condition. The same applied to cracked parking lot pavement. A four-lane highway turned to the right, but he continued into the business area where there seemed a better chance of finding food and gasoline. Shortly, a gas station and a Pizza Hut presented themselves. He bought a small amount of gas, and parked in a vacant area some distance from the fast food restaurant. He stretched his legs as he walked. It felt good. After sitting behind the wheel for hours, he welcomed the exercise.

Inside he placed his order and found a seat near a window. The pizza was filling, and with a nod to Jena, there was a salad. As he ate, he studied the old red truck parked in the empty lot. It felt right to keep an eye on the truck, probably a holdover from nearly losing it to a thief. He mused over plans for the pickup. There were probably parts dealers near Asheville, which wasn't more than an hour or so from the cabin. He hadn't decided how far to take the restoration, maybe just a paint job and a little repair to the interior. Still, if he really got into the swing of it, he could restore the F-150 to its original condition. The idea was almost exciting, a worthy project. That along with repairing the cabin gave him purpose.

He stood, dumped his paper dishes into the trash, stacked the tray, and made a quick stop in the restroom to wash. Refreshed, and with high hopes for the remainder of the trip, Micah stepped out into a bright afternoon.

Halfway to the pickup the world shattered.

The jolt was like a sledgehammer striking a mighty oak; the shock waves were almost audible. Micah fell to his knees, his hands skidding over sharp gravel that felt like glass. Across the street, the gas station's canopy collapsed on the four pumps and a car. Behind that, the store's glass front exploded; shards of the large windows flew outward. The vibrations in the earth set Micah's teeth on edge. The sounds of metal twisting and wood splitting made his head ring like a bell.

He knew what was happening, yet it was too enormous to accept. Buildings in every direction crumbled, shaken from their foundations. Trees bordering the parking area fell over, flattened to the ground. Cars on the highway skidded sideways, ending in ditches. The noise level rose as if a wrecking crane were knocking down every standing structure. Micah tried to get up. His legs shook and he fell...again he tried to stand. After the first mighty jerk, the ground continued to shake as if trying to settle into a new configuration. Amid the sounds of destruction, human cries arose, sounding like high-pitched screams. Micah thought they were voices. Yet the volume was too great; maybe it came from activated sirens.

As the trembling ground finally settled, Micah got to his feet. Now, his nerves more than the tremors made it hard to stand. The area had changed from a highway through a small town with shops on either side, to a jumbled junkyard. The Walmart far across a large parking lot was a gray pile of rubble; the front sign on end pointed toward a peaceful blue sky. A split in the pavement had opened between Micah and his pickup. The crack stretched from the flattened Pizza Hut, across the small side street, to the crumbled gas station. He turned back to the fast food restaurant. He couldn't remember how many people were inside. As he drew near, he saw a young man along with a girl working their way out of the ruin. Micah ran to help them.

In the vast vault of the sky, the whirl of helicopters came from the west. The beating of their rotors became the dominant sound. As Micah lifted a metal panel out of the way of the girl, the young man helped her step onto the pavement. They had lost their hats but from the shirts they wore it was plain they were employees.

"Anyone else in there?" Micah asked.

They both nodded. The girl was rubbing her bleeding arm, smearing the blood. The man had a cut on his forehead and didn't seem to notice it. The building was almost flat, the metal sides folded in. The best hope for survivors was in the middle of the building where the collapsed sides formed a steeple. Micah started searching for a larger opening in the wreckage.

"Hello, can you hear me?" he called.

"Yeah. Over here."

The young man followed Micah toward the voice. After pulling away more siding, they found a man and woman huddled under a table. In another booth a mother with a small boy had ducked under a table, too. All four customers were able to crawl outside through the wreckage. In the main aisle, where the counter had been, lay a girl in a uniform. The young man shook his head.

"That's Maylee. Is she alive?"

Micah duck waddled around a booth to reach her. She didn't seem to be breathing, but he felt a faint pulse in her neck. There wasn't room to do anything, and he was afraid to move her. The warble of sirens increased; it sounded like a horde of descending insects. Micah backed out of the wreckage on his hands and knees behind the young man. An ambulance and two police cars were near the collapsed gas station. The four Pizza Hut customers and two workers were standing beside the crack in the street. Micah called to them.

"Can someone find help? A girl, inside, she's hurt."

The man Micah had helped from the wreckage nodded. "I'll go." He hobbled toward the ambulance; his torn pant leg revealed a long cut near his knee.

Just as a fire truck arrived, a yellow flame shot skyward out of the gas station. The police urged everyone to move away into the middle of the Walmart's big parking lot. One of the attendants from the ambulance was examining the girl's bleeding arm, while she told him about her co-worker in the crumpled building. The other emergency worker tried to help the man with the wounded leg, but he shook his head and pointed toward Micah. When the medic reached him, Micah explained about the trapped girl. Then, he took him to the gap in the siding where they crawled through to the wounded girl.

"Can I help?" Micah asked.

"Go tell my partner to bring a stretcher."

The building seemed stable, but Micah worried about further shaking. In the parking lot a large group was gathered. They had come from the Walmart, and from surrounding businesses. Several of them had minor injuries. Some of the uninjured men were forming teams to dig through the rubble for victims. The four policemen discouraged such activity. They had herded survivors into the center of the lot and were intent upon keeping them safe. Hovering over the scene were two helicopters; they made wide circles as if surveying the surrounding area. Probably news stations covering the situation. Micah wished he knew what they could see. He wondered how widespread the destruction was, if more help was on the way, and if he could do anything to help.

Micah slowly turned in a circle, seeing wreckage in every direction. Four more fires burned in the immediate area, and the one fire truck was clearly overwhelmed. Maybe letting the piles of wreckage burn was best; it saved bulldozing them. There was not a cloud on the horizon, no chance of rain to put out the fires. Still, a downpour could turn the rubble to piles of slush, and hinder rescue efforts. The destruction demoralized Micah. It was the exterior reflection of his inner feelings; it proved the folly of human endeavor.

If death didn't show the futility of life, nature stepped in to deliver the ultimate proof. He stumbled to his pickup and climbed into the cab. The truck was an island of safety in a sea of danger.

He was in sight of the main highway running through town. Emergency vehicles roared back and forth, lights flashing, sirens screaming. Perhaps a hospital was still operational. More fires broke out and clouds of black smoke billowed up to meet the blue sky. The two previous quakes were warnings of the third greater one. There was no promise that the depths of the earth wouldn't continue to shift, even more violently. Aftershocks could go on for months. Feeling he needed to help in some way, Micah stepped out of the pickup. He headed toward the nearest police car. The local officers were probably in shock as much as anyone, but they should let the able-bodied help. A young policeman was standing beside the open door of his patrol car speaking on a cell phone. He kept repeating, "Yes. Okay, I understand." His light brown skin was shiny with sweat, and his black eyes shifted from side to side as if trying to watch everything at once. When he closed the phone, Micah spoke.

"Is there something I can do? Some of the uninjured men could search the rubble."

The officer looked to be in his late twenties. His partner was in the street directing what had turned into a steady stream of traffic. As many as could were leaving the area, heading west away from the danger.

Micah asked his question again, and this time got the officer's attention.

"What? Yes. Maybe you can help. They are evacuating the hospital. Ambulances and buses to take them to Little Rock. They need help loading them."

"I'm not local. Tell me how to find the hospital."

Before he could answer, another call came. The officer turned away and had about the same conversation as the last call. When he stopped, he gave Micah directions to the hospital.

"I don't know how clear the streets are between here and there."

"I'll find it. How big was this earthquake?"

"I don't know."

"Is it just this area?"

"No. Best I can find out, most of the river towns are hit, from Dubuque right down to New Orleans."

Micah took a step backwards. That was nearly the whole river. The old man at the filling station in Forrest City had spoken of water rising in St. Louis, and the news had told of flooding in Minnesota. It was like all the fault lines beneath the great basin were failing, one after another. It could mean more was on the way! Micah thanked the officer, who had turned his attention to other things, and ran to the pickup. Getting across the highway would have been difficult were it not for the officer directing traffic. Maybe not all electricity was out, but these traffic lights were. When he reached a side street, the going was easier. The standing houses made of brick or stone had some damage, but those built of wood looked like piles of lumber.

People were in their yards trying to gather trash, piling stacks of it near the curb. Micah wondered when the town could recover enough to pick it up. He felt as if the quake had hit only minutes ago, yet from the direction and length of shadows, it was late afternoon. Hours had passed; maybe he had sat in the pickup longer than he thought. Trying to find the hospital by the officer's directions didn't work. One street was blocked, and it took several turns to get back in the right area. When the hospital came into view, a line of two ambulances and three buses stood at the northwest corner. Micah parked in the lot beside the front entrance. The building looked intact until on closer inspection the cracks in the foundation were evident. They lined up with zigzag breaks running across the asphalt lot.

The two-story hospital built of yellow sandstone was 'L' shaped, with the emergency room in the back between the two wings. Micah entered the lobby where sofas and armchairs formed a line across the back wall, as if they had slid there. The big curved reception desk appeared undamaged and an older black woman was sitting behind it. In the hallways leading from the lobby, hospital employees, nurses and orderlies were rushing about. He asked the lady at the desk if they needed volunteers to help move patients. She tried to smile, but her dark eyes looked worried. She pointed to a hallway behind her.

"Go straight back, take the first hall to the right. They will tell you what to do."

It was a one-hundred-twenty bed hospital, with offices, pharmacy, x-ray, laboratory, and cafeteria on the first floor. As Micah passed the doors, he saw people salvaging supplies and boxing up records. An elevator and small waiting room were near the emergency room entrance. A line of patients in wheelchairs waited to be moved to the appropriate type vehicle. Nurses and other employees were quickly going about the evacuation. Micah looked for someone to tell him what to do. There was a gray-haired man in a blue suit standing in the small lobby giving instructions. Micah went to him. He was the hospital administrator. He told Micah to go outside and someone there would direct him. Micah's job was to assist in lifting stretchers into a waiting ambulance, or to help ambulatory patients from a wheelchair into a bus. It was an assembly line operation. There was noise from the vehicle engines, and shouts from people asking or giving instructions, and occasionally a moan or gasp. There should have been more expressions of pain, considering the condition of some patients.

The sun was low but the day still hot. Sweat ran down Micah's face, the back of his shirt grew damp, and other people were in the same shape. He and an orderly in a green uniform became a team. They took patients from the nurse at the door and conveyed them to a waiting vehicle. This day the hospital held eighty patients and all had to leave. The building might remain standing even with the cracks, but the utilities were gone. Electric lines, overhead and underground were broken, water pipes leaked, and there was talk that the town's main water line had ruptured. Moving the patients went surprisingly fast. There were two school buses and one church bus. The three buses provided plenty of room for sixty-five of the ambulatory patients. Of the fifteen other patients, only five needed to remain on cots. The ambulances carried two of the five on benches.

Due to the circumstances, getting them out of the area to another hospital took precedence over proper procedure.

The nearest hospital on the west side of the river was Forrest City. Although, after the third quake they too needed help and had none to offer. Hit three times, Forrest City had trouble of its own. Communications were not reliable, and flooding complicated the widespread destruction, while rumors and misinformation abounded. By twilight, the patients and hospital personnel who were to accompany them were on the road heading west. They would try for the nearest towns and keep going if they found no room. After the buses and ambulances left, food and drink magically appeared in the emergency room and at the desk in the front lobby. It was amazing how many women came to prepare and serve a meal in the face of such devastation. Micah accepted a ham sandwich along with a paper cup of lemonade and sat on the end of a sofa in the lobby. Others also took time out to eat.

Darkness descended and the only light came from battery powered lanterns, headlights, and the growing number of fires. After eating a quick snack, most of the workers left. They had homes and family needing help. Ten people remained. One of them was the older black lady who worked behind the desk. She had also taken part in preparing the food. For some reason, two young men started rearranging the lobby furniture, putting it back in the original places, Micah supposed. Three women repackaged the remaining food. One of them came to Micah holding out two sandwiches. She was short and round with a face made to smile, but it wasn't.

"Please take these," she said. "They will only spoil. We really should be at the stores gathering up canned food. Nothing else will last."

Micah took the sandwiches and thanked her.

She walked back to the other ladies and when they finished their job, they looked around as if in a daze. The two young men had wandered away and taken one of the lanterns with them. The remaining light sitting on the desk caused dark shadows to hang in the corners of the big room. As the rest of the people in the lobby left, a man took the remaining lantern. After that, the hospital grew silent except for an occasional clatter in a distant hall. Maybe it was something falling to the floor, or someone gathering up supplies. Moonlight filtered softly through the cracked glass doors and shone down from the clerestory windows near the ceiling. Micah noticed that several windows had lost their panes, although there was no broken glass on the floor. The pieces must have fallen outside on the ground.

As he sat on a sofa near the lobby doors, he considered sleeping there. It was more comfortable than the pickup, and he didn't relish the idea of setting out in the night. Best to wait until morning when there should be more information on the road and bridge conditions. It seemed unlikely that the river was impassable. Some bridges must have survived. Highway Patrol would have information. He took his cell phone from his shirt pocket, leaned back on the sofa and tried to get a signal. When nothing worked, he stood and walked around in the lobby hoping to find a connection. Landlines might be down, but maybe some nearby towers were still standing. Giving up, he went to the reception desk and picked up the telephone there. Not even a dial tone, just dead silence. Now would be a good time to own a satellite phone, Micah concluded.

He crossed to the lobby doors and looked out at the empty lot where the old red pickup stood like a deserted relic. It made him think of Taylor and Charlie Redman, which in turn brought thoughts of death. For the past few months the subject was always lurking in the back of his mind. It didn't take much to bring it forward.

A sudden weariness made him tremble, and his legs shook. He went back to the sofa, sat, put his legs up, stretched out, and closed his eyes. With his arm resting on his forehead, it shut out even the weak moonlight. He couldn't understand why his simple goal of reaching the cabin was this hard. He would need to leave the area, that was sure, go back west out of the damage. From what he knew of earthquakes, it would be a long time before the region was back to normal. The nearest unaffected city would have an airport, so flying over the river was an option. But traveling that way didn't include the pickup, and he didn't want to leave it. Maybe a boat of some sort, or a ferry. People would be wanting to go from one side of the river to the other, and they would set up some type of transportation.

Focusing on the immediate problem of his continued trip helped cover the raw, painful feelings that refused to heal. Traveling was a way of keeping busy. Having a plan, like moving into the cabin and remodeling it, helped occupy his mind. After what he'd lost, Micah hoped for an uncomplicated life and when the time came, an easy death. He'd appreciate this bit of mercy. He did not consider giving up and going back to California. He admitted that earlier the idea had floated at the edge of his thoughts, but with each roadblock, he grew more determined. As he relaxed against the sofa cushions, his confidence grew. There had to be a way across the river. He'd go south to the Gulf or north to Canada; it was a detour, nothing more. In the silence and darkness, weariness put him to sleep.

Six

Something hit the soles of Micah's boots and a hand roughly shook his shoulder. He jerked awake and sat up, blinking in the beam of a flashlight.

"What?" he stuttered.

"Who are you, buddy? What are you doing here?"

"Ah, ah, Micah Hanson. Guess I fell asleep."

As the light left his face, he saw a black police officer in a dark blue uniform.

"You can't sleep here. That your pickup out front, with the California plates?"

"Yes. Yes. I'm traveling through; the quake caught me here."

"Do you have any identification?"

Micah reached for his billfold, took out his driver's license, and handed it to the officer who put a light on it. He examined the license. Then looked back at Micah, and seeming satisfied, he returned it.

"You need to move on. The town is being evacuated, most are gone by now. Except for the looters."

Micah stood. "Looters?"

"Yes. They sift through stores, houses, anything they can get to. You're lucky they haven't found your pickup."

Micah looked toward the dark parking lot, a moment of panic making his heart race.

"Thanks for waking me. I'll be on my way now. Any news on how to get across the river?"

The officer lifted a lip in scorn.

"I doubt anyone will be crossing it any time soon."

"I could go south to New Orleans."

Now the officer laughed.

"You could, but seems they are worse than we are. Down there, the river broke through some levies and is taking another route to the Gulf. Come on now, you need to be on your way."

Micah followed the policeman out of the hospital and into the parking lot where a white patrol car stood beside his truck. He squinted at his watch, surprised to find it was three in the morning. He'd had a few hours' sleep; it accounted for his feeling rested. Darkness still prevailed but there was a hint of the coming dawn. Fires still burned and in the distance there was the occasional shout, or cry. The air smelled of oil and soot. The sound of gunfire startled Micah and he turned to the officer.

"What is that?"

"Nothing to worry you. Follow me. I'll get you out to the highway. Go west and keep going until you are out of this mess. I believe they are setting up FEMA camps near Little Rock, though they have damage there too. If I was you, I'd go all the way to Fort Smith before deciding what to do."

"That bad, is it?"

The officer opened the pickup's door and motioned Micah to get in, so he did. He put the key in the ignition and started the engine. The officer gave a wave, climbed into the patrol car and headed across the lot. Micah turned in the same direction to follow him. In the double headlights, destruction on each side of the neighborhood streets looked worse than it had in the daylight. The officer took a short route to the highway and pulled into the lot where a filling station had once stood. He stuck his arm out the window and motioned for Micah to pull around him. Micah drew alongside, parked, got out, and crossed to the driver's side of the patrol car.

"I want to thank you, and wish you the best for your town."

For the first time, the officer smiled.

"Good luck to you, too."

At the edge of town, Micah had to stop at a roadblock. Cars were parked across both traffic lanes, leaving a small opening in the center. It was enough room for one vehicle at a time to pass through. The area was brightened by headlights and floodlights on short poles. Two troopers were manning the barrier. Micah stopped behind the van traveling in front of him. After the trooper checked and waved the van on, he motioned Micah forward.

"Identification," the officer requested.

"Sure," Micah said as he pulled out his billfold.

"Far from home, aren't you?"

"I was on my way to North Carolina. Is there any news about river crossings?"

He handed Micah the driver's license.

"Stay on Highway Forty-nine. There will be traffic control at major intersections. All lanes are open to the west. No one is allowed east of Little Rock."

"What about the people who live between here and there?"

"Crews are sweeping the area, finding those who need help. Please, move along."

Micah nodded, pressed on the gas pedal, and did as instructed.

In places, the pavement had cracked. Micah drove slowly to miss the damage. Several vehicles were on the siding, either out of gas or facing other problems. He was soon near a road that turned straight north toward Forrest City. Micah hesitated, but continued northwest. The patrolman was right; it was best to get out of the area. The traffic was light, and he met only two cars going east. Maybe they had homes to check on, or they were volunteer help. The summer night was not much cooler than the day. The odor of water and vegetation gave the slight breeze a swampy smell. In the flooded areas, with fields and bushes underwater, the sun would soon put a rotten stench in the air. Micah longed to reach the cabin in the cool mountain retreat.

He had considered flying but he doubted he would be that desperate. Leaving the pickup was out of the question. He was sure he could get to his destination by driving north. The news about New Orleans and the Gulf ruled out a crossing in the south. The bridge on Highway 80 was a possibility. Even if the river had some course changes they should be in the more open land to the south. As he drove, Micah drew comfort from his determination. No matter how long it took, he would make it. He had never been to Iowa or Illinois; it would be an adventure. The vast expanse of his native land was amazing, and the diversity was astounding. Pick up a person in San Francisco's Chinatown and set them down in Austin, Texas, or Fort Smith, or his cove in the Smoky Mountains and they would feel they were on another planet.

He tried to plan a new route. The destruction in the town behind was hard to forget. The thought of the many other river cities and towns in the same shape was too much to imagine. In Little Rock, he'd get some reliable news. He'd been on the road for thirty minutes. Another hour and a half should get him there. The past afternoon and evening replayed in his mind. He wondered if the people pulled out of the Pizza Hut were okay, and the ones removed from the hospital? Where had the buses and ambulances taken them? Considering the size of the affected area, there could be thousands, even a million, people displaced.

The patrolman at the crossroad had spoken of a FEMA camp. There could be more than one, and Little Rock might not be far enough away to escape the confusion. The officer that woke him in the hospital had mentioned looters. Micah started watching for a spot to pull off the highway. He hadn't opened the pickup bed before leaving Helena, and he needed to check his supplies. Soon, there was a dirt road in the headlights and he slowed to make the right turn. The gravel and reddish clay of the road looked recently graded, with ditches on either side. Watching for oncoming cars, Micah pulled beyond the dirt road, carefully backed in and stopped. A quick check of the items in the truck bed would relieve his mind.

The cloudless predawn let the moon turn the scene into shades of blue to darkest black. As he walked around the truck bed, he inspected the cover. There was no indication of damage, and when he unlocked the tailgate to look inside, nothing was disturbed. He had hesitated to have a tailgate lock installed, but the security was worth it. Since the new bed cover wasn't original either, he'd gone ahead and done it. Taylor would have approved. Besides, if he restored the old pickup, many parts might be newer material. The guys at the garage had to make some adjustment for the lock but when they finished it looked fine. Micah folded the cover back one panel and reached for his backpack. Thoughts of looters made him decide to carry the bag in the cab, for there was a handgun resting beneath his new socks. He'd only ever fired the thirty-eight on a practice range in the gun shop. The pistol had seemed a necessary item to the business on the boardwalk. Because of Jordan, he had been especially careful to keep the gun in a secure place.

While the pickup bed was open, Micah took a bottle of water and a couple of granola bars from the small ice chest. He set the items on the ground, closed and locked the bed. Sitting in the cab, he put the backpack on the floor and unwrapped a granola bar. He ate slowly and washed it down with the water. It was quiet sitting in the moonlight watching the traffic on the highway. He looked across the dark landscape. If the quake had done damage here, it didn't show. However, the ditch on the east side of the road was full of water that shimmered with silver light. Occasionally it quivered, almost a dancing vibration with tiny whitecaps. Micah watched for a few minutes, started the truck, turned on the headlights, and got back onto the paved highway. He didn't like the looks of the water, especially when there wasn't enough wind to cause the disturbance.

Traffic was light, but still more than expected at this time of morning. At the intersection of Highway 79, it was almost a traffic jam because troopers had turned it into a four-way stop. Vehicles coming from the north added to the congestion, some wanting to continue south to Pine Bluff, and those on Highway 49 wanting to turn right. While waiting, Micah considered going south but decided against it. His goal was the far north because what the officer had said about New Orleans didn't sound good. He didn't know much about the Mississippi River except how powerful it was, and how levies and dams had directed its course. If the earthquake had knocked down the structures that kept this mighty river in check, it could be years before man again gained control. The cars, vans, and trucks edged forward. When Micah reached the intersection, the officer directed all traffic south. Micah shook his head and pointed north. The officer shook his head and pointed south with such determination that Micah turned left with the other travelers.

There was nothing to do but drive on. He'd find a way back to Little Rock, and once there reach a major highway north. It was almost five in the morning, and he'd not covered half the distance to Little Rock. It seemed he was stuck in a time warp. Still, driving in the dark on unfamiliar roads, and the fact that he had stopped for a while, could account for the feeling. The driving was slow on the two-lane road, even with both lanes open in the same direction. It appeared that this close to the river, no one could take any road north or east. Micah suspected some people knew of back roads that would take them where they wanted to go, but he didn't want to try it. Near the White River, his caution was justified. It was far out of its banks and he could see the water glistening in the spaces between trees. Beyond that, the open fields had a suspicious gleam, and the buildings on low ground beside the river had water near the roofline.

A man with a lantern was in charge of the river crossing. He allowed two cars at a time to traverse the high bridge. When they were out of sight, he sent two more. The bridge seemed steady but there hadn't been time for an inspection. If the structure should collapse, the two-car limit seemed wise. Micah followed a Jeep across. It drove fast, and he stepped on the gas to keep up, happy to get across. In the middle of the span, water rushed against the pilings a few feet below the bridge deck, but it was still dark and he didn't know the normal level of the water. The land was flat, with clumps of black trees, and nothing but dark ground stretching to a slightly lighter sky. Micah was tired of the Mississippi bottomland. It was too featureless. He realized he was being unfair. The rich basin supplied tons of rice, cotton, sorghum, corn, wheat, and crops that he couldn't even guess. If the river changed course it could damage the farmland. River towns had already been destroyed, and river traffic was disrupted. It was hard to believe the pipes carrying gas and oil beneath the river were still intact. What this earthquake could mean to the economy was staggering.

Micah drove faster, eager to reach a town or city that had accurate information about this disaster. It was an inconvenience for him, a delay in reaching the cabin. Yet, if things were as bad as he had begun to suspect, the entire country would suffer. The highway skirted most of the smaller towns. There was no way to know the extent of their damage, but at each intersection more vehicles added to the traffic. The pickup had used several gallons of gas and although it wasn't in danger of running out, it would be wise to fill up at the next chance. The twelve gallons in the truck bed were for emergencies only. Around five-thirty, the morning sky turned a light gray and to the east, a thin ribbon of pale pink rimmed the horizon. He could almost stop using the headlights.

The next road sign proclaimed a town ahead, and from the visible metal buildings, and tall silos, this town was near the highway. In hopes of finding a filling station, Micah turned off the main highway and took the business route. The streetlights were out. It might be there was no power, or perhaps they were on a timer and it was light enough. The storefronts were dark. A bank on the corner had a tumble of stone where one side had collapsed. There were only a few vehicles on the street. The center of town was about eight blocks long. As Micah neared the end of the main street, hopes of a filling station dimmed. Then, just beyond a used car lot, one came in sight. There were several cars waiting at the station's two pumps. Micah pulled in behind the last car. There were no lights on in the station. A man was operating the pumps and the big sign behind him said 'cash only' and a five-gallon limit.

Micah waited and watched. There was little talk, and each driver got his allotment and drove away. When the attendant stepped up to Micah's window he said, "Five gallon limit, cash only, pay up front." He sounded like a recording.

Micah took out his billfold and handed the man ten dollars.

"Great, but I'll only take four gallons, okay?" He figured he'd used about that much since the last filling.

"Good, my supply won't last long and no word of when another tanker will be here. Besides, I'll probably run out of fuel for the generator in another couple hours." He handed Micah a fifty-cent piece. "Rounded the price up, makes change easier."

As the man took off the gas cap and prepared to put in the fuel, Micah got out of the cab. He wanted information along with the gasoline.

"You get much damage around here?"

"Enough. Lots of flooding. We lost most utilities. The people out of town are on private wells, and without power, they're short on water. The city has emergency generators, but they won't stay up without a fuel supply."

"I came from Helena."

The man squinted up at him. "Pretty bad over there. Our clinic took some of their patients, but we're small and can't be sure we can take care of our own much longer."

"Do you hear anything from Little Rock?"

The man pulled the nozzle out of the tank, turned to hang it up, and gave a harsh laugh.

"I'd rather stay here and face what comes. People pouring in there from all up and down this section of the river. Emergency relief supposed to be available; I'm guessing those camps will turn into hell holes."

"And Pine Bluff?"

"Damage is about the same as us, I hear. The Arkansas is flooding them pretty good."

The driver waiting behind Micah scowled through his windshield. Micah got the message and quickly climbed back into the pickup. Driving slowly down Main Street, he could see the few restaurants looked closed. Even a convenience store was dark, and there was no one at the gas pumps. They were either empty or had no generator. He wished there was more in his ice chest. He should have picked up some candy bars when he bought the gasoline. He shook his head at the lack of forethought. He was accustomed to stopping any time to buy whatever he needed. Until now, he'd not been seriously concerned. He had only to get out of the earthquake's range, find a way across the river, and life would be back to normal. Whatever that was! He suddenly realized he should have used the restroom at the gas station. It wasn't quite daylight; perhaps a country road would serve.

A half mile on, at the edge of town, a dirt road came into view. There wasn't much traffic and Micah decided to risk a stop. He turned right onto the side road. The pickup jerked and bumped. The road had deep ruts with water standing in them, a bad place to be stuck. Micah turned off the headlights, and stepped out, careful to stand on the higher ridges. Flooded fields stretched away on either side of the road. Far ahead was an unpainted house with a low overhanging porch roof. He didn't see any lights. Either the people were not up yet, or had no electricity. Still, it was almost light. This was not an ideal place to stop, but becoming more necessary every minute. It had better be done quickly, but with as much discretion as possible. He stepped around the front bumper and going to the passenger side, opened the door as a shield. The road was already wet, and the ditch full; wouldn't even be a wet spot to mark his stop. He unzipped, and sighed with relief as the stream dwindled. Feeling much better, he closed the door and, watching the ruts, started around the front of the pickup.

A deep throaty growl made him look up from the ground. Standing a few feet from the bumper was a large dog. Its stiff legs were spread, and its black lips drawn back over long white teeth. Micah froze, swallowed, and judged the distance back to the door he'd just closed. The big shaggy dog stared at him. Micah tried not to stare back. He'd heard canines didn't like that. The growl rumbled deep in the dog's throat, mixed with a snarl, and the animal took a step forward. It looked about knee-high, and probably weighed around seventy or eighty pounds, although the heavy shaggy tan-and-black coat could be deceiving. One short ear stood straight, the other flopped over. Micah looked down the road toward the house he'd clearly trespassed. He edged around to the middle of the bumper while the dog tracked his progress.

When he reached the fender and took a step backward toward the driver's door, the dog swiftly made a half circle in the road to come even with the door. The brown eyes shifted between Micah and the door. Micah slowly turned to face the dog. He kept his hands at his sides.

"Easy, boy...or girl. I won't hurt you. Just stopped to pee."

He took a step closer to the door.

The big dog sprang forward, placing itself between Micah and the door. The dog's ragged coat brushed Micah's jeans. Micah looked toward the house, hoping someone would come if he yelled. He could rush the dog, push it aside, get the door open, and jump inside. But the dog might bite him, and from the way it was acting it could be rabid. Micah didn't want to take the chance. It was remotely possible he could make friends with it, or show some authority and make it leave. They couldn't stand like this forever. Maybe he could outwait the animal.

"Go home, get out of here. You go your way, I'll go mine. Git!"

The dog pressed against the door, tilted its head, and seemed ready to stay there. It had stopped growling. That was progress. Micah still didn't try to touch the dog. He didn't want to lose any fingers.

"Oh, come on now. Move."

It did, toward Micah, who took a step backward, his heel squishing in the mud. As he did, the dog pressed steadily forward with him, putting more distance between them and the pickup. After another step in the direction of the house, Micah had the feeling he was being herded. To test the thought, he took a step to the side avoiding a large puddle. The dog lowered its head and growled, moved sideways to track him. Either this dog wanted him to go somewhere, or it was getting ready to attack. He took two steps toward the pickup and the dog lunged at him. The vicious growl returned along with the bared teeth. Micah stopped. The dog stopped. With its eyes glowing, it seemed to study him. After a long minute, it slowly came to Micah's side, lifted its head, and gently gripped his shirtsleeve. When the dog tried to tug him toward the house, Micah gave up and started walking.

He thought of driving the pickup to the house, but he was sure the dog wouldn't understand. Besides, there seemed a good chance of being stuck in the mud. It was about a quarter mile to the house. The frame structure had a long front porch with a sagging roof. Two old cane chairs and a line of potted plants stood on the worn board floor. Micah stopped at the bottom of the two steps leading to the porch. The house was silent and dark. The dog stood beside Micah. When his nose gave Micah's leg a nudge, Micah nodded.

"Hello," he called loudly. "Anyone home?"

There was no answer. The dog whined and trembled. Hating what he was about to do, Micah moved up the steps onto the porch. He stopped again and called out, shouting this time.

"Hey, anyone in there? Answer me. I'm coming in!"

When there was no reply, he stepped to a window next to the door and peered in. A thin curtain dimmed the view into a dining room. There was a large round table with several chairs around it; he couldn't see past the table. He called out again and moved to the side to grasp the metal doorknob. As the knob turned, he eased the door open. When it was but a quarter open the dog pushed past him and into the house where he started barking. The sharp, loud noise was unnerving. As Micah came into the front room, the dog continued to bark and almost dance between Micah and a door leading to the next room. He followed the dog into the dining room he'd seen from the window. Beyond the round table was a wide space before leading into a kitchen. Faded green wallpaper with a leaf design covered the wall. A tall oblong section that showed the original darker green was empty.

The big china closet that had stood against the wall between the kitchen and dining room was lying on a small black woman. Her head, shoulders, and arms stretched out before her with the heavy cabinet resting on her back and legs. The dog hovered near her, whining. Micah knelt beside her and touched her throat looking for any life. Although, it seemed clear she had been dead for a while, maybe a day. The body was cold. A dried trickle of blood ran from her mouth to the floor. Micah stepped into the front room and took out his cell phone. He waited a couple of minutes, but could not get a signal. He didn't know what he felt more: sorrow, pity, anger, or just a deep despair.

The dog left the lady's side and came to Micah, who reached down and rubbed its head. The dog put its head back and howled. The long drawn out sound sent chills down Micah's back and at the same time a similar longing to vent his pain. The dog sat and looked at Micah, and Micah stared back.

"What do I do now? Is there a phone?"

The dog didn't answer so Micah looked around. Not finding a phone in the living room, he went into a hallway that led to a bedroom and another doorway into the kitchen. A chair lay overturned on the linoleum-covered floor and some dishes lay broken. A screened porch stretched across the back of the house. Since he couldn't find a phone, there was nothing to do but drive back into town.

"You stay here," he told the dog.

When he stepped off the porch and started down the road, the dog followed. Micah stopped several times and tried to make it go back, but it would not. When they reached the truck, Micah opened the driver's door, and before he could stop it, the dog leaped into the cab. Micah tried to pull it out, but it wore no collar and tugging on the fur and loose skin didn't help. After trying to wrestle the dog out of the pickup, Micah stopped. The dog couldn't stay at the house anyway. Someone in town should want to take it.

"Okay. But no more growling."

Micah backed out of the dirt road, not wanting to risk a turn in the soggy ground. He headed back to the last small town and, not knowing where else to go, returned to the gas station. In the entrance, a closed sign hung between two oil drums. Either they were out of gas or the generator was. The large garage door was open, so Micah drove in, parked, told the dog to stay, and went into the station. The man was behind the counter.

"Don't you believe in signs?" he asked.

"I do," Micah answered. "I'm here because I need to find help, I guess the police. Can you direct me to the station?"

The man came from behind the counter, a frown on his dark face.

"Hey, I remember you. Old red pickup." He looked out the glass front and nodded. "Yeah, there it is."

"I was on my way out of town and pulled off on a dirt road, forgot to use your restroom, and a dog wouldn't let me leave. I'm sorry to say I found a dead lady there. The china cabinet must have fallen on her. I have her dog out in the pickup. I need to notify the police or someone who can find her family."

The man's mouth hung open and he shook his head. He moved back behind the counter and picked up a phone. He dialed and immediately got an answer. Micah listened as he talked.

"...that's right. I think it must be Miz Rose. She lives out that way. Sure, he's here. He'll wait, he's got her dog."

He hung up and turned to Micah.

"If you wait, Officer Howard will be right over. He'll go get her daughter, Lilla. She lives in town."

Micah looked at the rack of snacks behind the counter and remembered his earlier regrets.

"Might as well buy something while I wait," he joked.

"Hey, glad to make a sale even in sad circumstances."

Micah picked out four Payday bars, two Butterfingers, and a bag of pork rinds. Jena would not approve, but he was running on nerves and needed the quick energy. He wouldn't eat them all at once. Actually, his stomach felt too upset for any type of food. The man stuck out his hand to shake.

"Name is Leland Howard. Officer Howard is my brother."

Micah shook hands with him. "I'm Micah Hanson."

"Like in the Bible."

"What?"

"You know, the book of Micah, an old-time prophet."

"I don't know about that. Just a name my parents gave me."

"Was her place much destroyed?"

"I guess not. A couple of things overturned, some broken dishes. The china cabinet..."

"Yeah, maybe it started shaking and she tried to steady it." Leland frowned. "Little old thing like her. Hope she didn't suffer." Leland went toward the station's door. "There's Billy now."

Micah followed him out to the area between the station and the pumps. A black police car came to a stop beside them. A young black woman was in the passenger's seat, her hair in a dozen braids, and she wore gold eye shadow. A tall, thin black officer got out on the car's other side. He came around to Leland and Micah. The woman rolled down her window and stared at Micah. Leland made the introductions and Officer Howard narrowed his dark eyes.

"How come you was out there?"

Micah held the bag of candy bars and wondered if he should have backed out of the dirt road and gone on his way. He tried to smile.

"I stopped here for gas, but forgot to use the restroom. I pulled in on the first dirt road, and well, hope that isn't a crime." He again tried to smile.

"How is it you ended up at the house?"

Micah gestured toward his pickup.

"It was the dog. At first, I thought it was going to attack me. I tried to leave, but it got between the pickup door and me. I finally got the idea it wanted me to follow. I shouted several times, and when I didn't get an answer I went in."

The woman leaned out the window. Her hand visible on the window edge had long blue nails. She looked up at Officer Howard.

"You believe him?" Her tone expressed suspicion.

He glanced down at her.

"We'll see after we go out there. Come on." He motioned to Micah. "Get in the back."

"I can follow you. Don't want to leave my truck. Where can I put the dog?"

Officer Howard turned to Leland.

"You watch the truck for him. This won't take long."

"I'm closing up, Billy. I want to get on home. Jewel wants me to help clean up things from the quake."

"I said it won't take long. Get the dog inside the station."

Leland shook his head and started for the pickup. Micah hurried after him. When the dog was out, Micah rolled up the windows and locked the truck. Leland bent over, holding onto the dog by the nape of its neck.

"Didn't need this," he muttered.

"I don't either," Micah replied. "Wish I'd left the dog out there and gone on."

The dog barked, pulled against Leland, and tried to go with Micah. Leland took the dog inside the station where he had to shut the door to the garage section to keep it from going to Micah. The dog and Leland stood staring out the front window as Officer Howard drove away. In minutes, they were out of town and halfway to the dirt road. The woman turned and looked at Micah.

"I'm Lilla Banes. We think you found my mother, Rose Harris."

"I'm sorry."

She turned to face the front. The dirt road was ahead on the right. Micah gestured toward it.

"There, that's the place. I didn't drive all the way in. I was afraid of getting stuck."

Officer Howard nodded. "Yes. We haven't had rain, but creeks and rivers are rising anyway. Probably caused by the earthquakes."

He drew up in front of the house. The yard was mostly dirt, a few weeds, and a strip of grass near the porch. Lilla opened her door and got out before Officer Howard did. Micah quickly followed. The house looked the same, but this time Micah noticed how the front porch sagged to the right. One of the short posts holding it was cracked. The officer and Lilla entered the house and Micah lingered on the porch. He heard Lilla say, "That's her all right. Crazy old woman."

There wasn't any grief in her voice and it hurt Micah; he wasn't sure why. He didn't know the old woman, but he'd felt sad upon finding her. She must have been a nice lady; she certainly inspired loyalty in her dog. Micah watched through the open front door as Lilla and the officer went through the four rooms and out into the back screened porch. In minutes, they returned to the front porch. Officer Howard turned to Micah.

"Looks like the quake jarred the china closet loose and it fell on her. From her position face down, I'd guess she came from the kitchen and it knocked her flat."

Lilla stood twisting one of her long braids. "What you going to do?"

"First off we'll get the doctor out here. He can arrange for the funeral home to come out. Not much else to do that I can see."

Micah stepped to the ground, started for the patrol car, and the others followed him. He quickly settled in the back seat and couldn't wait to get back to town. There hadn't been any reason to accompany them. Leaving his pickup made him nervous, besides all the time wasted. He should have been in Little Rock by this time. The rerouting by the patrolmen was a disappointing delay. It appeared Pine Bluff was the next major stop before going north again to Little Rock. This tour of middle Arkansas was a total waste, and there was still the problem of finding a way across the river. As the officer drove down the dirt lane back to the highway, the mud splattered onto the car doors, making a sloshing sound. The ground seemed mushier than when Micah had parked there. Lilla drummed her long fingernails on the dashboard.

"I told her a million times to move into town. When she couldn't drive any more, well, you'd think she'd had some care for me. Had to drive out here, haul her to the store, and back again." Lilla turned to Billy Howard. "I offered to buy stuff for her and bring it out, save half the trip; you think she'd do that? Course not! Said she needed to pick out things."

Officer Howard didn't answer, and Micah was more than content to keep silent. When the filling station came into sight and the old red pickup was where he'd left it, Micah relaxed a bit. As soon as the patrol car stopped near the station, he opened the car door and stepped out. Officer Howard went around the front of the patrol car and stood facing him.

"Hope you don't mind, I need you to sign a statement."

"What?"

"How you found Miz Rose. Won't take long."

Leland had opened the station door and the dog bounded out. It lunged at Micah and landed against his leg, making him stagger a step to the side. He frowned down at it and tried to move away.

"Ah, can someone take this dog?" Micah asked.

Lilla was still in the patrol car. She looked out the window to yell at Leland.

"Leland, get that dog. Tie him up and call someone"

"I don't see how that's my job!"

"Well, I sure don't know what to do with him. Okay, just turn him loose, but he better not follow me. I got enough to handle; you should see the mess I have to clean up in the beauty parlor. Billy Howard, please take me back there right now! Those lazy girls I left cleaning won't do a thing if I'm not there."

Officer Howard looked at his brother.

"I'd appreciate it, Leland, if you'd do something about the dog. Call the pound, and if there isn't anyone there, take him out back and shoot him. Can't have animals running around, not with all this other. Be more merciful than letting him starve." He turned to Micah. "Come on, follow me over to the police station. It's only a few blocks."

Micah looked down at the dog.

"Does he have a name?"

Lilla squinted, the golden eye shadow flashing in the morning sunlight.

"Bo! She called that vicious animal Bo. Stupid dog and stupid name. You should saw what she spent on dog food, crazy old woman."

Bo lifted his head, bared his long white teeth, and a growl rumbled in his throat. Lilla pulled her arm back inside the car.

"Leland Howard, you do like your brother said. Take that mangy thing out back and shoot it. I'd do it myself if I had time!"

Bo pressed against Micah's knee. He could feel Bo's shoulder tremble, and Micah dropped his chin to his chest. He surely had problems enough. Still, it might not take long to give the dog a little help. Before he could decide what that help could be, Office Howard tapped him on the shoulder.

"Come on, follow me. I'll drop Lilla back at her shop. The station is just a block over from there."

Leland gave Micah a small smile.

"Want to help me peel that dog off you? Guess I can get rid of him; no one else will."

Bo lowered his head, flattened his ears, and displayed his sharp teeth. When Leland reached toward the dog, Bo gave a threatening snarl. Leland quickly drew back. Officer Howard shook his finger at his brother.

"Get on with it, Leland. We don't have all day!"

Micah put out his hand to stop Leland.

"Wait, I'll take care of it...him...Bo."

Leland looked relieved.

"Thanks. I'd take him, but I got three of my own, and I don't relish putting a healthy dog down."

Officer Howard was in the patrol car, the engine running. Micah hurried to his pickup, Bo keeping stride. When the patrol car made a turn out onto the highway Micah started the truck and followed him. As the officer drove into the middle of town, the streets showed more damage than the highway. Perhaps the pavement was not as strong, or the ground rolled more in that area. The patrol car pulled to the curb in front of a storefront. The painted window read, *Cut and Curl*. Lilla left the patrol car, slammed the door behind her, and hurried into the beauty shop. Officer Howard took off down a cross street and they were soon in the police station's parking lot. The one-story brick building seemed undamaged, but upon a second look, two windows had cracks from top to bottom.

In the pickup, Micah rolled up the windows halfway. It was unnecessary; he was almost certain Bo would not run away. If he did take off it could solve one problem. As Micah walked around the front of the pickup, Bo sat in the passenger's seat, his tongue out, his gaze following Micah's every step. The dog had an unsettling expression. Something in his brown eyes said he was fierce, or maybe crazy. If Bo had been in the pickup in Oklahoma City no one could have taken it. Micah pushed through the doublewide glass doors and into the police station. Officer Howard took him to a small office where Micah again explained how he'd found Mrs. Harris. He signed the statement and stood to leave.

"You mentioned the pound; what kind of place is it? Do they try to find homes for stray animals?"

Howard stepped from behind his desk and came to open the door for Micah.

"It isn't a big place, runs mostly on donations. Sometimes a dog is adopted, but they can't afford to keep them indefinitely. Listen, don't worry about it. I'll give you directions. It is enough that you drop the dog off there."

As Micah followed Howard down the hallway to the front entrance, the dog situation created turmoil in his mind, and made his heart race. Just do it, take the dog to the pound, drop him off and get out of town before something else happens. He'd vowed to stop becoming involved. From then on, he'd not stop for anything less than an avalanche across the road, and that wasn't likely in this flat country! With his hand on the metal push bar, Micah turned back to Officer Howard.

"Is there a veterinarian in town?"

"Yeah. Doc Simpson, over on seventh street. I know he won't take the dog. He sometimes boards animals, but with all the disruption and lack of utilities, he probably can't do that now."

"Seventh Street, how do I find it?"

"Go left onto Main, at the next corner make another left, go four blocks, turn right, and he's in the middle of the block."

Micah thanked him and when he reached the pickup, he could swear Bo smiled. He started the engine, swung through the parking lot and turned left onto Main Street. Driving slowly through town, more and more damage appeared...some cracked pavement, broken windows, and crumbled brick. Several street signs were leaning over and a suspicious amount of water ran in the gutter near the curb. Hard to know where it came from, maybe broken water lines, or from some creek like the rising water in the open fields. The vet's property had a small sign near the sidewalk; the house sat far back across a lawn with a long drive leading to a metal building behind the house. Micah stopped near the trim, white board house and got out of the pickup; Bo started barking.

"Hush. Stay. Let me see what's up."

Micah had trouble believing he was talking to a dog, and even more disbelief that the dog understood. He stepped to the front door and rang a small bell hanging from an extended metal rod. There was the sound of movement from inside the house, and in seconds, the door opened. A short, round, blonde woman wiping her hands on a blue apron looked up at him.

"Yes?"

"I have a dog."

"Take it around to the back. Melvin is out there."

Before he could answer, she closed the door. Micah shrugged, jogged down the two porch steps to the walkway, and got into the pickup.

"He's out back," he told Bo.

The dog wrinkled his forehead and leaning forward, peered toward the metal building. Micah drove slowly past the house and stopped near the fenced-in back lot. Leaving Bo in the cab, he opened the metal garden gate and went to the outbuilding. He could hear a couple of barking dogs. Maybe the doc wouldn't mind taking another, especially if he received extra payment. Bo was a smart dog, he'd look better cleaned up. Someone would want a good guard dog. This was the best Micah could do for him. Bo would have a better chance here than thrown into the pound. The building had a doublewide door that stood half-open. Micah poked his head around the door.

"Hello? Anyone here?"

"Be there in a minute," a man's voice called from the dim interior.

Melvin Simpson came to the front half of the building and into the light. He was a couple of inches shorter than Micah, and wearing a sleeveless tee shirt and jeans. With his thinning gray hair and lined face, Micah guessed the vet to be around sixty years old. Still, he looked strong. Muscles corded his long bare arms.

"Just cleaning out the back. What can I do for you?"

"I have a dog that needs a home. I thought if you'd take him, clean him up a bit, someone might want him. I'll pay a good amount. I want to give him a fighting chance."

"Is he your dog?"

"Mine? Oh no. I came by him due to an unfortunate circumstance."

The vet stepped out into the sunlight and closed the open side of the double door. Micah pointed to the pickup.

"I have him right out there. I know this might be asking a lot, because of the disruption from the quake, but I don't know what else to do for him."

Doc Simpson left the enclosed yard and Micah followed. When they were close to the pickup, the doctor told Micah to let Bo out. He hurried to comply. The doctor would see what a fine dog Bo was, and the extra money could be an enticement. Micah opened the door for Bo. The big dog didn't move.

"Come on."

Micah reached into the cab to take Bo by the loose skin around his neck. Bo didn't snarl, but he settled back against the seat and became as heavy as a large bag of cement. Micah turned toward the doctor.

"Can you help get him out?"

Micah stepped away and the doctor took his place. He looked Bo over and pointed his finger in the dog's face.

"Now you get on out here, Hobo. We won't have any trouble."

The dog hung his head and edged toward the open door, made a limp leap and landed at the doctor's feet. Doc bent over and patted Bo's head.

"There, that's a good dog. No shot today, where's your collar?"

Micah felt a bit jealous at how Bo obeyed the doctor. Still, he was a veterinarian and he knew how to handle animals.

"You called him Hobo."

"That's right. This is Rose Harris's dog. Where did you find him?"

Micah leaned against the pickup fender while the doctor rubbed Bo, or Hobo's head. He repeated the story of how he came into possession of the dog. It was a relief to know that the dog would be among friends. Since the doctor knew him, he'd be sure to find a good home for him, or even keep him.

"Don't guess Lilla wants him, does she?"

"No. She seemed to have a strong dislike for the dog."

"She objected to her mother spending money on it. Hobo wandered onto Rose's place several years ago; that's why she named him Hobo. She brought him in and he was a mess, skinny, needed shots and worming. We took care of him and he turned out to be a great comfort to her. Sure sorry to hear that she's gone. Haven't heard of any other deaths associated with the earthquake, but I'm betting there are plenty to the east."

Micah hadn't thought of the deaths. Damage was all he'd seen, except for Bo's owner. He hadn't thought about much other than getting across the river. The enormity of the disaster hadn't truly registered with him, even though he'd seen the people in trouble and at least one town destroyed. For a moment, he had the sensation of dreaming. It was unreal to be in a small Arkansas town trying to arrange accommodations for a dog. He blinked in the bright mid-day sun. Under his feet the earth shook. It blended with the trembling of his body. He looked at the doctor.

"Did you feel that?"

"What?"

"Nothing. I've been traveling for a while. My legs are shaky. How much will you charge to keep the dog? You probably already know a family who can take him."

Doctor Simpson shook his head.

"No, can't say I do. As for boarding him, I have two small dogs now. Their owner is away on vacation. I've contacted them, and they'll be back shortly. With no utilities, I can't take care of any animals. I'm drawing water out of a cistern, but we can't drink it. I could give Hobo a bit of a cleaning, and probably wouldn't hurt him to drink it."

"And what, turn him loose or put him at the pound?"

"They aren't taking in strays either. We have trouble enough taking care of humans. I've heard the earthquake will affect millions of people, from the Missouri River to the Gulf. We'll either end up providing housing or helping set up temporary camps. Besides all that, we're going to have a shortage of supplies that come from the east. Even airports are shut down, lack of fuel, disrupted pipelines…" Doc's voice trailed away.

The actual seriousness of the situation slowly settled into Micah's mind. Even so, people were trying to act normal: Leland selling what gas he had, Lilla cleaning up the beauty shop, and the police department trying to continue operations. The undertaker would collect poor Mrs. Harris, even though the ground may open and cough up all the buried. Micah again felt the earth vibrate. The doctor didn't seem to notice or else he chose to ignore it. No one would bother with Bo. The vet might give him one meal and turn him out, or worse, destroy him. Bo looked up at Micah and held stone still.

"Do you have time to get this dog cleaned, and maybe trim his shaggy coat?"

"That I do! Won't take long. There's a Dollar General open, big run on groceries and survival stuff, but you can probably find dog food. Dry be better for traveling."

Feeling under some strange spell, Micah found the market, bought two large bags of dog food, two bowls, a leather collar, and a length of chain. He also bought a roll of paper towels and spray cleaner for the cab's seat. When he returned to Doctor Simpson's, Hobo looked transformed. He was still a big brown and black dog, but his fur was soft and clean. His brown eyes and black nose were clearly visible, no longer hidden in a tangled mat. As Micah buckled the collar around his neck, Bo stood still. When he shook his head, the metal tag the doctor affixed there jingled.

It was mid-afternoon by the time Micah and his dog were back on Highway 79 heading toward Pine Bluff. Micah glanced at the dog who was sitting tall in the passenger's seat.

"I'm not calling you Bo or Hobo. That's no name for a respectable dog."

The dog chuffed and turned to stare out the side window.

Seven

The traffic heading south on Highway 79 picked up in both number and speed. There were cars, vans, and trucks. Truck beds were piled high with possessions, some loosely tied that wobbled and threatened to fall. Micah wondered what would happen if things fell onto the pavement. There wasn't room to swerve. Ditches full of water on either side of the road glistened in the afternoon sun and the fields beyond flashed with swollen ponds. The open land stretched brownish-red between row crops under a cloudless blue sky. Lines of dark green trees formed distant boundaries, or stood sentinel alongside the highway. At intersections with rural dirt roads, an occasional vehicle joined the southbound rush. Pine Bluff was in for a swarm of refugees despite the flooding there. The summer air rushed in Micah's open window. The noise of engines along with the odor of exhaust fumes, made the wind hot rather than refreshing. Perhaps it was his imagination, but there seemed to be a sense of desperation hanging over the fleeing procession.

The tied-open back doors of a white cargo van in front of him revealed two pet carriers. It looked like they had been crammed in after the van was full of boxes and suitcases. Two unconcerned tabby cats slept in one cage; in the other a nervous brown terrier bounced around on shaky legs. Micah glanced at the dog beside him.

"See how lucky you are?"

The dog ignored him.

"Won't answer? Maybe if you had a name you would. Rex? Spot? Myron? Bert?"

The dog gave a disgusted frown and returned to staring at the back of the white van.

"I suppose you'll let me know when you hear a name you like."

"Woof."

"Oh, come on. You're not near fierce enough to be called Wolf."

The dog growled, a menacing rumble deep in his throat.

"Okay, you're a tough dog. Still, you are a dog, be proud of what you are. How about *Perro*?"

The dog slumped in the seat and rested his chin on the dashboard.

"Don't speak Spanish, huh? Well, you're a fine dog anyway."

The dog came to attention. He turned to Micah and gave his hand a wet lick. Then he sat up straight, expanded his chest, and cocked his ears forward.

"Dog it is, then."

Dog turned his head, said, "Chuff," and rattled the tags on his collar.

Micah laughed.

The blare of a car horn behind Micah startled him out of his conversation with Dog. He looked in the side mirror to see an angry man in a blue Honda nearly riding the pickup's bumper. Micah waved his hand and pressed on the gas pedal. He'd fallen a small distance behind the white van. The stream of vehicles was moving faster, nearly five miles over Micah's normal sixty. The empty bottomland stretched away on either side of the two-lane highway. Some fields had low growing green plants in long rows; others had something that might be sorghum heading out. None of the fields was dry, and if the water increased, they might be in danger of flooding. With no small town in sight, Micah checked the fuel gauge. It was a nervous gesture because the tank was full only a few hours ago.

Several times Micah thought he felt the pavement roll. He tried to believe it was his nervousness, or at the most some slight aftershocks. It was too frightening to think that yesterday's and today's earthquakes were leading up to something much stronger. He understood the San Andreas Fault. In many places, it was visible above ground, especially along roads where the different colored plate rocks mark the rift. The thought of a major California earthquake was frightening. However, the famous fault line was so familiar that most people didn't worry about it. Especially, the myth of half of California falling into the sea. That was an impossibility, as the plate moving northwest wouldn't sink, but only slide to the north. In eons to come, Los Angeles could find itself adjacent to San Francisco. Landslides can change the coastline, but the state would remain intact. Perhaps it was knowledge that made living on the huge fault bearable. While shaking ground in the middle of a stable continental plate was more frightening. That meant the earth might at any time tear itself apart. Scarier still was that people living on the thin upper crust had no control. Like all other creatures, they had to survive the best they could.

Since the 1930s, California had enforced stricter building codes. With each quake, more regulations appeared. The older buildings were retrofitted and new construction consisted of reinforced walls, tied-down foundations, and other shake-proof measures. Micah recalled hearing of a new housing development that survived a quake greater than magnitude five without so much as a broken dish. Some of the nearby older buildings lost bricks and suffered foundation cracks. With such news reports, people had reason to hope survival was possible. Still, if a truly huge earthquake hit towns sitting directly on the fault, such as San Bernardino and Palmdale, they would be in deep trouble. Micah shook his head, thinking he'd left all that behind.

The traffic started to slow. Micah pressed the brake, tapping it to stay far enough behind the white van. For a bit the line came to a complete stop; horns blared. Micah stared ahead trying to find a reason. It made him nervous sitting trapped between the white van and the blue Honda behind. Pulling off the highway to go around was out of the question. There was no way to know how deep the water was in the ditches, and the fields beyond were soggy. Dog whined. Micah nodded and swallowed to bring moisture to his mouth. When the vehicles in front started moving, he relaxed a bit. Soon they were gaining in speed. A warm breeze through the open window cooled the sweat on his forehead. But the smell of rotting vegetation along with engine exhaust tempted him to roll up the window. He would have, except that Dog's shaggy coat seemed to absorb moisture and add an aroma of its own.

About a mile ahead, Micah found the reason for the delay. An empty gray Chevrolet sat in the left-hand ditch. It must have run out of gas or had engine trouble. Micah wondered where the occupants had gone; probably picked up by another driver. The sight of the mishap tightened Micah's shoulders; it could happen to anyone. Again, he glanced at the gas gauge. The extra gas in the truck's bed was a comfort, but also a worry. He wondered how others might react if he pulled over to refill the tank. They might need gasoline, too. The Ford's tank held about nineteen gallons. It should take him around two hundred miles, but he didn't want to reach empty. He'd buy more gas at the next opportunity. The flat fields stretched on forever with thin knee-high green plants in curving long rows. A road sign declared this the rice growing capital, and Micah believed it. The water standing between the rows gave him hope that it was irrigation and not flood waters. When the roadside ditches filled to the highway's verge, the hope diminished.

Leland, the gas station's owner, had said the Arkansas River around Pine Bluff had risen. If what Micah was seeing in the ditches and fields was an indication, he worried about conditions to the south. He didn't want to go to Pine Bluff, or to cross the Arkansas River. He hoped to find a highway northeast of the river and take it to Little Rock. While he speculated about a route, and how to leave the enforced caravan, his cell phone rang. Micah and Dog both yipped, startled out of their tension.

Micah held the phone to his ear. "Hello?"

"Micah, where are you? I've been trying to reach you."

"Oh, hi Harry." Micah turned to Dog, who was glaring at him. It is my attorney, Micah mouthed and Dog cocked his head.

"Harry, I meant to call you. Is everything all right?"

"It is. Just worried about you with the Mississippi upheaval. Who the hell would have guessed something like this? Where are you?"

"Still in Arkansas. I didn't get across the river before it hit. I'm going north to find a way around the mess."

"This disaster is the only thing on the news. It can't be as bad as they say, can it?"

"It's hard to tell, because all I see is just what is around me. I suppose the media has aircraft shooting pictures. You probably know more than I do."

"From news reports, the quake did damage from Minnesota to the Gulf. You might have to go to Canada to reach the eastern states."

For the next few miles, Micah talked with Harry Miller. It calmed him to know that short, plump, gray-haired attorney Miller was taking care of his affairs. Harry had hired movers to pack and place in storage everything from the apartment above the business. He had little trouble terminating the lease on the sandwich shop and a settlement from the trucking company was proceeding. It did startle Micah to hear that Harry had paid three months' advance storage fee, thinking it would give Micah time to arrange the cross-country move. *Three months.* Micah doubted he'd be ready to call for the personal belongings that soon. Harry didn't have a timeline on the accident settlement, but when he did, the plan was for him to deposit the money in Micah's bank. The idea of money from the death of his wife and son made his stomach churn.

After he'd said goodbye to Harry and put the phone back in his pocket, the good feeling that Harry's voice produced faded like a wisp of smoke. Staring ahead at the line of vehicles, his hands clutching the steering wheel, his mind numb, Micah recalled the first three months after the accident. More accurately, he didn't remember. The first thing he truly remembered after the funeral was hiring Harry.

Three months later, he called Harry to tell him he was leaving. He filled the backpack and hit the road. What he did during the months between was a blank. He might have sat on the beach watching the waves. He must have eaten because he didn't starve, although he did lose weight. He remembered the grief counselor Nina Sims. But mostly, that time was a black hole and he was content to leave it that way. Digging through memories reopened the wound, and he was barely surviving.

Micah reached over and shook Dog's shaggy shoulder.

"We all have a past. Right, Dog?"

Dog hung his head.

Harry had assured him everything in California was fine. He hadn't mentioned that the gravestones were standing in their proper place, but Micah knew they were. When the ground sufficiently settled, Harry was to check on the placement. Harry only alluded to the painful subject by saying he'd concluded the cemetery matters. When Micah hadn't asked for details, Harry changed the subject to the earthquakes, which Micah appreciated. Thinking about anything else was preferable, even the disastrous quake.

Harry said the rising water Micah mentioned wasn't a surprise. The ground crumbled around the mouth of the tributaries up and down the Mississippi making huge earthen dams. South of Greenville, the land sank. It tumbled great sections of forests into the river, causing dams of a different kind. Both of these made the water spread into every low space. The hope now was for dry weather in the Midwest. A deluge would make the disaster worse. Pictures from the Gulf showed everything around New Orleans under water. No one could say if it was flooding from the river, or ocean encroachment. The earthquake had taken down buildings in Baton Rouge where large sections of town sank to reported depths of ten feet. Entire blocks dropped below normal ground level. Harry said there were guest geologists on every television station with just as many opinions as to what was happening. The last Harry heard liquefaction was to blame. The silt and sand turned to slush that subsided and caused the Gulf to expand.

As Micah considered what he'd learned from Harry, the idea of an expanding Gulf seemed reasonable. If the land sank, the sea would rush in. Especially when there is no flow of fresh water from the north. If damp sandy soil starts shaking, and the underlying limestone or granite has cracked or completely pulled apart, the ground will subside. It was possible the liquefied soil would wash out into the Gulf and form new barrier islands. At this stage, no one knew what changes the earthquake had made. He and Harry had agreed it would take months if not a year to assess the damage.

Dog began to fidget and whine. Micah studied the road ahead. He didn't see a place to pull over. Both lanes of the highway were filled with traffic, and the roadway siding was too narrow for parking.

"Hang on, Dog. I could use a stop myself."

A gravel driveway was coming up on the right, some kind of long metal building with an American flag on a tall pole in front of it. A couple of mobile homes completed the complex. It looked like a small rural post office and Micah drove on; they might not appreciate becoming a rest stop. Several miles to the south, a dirt road leading west presented itself. It wasn't clear how to turn around and get back on Highway 79, but the stop was necessary. Half a mile off the highway stood an abandoned barn with a shed leaning beside it. He and Dog made good use of the area behind the barn. Dog decided to explore and it took Micah longer than he would have liked to persuade Dog they should go. Once he had cleaned Dog's feet and disposed of the dirty paper towels, Micah sat behind the steering wheel staring at a grove of trees across the road.

All the ground was damp if not outright standing with water. A faint odor of sulfur mixed with the smell of rotting vegetation. One car sped past, a rattling old rust-colored Chevy. The man and woman glanced at Micah's pickup and quickly turned away. Micah wondered why he didn't start the engine, but it just seemed easier to sit there. Dog pawed at his thigh and bumped his shoulder with his nose.

"What, you ready to leave?"

Dog stared at him.

"You hungry? You can't be thirsty. I saw you drinking some of that swamp water. Really shouldn't do that, no telling what's in it."

Maybe having something to eat wasn't a bad idea. The late afternoon sun put a sheen on the muddy dirt road and the western sky was bright. In less than four hours, it would be pale with twilight. Still, Micah couldn't move. Thoughts of sitting there forever were inviting. It didn't make any difference if he drove on or not. He could put his head down on the steering wheel and sleep. As he welcomed the thought of sleep and his eyelids drooped, Dog barked! A sharp, jarring sound. It jolted Micah out of slipping further into a dark, despairing place.

After providing Dog with a bowl of dry food, Micah ate some of the beef jerky from his supply and they both drank water. This time Dog lapped bottled water from his dish while Micah finished the bottle. He knew there was something wrong in his head, or maybe it was his heart. Time didn't flow right. Things that should take minutes stretched to half hours, and days ran together. He didn't know how to fix the problem. If taking one breath after another wasn't automatic he might stop breathing. When the sinking darkness again threatened to settle over him, he looked around at the empty countryside.

"We can't stay here, Dog."

He turned the key in the ignition, put the Ford in gear, and pulled out of the abandoned barnyard. He went east on the country road, and in less than a mile reached the intersection with Highway 79. The traffic wasn't as heavy, but it was just as fast. When he saw an opening, Micah pressed on the gas pedal and re-entered the parade of fleeing quake victims.

A medium-sized delivery truck was in front of him. The rear door had an arched sign reading Helm's Bakery. It didn't seem likely that the truck was making a delivery. Still, maybe some stores were staying open. Returning to normal as quickly as possible made sense. People couldn't give up. If they did, the losses would be greater. A few months ago, Micah had thought of giving up despite his promise to Jena. That was when he decided to walk to the cabin in North Carolina. He had thought the long trek would help him heal. Micah shook his head and snorted. He doubted he would ever heal, not if it meant forgetting his family. However, the move did accomplish two things. It got him away from the scene of his sorrow, and it forced him to keep functioning. Maybe that was enough. He was ready for any improvement, even a small one.

A pickup stood stranded on the left side of the road. It was scarcely off the pavement, and traffic swerved around it. The empty truck could have run out of gasoline. Barely a mile beyond, a blue Honda sat on the narrow right verge. A man and woman were standing in front of it. Micah turned to take a second look. He remembered the blue Honda behind him earlier. He wanted to stop, but the small yellow Corvette crowding him had already tried twice to pass. He could turn around and circle back, but with traffic flowing in one direction there wasn't a chance of that. The couple must have a cell phone; oh wait, Micah fumbled in his pocket. He could put a call in to highway patrol for them. The delivery truck in front slowed; it caught Micah by surprise, and he dropped his phone. When he uttered a curse, Dog growled. The phone slid under his backpack on the floorboard. It would have to stay there for the time being. As more people were fleeing the destruction and the flood, stalled cars were only the start of trouble.

The line of vehicles slowed to a crawl, and it was difficult to see around the boxy delivery truck. A few minutes later, a T intersection was visible as were two black and white patrol cars. They were parked nose-to-nose blocking the highway south. Two policemen were directing traffic, while two more stood beside the patrol cars. The officers were armed. The men on the road were wearing holsters carrying pistols. The two leaning against front fenders had rifle butts propped against their hips. The barrels pointed skyward. Dog pressed toward the dashboard, his ears forward. He looked as tense as Micah felt. When they reached the intersection, the patrolman was gesturing for him to turn right on a two-lane paved road heading north. Micah stopped, leaned out the window, and yelled, "What's happening?"

The tall black patrolman frowned and kept pointing to Micah's right.

"Move on. Two-way traffic ahead."

There was nothing to do except follow directions. Highway 13 headed north; that was good. The sooner he reached a major interstate the better. A green highway sign indicated a small town ahead, and the town of Carlisle, twenty-nine miles beyond that. Micah remembered Carlisle was near Highway 70, which ran parallel to Interstate 40! This progress was encouraging. The patrolman was right. Traffic on Highway 13 did flow both north and south. The yellow Corvette found a break and whipped around Micah's pickup. It was a relief to get it off his rear bumper. The roadside appeared normal; no buildings falling down, except from age. The area was more populated with houses visible from the highway, and clumps of forest between stretches of vast fields. The sun was near the horizon and long shadows from the trees stretched across the pavement.

Having head-on traffic seemed strange after the frantic rush away from the quake area. The peaceful surroundings made Micah wonder if he'd hallucinated the last two days. The only thing that seemed out of place was the number of cars on the road. Then the highway traversed several creeks where the damage was apparent. One long bridge with cement side rails stood above the water, but the land surrounding it was flooded. Smaller streams with bridges across them became low-water crossings. Micah slowed the pickup, but oncoming traffic and the vehicle in front of him plowed through, sending wings of water to either side. Micah managed to roll up the windows in time to stay dry, but the windshield was flooded. Micah turned on the wipers. Dog stood and fiercely barked at the attack.

"Easy fellow, no threat."

Dog gave him a hard 'are you sure?' stare.

No, Micah thought, he wasn't sure of anything. It was starting to feel as if he'd drive forever, led down one endless highway after another. Still, the situation was looking better. It was more than a half hour to Carlisle; another forty-five minutes to Little Rock, and it would still be daylight. As the air in the cab grew stale, Dog being a big contributor, Micah rolled down the windows. A musty smelling breeze whipped in and Dog lifted his nose as if sensing each intertwined odor carried on the ribbon of air. Micah marveled at the animal's senses, but he didn't envy them. The growing smells of stagnate water was enough for him. Ways of getting across the river filled his mind. He couldn't wait to reach a place where he could either fall apart or lie down and die. He didn't know which he preferred. Two cars honked and passed him. He'd drifted, his foot easing off the gas pedal.

The late afternoon turned a brilliant gold as if the sun wanted to leave a lasting memory to carry through the black of night. Upon reaching Carlisle, Micah had a choice, Highway 70 or Interstate 40. The small town of around three thousand offered both. It was also home to several huge grain elevators and warehouses. This was rice country, along with corn, soybean, and sorghum. There had been big elevators in western states too, but those stored wheat. The Arkansas countryside did not look right for wheat even to a city dweller such as Micah. Another clear observation was that Carlisle was host to more people than it could handle. It appeared others, like Micah, needed time to decide upon a direction to take.

Civilian traffic directors manned the intersection of Highways 70 and 13. With most of the population near the river fleeing the area, they swamped the small towns. Yet, there didn't seem to be any panic. Occasionally, tempers flared. He'd seen men standing beside gas station pumps shaking their finger in some other man's face. There were parked cars with open doors where scolding women cleaned the cheeks of small red-faced children. Micah saw more anger than fear or panic. These people chased from their homes were not the victim type. Whatever nature, or anything else, threw at them they looked as if they'd fight. They were the strong heart of the country. The rich soil of the Mississippi Basin provided abundant crops, but that didn't mean this bounty came free. Farmers, independent or corporate, faced nature's fickle temperament. Too much rain, too little rain, the wrong temperature, insects and disease destroying plants. It was a constant battle. Considering this latest natural catastrophe, people had a right to look angry.

Micah pulled into a Conoco service station and waited in line to buy the allowed five gallons of gas. It was twenty cents more a gallon than at the last station. This seemed strange because the top oil producing states were all west of the Mississippi River. It should be states to the east of the river experiencing the price hike. However, if the big pipelines running under the river had ruptured, the cost to the oil companies was beyond knowing. As he waited in line, Micah got out of the pickup and started a conversation with the man behind him. The man looked to be around fifty years of age, with a lean tan face and a thatch of sun-bleached hair turning gray at the temples. He stood leaning against his truck's door. Micah shook the man's rough, dry hand.

"How are you doing?" Micah asked.

"Okay, considering. See by your plate you're from California. What you doing here? Just come to bring us some of your misery?"

Micah half smiled and his laugh sounded weak. "Kind of looks that way. Sorry."

The man shook his head. "No, I'm sorry. Just being hateful. Never thought this could happen."

"Have you suffered much loss?"

"One hundred sixty-nine acres of rice all under four feet of water. I planted early this year; ten days under water is about the limit it can stand."

Micah didn't know what to say other than 'sorry.'

"Oh, we've survived floods before. Even have crop insurance, but you know how that goes. The fine print usually wins out. Don't have any idea what the insurance on the house will pay. Probably be a big discussion over the cause of the damage. Was it flood or the quake that moved it off the foundation? Course, I don't have earthquake insurance." The man threw his head back and gave a harsh laugh, revealing a mouth full of strong square teeth.

The truck in front of Micah pulled up to a pump. Micah again shook the man's hand.

"I hate to keep saying I'm sorry, but I really am. But with a disaster of this size the government will step in." Micah pointed to the vacant space in front of his pickup. "I better go. Good luck to you."

The man nodded and slipped back into the driver's seat. "Same to you, mister. Should have stayed in California, right?"

Micah jogged to his pickup and got behind the steering wheel. Dog whined and tried to push past him.

"Not now, Dog. There's a vacant lot ahead."

People were using the empty lot for a dog park, and under the circumstances, Micah doubted anyone would object. When the gas tank had an additional five gallons in it, he paid the attendant, who was happier with cash than the credit cards some were using. Then he pulled past the gas station to park at the edge of the empty lot. There were about seven other dogs in the lot, some of them were on leashes, some were not. Micah didn't trust Dog so he fastened the chain to his collar. Dog raised his shoulders in a huge sigh and shook his head, making the dog tags rattle. Micah opened the pickup door, and stepped out letting Dog follow him. He locked the pickup behind them. The procedure of Dog finding a suitable place to do his business was long and involved. There were no trees on the lot, the free ranging dogs wanted to communicate, and Dog seemed humiliated. Micah let the chain out to its full length and turned away. After a while, Dog trotted back to stand at Micah's side. From Dog's attitude, Micah knew he was much happier.

It was six-fifteen and there was still plenty of daylight. Micah eyed the Sonic Drive-in on the other side of the vacant lot. His stomach rumbled, making dinner seem a good idea. The place was crowded, even a line at the door for inside service. If he judged the sky correctly, there was time enough to eat and still make it to Little Rock before dark. He kept Dog at his side and walked to the drive-in. After a thirty-minute wait, he left with two huge hamburgers, fries, and a vanilla malt. As they walked back to the pickup, he balanced the food and kept Dog on a short chain. He set the takeout on the bed cover and filled Dog's bowl with kibble. As Dog gobbled his food, he kept an eye on Micah's hamburger. In the end, half of the second burger was his.

"But I don't share the shake," Micah told him. "Water is better for you anyway."

Dog didn't argue.

Fueled, fed, and ready to travel, Micah made a quick stop at the Conoco restroom. The nearby interstate was a straight shot to Little Rock. He had passed by that city two days ago. It was discouraging to be going back, yet it seemed the best way to reach a highway north. With Dog settled beside him, Micah started the pickup.

When the ground heaved, rumbled, and did a hard jerking roll toward the west, Micah killed the engine. He stiffened and gripped the steering wheel. The filling station behind him rose and fell. The clang of metal, the clatter of collapse, and the burst of exploding neon signs made him duck. The Sonic Drive-in beyond the vacant lot tossed like a ship on a stormy sea. The vehicles parked beneath the drive-in's canopy disappeared under a mound of twisted roof. The building lost half of its structure to a widening crack in the ground. Dog alternately barked, growled, and whined. Micah knew how he felt. It was tempting to start the pickup and try to drive away, but the highway's pavement was buckling and breaking apart. Micah's stomach threatened to give back the hamburgers, and the malt came up in his throat. He swallowed.

"Be calm," he told Dog, who paid no attention.

Across a distant field, a long line of trees shook before toppling to the west, leaving a barricade of exposed roots and mounds of dirt. Micah looked in the rearview mirror at a sudden sand storm. A plume of white shot high into the air, spraying sand in all directions. Micah quickly rolled up his window while the pickup vibrated and rattled. Dog dropped onto the floorboard, smashing Micah's backpack. Shouts and screams pierced the air between the screech of twisting metal and the thud of falling buildings. About a block south, behind Micah's location, what sounded like a great implosion shook the ground in a different way. The thump and swoosh came seconds before a huge fireball erupted. A gas station's underground tank must have ignited. When the quake hit, a man in camouflage jacket and dark green ball cap was in the vacant lot walking two black and white English Setters. He staggered and spread his legs trying to balance. The two dogs dropped to the ground trembling. An instant later, the man fell beside them.

The shock felt stronger than the one in Helena, and it seemed to last longer. On the edge of town, there were fewer buildings to destroy. Micah wondered what might be left of the town proper. The first shaking in Forrest City was a warning, as was the stronger one on the highway south of there. Both of them led up to the destruction in Helena. There had been small tremors between the quake in Helena and this major jolt. People had grown accustomed to a little shaking. Oklahoma and Arkansas shook almost every day. It was blamed on the increased oil drilling activity and more fracking. Seismographs recorded the minor tremors under magnitude 2, and even a magnitude 3 was not concerning. When a magnitude 4.5 hit hard enough to knock dishes off a shelf people took notice. But there was nothing to do except shrug and sweep up the broken china. The only protection against an earthquake was to be where it wasn't!

Micah gripped the steering wheel and waited, expecting any second for the pickup to drop into a hole. The soil in the great Mississippi River Basin was fertile and good for growing crops, but the loose sandy loam turned to a quivering slurry when shaken hard enough. If the pickup's four tires stayed on solid ground, Micah intended to drive away.

The heavy jarring had stopped. Micah wiped sweat from his upper lip, and taking hold of Dog's collar pulled him up onto the cab's seat. People started to move about. One woman carrying a small child ran toward the Sonic Drive-in, her mouth open in a scream. People were in the vehicles trapped under the collapsed canopy. Micah shook his head trying to clear it, as he flashed back to the destroyed Pizza Hut in Helena. He should try to help, but there were enough uninjured people to do that. If this quake was as strong as he thought, the damage in town was extensive. Even Little Rock, about forty miles away, could have damage. He wondered how far west he'd have to go to escape.

Micah recalled some earthquake facts. Anyone living on a major fault probably knew more than he realized, but it was like cancer information. It was put aside, convinced it would never happen to you. In Helena the first thing he had felt was a hard jolt. At the time, he hadn't thought about what it meant, but the sudden hit was because of being near the epicenter. Helena was close to, if not, the center of that quake. Forrest City and the shaking on the highway heading south had both been a wave-like rolling motion. Those were distant from the center, and lasted longer. At the time of the Forrest City tremors, news had also come from as far north as Minnesota. A few experts had speculated that a small fault in the north had ruptured, and stressed the underlying bedrock of a larger fault. Judging from the lighter damage these first quakes caused, they were probably more than fifty miles under the surface. While the two stronger ones were closer to the surface. The deeper in the earth the fracture occurred, the less the damage. The shock waves had time to weaken and cause less destruction. If any earthquake was harmless, it would be one at least three hundred miles deep and far from any settled area. Quakes such as that probably happened more times than anyone guessed.

It was hard to judge a quake's strength without knowing how deep the initial rupture or how far away it was. All Micah knew for sure was that he was caught in some chain reaction and the earth was making changes in its crust. People live on the earth's skin, floating tectonic plates. These change positions based on the movement of the more fluid mantel. Sometimes they break apart because of pushing against one another. Most people know of 'plate movement,' how pressing together, or passing each other, they create stress. When enough stress builds up, a break occurs. Most of the world's major fault lines are at the edges of these tectonic plates. Micah sat in the middle of a continent thousands of miles from the edge of a plate, and he was worried.

He hoped this round of shaking was the last. With two days of breaking, the underground pressure must be eased enough to let the surface settle. Still, rumbling and shaking can go on for months after an earthquake. Dog nudged Micah and whined, his body quivering. Micah put his arm over Dog's shoulders. Dog had seen his last owner flattened under a huge china closet after the earth shook. He had reason to fear.

"Okay, fellow, we'll get out of here."

Micah started the engine to back away from the vacant lot. He edged past a parked van, and set the pickup's front tires on Highway 13. He waited for two cars to creep by. There were no speed demons under these conditions. The pavement had cracks, and in one place the verge had dropped off into a deep trench. Micah didn't stop to investigate. He was heading north toward Interstate 40 as quickly as possible. If he could get on the interstate west toward Little Rock, that was all he'd ask for this evening. It was still daylight, the sun near the horizon shooting strong hard beams onto a broken countryside. Thankful for the remaining light, Micah pressed on the gas pedal. He was anxious to leave the area, but he saw what looked like white sand on the road. He frowned and slowed the pickup. Coming closer he found it was a layer of pure white sand. It made a great circle covering both lanes and out into the ditches, where water soaked part of it. Micah hesitated before slowly driving through it. It was a sand blow. He'd seen one behind him during the quake. This sand came up from the depths. It was sent skyward under immense pressure, like a boil erupting. On the far side of the sand, Micah wiped his sweaty hands on his thighs and shook his head at Dog.

"Hope there isn't more of that stuff."

Dog sat stiff, staring straight through the windshield. He clearly didn't intend to let down his guard.

The roadside businesses were far apart so when they cracked, crumpled, or fell they didn't hit another structure. A long brown two-story building looked as if it was either an apartment house or a motel. Its sign lay upside down on the ground. Micah kept his gaze on the road, watching for damaged pavement. Shortly, he reached the interstate's on-ramp. He could make the right turn and head toward Little Rock, except he'd have to wait in line. However, the vehicles which were in line were trying to back out. They maneuvered from one side to the other in an effort to turn around. Something was blocking the forward progress.

No one would head east unless he had a home in that direction. Most of the drivers must be trying to go west. Micah quickly backed up and drove forward toward the Highway 13 overpass. He'd try the ramp on the other side. Even if it headed in the wrong direction, he could drive over the interstate divider and get where he wanted to go. Soon as he gained the rise to the overpass, he saw the problem. He put his foot on the brakes to stop before driving over the edge of a yawning gap in the road. The overpass bridge had fallen, blocking all four lanes of the divided interstate below. The on-ramp behind him was useless, for it was a mass of autos trying to untangle themselves. The open field to the left was flooded, and trying to cross it didn't seem wise. Beyond that, the embankment to the interstate looked too steep, and there was no way to reach the other side. He made a short jack-knife turn and, heavy with discouragement, drove south on Highway 13. There was still Highway 70, and it didn't have an overpass that could collapse.

He'd hoped to miss seeing what had happened to the town, but it was much as he suspected. The water tower's metal legs had broken, dropping the tank to the ground where it lay smashed atop its supports like a dead spider. Sirens and other alarms cut through the late afternoon. There were several cars in the ditch, and he stopped once for a fire truck that whipped around him. Toward the center of town, two separate blazes shot flames above rooftops, and a section of one tall grain elevator had crumbled into a pile of rubble. Micah hurried on, looking for the Highway 70 intersection. All he wanted was to outrun the devastation. Running was becoming a habit, and he didn't mind. It made sense to him. He didn't feel up to fighting pain and trouble. There was no chance to win; leaving it behind was a good option. Trees on either side of the highway had suffered random uprooting, some completely toppled, others leaning into those still standing.

There were telephone poles snapped off with lines sagging to the ground, others tangling in the branches of ruined trees. The world around Micah mirrored his emotional state. With his family gone, his balance was unsteady, leaving nowhere solid to stand.

There was nothing left upon which to base a life. He didn't look for answers. He would survive his physical and emotional earthquakes, or he wouldn't. Jena used to accuse him of being stubborn. She had probably been right, because he intended to reach the cabin in North Carolina or die trying. There was no good reason for this goal now any more than there had been when he left California. A kind, compassionate person would stop, turn around, go back to the ruined town, and find a way to help. As the huge yellow/orange sun settled lower in the sky Micah pressed his lips together, narrowed his eyes against the blinding fire, and stepped on the gas pedal.

A short distance out of town at a farm supply, the tractors, trailers, and mowers lay tossed about like toys. The big one-story metal building sagged in the middle, both ends tilted skyward. The concrete slab beneath must have cracked in the center, or a fissure opened beneath it. Farther along the two-lane highway, standing trees lined both sides. It gave hope that the damage was at an end, until a low concrete-railed bridge came into view. Several vehicles ahead had stopped; an equal number stood on the opposite side of the bridge. The right-hand lane near the middle, along with its railing, was gone. The slow flowing creek, partially dammed, spread to either side. The left lane looked stable. Micah killed the pickup's engine, opened the door, and stepped out onto the road. Three men across the creek were walking toward the damaged bridge. Micah walked past a car with a gray-haired woman driver. With the window lowered, she yelled at him.

"What are you doing?"

Micah shrugged and continued to walk. A man in a white van pulled into the left lane and started backing east. Plainly, he didn't intend to attempt a crossing. On the opposite side, a little blue Volkswagen did the same. Micah hesitated at the edge of the bridge, but started across, while a short, bald man from the other side came toward him. They met near the middle. His white shirt, under bib overalls, was yellow with age while his drooping white mustache was tobacco stained.

"What do you think?" he asked.

Micah walked to the edge and peered under the hanging roadway. At both ends, the concrete supports were undamaged. The middle one had lost the tip of its right arm, but the left looked strong. Micah returned to the man.

"I wouldn't advise anyone to drive over this."

"Me neither, but I got kin that needs help down the road. I figure it might hold up for a while before the water washes out the rest of it."

"So you're going to risk it?"

The man nodded, shifted something in his cheek, and turned away. He walked back to the two men waiting at the far edge of the bridge. Micah hurried back to the first car where a young man and woman peered anxiously at him. He explained what he'd seen. Both of them raised their eyebrows and the woman's blue eyes grew wide.

"You turn this car right around, Bob Whittaker. There's nothing we need over there."

Bob smiled up at Micah. He nodded toward the two vehicles between his car and Micah's pickup.

"Guess we'll be turning around. You going to tell the others?"

"Yes. Why don't you wait and see if they will back up to give you room to turn around?"

"Okay."

Micah stopped beside the rusted, brown Chevy pickup next in line. He repeated the information and received the same response from the dark-haired young woman driver. The two small boys on the seat beside her explained her choice. When he reached the older lady's tan Buick, she was already trying to turn around. Micah waved to her, got into his pickup, and backed almost an eighth of a mile to give them all room. Across the damaged bridge, autos were performing the same maneuver. The scant east/west traffic arriving on the scene seemed to grasp the situation, and some of them were backing up or pulling to the edge of the pavement. Soon there was no one between Micah and the bridge. He put the pickup in gear and slowly drove ahead, stopping about fifteen yards from the bridge. On the far side, the short, bald man, true to his word, rolled forward in a topless, dark green Jeep Wrangler.

The Jeep crossed the bridge abutment and slowed, as if taking a deep breath before tackling the bridge proper. Micah didn't know the weight of the Jeep versus his pickup. It was a good bet the pickup weighed more, especially the older model with more metal parts. The Jeep came slowly over the bridge, which Micah considered wise; no point in setting up unnecessary vibrations. Once across, the Jeep pulled even with Micah's pickup. The man's bald head was dripping sweat, and not all from the sun was Micah's guess. He smiled up at Micah.

"I'm a danged fool. But I wouldn't have missed doing that for all the world."

Before Micah could answer, the man gave a rebel yell and sped away. On the far side, several newcomers to the situation either parked or turned back. Behind Micah, a few others did the same. The sun was setting, but the rays were still a horizontal blaze. They turned the water to shining wine and put a glare on the blacktop. Micah looked at Dog.

"What do you say, can you swim?"

Dog cocked his head and glared.

Micah put the Ford in gear. He drove up the abutment and, following the Jeep's example, eased onto the bridge. With the window down, he listened to creaks that sounded like metal stress, or nails pulling out of aged wood. His throat turned dry and from the corner of his eye, he saw Dog trembling. This increased Micah's anxiety. He resisted pressing the gas pedal to the floorboard.

He could have turned around; there had to be other roads to Little Rock. He'd never done anything this insane. Breaking into the auto parts lot might qualify, but this seemed more dangerous. Maybe he had a secret death wish. He'd heard of a woman who, after her husband's death, left her doors unlocked, not caring what could happen. She claimed that the worst already had. Micah understood her reasoning. When life takes such a drastic turn, there is a great feeling that nothing else matters. Take away everything a man has and he loses all fear. Then, depending upon his character, it makes him either brave or dangerous.

As he crept across the bridge, the sun settled lower like a huge ball of fire at the end of the highway. He squinted against the blinding glare. Micah didn't feel dangerous, but no one should mess with him either. When the pickup's front wheels touched the far side of the bridge, he drove faster. On the pavement proper stood a young man waving at him. Micah slowed, and when he drew even he stopped. The guy looked young, certainly under thirty, wearing jeans and a white shirt, along with a cowboy hat. His smile was lopsided, giving him a daring look. The young man pointed to a pickup with an attached horse trailer.

"Hey, mister. How bad is it? Think my rig can make it across?"

"Don't try it. It isn't worth the risk."

"I saw the Jeep make it, and you did."

"That man in the Jeep is a nut, and I'm no better. It isn't safe."

As they spoke, a siren sounded. Coming from the east a black and white patrol car soon reached the far side of the bridge. Micah smiled, grateful that some authority had arrived. A patrolman got out of his car and started talking to some of the people gathered there. Micah nodded to the young man.

"There is your answer. He'll close off that side and someone will probably be here shortly to do the same on this side."

"Yeah, probably."

He looked disappointed, but Micah was glad. Risking *his* life was one thing, that of someone else entirely different. Micah drove away. In the rearview mirror he saw the pickup with the horse trailer backing from the bridge. The other three cars were doing the same. It was a relief to have made it across the bridge. If he'd had to go back and find another way, it could have meant more hours wandering around the middle of Arkansas. No offense intended to the state, but he felt trapped. The sun had at last sunk below the horizon and the lavender-gray of evening brought a soothing calm. In about thirty minutes, he'd need the headlights. If it hadn't been for the last upheaval and the detour to Highway 70, he would have reached Little Rock before dark. Now, he'd barely make it, if nothing else happened. Dog curled up on his side of the bench seat, his nose buried in his tail. Micah thought he was asleep until he saw two black eyes staring at him out of the tan and black fur.

"We're almost there," he told Dog.

Dog snorted.

Micah ignored Dog's lack of faith, although he wished it wasn't this late in the evening. Nighttime driving was worrisome, especially with the blocked roads and confusion caused by the damage. Part of the time, trees lined both sides of the two-lane highway, and traffic was light. Micah saw a pickup that looked even older than his Ford, and later a small gray car that was creeping along. He drove faster, trying to outrun the night, hoping to reach a city with lights before total darkness. Occasionally a metal building housing some type of business popped into sight. In low spots, water stood over the pavement and covered the fields. Worried about road damage hidden by the water, Micah drove through it slower. Many telephone poles leaned, dragging the lines with them. When he reached a small town, the highway curved through it revealing a surprising amount of destruction. There were brick buildings with rubble piled on the sidewalk, and broken storefront windows. Several people on the street were doing what they could to make repairs.

At one intersection, there stood a slightly bent Interstate 40 sign. Micah nearly cried out in delight and signaled a right-hand turn. The stoplights were not working. Instead, a man in a yellow vest manned the center of the street directing traffic. To the left, a two-story building had collapsed. Part of it lay in the street where two men were trying to remove the large chunks of concrete. An ambulance idled in a lot nearby. When the traffic director motioned to him, Micah wished the best for the town and turned north. In the distance, flames flickered against a purple evening sky. In an earthquake, pipes and lines broke and fire followed. There was nothing to do but keep driving. He wasn't part of this community, and he shouldn't even be there.

Soon out of town, he came to another bridge, this one still intact. There was an officer limiting the crossing to one vehicle at a time. Micah was grateful to be getting across, no matter the short wait. It was almost dark and a metal building near the bridge had emergency lighting set up on makeshift poles. Night was going to make the situation worse. Near the interstate on-ramp, a Shell service station was still open. A large hand-painted sign declared cash and a ten-gallon limit, and the line was short. Micah didn't hesitate to take advantage of the chance to refuel. Afterward, feeling too weary to move another mile, Micah headed for a tumbled down structure. It looked like an abandoned carwash or drive in. The roof of the stalls sagged, and it didn't seem stable. Rather than risk further collapse, Micah drove behind it. He parked at the back of the paved lot near a line of trees.

"Okay, Dog. This is it. Home sweet home. At least for the night."

The arrangement suited Dog. The trees provided privacy, and once he'd eaten, he seemed content. He made his bed on the pickup's seat beside Micah. Of the two, Dog's rest was the more comfortable.

Eight

Sometime in the dim early morning, Micah couldn't sleep any longer. He got out of the cab and stretched the kinks out of his arms and legs, and he and Dog used the trees for a urinal. When they were back in the truck, Micah pulled out onto the pavement. Down the road, he found the on-ramp for Interstate 40. The plan was to drive west to the Highway 65 exit and take it north to Springfield, Missouri. From there he'd go to Kansas City where there should be information about the Mississippi River bridges. Never had a river been this hard to cross.

Even before daylight, the interstate was busy. A stream of bright headlights in one direction, and red taillights in the other. Some of the vehicles had suitcases tied on top, while truck beds held boxes and small pieces of furniture. The fracture down the Mississippi basin had displaced thousands of people. Micah wondered where they would go. Hundreds of empty acres surrounded those Midwest towns and cities, but the land belonged to someone. He doubted the owners would invite others to move onto it, certainly not without compensation.

Sometimes the enormity of the damage done by the series of earthquakes sent a chill down Micah's back, at others he could not grasp so large a tragedy. If pipelines and cables running beneath the river had broken, the entire country would suffer. The destroyed bridges at Memphis carried more than vehicle traffic. They held railroad tracks, and probably conduit pipes for electricity and communications as well. The best chance of a bridge still standing was to the north. From the little news he'd heard, none to the south remained. Dawn found Dog and Micah in North Little Rock near Highway 65. Micah looked ahead toward a big cloverleaf intersection where the on-ramps were crowded with cars entering and leaving the interstate. As the sun rose behind Micah, shedding a rosy light over the scene, he was glad to be heading west. It was much easier on his eyes. Beside him, Dog stirred and gave a short whine.

"You drink too much," Micah told him, but still started searching for a place to pull off the interstate.

A Love's Travel Stop appeared and he took the service road to reach it. The entire lot was crammed with big rigs. Many of them were parked in rows along the side of the tree line, others stood at the back of the property. It looked like a tractor trailer dealership. Cars and pickups had squeezed into smaller spaces, or waited in line at the gas pumps. Much as Micah wanted to keep the Ford's tank full, he didn't want to wait. His heart beat faster as if that would get him out of the area sooner. He parked between a van and a truck with a camper shell on the bed. He killed the engine, stepped out of the cab, and Dog jumped out the door behind him. Micah grabbed his collar.

"Not so fast. This is no place for you to run free."

Dog gave him a resentful look, but remained at his side while Micah found the chain and fastened it to his collar. As they walked to the rear of the lot and stepped into the woods, no one seemed to notice them. They were too busy with their own problems. Micah took a chance and stepped behind a large oak where he unzipped and watered a patch of dead brown leaves. There was no way he intended to stand in the long line for the restroom. Trying to buy food also seemed out of the question. He'd have to make do with what was in the small ice chest.

What he really needed was to reach an unaffected city where he could restock his supplies. Maybe even find a motel for a good night's rest, and finally get across the river! Dog didn't stop to sample the many smells under the trees or to investigate the huge tires of the big trucks. He plunged ahead, putting a strain on the chain. Micah ran to keep pace. Reaching the Ford, he unlocked and opened the door. Dog stood patiently waiting until there was room for him to jump onto the seat. Micah was anxious to get back on the road, and Dog's actions made him more so. There was something in the air, a sense of desperation or great danger. It was hard to explain. Perhaps it was the crush of so many scared and worried people. The big rig drivers stood in groups talking, some drinking from insulated cups or thermoses. They must be talking about the road conditions, and Micah wanted information, but he was too nervous to make the effort. The best course was to drive on. He'd find out soon enough if there were closed roads or other problems.

The next five miles of pavement seemed cracked more than usual; some overpasses had lost chunks of their railings, and there were uprooted trees. In the full light of day, in-town flooding to the south of Interstate 40 made side streets look like creeks. Little Rock was almost one hundred-forty miles west of the epicenter. There shouldn't have been such damage. The backed-up Arkansas River accounted for flooding, but the broken pavement and trees had to be from earth movement.

Micah was near Highway 65 when the eastbound lanes to his left rose up, throwing vehicles into the median. When the wave hit the ground under Micah, it tossed the pickup into a metal guardrail, which was all that kept him out of the ditch. The screech of metal against metal was like magnified fingernails on a blackboard. Dog yipped and landed in the floorboard. As the pickup slid along the verge, Micah automatically pumped the brake, and managed to pull away from the rail before it turned into a concrete guard. He gained control of the pickup and stopped on the roadside.

The shaking came in two parts. The rolling wave threw the pickup against the guardrail, and then just as Micah parked, a hard jolt struck. The pickup bounced in place, Micah's head hit the ceiling, and he bit his tongue. He could taste the blood, and Dog slammed against the door. Dog whimpered and tried to scramble onto the seat. Micah grabbed Dog's collar and pulled him up beside him. They both sat shivering, expecting another pounding. After a few minutes with only mild quivers, Micah carefully opened the door and set his feet onto the blacktop. He remained half-seated, surveying the scene. Ahead, a small green car lay smashed against the concrete guardrail. A tractor trailer was on its side in the median behind a four-car pileup. This part of the interstate looked like the biggest traffic accident in history. Reaching up to grasp the edge of the roof, Micah stepped up to stand on the bottom of the doorframe. As far as he could see in either direction, the view was the same.

People were climbing out of vehicles, running to help others, while some staggered around looking as stunned as Micah felt. He knew the pickup had been damaged, probably long scrapes where metal had ground against metal. He jumped down to the pavement and started around the front of the truck, slamming his palm against the left front fender, angry over the damage to Taylor's truck. Sure, accidents happen, but he was a careful driver. He watched what other drivers were doing and stayed out of their way. Now a quake from nowhere had made it certain the Ford would need bodywork along with everything else. Micah understood the rolling wave-like action of the first part of this quake. The fracture was probably far away to the east, but the second hard jerking jolt was a more direct hit. It made him wonder if a distant fault had set off a closer one.

Stepping around the right front fender, he saw what he had feared. Still, it wasn't too bad. The scrape started on the door panel near the bottom and ran to the back wheel well. Past that, there was no damage. He must have pulled away in time to save that much of the body. He bent down to examine the scar. It was about four inches wide, but not at all deep. The loss was mostly paint! A point in favor of older trucks. Plastic would never stand up to a metal guardrail. He patted the wounded pickup, shook his head, and started around the rear of the Ford. Some cars that were drivable had pulled back onto the road. They weaved around parked and wrecked autos, while dodging cracks and upheavals in the pavement. As Micah stepped around the bumper and walked by the left rear fender, a small speeding black car whipped by a parked van and whizzed past him. It almost hit the pickup, and all but struck Micah. He wasn't sure, maybe it had hit him. He spun around, losing his balance, and slammed against the back fender as he fell. It all happened in an instant. His last thought was I'm going to hit the bumper. As a bright light flashed behind his eyes, a pain shot through his head.

The next thing Micah knew, a dull ache pounded inside his head which was resting upon something soft. He opened his eyes to see a woman staring down at him. He tried to rise, but she pressed against his shoulder.

"No, just stay down. Be glad you're awake." She smiled and her blue eyes crinkled at the corners. A cloud of gray hair framed her round face.

"Where am I?"

"In the back of our pickup. My husband, Rory, and I found you after that car hit you."

Micah touched his head. "Don't think it hit me."

Staring straight up, he saw the sky was pale blue with a few sunlit clouds. Looking beyond his boots there was a pickup tailgate, and to his right sat the wife of Rory. She placed a cold, damp cloth on his forehead while the truck bed bounced and nausea rose in his stomach.

"Where is my truck?"

"Behind us. Our son, Sammy, is bringing it."

"Where to?"

"We're taking you to the church. The hospitals are all full. There is a camp set up on the church grounds. This isn't the first shockwave to hit here, but Lord have mercy, it's the worst!"

"My dog..."

She frowned, her forehead like a furrowed field. "Didn't see any dog. You sure you have one?"

Micah closed his eyes and rolled his head from side to side, and it brought a stabbing pain to his right temple. He quickly stopped, keeping his head still on the pillow. Mrs. Rory smiled.

"You just rest. There is a big bruise above your eye, and a knot on the back of your head. We figured you hit the front on the truck bumper, must have smacked the back when you fell to the pavement."

The woman put her hands on either side of his face, and stared into his eyes. "Pupils don't look dilated. Here now, follow my finger."

As she moved her index finger from left to right and back again, Micah did as she said. Strangers had picked him up and he was grateful they were kind, caring folks, but he'd probably lost Dog. He was unable to explain the deep sadness it produced.

"I'm no doctor, but I've cared for plenty of the injured from broken limbs to worse head bumps than yours, and I'm guessing aspirin and a couple days' rest and you'll be okay. What are you doing so far from home, anyway?"

The California license plate gave him away every time. He didn't have the will or the energy to try to explain

"How far is this church?"

"We're almost there. It's slow going because of the chunks of missing pavement. It's not more than a couple of miles from where we found you. Just a mile down the interstate and a mile after the turnoff."

"Very far out in the country?"

Mrs. Rory laughed. "We're on the north side of town, still in the city limits; just seems like country because everything is so spread out. Not like true downtown."

He couldn't keep thinking of her as 'Mrs. Rory.' She was too much a person in her own right.

"What's your name?"

"Oh, I'm Hazel. We are the Coopers, Rory and Hazel. Our son, Samuel is married to Rita and they have two nice boys. There now, that's the immediate family." She laughed aloud. "You don't want a list of the extended bunch. We've enough kinfolk to sway an election."

As the truck slowed and turned to the right off the interstate, Micah raised on his elbows to look around. There was a Conoco gas station at the intersection, along with a long metal building of some kind. The gas station's sign hung bent to one side, but the building was still standing. Evidently, it had gasoline because there were cars at the pumps. The Ford was close behind the Coopers' pickup. A blond young man with a broad smile gave a wave through the windshield. Micah wasn't happy with someone driving the pickup. Even though he was hurt, he wanted to escape the tender care of the Coopers. Ungrateful, thinking only of himself. Yes, he was all that, but it was hard to think of anyone else. He could not believe his simple plan had gone this far astray. If planes were still flying, the best course might be to get a taxi to the airport, leave the pickup and its contents with the Coopers for their trouble, and fly to Asheville.

He could call Harry Miller, and find out how the settlement was going. If the money was there, he'd have it transferred to a North Carolina bank. He could buy a new pickup and drive it to the cabin. Unless, of course, the Smoky Mountains had fallen or the Atlantic Ocean had swept in to cover the state! Micah didn't recognize himself. He didn't let setbacks cause such disturbance in his emotional nature. Things happen in life. If one way is blocked you go another. There are always choices. There is no profit in becoming sullen and sarcastic! Since the deaths of Jena and Jordan, he had felt self-pity lurking in the shadows. It was a grinning death's head, waiting to infect him with misery and defeat. To keep this destructive emotion at bay, he had put up a barrier. It was the mental image of his lost family, how they had loved and depended upon him. They were gone, but if he failed to live up to their opinion, he might as well be dead, too.

Micah lowered himself to the pillow and tried to control the ache in his heart. It rivaled the pain in his head. First things first. He'd thank the Coopers, reclaim the Ford, and move on. Farther from the earthquake damage, there were undamaged motels. Springfield should be far enough away. He might even make a pass back along the interstate. Maybe Dog was still in the area. The Coopers' pickup hit a stretch of rough road and he and Hazel bounced like corn in a popper. It only lasted a couple of minutes. Hazel stood and pounded on the top of the cab.

"Rory," she yelled. "Watch it, you nearly tossed us out!"

Seconds later Rory drove into a wide graveled lot. At the rear of the property was a big yellow metal building with a steeple that looked something like an oil derrick atop the silver metal roof. There were wide brown double doors facing the parking lot, with long narrow windows on either side. The muntins in the amber glass formed tall crosses in each window. Rory parked diagonally in front of the church. He jumped to the ground and came to the back of his pickup, where he lowered the tailgate.

"Hazel, help our patient out."

Rory Cooper looked about sixty years old, but still strong and vigorous with a stocky build, just a bit too fat. His blond hair had pale silver streaks. The two light colors blended; it would be hard to tell when the man turned completely gray. He stood waiting for Hazel and Micah, a friendly welcome in his brown eyes. Rising to his feet was more difficult than Micah expected, and he had to accept Hazel's offered arm. When they reached the rear of the truck bed, Micah leaned forward and Rory's strong hands took Micah's elbows. Rory almost lifted him out of the truck. Micah stood for a second, getting his legs to support him.

"Take it easy," Rory advised.

Micah nodded and put a hand on the fender to steady himself.

Hazel jumped down to the ground and pointed to where Samuel was parking the Ford at the corner of the church. A short distance from the church's east corner stood three travel trailers. A couple of children sat on the steps of the nearest one. When Samuel got out of Micah's truck, he waved at the children and they waved back. Micah turned to Hazel.

"Those your son's children?"

"No, his boys are older than that. Those poor little tykes live south of here where the river flooded. If that's not bad enough, the foundation cracked and their house split down the middle."

Micah started to hobble toward his truck. "Good thing they had a travel trailer to move into," he said over his shoulder.

Rory stayed behind to latch the tailgate, while Hazel hurried to walk with Micah.

"They don't have a trailer. Those three are donations from church members. We expect FEMA to deliver some before too long. We have water hook-up, and the church is on city sewer. Some of the men are working on figuring out the connections. Thank God it isn't raining!"

Samuel waited for Micah and Hazel to reach the Ford. He looked to be about thirty years old, a younger version of his father except for his mother's blue eyes.

"What year is this old Ford?" he asked. "Sure seems in good shape."

"A nineteen seventy-nine."

"Wow. It's older than I am." Samuel laughed. "I left the keys in the ignition. You want me to get them for you?"

"No. I'll climb in and be on my way." He turned to Hazel. "I am very grateful for your help."

There were cars coming and going in the parking lot. Some of them dropped people at the church door and others were delivering food and bottled water. One car stopped near Micah's pickup. The man driving climbed out and rounded the front bumper to reach the passenger side. There he helped an older woman to her feet. She was clutching a tiny white poodle; the dog was trembling, and she was whispering to it. Hazel shook her head.

"That's Mary Gains. Poor old thing, we buried her husband a couple of months ago. Now her house isn't safe to live in." She turned to her son. "Sammy, go help her get settled. Then tell your dad to make another run down the interstate. See if he can find anyone else."

Samuel nodded and took off. She called after him.

"Remember, bring back only those not needing a doctor. Call the ambulance for the others."

She turned to Micah.

"Well, let's get you settled."

"Oh no. I won't bother you, looks as if you have plenty to take care of. I'll manage."

"Nonsense! Now you just come along. I went to all the trouble of picking you up and I will not let you go until I'm sure you're okay."

Hazel stepped to the truck and, reaching inside, removed the key and pointed to the backpack in the passenger floorboard.

"You want that brought inside, or shall we lock it in the truck?"

Micah's head pounded, his throat was dry, and every muscle seemed to ache. He tried to remember when he'd last slept or eaten. He'd spent most of last night in the truck. He and Dog had eaten what they had with them, but neither the food nor the rest were much help. His stomach quivered and his legs trembled. He struggled to stay upright. Maybe a short rest wouldn't hurt, and it would be a chance to recharge his cell phone. He leaned over to take the charger from the bag and closed his eyes against a dizzy feeling. If he fell, Hazel would never let him go.

"I don't want to be any trouble. Here, give me the key. I'll lock the truck."

Hazel handed him the key. He managed to lock both doors, and put the key into his jeans pocket. She stood watching. The look in her eyes said she knew how weak he was. He suspected she let him manage alone to prove her point. The small exercise did tire him. She took his arm.

"We'll go in the side door to the recreation hall. We have cots set up in there."

The hall was large, maybe half of the building's total area. The kitchen was in a far corner, divided from the open space by a long counter. Three tables stood just beyond the counter. Two of them held boxes of groceries, while the other was set up with paper plates, cups, and big trays of sandwiches. Women in aprons buzzed like bees, the kitchen their hive. The other end of the hall served as a resting space. Micah judged there were nearly thirty cots in neat rows. Half the cots held either people or personal belongings, reserving the cot while the occupant took advantage of the refreshment table. Young children napped on cots while older ones played games. Several smaller ones were sitting in the middle of their beds sobbing. They didn't look injured, but the earthquakes were enough to make anyone cry.

In the corner opposite the kitchen, two cots served as seating in front of a large-screen television. Two old men and four younger ones kept their gaze on the screen. Micah felt drawn to it. The sound was low, but he could see it was a newscast. Hazel shook her head.

"You men...can't get enough of the news. Doesn't matter what's happening elsewhere, we have to deal with our neighborhood. All right, you go see what the experts are saying. Promise me you'll get something to eat and find yourself a cot. Okay?"

Micah nodded. "I promise. I'll eat and rest before leaving. I hate to ask, but does anyone have some aspirin?"

Hazel held up a plump finger. "You wait right here." She hurried to the kitchen, and returned minutes later with a small bottle of Advil. "Here you go."

"I'll only take a few; can I pay for them?"

"No, you keep it. We have a friendly pharmacist who provided samples. Just mind the instructions."

Micah said he would, and as Hazel headed toward the side door, he opened the bottle and dry swallowed two capsules. When he almost choked, he hurried to the long table where bottled water sat on one end. He drank half a bottle, and started back toward the television area. But when a wave of weakness hit, he turned away and found an empty cot. It was in the last row near a wall outlet, making it easy to recharge his cell phone. He put the Advil in his shirt pocket, stretched out on the cot, made a pillow of the provided cover, and was instantly asleep. When he awoke, the large recreation room was silent in the dim light of early morning. The first faint sun rays brightened the high clerestory windows along the east side of the building. Some of the cots were empty, but held rumpled blankets, indicating someone had spent at least part of the night there. In other cots, children ranging from infants to teenagers still slept; a few adults were also asleep. Even in a foggy condition, he realized he must have slept half a day and all night.

He lay looking up at the underside of the metal roof. When he was fully awake, he didn't move. His stomach felt nauseous, and it seemed to spread to his entire body. It was like a poison making his arms and legs numb. He probably couldn't move even if he wanted to. The word *sick* marched through his mind. He felt as he imagined a wounded, dying animal must feel. He loathed self-pity, giving up was against his promise to Jena, but where could he find the resolve to continue? The idea of reaching the North Carolina cabin and settling into some sort of life had begun to fade. What had made him think living there would bring peace, or make life bearable? Maybe he'd started this trek more to run away rather than to reach a destination. He could keep on the move, run until he wore out. Then die in some town with enough money in his pockets to bury him. Although, putting such a burden on strangers held no appeal. Near the end, he'd find someone the way Taylor had done, but he didn't even have a burial place in mind. And certainly no friend would be waiting there. If he had the energy, he'd laugh at the sorry creature he'd become. Worthless, of no account to anyone, especially to himself. Micah shook his head to dislodge such thoughts. They came too close to a pity he didn't deserve.

As an adult, Micah had never depended upon anyone, and he had enlisted in the Navy at eighteen. While he was serving six years, both his parents had died. His father had shot his mother before killing himself. With no siblings, and no close extended family, he drifted until he met Jena. At first, the thought of marriage was frightening. His parents were his only example, and theirs had been a strange relationship. They spoke of love, but the constant bickering and bitter jealousies denied it. They had treated Micah well, and always provided for him. No one observing the family would have seen the inner strife. During his youth, Micah had tried to understand his parents, many times playing the mediator, but never bringing peace for long. When he was older, he gave up and left. One night he saw an old 1966 movie on television, the script adapted from an Edward Albee stage play. It was a close portrait of his parents' marriage. The story was disturbing rather than entertaining, and gave no insight to such behavior, leaving Micah as unknowing as before.

He had explained his past to Jena, and worried that she'd walk away. Her laughter was like a refreshing rain. "Oh, Micah," she had said. "You are a kind loving man, not responsible for the actions of others." She had opened his eyes. He could determine his character, and if anything, his parents were a cautionary tale. He and Jena were free to build a good life. With her, he dropped the burden of the past and gladly picked up a healthy, happy future. Without her, there were black clouds on the horizon, and he wasn't sure he could survive them alone or that he wanted to. He didn't know how life had come to such a state. Just as he didn't know why his parents had had a miserable life, his father ending it in such a horrible fashion. There were no answers. A mild ache behind his eyes caused him to touch the slight swelling on his forehead. Examining further, the larger lump on the back left his fingers slightly sticky with blood. He fumbled in his pocket for the Advil, started to take one, and decided to wait until he'd had something to drink.

Several women appeared in the kitchen area, and three more came through the side door, each carrying large, covered baking pans. The room came alive; only a few small children still slept. The aroma of coffee filled the air, and soon the smell and sizzle of bacon frying joined it. Micah's stomach rumbled despite its queasiness. He suspected the sick feeling was more emotional than physical. It was a pity because food could cure the one whereas there was no remedy for the other. He carefully swung his feet to the tiled floor. As he sat, making ready to stand, the floor lurched and quivered, causing kitchen utensils to clatter. People froze where they were, not daring to move. One more tremble and the floor grew steady. A momentary pause and everyone resumed moving and talking, chattering on as if nothing had happened. People quickly adjusted to the small aftershocks. Men with cups of coffee gathered at the television to hear the latest news. Micah's legs shook, but as he moved between the rows of cots, making his way to the kitchen, he grew stronger.

A smiling lady in a blue apron over a tee shirt and jeans offered him a cup of coffee. No one questioned his being there. She pointed to the next table.

"Scrambled eggs, pancakes, and bacon will be ready in a few minutes."

A tiny girl in pink overalls darted by her. She spun around, scooping the child into her arms.

"Jenny's mother," she called loudly. "Where are you?"

A young woman with long brown hair ran from the door leading to the hallway. She took the child.

"Sorry, just went to the restroom for a minute. I thought Dan was watching her."

The older lady raised an eyebrow and pointed to the television.

"There is your Dan."

They both laughed and Jenny's mother hurried away with her squirming child.

Watching the exchange, Micah sipped the hot coffee. Just that minute of the two women laughing, the energetic little girl, and the smell of breakfast cooking brought tears to his eyes. He quickly turned away, walking toward the television. They were so much like a loving family, sharing a warmth that was absent from his cold barren world. If this was his lot in life, the quicker he accepted it, the better off he'd be. A hard, icy heart didn't ache. A real man didn't sit around crying over his losses, he faced facts and got on with life. As Micah stood at the end of a cot in front of the television, a thin, gray-haired man scooted aside and pointed to the spot he'd vacated. He wore a blue, short-sleeved shirt under overalls that looked years old, but ironed to perfection.

"Have a seat. Not a lot of news, but interesting to see how far spread this thing is."

Micah sat. "Thanks. I haven't heard much lately."

The old man put out his hand. "Arnold Bitner is the name."

Micah shook his hand. "Micah Hanson."

The television started five minutes of commercials and Arnold turned pale blue eyes on Micah.

"Haven't seen you around," he said politely. "New hereabouts?"

Arnold looked almost as old as Taylor had been. Both of an age to have seen a great deal of life, but they didn't seem hardened or bitter. Maybe they hadn't suffered many losses or hardships. Micah set his coffee cup on the floor between his boots and gave Arnold the short version of his trip. He left out his experiences along the way. It was enough to reveal that he'd lost a family and was heading to North Carolina.

Arnold nodded. "Pretty country west of Asheville. Had a cousin lived around there. Course that was ages ago. Heard him tell of the good hunting close to his place." Arnold gave a raspy laugh. "I vowed it was better here in our Boston Mountains! Doubt he believed me."

Micah wondered if Arnold had heard the part about his losing Jena and Jordan. The old man went on about seemingly unimportant things.

"I've lived here all my life. The family had a big farm, eight hundred sixty-eight acres. By the time my papa inherited, only had three hundred acres left. Man, if it wasn't drought it was flood. When we had a good crop, the prices were bottom low. When the prices were at the top, most likely our crops failed." Arnold chuckled. "If Little Rock hadn't grown out to meet us, that land might never have paid off. The developers saved us. A Big Agra company bought out the rest."

"So you don't farm any longer?"

"Not me, nor any of my boys. All three went away to colleges." Arnold shook his head. "They are spread from Canada to Texas. Now me and Agnes live in town. Well, I guess we still do if we can repair the house. I'm going out today and see what's what."

"Agnes is your wife?"

Arnold gave a crooked smile, revealing a set of dentures. "No. My wife passed ten years ago. I guess Agnes is a funny name for a cat, but she once belonged to a lady named Agnes. Agnes, the lady not the cat, moved away. Went to a rest home. Asked me to take the cat. I couldn't think of a name, kept calling it 'Agnes' cat.' Finally, it got to just Agnes for short."

The talk about Arnold's pet settled a lump of sorrow in Micah's chest. He couldn't imagine what had happened to Dog. He hoped a car had not hit him. Dog had probably decided it was too dangerous in the truck and headed out alone. He'd be okay. Dog was resourceful, Micah silently laughed. Between them, Dog was better able to cope.

The television commercials ended and the news returned. The men sitting on the cots stopped talking, all attention on the screen. Five other men came from the kitchen area carrying paper plates filled with eggs and bacon. They stood behind the cots to watch the show in progress. The breakfast smells made Micah's mouth water, but he stayed seated next to Arnold. The news anchor, a young dark-haired man, interviewed a geologist from California. The network probably thought viewers would be impressed with someone from a more earthquake-prone area. The anchor and the expert stood before a huge interactive map, the expert holding a long pointer. On the map, he drew a big circle from Fort Smith going west to Oklahoma City north to Ponca City and Bartlesville, and south to the Ouachita Mountains where they entered Arkansas. Inside this area, Pawnee was north of Stillwater and Cushing was to the south.

He explained that the area was important because of several fault lines running east and west through it. Some of the Oklahoma faults had remained dormant since the age of dinosaurs. He hesitated to blame the recent increase in activity to oil drilling, the injection of wastewater, or the 'fracking,' because other areas such as North Dakota employed the same methods without causing earthquakes.

"If the area were fault-free, the drilling would not cause tremors," he said. "And even with the faults, there is no real proof that oil production awakened them."

Several men viewing the program gave loud guffaws. One of them spoke out, "Wonder which oil company is paying him?"

A man behind Micah said, "Probably all of them. That guy will be rich before this is over."

This caused a general round of laughter. Arnold raised his hand.

"Hush. I want to hear why we are suffering because of Oklahoma's problems."

The men grew silent, except for the sounds of eating and drinking. The geologist continued making marks on the electronic map. He drew long wavering lines to represent the faults. They extended into Arkansas as far as Little Rock. Next he moved farther east on the map and drew a large oblong shape encompassing Forrest City, then south beyond Marianna and down to Helena Arkansas. This, he explained, was a newly discovered fault, resting on the eastern part of Crowley's Ridge. This ridge was some two hundred-fifty feet higher than the surrounding land. Millions of years ago, it might have been an island between the Mississippi and the Ohio rivers.

"The area I've outlined is the location of the Marianna Fault. It is not a part of the well-known New Madrid, which is..."

The television anchor broke in. "Can you give an estimate of the damage caused by the current series of quakes?"

The geologist appeared startled, blinking as he turned away from his map.

"No, no. I doubt we will know the extent for a long time. I'm trying to point out how disturbances in one fault may have triggered a chain reaction."

With that, the geologist returned to the map. The anchor tried to look interested. The network had hours to fill with disaster coverage, and so far, none of the experts had definitive answers. The program switched to pictures of the almost totally destroyed cities of Memphis and Baton Rouge, while New Orleans was under water. The damage came in various forms: broken buildings, damaged bridges, cracked highways, fires, and backed-up rivers flooding along with huge changes to the land. Great sections of ground either had dropped due to liquefaction or rose from pressure.

When the station switched back to the geologist, he was saying, "...it is possible the growing number of earthquakes in Oklahoma exerted pressure, causing strain on northeastern Arkansas faults such as the Fayetteville fault, which in turn unsettled the Marianna. This shifting could have easily unsettled the New Madrid seismic zone."

"You feel the disruptions started in the west?"

The geologist shook his head. "I didn't say that. As you know, a quake in this current series hit Stevens County in Minnesota. That is normally a quiet area, but it is in the Great Lakes Tectonic Zone. It was a magnitude four, with little local damage. However, an immediate shock followed in a most unlikely place, Davenport,

Iowa. Following that, the first magnitude four point five we felt here in Arkansas, its epicenter the Missouri Bootheel."

"Isn't that right on the New Madrid fault?"

"Yes, however it isn't a single fault, it is made up of several. Such as the East Prairie Limb, the better-known Reelfoot Thrust Limb, and the Blytheville Arch, and others. What I'm pointing out is that with the recent activity in Oklahoma combined with the northern earthquakes, it might have been enough to set off the series of much stronger quakes."

Another reporter broke into the newscast.

"We have just received information on the condition of the fifteen nuclear plants located in the earthquake zone. All of them are offline with no apparent damage. None will be restored to power until every measure has been taken to ensure they are in perfect condition."

Arnold's elbow nudged Micah's ribs.

"Notice they aren't saying much about the oil pipelines. Bet we'll be swimming in the stuff before this is over."

Micah nodded. He couldn't imagine that the miles and miles of pipe from Cushing to Memphis had withstood the shaking. There was no way of knowing how many had ruptured.

When the broadcast returned to the local station, a young woman had replaced the male anchor.

"So you are saying we can't actually pinpoint which fault activated first."

The weary geologist had stepped away from his map.

"The earth is honeycombed with faults. Earthquakes happen anywhere between the earth's surface and to about four hundred thirty miles below the surface. The deeper the epicenter of the quake, the less it is felt on the surface. The waves dissipate with distance. Deep quakes, felt only slightly on the surface, might put stress on faults closer to the surface, and bring on the destruction we are seeing now."

The men standing behind Micah left, dumping their breakfast paper plates in a large trashcan beside the hallway door. The news stations repeated report after report on damage assessment. There was a rolling banner telling what FEMA was doing, where to find aid, how many people were affected. And how overcrowding extended to hospitals as far away as Houston and Oklahoma City. Hazel Cooper was right. It didn't matter what was happening state or nationwide, they had to deal with the local situation. Micah turned and looked toward the recreation hall's kitchen where a line reached from the cots to the tables. Adults and children picked up plates and utensils and passed by the serving area to receive their breakfast. Arnold stood and arched his back.

"Well, don't know a lot more than I did before all that reporting! You had anything to eat yet?"

"No. I can find something on down the road. Don't want to put a strain on the resources here."

Arnold laughed. "Church women like nothing better than to feed everyone in sight! Food turns up like magic. I've never seen a skimpy meal around here." Arnold wrinkled his forehead, a distant look in his eyes. "I was young and now I'm old. Yet I have never seen the righteous forsaken or their children begging bread."

"What?"

"Just something from the Bible. Guess all the bounty made it pop into mind. Come on, we'll both have something. They'll be insulted if you walk out on their cooking."

Micah was hungry, and his head still hurt. The coffee had helped, but the odor of frying bacon overcame his desire to leave. He followed Arnold to the rear of a short line. After they filled their plates with bacon, eggs, and toast, Arnold led them to a place at the end of a table. Micah found two folding chairs for them. The food was the best Micah had eaten in days. Arnold wrapped a piece of bacon in a napkin and put it beside his plate.

"For Agnes," he explained. "She loves bacon."

Micah wondered where Dog was, and if he'd found any food. Arnold's pet was lucky.

"Where is she?"

"Oh, I left her shut in the bathroom. She hates that, but I wasn't sure the rest of the house is safe. My friend Jackson is supposed to show up to help me see what needs doing at my place." Arnold looked toward the hallway entrance. "Hey, there he is now! Jackson, over this way." Arnold stood and motioned to his friend.

Jackson was a brown version of Arnold. An old man with a frizz of short white hair above a smooth dark face holding faded brown eyes. He wore a long-sleeved white shirt, starched to a shiny finish, and his overalls held as neat a press as Arnold's. As Jackson shook hands with Arnold, and they clapped each other's shoulders, they looked identical in height and weight. Micah envied their friendship. Arnold drew Micah forward.

"Jackson, this is Micah."

Jackson frowned. "You don't look too good, boy."

"Micah lost a wife and a son just a few months back," Arnold spoke quickly.

"Yeah, that can account for his hollowed out look. How'd he come by the other injury?"

"The quake caught him out on the interstate and he got hurt. He's trying to get across the Big River to North Carolina."

Jackson shook his head. "He sure enough looks like he's 'bout to cross over something!"

Arnold turned to Micah. "Don't pay Jackson any mind. He's a great one for teasing."

Jackson patted Micah's shoulder.

"Just trying to keep things cheerful. Lord knows we need it during these trying times. Hope you didn't take offense."

Micah smiled. "Not at all. I suspect I do look a wreck. I'm grateful to the kind people here who gave me a bed and something to eat."

Jackson nodded. "Yes, they are kind folks. Say, you want to come out with me and Arnold?"

"Why don't you?" Arnold broke in. "Jackson used to be an insurance adjuster. He knows all about house damage and what it might take to repair it. Could be interesting for you, seeing you have an old cabin to fix up."

It was tempting to go along with the two old men. They were trying to help him in the only way they knew, and their friendliness was like a warm blanket. There were no expressions of sympathy, just an offer to get on with living.

"Thanks, but I should find out about the roads north and if there is any possibility of crossing the river up that way."

Jackson squinted a milky brown eye at him.

"From what I hear, there isn't a bridge open from Duluth to New Orleans. Might be you could get north of there and work your way around the Great Lakes. But east of the river isn't in much better shape than we are."

Arnold produced a toothpick from the top pocket of his overalls. "Sad, just sad times," he said, rolling the toothpick between his lips.

Micah was stunned. He'd heard about the widespread destruction, but it was hard to take in.

"Where'd you hear that there were no bridges open that far north?"

"I have kin in Tennessee and Kentucky. My son works for the Department of Transportation in DC. He's been calling to see how I am. I don't know if all his information is accurate, but if it is, then the whole country is affected."

Micah's heart sank. Maybe he never would find a way across the river. Even the small voice which had first protested the journey seemed to confirm. 'See I told you,' it whispered. The bacon and eggs turned sour in his stomach; he bowed his head and swallowed. Arnold took his arm.

"Hey, you all right? Jackson, here help me get him seated."

"He sure turned pale," Jackson said as they led him to a nearby cot.

Micah tried to stand straighter. He felt foolish, ashamed. There was injury, death, and destruction all around and he was weak. He sat and, lifting his shoulders, took a deep breath.

"Thanks, I'm okay. Don't know what's wrong with me. Got dizzy for a minute."

Jackson leaned over him. "Might be that lump on your head needs looking at."

Hazel Cooper stepped between Jackson and Arnold.

"Here, what's wrong with my patient?"

The three men looked at her.

"He near passed out," Arnold said. "Might need to see a doctor."

Hazel sat beside Micah and took his wrist in her hand.

"Not much hope of that. Every medical facility from here to Oklahoma City is crammed with injured. You two go on, I'll sit with him for a bit."

Arnold smiled around his toothpick.

"Might be best you rest here, Micah. Come on, Jackson. Agnes will be clawing at the walls to get out."

Jackson nodded and smiled at Micah.

"This life is made up of trials and temptations. How we respond tells what a man's made of. If you stay around, we'll catch up with you later."

When the two headed for the side door, Micah was sure he wasn't pale now; his face burned with embarrassment.

"I don't know what happened," he said.

"Hush, I'm trying to take your pulse."

Micah sat still. He doubted Hazel's medical skills, although it was comforting to have her beside him. She seemed satisfied with the beat of his pulse and taking his chin, turned his head toward her.

"Look straight at me," she said. Her bright blue eyes studied him.

Micah complied.

"Now roll your eyes to the left...now the right."

Micah did.

When she touched the bruised lump on his forehead, he flinched.

"Maybe if we put a cold compress on that it will go down faster. Let me check the spot on the back of your head."

She examined his head, stood and hurried to the kitchen. She came back with a wet washcloth and a baggie of ice which she handed to him. She used the wet cloth to clean the small cut on the back of his head.

"There," she said. "You'll live, but you should rest today. There isn't any place for you to go anyway. Rory and I have been out on the roads. The passable ones are a traffic jam. Buying gasoline is hit and miss. The stations that have gas don't have electricity, and the ones that have power don't have any gas." She shook her head. "Just a big mess!"

"Jackson said *all* the bridges across the river are out."

Hazel chuckled. "Jackson thinks he knows everything because his son is with the government."

"He might be wrong?"

"I don't know. If I were you, I'd rest here a little longer. With our world turned upside down, it seems safer to stay put. I'll tell Rita to check on you later."

Hazel stood, patted his shoulder, and hurried away toward the hallway door. Micah sat with the ice pack in his hand. Rita, she was Hazel's daughter-in-law. If he remembered that, his mind was probably all right. *His* world turned upside down three months ago. Micah leaned back and held the ice to his forehead. He suddenly realized Jena had been gone longer than three months. He took the ice pack away. He couldn't believe so much time had passed. It was almost five months. He'd said three months for so long, it seemed it would be forever three months since losing his family. Where had May gone? Time was playing games with him. Yes, it was May that was missing. He had set out on the trip in June. It must be near the end of June now, but in his situation, time didn't mean anything.

Micah stretched out on the cot. The laughter of children playing echoed in the recreation hall. The clatter of cookware came from the kitchen, and the low drone of the television faded as he fell asleep.

He awoke with a start, making his heart pound. For a second he didn't remember where he was. He sat up; the icy baggie held sloshing water. He ran his hand through his hair to smooth it. Looking around he found fewer people in the hall. In a far corner, a semi-circle of chairs faced a chalkboard. Older children were sitting in the chairs, while a young woman was writing on the board. Some sort of class was in session. Most of the cots had blankets neatly folded at their foot. In the kitchen area, long tables held only bottled water, a coffee urn, and a tray of fruit. It appeared the church families were going about their day. Micah stood; his legs trembled a bit, but overall he felt stronger.

He picked up the light blanket, shook it, folded it, and placed it at the foot of the cot. He headed for the hallway door, but as he passed the kitchen, he stopped for a drink of water. He used a cup from the cabinet and drank water from the tap. No sense opening a bottle for a couple mouthfuls. He rinsed and dried the cup, and again headed to the hallway. Just beyond the door were restrooms. When he entered the door marked 'men,' the scene reminded him of a school facility. A row of four sinks with soap dispensers stood across the room from five toilet stalls. Micah had the room to himself. When he looked into the mirror above the sinks, he understood Jackson's remarks. It wouldn't take much more pallor, or darkness under his eyes, to make him look dead. He passed his hand over a cheek dark with stubble. Maybe he should forget about shaving. Why bother?

He used the toilet, went to a sink and lathered his hands and face with soap. When he rinsed, and poured water over his entire head, a slight red stain ran from his hair. He rinsed again and the water was clear. It wasn't much of a cut. He used a handful of paper towels to dry, pulled a small black comb from his back pocket, and carefully combed his brown hair. The image in the mirror looked clean but lifeless. Micah turned his lips up in a smile, trying to bring some light to his eyes. His eyes were brown but always looked bright because of the gold flecks in them. He frowned and leaned forward, looking for those highlights. They seemed gone, but it didn't matter; not much about him was normal now.

When he left the bathroom and started toward the nearby exit, a short, slender young woman came hurrying toward him. She had long black hair pulled back in a ponytail, a pretty smile, and sparkling black eyes. Her rolled up jeans were above white socks and blue sneakers; the gray tee shirt had the emblem of the American flag across her chest. She waved at him.

"There you are! You are Micah Hanson, aren't you?"

Micah admitted that he was.

"How do you feel?"

"Okay. And you are?"

She laughed and her cheeks dimpled.

"Rita. Sam's wife. Hazel told me to see about you. If you are okay, I could sure use some help. I have a truckload of supplies. I picked some up from a government distribution center, and the rest from individual donations."

Rita started walking toward the main exit and Micah hurried to stay beside her. At the end of the hallway, double doors led to the sanctuary, while another set to the right were marked exit. Rita pushed through them to the outside. It was mid-day, a cloudless blue sky stretched high above them. The parking lot was crowded with an assortment of vehicles and Rita pointed to them.

"Lots of them are out of gasoline. Some of the men are picking certain trucks and buses to use as common transportation. They siphon gas out of the others and store it to use in the designated ones."

Micah nodded. It sounded like a good plan. Rita stopped beside a big white Chevrolet stake-bed truck filled to the top with boxes and black plastic garbage bags. Rita unhitched the back rail and, stepping up on the bumper, jumped into the truck bed.

"I'll move things close to the edge, and you can pick them up from there. We'll get them all into the hallway and people can sort them out from there." She looked down at him. "You sure you feel all right?"

Micah nodded. Rita smiled and started moving boxes. Micah took the first one, carried it to the double doors, and shifted it around trying to open one side of the door. It suddenly opened outward, almost shoving Micah and his load aside. A teenage boy came out, a surprised look on his face.

"Wow, I'm sorry. Here, let me help."

Micah shifted the box to the boy, opened the door, and, using the wedge at the bottom, propped the door wide open. The boy carried the box inside.

"Where does this go?"

Micah pointed to the far wall. "Over there should be fine."

The boy smiled. "Should I stay and help?"

"Ask the boss out in the truck."

They both walked to the truck where Rita had several boxes and one cardboard barrel moved to the back of bed. The boy looked up at her.

"Do you need more help?"

Rita gladly accepted, and in less than thirty minutes, the truck bed was empty. A line of supplies sat along the hallway wall. The teenager went his way while Rita thanked Micah for helping. She smiled a lot and her dark eyes sparkled. The damage around her didn't seem to affect her. She patted his shoulder.

"Come on, we've earned a glass of lemonade. I saw a pitcher of it in the refrigerator."

Micah followed her into the kitchen where she found two paper cups and filled them. As they leaned against the counter, Rita studied him.

"You still trying to find a way across the river?"

Micah thought for a minute. He'd been asking himself that question. When he didn't answer, Rita laughed.

"It's okay. I'm nosy. Who knows what they are going to do now."

"What are you going to do?"

"I suppose I'll do whatever Sam decides. I'm betting we'll stay right here and see about rebuilding. Our house lost a corner bedroom along with the garage. Such a mess! Mom gave me a great piece of advice. She said, 'Smile and the world smiles with you. Cry and you cry alone.' She's right, cheerfulness is contagious."

Micah finished his lemonade and crumpled the paper cup. He couldn't help smiling.

"Your mom is a smart lady."

Rita laughed. "I better go. I have two wayward sons to catch up with. They think this disruption is an opportunity to get into trouble. Thank goodness Sam will be back tomorrow."

"Where is he?"

"Kansas City. He found a place willing to sell four generators. They promised to hold them. He has a cousin who owns a lumberyard up there. He set aside some building supplies. Just hope we get a fuel supply to make those generators worthwhile."

With that, Rita hurried away. When the hallway door swung closed behind her, the room seemed darker. Sam was a lucky man and Micah hoped he didn't have a moment's trouble bringing back the supplies. Micah knew he must make a decision. The people here were welcoming, but he didn't feel it was the place to stop. He supposed he could make some sort of life here, join old guys such as Arnold and Jackson. He didn't feel he'd fit in with Sam and other married men. They had family involvement and didn't have time to spare. He was happy for them, and wished they'd keep their families together for years and years. It was a strange feeling, but whenever he saw a happy couple, a bubble of joy swelled in his heart. He didn't understand it because his loss was still painful. Maybe seeing others, for the time being spared this sorrow, brought a measure of comfort. Micah started for the recreation hall exit. He wasn't emotionally equipped to figure out his complicated feeling, and he'd leave that to the experts.

Right then, he needed to check out his pickup. It still ran well, as evidenced by Sam driving it to the church. He remembered locking it and the key was in his pocket. The damage to the right side was regrettable, but he'd have it repaired. However, there probably wasn't a garage in the quake area that was up and running, and parts and paint might be in short supply. All this suggested that leaving was the better choice, and repair to the truck could wait. When he stepped through the door to the parking lot, Rita's truck was gone and a car had taken its place. A woman was struggling with two small children and a box filled with groceries.

"Can you get the door for me? Please," she called to Micah.

Micah quickly turned and opened the door, holding it wide enough for the lady to struggle by. The two little girls at either side held onto the tail of her long shirt.

"Do you need any more help?" Micah called after her.

She looked back over her shoulder. "I can manage. Thanks anyway."

Micah let the door close and started walking toward the corner of the building. The early afternoon sun was high, the sky cloudless, but the smell of rotting vegetation told of flooded fields and ditches of standing water. He remembered that Hazel had thanked God it wasn't raining. If there *was* something to be thankful for, it was the dry condition.

Nine

There were vehicles parked all along the side of the recreation hall. He didn't see his truck until he walked past a white church bus. There, on the other side, stood the red Ford pickup. Micah rushed forward, a growing happiness in his heart, for it was a homecoming of sorts. He fumbled in his pocket for the key, but stopped, startled by a loud snarling bark. As Dog squirmed from under the truck, his head visible, the barking stopped and the rest of his shaggy body appeared. Dog stood, shook hard enough to make his coat roll from side to side, and looked up at Micah. Then he lowered his head, whined, and did a slow tail wag.

Micah dropped to his knee, grabbed Dog around the neck, and touched foreheads with him. Dog immediately stiffened and pulled back a bit. Filled with joy, Micah laughed.

"Don't go in for mushy stuff, huh?"

Micah stood and started to unlock the pickup. Dog did another hard shake to remove bits of leaves and twigs from his fur before leaning against the truck door and looking up at Micah.

"I bet you're hungry. Move, so I can open the door."

Dog stepped backward and continued to stare at Micah. He didn't stop until a bowl of his dry dog food was on the ground before him. Dog turned all his attention to eating. If Dog had been out there the whole time, Micah felt bad. When Sam drove, Dog must have followed the pickup. Still, no one had mentioned a dog. Hazel hadn't seen one. If he'd been in the pickup, Sam would have known. Micah patted Dog's head. Another of Dog's mysteries. Whatever way he came to find the pickup, Micah was ridiculously glad!

Dog licked the bowl clean and, running his long tongue over his lips, lifted his head and surveyed his surroundings. Micah picked up the bowl and walked to the side of the building where he found a water faucet. Dog followed and drank an entire bowl of water before trotting back to the truck. Micah opened the truck bed and took out the roll of paper towels to dry the bowl. It was comforting to see that everything under the bed cover was as he'd left it. The red gasoline cans sat in a row behind the cab, the camping equipment, still in the boxes, along with the duffel bag and tools seemed like a fortune in goods. Here was everything a person might need to survive. He closed and locked the bed's black cover. When he opened the cab door and started to get behind the wheel, Dog pushed around him and leapt onto the seat. He moved to his side and sat up straight. Micah climbed in, and reaching to the passenger side floorboard, picked up his backpack. With it on his lap he sorted through and found clothes, pistol, and money all safe. A miracle in itself.

He dropped the bag back onto the floor and sat staring through the windshield. He could put the key into the ignition and drive away. He wasn't sure how to get back on the interstate, and wondered if he should. Side roads might be less congested and faster. Once away from the city, he could angle west toward Highway 65, and take that north to Springfield. It probably wasn't far enough away to avoid the upheaval. If he bought some groceries along the way, he felt strong enough to keep driving until he did reach a safe place to stop for a rest. Rita had said Sam was in Kansas City gathering supplies, and surely, that city was far enough away. With the change in his destination, Micah picked up his cell phone and checked the mileage from Little Rock to Kansas City. He could be there in a little over six hours.

After resting in Kansas City, he'd continue north, and if there wasn't a way through the Great Lakes area he could try Canada. Still, he didn't have a passport. He could sneak across and sneak back, but he doubted it would come to that. The Mississippi River wasn't that wide in Minnesota. At the headwaters, it was as narrow as twenty or thirty feet, and as shallow as three feet. He suspected that it was several faults shifting that caused the quakes, like a chain reaction. And even if an earthquake had hit that far north, it probably didn't damage the bridges.

Since time didn't matter, as long as he reached the cabin before winter, he'd try various places along the river. The first intact bridge would be his route out of this disaster. The disruption of fuel supplies and commerce between the east and west of the country could go on for a year or more. However, once on his land in North Carolina, even with a shortage of supplies, he'd find a way to survive. The whole idea of the cabin was to live out his years in peace and privacy. He'd seen enough of the world and its troubles. Beside him, Dog whined and fidgeted on the seat.

"Ready to pull out of here?"

Dog nudged him with his nose and said, "Woof."

"Okay, but I won't feel right about leaving without saying goodbye and thanking some of these people."

When Micah started to open his door, Dog slumped in the seat and turned his head away.

"You stay here. Don't move."

Micah rolled the window down a few inches and firmly shut both doors. Although he wasn't sure that, if he tried, Dog couldn't open them. When he reached the side door to the recreation hall, he saw Rory Cooper's pickup come speeding into the parking lot. Directly behind him was the truck Rita had been driving. Micah stopped beside the door to wait for them. They could say goodbye to Arnold and Jackson for him. The pickup and the larger truck stopped in the first row of parking. Hazel, Rory, and two boys climbed out of Rory's pickup while Rita jumped out of her vehicle and ran toward them. As they came toward the building, they were all talking at once, and with worried looks on their faces. Something must be wrong. Micah started to speak, but they didn't seem to notice him. Micah opened the door and all five of the Coopers rushed past him and into the hallway. Inside, they hurried into the hall and Micah followed.

"You keep the boys. I'm going." Rita was almost screaming.

Rory put his hand on her shoulder. "Listen, Rita, I can make the trip easier alone. I'll bring Sam home. Your place is with your sons. You know Sam would want that."

Hazel was frowning, her round face set like stone.

"Rory, I know how she feels."

Rory glared at the two women. "I'm not fighting both of you. It's settled. I'll be back with Sam in the morning!"

"Just how are you going to drive two trucks back?" Rita asked. "We can't leave the supplies up there. We need them! Besides, you aren't going to keep me from going to Sam."

Hazel put her hand on Rory's arm.

"We need you here. Some buses are running. Let Rita take one. She can drive the supply truck back."

Micah couldn't keep quiet. "What's happened? Why does Rita need to go to Kansas City?"

Hazel, Rory, and Rita turned to him.

"Sam's been hurt," Hazel said. Her bright eyes were a stormy dark blue.

Rita looked close to tears. "Thank God he's not dead. Savages, rotten people."

Rory looked pale but he squared his shoulders and nodded at Micah.

"Sam is okay. Take more than a busted arm and a few broken ribs to stop him. We had to make him promise not to drive back on his own."

Hazel shook her head. "If Sam could drive back on his own, we wouldn't be having this conversation. I suspect he's hurt worse than he's saying. And how are we supposed to make up for the lost generator?"

"Jerry said he can get us one from Lowe's in Springfield," Rita said. "He called a friend there and he took it to his house to hold for us."

Micah leaned toward Rita. "Who is Jerry?"

"He's Sam's cousin, the one with the lumberyard in Kansas City."

She turned back to the others.

"It will take longer on the bus with all the stops, but bus lines get gasoline preference. At least I'll be sure of getting there. Hazel is right, Rory, you can do more good here. Besides, you are the only one that can keep the boys in line."

The three adults almost smiled. Micah held up his hand.

"Wait. If Rita needs to go to Kansas City, I plan on going through there. I came in to say thanks and tell you I'm leaving. She is welcome to ride that far with me. That is, Rita, if you don't mind sharing with Dog."

Hazel tilted her head back and raised an eyebrow.

"You going on about having a dog again? You mentioned it more than once when we picked you up. But I told you, we didn't see a dog."

Rory squinted. "Listen, you sure you feel up to leaving?"

Micah laughed. "It's okay, I'm fine. I do have a dog. He followed the pickup here and has been staying under it. I thought he was lost until I went out there today."

"Is he a medium to large shaggy brown and black, with a threatening snarl?" Rita asked.

"Sounds like him."

"I saw him last night drinking from the roadside ditch; I figured he was a stray."

"Do you think you could stand riding with him for six or seven hours?"

"No worse than being on an overcrowded bus."

Hazel clapped her hands. "That settles it. Rita will ride to Kansas City with Micah. She can decide when Sam is well enough to make the trip home."

After more discussion, and when Micah told Rory of the extra gasoline in the pickup which would ensure their arrival in Kansas City, he agreed to the plan. Rita was as eager to set out, but she pulled Hazel aside and gave a long list of instructions concerning her two sons. Rory gave Micah the address where Sam was staying with Jerry Harmon.

"Jerry is my sister's boy. They lived here until her husband's father died and left them the lumberyard up there. Sam and Jerry are close as brothers. Makes us feel better knowing he's with Jerry."

Micah did his best to assure Rory he'd safely deliver Rita to her husband. He liked the feeling of doing something to help the ones who had helped him. He also realized that for almost an hour he hadn't been thinking of himself. The sensation was such a relief he felt guilty for forgetting Jena and Jordan, and the familiar heavy ball of sorrow dropped like a rock into his heart.

Rory rounded up his grandsons, seven-year-old Rick, and nine-year-old Joey.

"Get over here and kiss your mother goodbye." He spoke gruffly but there was an underlying pride in his voice.

Hazel made a fuss of hugging and kissing Rita, telling her not to worry about the boys, just take good care of Sam. Rita smiled and warned her sons what would happen if they didn't obey their grandparents. The two youngsters, Joey dark as his mother and Rick fair like his father, solemnly promised to behave. Micah thanked them again, and with all the goodbyes concluded, he and Rita hurried out of the building. Once in the parking lot, Rita ran to the big Chevy truck and retrieved a small canvas bag. When they reached Micah's truck, he opened the door and introduced Dog to Rita.

Dog was silent.

Micah took his backpack and Rita's bag and put them in the truck's bed, carefully locking the cover and making sure everything was ready to set out on the road to Kansas City. When he returned to the front of the pickup, Dog was standing outside the driver's door waiting for him. Rita was in the passenger's seat. Dog leveled a questioning gaze at Micah, who wasn't sure how to proceed. Rita pointed to her door.

"Bring him over here."

Micah went around the front of the pickup with Dog at his heels. Rita raised her feet to the edge of the seat and motioned to Dog.

"Get in," she said.

Dog looked to Micah who nodded. With a heavy heave of his shoulders, Dog sprang up and settled in the floorboard. Rita put her feet on the floor next to the door. Micah shrugged and slammed the door. He doubted they would ride in that position the entire trip, but it was good enough to start. He pulled out of the parking space at the end of the building and when they rolled by the recreation hall door, Rita's family was standing there to wave goodbye. Rita directed him through a couple of streets until he saw the sign for Interstate 40. Hazel was right about the heavy traffic. The shortage of gasoline didn't seem to be having much impact in this area. Rita told him to follow I-40 westward and then take I-49 north.

"It may be marked seventy-one, but it's the same thing," she said. "Past Kansas City you could take interstate twenty-nine clear to the Canadian border. You could try going east out of KC but that would put you in St. Louis and I've heard the flooding is really bad there."

Micah kept a watch on the traffic, which was erratic due to sections of pavement being blocked with sawhorse barriers. Drivers were cautious, but in areas without damage, they made up time by speeding. There were few highway patrol cars except at major intersections and in areas of heavier damage and detours. The huge amount of destruction spread the authorities thinly across the state. It was up to citizens, such as the ones at Rita's church, to fend for themselves. Micah drove as fast as traffic and conditions would allow, but it still took twice as long as it should have to reach Conway. He couldn't help but think how many times he had retraced his tracks. Every time something happened to turn him back west, he superstitiously wondered if it had some meaning. Yet, each time nothing prevented him from again heading east. After Conway, the pavement was better. Some buildings visible from the highway showed damage, the ditches brimmed with water, and some distant fields had a suspicious sheen. The Arkansas River coming out of Oklahoma near Fort Smith followed Interstate 40 all the way to Little Rock. In places, it lapped at the interstate embankment. The earthquake damage at the confluence of the Arkansas and the Mississippi rivers accounted for the flooding as far west as Fort Smith.

How long the flood conditions might last was anyone's guess. The rivers kept flowing south out of Kansas into Oklahoma, and once into Arkansas they flooded the riverbanks. Micah couldn't wait to get away from the soggy ground. He was eager to hit Interstate 49 and go north away from the river. He and Rita continued in silence beyond Russellville and Ozark where barriers blocked the turnoff because of high water. The landscape of low rolling hills stood thickly forested with oak, hickory, and cedar. The pavement had some cracks, but they were easy to avoid. It was hard to tell if the crumbling roadsides were due to wear, or tremors from the earthquakes. As Micah neared a county road, Rita pointed to the supports of the overpass. The right-hand side of the structure seemed buckled. It was folded back into the bank, and the county road was blocked, but the interstate beneath was clear. Road damage was intermittent, and kept Micah constantly on guard.

At Alma, Dog made it necessary to stop. He'd clearly decided that driving for an hour and a half longer than the two hours it should have taken was reason enough to stop. Micah agreed. His shoulders were stiff from holding them rigid. There was a small empty field behind a Kentucky Fried Chicken restaurant which met Dog's needs. Rita and Micah decided they should take a rest, too. It could be another five or six hours to Kansas City, depending upon circumstances. They would arrive in better condition after a good meal.

Back on the road, Micah took the sweeping loop north to Interstate 49 which headed toward Fayetteville. Rita seemed more relaxed, and he felt the same. The traffic had thinned. Fewer of the gas stations had 'out of gas' signs, but the five or ten gallon limit still applied. Rita patted Dog's head and smiled at Micah.

"Thanks for letting me ride along."

"Hey, no problem. I told you, I was heading this way."

"Yes, but I would have hitchhiked if I had to. You don't know how I feel; I *have* to be with Sam."

Micah understood more than she knew. He just nodded. A flush rose in Rita's cheeks.

"I'm sorry, Micah, what I said was thoughtless. I heard about your wife. I can't imagine how it must feel. What was her name?"

Micah's throat tightened. He hadn't said Jena's name aloud in months, but her name was constantly in his mind. Rita put her hand on his arm.

"Never mind. You've probably heard how 'fools rush in where angels fear to tread.' I shouldn't have asked."

"No, that's all right." Micah stiffened his jaw and said, "Jena. Her name is, *was* Jena."

Rita sat silently looking at her hands folded in her lap. Micah's eyes burned and the highway blurred. He blinked hard and the road cleared. He could not go on feeling this way. The burden was too heavy and it could crush him. Self-pity had to be the cause of it; he was sorry for himself, but he had no right to be. He wasn't the one who had died. Yet, sometimes he felt that Jena was the lucky one, and he was strangely grateful that she didn't have to endure this. The many contrasting emotions that scrambled his brain made it hard to think straight.

"My son's name was Jordan."

"Micah, you don't need to go on."

"They were both killed in a car wreck. Jordan died right away. They said he didn't suffer. Jena lasted a week in the hospital. It happened last February."

"You must be so angry."

Her words hit with an unexpected impact. Yes, yes he *was* angry. He was more than angry, furious came closer. As he acknowledged the rage, a sense of helpless futility swamped him. Under the sorrow was outrage because he felt robbed! Life, fate, whatever, stole from him what he prized most. The frustration of not being able to 'fix' this injustice was maddening. His face burned, his chest expanded, and he was ashamed of this physical evidence of his emotions.

"I've never lost anyone close to me," Rita went on in calm conversation. "My parents are both alive. I have two brothers and a sister. They have families, and their children are all doing well. You met Hazel and Rory. I never knew their parents. They were gone before I met Sam. I've heard that losing a child is the most painful loss of all."

Micah nodded. He hadn't separated Jena and Jordan. The sorrow was one huge black storm that encompassed them both.

"I thank God almost every day that my boys are healthy," she said. "I know something could happen to one of them, but I try my best to keep them safe and trust God they will be."

"Maybe I didn't thank God enough for my family. You think they weren't kept safe because I wasn't grateful for what I had?"

Rita clasped her hands to the sides of her head. "Did I do it again? Babbling on, saying something that could hurt."

Her reply let Micah know how bitter he'd sounded. His heart softened. He was happy for Rita's good fortune thus far. One of the few things that gave him pleasure was seeing safe, happy families. No matter how painful his loss, he never wanted others to suffer the same fate. The rotten downside was that he knew someday Rita would face this same trial. He glanced at her and smiled.

"No. I'm glad your family is intact. I hope you have many long years of happiness. That your sons grow up healthy and strong. That you and Sam live to see your grandchildren."

As they traveled deeper into the Ozarks, the land lay like a rumpled green blanket, building toward more narrow valleys and steeper hills. They rode on in silence for several miles. Dog looked up from the floorboard and whined. There was a questioning look in his brown eyes. During the conversation, he had stayed curled at Rita's feet. Now he looked disturbed, as if he sensed something wrong. Rita patted his head and he licked her hand.

"Guess you've made friends with Dog."

"You call him dog. Is that his name?"

Dog's ears stood up and he shivered. He clearly understood they were talking about him.

"I guess it is strange, but I haven't been functioning normally. He's lucky to have a name."

"Where did you get him?"

Micah spent the next few miles explaining how he and Dog met. Rita looked interested.

"That lady's daughter didn't seem very nice. Good thing you took Dog, she really might have killed him." Rita patted Dog again and he squirmed with pleasure.

"He's been company for me. I'll appreciate having a dog when I get to the cabin."

"Tell me about the place you intend to settle."

As they neared Fayetteville, Micah finished telling Rita about the cabin on the twenty acres in North Carolina. His telling was as he remembered it years ago, but it might not be the same now. Still, it was his destination and about all that kept him going. Rita looked out the window as if she were seeing what he described.

"Sounds nice. No wonder this earthquake is upsetting. Well, it is upsetting for us all but it stops you from reaching the rest you are looking for." Rita put her hand on his arm. "I hope you reach your cabin, Micah, but remember...wherever you are, there you will be."

Micah frowned and quietly laughed. "You are trying to say I can't run away from myself. Right?"

"Like I said, I can't know how you feel, but I'm sure there is purpose behind every life."

Micah let that go unanswered. If there were some purpose in his being alive, he couldn't see it. Jena had been Catholic, intended to enroll Jordan in a Catholic school. She hadn't insisted that he attend church, but she said she prayed for him. He'd left that out when telling Rita about his family. When he was silent, Rita continued, "I hope you find what you are looking for, Micah."

What *was* he looking for? Thus far, all he'd thought about was getting away from the scene of his pain. Yet, as Rita had pointed out, you can't run away from yourself. She watched him expectantly, obviously wanting a reply.

"Maybe I'll find peace," he offered. "I guess that's about all a person can expect."

Rita sighed. "Maybe so. No one is happy all the time, even when things are going all right. Just remember, peace isn't a place."

"I know." Even as he said it, the hope remained that he would find peace in the cabin.

Rita turned to watch the passing scene. Micah wondered if he'd told her too much, but the road conditions cut short his concerns. In an area where north and southbound lanes were divided by some distance, and both spanned a valley by long bridges, traffic was backed up. Drawing near, it was plain the southbound bridge was impassable. At least two of the tall T supports under the highway had lost concrete, exposing some bent interior metal. Micah stared ahead while Rita and Dog grew stiff and silent.

Both north and south traffic shared the northbound lanes. Highway patrol was set up at either side of the detour. Micah waited in line until the signalman waved him on. It was a short wait. Most of the traffic was commercial, and Micah saw only two passenger cars. When they were beyond the destruction, north and south lanes were again occupying their original course. Micah and his passengers heaved a collective sigh of relief. The random destruction was nerve wracking.

Around Fayetteville, the green mountains rolled away in the distance under the vault of the high, bright blue, cloud-streaked sky; both seemed to stretch into forever. The traffic was a bit heavier but there were a surprising number of people on foot. This made Micah glance at the truck's gas gauge. Ahead stood an information sign advertising food, lodging, and gasoline.

"I should stop," he told Rita.

She nodded. "We could all stand a rest."

The Phillips station had three stalls with six pumps, but four of them had 'empty' hoods over the nozzles. The other two were in use and no other cars were waiting. The large hand-painted sign near the roadway read 'private vehicles five-gallon limit, commercial ten.' Micah wondered how long it might be until the gasoline shortage ended. The broken pipelines could take months if not years to repair. However, tanker trucks could deliver to the filling stations, if the refineries were still in operation.

Rita and Dog got out of the truck to walk around while Micah entered the station to pay cash for the allotted five gallons of gas. The station attendant was an older man wearing a red ball cap and a wide leather belt around his thick waist. The belt had a holster attached on the man's right hip, and the butt of a pistol was visible above a safety strip over the hammer. Micah pointed to the gun.

"You have much need for that weapon?"

The man didn't smile, his eyes narrowed, and his heavy jowls quivered.

"You bet, bub. I've been threatened more than once. Serve them right if I locked the place down."

Micah had his billfold in hand counting out the money for his purchase.

"I'd have thought things would ease up this far from the center of the quake."

The man took Micah's cash and stepped to the register.

"Nope. I suspect it will get worse before it gets better. There are refineries in thirty different states, but Texas, Louisiana, and California do almost half of the refining. Guess you've heard about Louisiana and southeast Texas."

"No, well, yes, I did hear Baton Rouge and the Gulf were in trouble."

"Hah!" the man gave a harsh laugh. "Trouble? I'd say more like wiped out! New Orleans might as well give it up. The mouth of the river was already below sea level. Only thing that kept the ocean from rushing in was the out flow of fresh water. When the quake caused the land to sink, the river over ran its bank, spreading all over creation. It let salt water rush in clear up to interstate ten."

Micah didn't know what to say. If the man was right, gasoline might be in short supply for a long time. He put his change in his pants pocket.

"Guess people will be doing a lot more walking."

Now the man did laugh. "That or riding hay burners."

Micah pushed open the glass door and walked to the pickup before the term 'hay burners' registered. Horses. Not a bad idea. When he reached the cabin, he should look into buying a horse. A dog and a horse...maybe he'd live like a frontiersman. Still, if the shortages continued, horses might be out of his price range. As Micah took the allotted gasoline, and put the gas cap back into place, Rita and Dog climbed into the truck. It was mid-afternoon. The sun was high overhead, and with no breeze, the temperature rose. When Micah pulled onto the highway, two cars drove into the gas station. He didn't tell Rita the attendant was armed. Considering Sam's attack and robbery, maybe times were more dangerous than he realized. He did tell her what he'd learned about the destruction in the Gulf area.

"I'm pretty sure there are refineries east of the Mississippi," he said. "But I don't know if they can supply all the needs of those states."

Rita rolled her window down lower to help cool the cab.

"It will be a mess for a long time. I imagine the church congregation will survive. We'll find a way. Soon as the flood water goes, things will get better." Rita turned toward Micah. "Listen, I don't mean to be giving advice, but when you get where you're going, you should find a good church."

Micah shook his head and raised his hand from the steering wheel. Before he could speak, Rita cut him short. "I know, I know. Until you understand, church just seems like a bunch of 'do gooders' telling people how to live. But that isn't the heart of it, Micah. If people don't believe in an Almighty, it makes their lives useless. It makes humanity worthless. A man is no better than Dog here." Rita patted Dog's head and laughed. "No offense, Dog."

Dog licked her hand and didn't seem in the least offended. Micah decided he wasn't either. Rita had her belief and he was glad for her. True or not, it seemed a stabilizing force in a world racked by natural disaster and human cruelty.

As they drove through Bella Vista, Arkansas, many of the fast-food restaurants appeared closed. Upon looking closer, there was visible damage to some buildings, much more than to be expected this far from the epicenter. Although Micah wasn't clear on where each quake's center occurred. Maybe smaller faults account for damage in more distant areas. Rita had grown silent, and from the slump of her shoulders and the occasional nod of her head, she was drifting into sleep. Dog, curled on her feet, seemed napping, too. Micah rolled his window down a bit more and let the breeze cool him. As the sweat dried around his shirt collar, he realized how tense his muscles were. He was stretched to the breaking point. This was a new emotion since leaving California. Yet, maybe it had been there all along hidden under the sad and lost feeling, and the painful attacks of sorrow. He had almost grown accustomed to those. Rita had made him aware of the anger lurking beneath his grief. He had to acknowledged that she was right. He had been angry from the start, and strung tight as a piano wire, too.

The highway cut through low green mountains. In places, granite and limestone cliffs flanked the road. There was little traffic; twice he saw men on horseback, and just before reaching the Missouri state line, there was a wagon drawn by a mule. Evidently, people were adapting to the gasoline restrictions. Heading into Missouri, Micah examined the source of his nervous tension. He wasn't afraid of anything physical. If anything, his anger made him of more danger to others than they were to him. He had begun to understand that he was a man with nothing to lose. He would regret the loss of personal possessions, and losing Dog would be a blow, but he'd get over it.

The afternoon sun put a glare on the pavement making it shimmer. Micah narrowed his eyes against the brightness and thought about his emotional condition. He realized he must make a decision. He could let the anger, tension, and bitterness welling up in him rule, or he could fight the destruction to his character. He almost laughed at such thoughts. Truth was he never dwelt upon such things; in each situation, he had done what felt right and moved on.

Rita shifted in her seat and leaned her head against the half-opened window. She looked uncomfortable, but it didn't seem right to disturb her. The sagging of her jaw said how tired she was. The last week had put everyone through an enormous strain. Psychologists would probably do studies on how this disaster affected the population, maybe finding it even shortened life spans. Micah could already see changes: displaced families, destroyed businesses, lost jobs. Still, he had little doubt that, given time, the area would recover. Just across the Missouri line, there was a convenience store with gas pumps out front. Micah glanced at the truck's gas gauge and slowed to make a right turn off the highway. It seemed only prudent to keep the tank topped off as often as possible. As he pulled to a stop near a gas pump, Rita moaned and leaned back against the seat. He watched for a moment before quietly opening the door and stepping to the ground. If she didn't wake up, he'd let her sleep. It was about an hour to Joplin where they could all take a rest. The limit on gasoline at this station was three gallons. Micah didn't argue, but if this kept up, people wouldn't be able to make it from one small town to another.

When Micah got back into the pickup, Dog lifted his head but didn't bother to move or make any comment. The divided highway skirted most of the small towns along its route. The pavement was in good shape, but in places the concrete divider between the north/south lanes had crumbled. Large hunks blocked part of the near lanes. In the light traffic, it was easy to avoid them, but it was a relief when the divider became a wide swath of grass or gravel. Near Pineville, the highway crossed the Elk River. Micah could see it was normally a medium-sized river, but now it was far out of its banks. Water shimmered beneath oak and cedar trees and put a sheen on a valley field. Something had happened to even this river. Micah had heard of the fracking in Oklahoma disturbing fault lines in Arkansas. Maybe the huge shifting in the Reelfoot Rift set off a chain reaction in the other direction. Micah looked forward to getting some accurate news.

As the afternoon wore on, the countryside changed from looking like a rumpled green blanket to some open fields. Still, there was the feeling of being on some kind of high plateau. The information signs gave clear directions and the highway bypassed many smaller towns. Near Neosho, Missouri, when the Highway 60 intersection appeared, Micah looked wistfully toward the east. Traveling on, his heart picked up a beat when I-49 met with I-44 that led to St. Louis, but he stayed on his route north. If St. Louis was the disaster everyone said, there would be no bridges open there. Micah drove past Joplin. Rita hadn't stirred and Dog rarely did more than give a deep sigh and change positions. Halfway between Joplin and Kansas City, Rita awoke. When she moved her legs and pulled her feet up onto the seat, Dog gave a startled half bark. She reached down to pat his head and he quickly settled back onto the floorboard. Dog and Rita were getting along fine. Dog would probably miss her. Micah suspected he might too.

Rita brushed a strand of dark brown hair back from her forehead. "Where are we?"

"About an hour out of Kansas City. You haven't missed anything."

"Didn't think I would. How do things look up this way?"

"A bit of flooding, some building damage, other than that just hills, some rougher than others. This is mostly what they call the Ozarks, right?"

Rita nodded. Micah frowned.

"I thought it would be more mountainous. Like the Rockies or even the Appalachian chain."

"Nope. We here in the middle have a whole different setup."

"How's that?"

"I'm no expert, but this area wasn't raised like those mountains you mentioned. It started out high, like a big plateau. Over time, earth washed away as rivers and rain cut into the land. I've heard the Ozarks were carved out, not raised up. That's why the roughest and craggiest parts are near the rivers."

"Huh, interesting. Must have taken centuries."

"Probably a lot longer than that. None of us ever live long enough to see real changes in the earth." Rita clapped a hand over her mouth and exclaimed, "No, that's a lie! We are seeing a huge change. It's changing right under our feet!"

Micah only nodded. Until they could get pictures and reports of how the earthquake had reshaped the Mississippi basin, they could only guess at the changes. The upheaval had disrupted lives and created huge obstacles to everyday living, but there was no doubt humanity, like a colony of ants, would rebuild as quickly as possible. As they drew near Butler, Missouri, Micah felt the trip would never end, and Rita looked as if she shared the feeling. With a Conoco station ahead, Micah turned off the highway.

"You need a rest stop?" he asked.

Rita nodded and Dog suddenly came alive. While Micah bought another few gallons of gas, he noticed a patrol car parked near the intersection. He hadn't seen much authority since leaving Arkansas. Maybe things were calmer up here, or all law enforcement was helping in the disaster area. Micah drove the pickup to the edge of the station's pavement and let Dog out to take advantage of a vacant lot. As he waited, Rita came out of the ladies' room and stood with her cell phone to her ear. She nodded several times, gave a weak smile once, nodded some more and put the phone back into her shirt pocket. When she came close to Micah, he could see she was crying, but she quickly brushed the tears away. He gave her a questioning look, and she managed a smile.

"We're almost there. I spoke with Sam. He is so grateful to you for getting me here." Her voice wavered and a tear tried to roll down her cheek. It seemed to make her angry, for she roughly wiped it away. "I don't know what's wrong with me! I'm stronger than this."

"You're just tired. Me too. If it wasn't wimpy for a guy, I might start crying."

They both managed to laugh. Dog came flying back out of the weeds and lunged against Micah's legs.

"Hey, don't knock me down. Rita, how about a cold drink to take with us?"

She nodded. They left Dog in the pickup with a handful of dry dog food, and went into the station. In addition to a couple of Cokes, they bought some Slim Jims and two Snickers candy bars. Once back in the pickup, Micah pulled onto the highway while Rita managed the refreshments. Dog eyed the beef jerky hopefully, but had to be content licking up a stray pellet of his own food. A few miles down the road, all three were more alert and looking ahead to the end of their journey. However, the closer they came to Kansas City, the more law enforcement they saw. Most of the men wore brown uniforms and carried weapons. There were patrol cars parked at intersections, while yellow sawhorses blocked some of the side roads. In a couple of places, they saw vehicles stopped on the roadside, the occupants standing with their hands on the car's roof while officers examined them. Rita turned to look back as they passed what appeared to be arrests.

"Jerry said there was looting," she said.

"I don't like the sound of that."

"Neither do I. Especially after Sam's awful experience. Thank goodness Sam and the truck with the supplies are both safe."

They drove on in silence until reaching the south edge of the city where Rita leaned forward to read the exit signs.

"The lumberyard is on a frontage road. It isn't far from here."

As she watched for the turn, she was tense, almost trembling, her hands clasped in her lap. Dog settled closer to her knees and gave a sympathetic whine.

"There, up ahead. I'm sure that's the exit."

Micah nodded and took the descending side road. When he reached the stop light at the bottom of the off-ramp, Rita pointed to the right. Micah made the turn. Less than a block away they came to a north/south cross road. Rita directed him to another right turn which headed them back south. There were a few scattered businesses: an auto repair, a small strip center, and a gas station. Beyond these stood the lumberyard. It was a large white building sitting on a wide gravel lot surrounded by a high chain link fence. The big doublewide gate had a heavy chain with a padlock. Above the building's main entrance was a sign with Harmon Lumber in yellow letters trimmed in brown. As they pulled closer, Rita was on her phone. She pointed Micah to a small driveway on the far side of the lot.

"Jerry is around there. He'll open a gate for us."

As Micah turned the corner of the enclosure and pulled past the building, there was a man standing beside a metal gate. He supposed this was Jerry, for the man motioned Micah through the gate and pointed to a parking space behind the building. Two large brown and tan dogs danced around his legs as he went to secure the gate. When the pickup came to a stop, Rita opened the door and jumped out. Dog was fast on her heels where he quickly joined the other dogs. While Rita embraced Jerry, she turned and motioned to Micah.

"Come meet Jerry."

Micah removed his hat, placed it on the dashboard, and stepped out of the pickup. A short distance behind the business was a lawn surrounding a craftsman-style house. The high security fence also enclosed the house. A short, heavyset woman with curly blonde hair stood on the covered front porch. She was waving and calling to Rita. Rita ran toward the porch, leaving Jerry and Micah to their own introductions. Jerry Harmon was a bit shorter than Micah and looked near his age. Jerry had brown hair in a short buzz cut; his round face held large brown eyes. Holding out his hand, he came toward Micah.

"Glad to meet you, friend. We can't thank you enough for bringing Rita. Sam will rest better now that she's here. Come on into the house. Mary, my wife, has been cooking all day. You like pot roast?"

Micah shook the man's hand and Jerry drew him toward the house. Jerry yelled at his dogs, sending them running toward the side yard. Dog stopped and looked back at Micah before running after his new friends. Jerry laughed.

"Big dog you got there. What's he good for?"

"Not much," Micah admitted.

Jerry clapped him on the shoulder. "Well, that's the best kind."

As they climbed the three concrete steps to the wide porch, Mary was all smiles.

"You are welcome, Micah. You'll stay the night. We have plenty of room."

As he crossed the porch and entered the house, a wave of melancholy passed over him. So many people treating him like family, and yet he'd never been this lonesome. A hollow feeling in his chest made it difficult to smile as he greeted Jerry's family. It didn't seem right to feel so alone among these good people, until he realized that the ones he was lonesome for were gone forever.

Jerry and Mary had three teenage daughters. They all looked like Mary: blonde, blue-eyed, and plump. They each said 'hello' to Micah, turned, and disappeared into the depths of the house, busy with their own interests. Rita entered the living room from a side hallway.

"Micah, come see Sam. He will want to thank you."

Micah obediently followed Rita down a wide hallway, its pale green walls covered with family pictures. She stopped at the third door on the left and waved Micah through. He stepped into a large bedroom with windows looking out onto the front lawn and the back of the lumberyard. A four-poster bed with a nightstand beside it held Sam Cooper. He was sitting up with a pile of pillows behind him. His left arm was in a sling, and his bare chest tightly wrapped in bandages, but his face captured Micah's attention. Above his left ear, a patch of his reddish blond hair was missing. It revealed a line of stitches that held the scalp together, and the cut was an angry red. A dark purplish-blue bruise covered that side of his forehead and down to his swollen eye. Below that, his cheek and jaw were every bit as stormy dark blue as his forehead. He held out his right hand.

"Glad to see you, Micah."

A cut lip caused his speech to be a bit slurred. Still, his lopsided smile was warm, as were his blue eyes. Sam was much like his father, Rory, in build but thinner in the manner of a younger man, although he had his mother's blue eyes. Micah stepped to the bedside and shook his hand. Rita sat on the edge of the bed at Sam's feet and watched him carefully. Micah could see her assessing her husband's injuries and planning the trip home. She was back to being her strong helpful self. The weakness had come when she didn't know exactly what they were facing.

Sam pointed to an armchair near the bed.

"Sit down and visit awhile. Gets lonesome in here. Everyone is too busy to talk. You look over your little mishap. Guess you're back on the way to North Carolina."

Rita stood and headed for the door.

"I'll be back after I help Mary with dinner."

Micah sat and asked Sam how he felt, remarking that the bruises looked painful and wondering how it had happened.

"I've felt better, I can say that. I'd just finished loading the truck and stopped at a station for gas. Two guys came at me, one from each side. They had baseball bats. A third one pulled around in a pickup and while one finished beating me, the other two stole a generator. If a car hadn't drove in, they would have taken more. I feel stupid! I should have had someone with me, or at least been armed."

"Doesn't sound as if you would have had time to draw a gun."

Sam shook his head and winced. "Probably not. Some people have no shame. Things get bad and they take advantage. I'd be careful traveling through this area alone...still, having the dog can't hurt."

As they continued to talk, Micah found there wasn't anything about himself that he could tell Sam that he didn't already know. It seemed what one family member knew spread through the rest by osmosis. Sam didn't learn anything new about Micah, but Micah learned a great deal about the earthquake damage and the civil disobedience. Nearly all of the first responders, Red Cross, FEMA employees, and at least half of the law enforcement in the city had headed to the disaster area. Sam thought it was getting a bit better since the National Guard had installed units in the city, and the curfew helped.

"I was surprised at seeing damage this far away from the center of the quake," Micah said.

"It is strange. We hear there are more faults in this area than we realized. You being from California this must be normal for you, but it is strange to us. Did you know about something called the Cascadia fault? You probably do...it's some kind of fault north of California."

Micah nodded. He did know. Everyone always talked about the San Andreas but a fault north of there, just off the Northwest coast, could produce an even greater quake. Something about a subduction zone where earth plates meet. If this became active, it could affect Northern California all the way up to Vancouver Island in Canada. Micah told Sam what he knew about it.

"I guess the whole west coast isn't that stable," Micah admitted.

"Yes, but that isn't the big news."

"No?"

"Ever hear of something called the crack across America?"

Sam's one blue eye, the one completely opened, sparkled. He was warming to the subject. It was probably something he'd learned from the constant 24/7 news reports. Micah wished he'd had time to watch more, but he'd been busy driving. He shook his head.

"Get this...a giant fault about a thousand seven hundred miles long runs from the far northwest, going southeast, right through a big volcano in Yellowstone park and it keeps going. Guess where it passes through on its way to the southern Appalachian mountains?"

Micah shrugged. Sam sat up straighter, his injuries seemingly forgotten.

"Right through the New Madrid area!"

"I guess none of the ground under us is very stable."

"You can say that again. Some geologists think a second crack comes out of the northeast, runs south down the west side of the Smoky Mountains and crosses with that crack coming from the northwest. Do I have to tell you where?"

Micah had nothing to add, and there was no need. Sam was intent upon his revelations.

"Again, right through our famous New Madrid. If you think about it, the whole Mississippi basin has to be there because of some underlying fault."

The subject was interesting, but Micah wanted to be on his way. If the center of the country crumbled, he could do nothing about it. He didn't understand his urge to be on the move. He suspected animals must feel it when they migrate. He'd agreed to stay for supper and even the night. However, he was sure he'd be gone at daylight. Rita came through the bedroom door. She saved him from hearing Sam continue to explain how the basin was a failed attempt, millions of years ago, of two tectonic plates to separate. If they had pulled apart, land east of the Mississippi River might be a different country, and the river a tongue of the Atlantic Ocean. Rita smiled at Sam.

"If you are well enough to talk Micah's ear off, you can come to the dinner table. Micah, help me get him out of bed."

Between them, they stood Sam on his feet. His wide smile split the cut on his lip and it welled up with blood. Rita grabbed a tissue and handed it to him. Declaring there was nothing wrong with his legs, Sam made his way down the hall to the dining room.

Jerry was right, for his wife *was* an excellent cook. The long table held a giant platter filled with beef and vegetables. Surrounding it were side dishes of green beans, red Jello salad, and corn. A large plate of biscuits sat at each end of the table; Jerry and Mary sat at either end. Their three daughters on one side sat opposite Sam, Rita, and Micah on the other. After a short prayer, the feast started. To Micah it was indeed a feast. He'd not had a home cooked meal like this in many months. As they ate, they talked of getting Rita and Sam back to Little Rock. Mary suggested Jerry go with them, but Rita protested, as Jerry couldn't leave the lumberyard. Mary scoffed at that.

"Between the dogs and the shotgun, I could manage!"

Everyone admired her spirit, but Mary couldn't defend the property alone. The three daughters were quiet, but when spoken to politely replied. Considering the circumstances, the Harmon and Cooper families seemed composed and ready to face what came their way. After dinner, the daughters took over clearing the table while the adults went into the family room where Jerry turned on the television. The clatter and chatter from the kitchen said the girls were happily and quickly getting on with their chores. Sam sat on a loveseat with Rita beside him. Jerry pointed Micah to a recliner while he and Mary headed for the sofa. Before taking the offered chair, Micah looked toward the front door.

"I should see about Dog. I need to feed him."

Jerry smiled. "Already done. I fed him along with the mutts. He'll find a sleeping place either on the porch or around back somewhere."

"You keep the dogs to help guard the place?"

"They aren't much to look at, but someone put a foot wrong and they might lose it."

All the television channels were airing earthquake reports. They ranged from local information on road closings to speeches from the President, and foreign dignitaries who pledged to help the country through this disaster. The destruction seemed random. Sections of cities were without utilities while others still had water, sewer, and electricity. It depended upon what pipes were broken and how they linked with others. Towns leveled by the earthquakes and those destroyed by flooding looked hopeless. Jerry commented that it would be better to bulldoze them and start over, if at all. Damage to roads, bridges, and communication lines depended upon how close they were to the spider web of lesser faults. While they were watching television, Micah felt a vibration under his feet. He looked up at those in the room.

They were all instantly quiet. Everyone felt the minor tremor. Mary lifted her chin and drew a deep breath.

"I was never aware of these tiny quivers before."

Rita nodded. "I know. I wasn't either."

Micah understood. The earth really was always moving. Little quakes, anything under a 2.5 magnitude were only detected by a seismograph, and there were close to a million of them a year. A magnitude 3 might catch a person's attention; however, after a massive quake even the smallest tremble was frightening.

When everyone decided it was time for bed, Jerry showed Micah a small guest room behind the kitchen. The connecting bathroom with a stall shower was a pleasant surprise. After surveying the accommodations, he went outside to collect his backpack from the pickup. Yard lights at the four corners of the lumberyard's building dispelled the night. All three dogs came to greet him while crickets set up a clatter in the shrubbery. Things seemed peaceful. The side trip to deliver Rita to Sam was more rewarding for him than he could have imagined. A wonderful meal, nice people, a refreshing shower, and a night's sleep deeper than he'd had in months.

Ten

Micah awoke as the first pink rays of morning brightened the bedroom window. When he threw back the bedcovers and placed his feet on the hardwood floor, he felt the vibration. It lasted mere seconds, but long enough to bring a rush of adrenalin. It was past time to be on the road. He shaved, brushed his teeth, and dressed in the wrinkled yet clean clothes from his backpack. He hid the dirty clothes, fearful that Mary would insist upon washing them before he left. It seemed impossible after last night's meal, but he was hungry. The smell of coffee and bacon told him he wasn't the only early riser. Indeed, the kitchen was a busy place. Rita was preparing a tray for Sam, Mary was turning pancakes, and Jerry was drinking from a large coffee mug. They all turned to greet him.

"Did we wake you?" Mary asked.

"No."

"Maybe it was the shaking, nearly threw me out of bed!" Rita said as she left the room carrying Sam's tray.

"I felt a tiny tremor," Micah admitted.

Jerry raised eyebrows over his big brown eyes. "You didn't feel the one about forty minutes ago?"

Mary pulled out a chair from the kitchen table and motioned for Micah to sit. She was wearing a blue housedress covered in yellow daises, her blonde hair a mass of uncombed curls.

"That was the one that woke us up! Scared the daylights out of me. I didn't think we were in danger this far from the big river."

Mary put a plate of pancakes and bacon in front of Micah, while Jerry poured a cup of coffee for him.

"Calm down, Mary," he said. "These are only aftershocks. The news said they can go on for weeks."

"But so far from any fault lines!"

"Now, we don't know that. Didn't you hear that geologist, the one laying out a map of the whole area? Listening to him, you'd think there isn't a stable piece of ground between Oklahoma and the river."

Micah ate in silence, but he was wondering how he'd ever complete the journey. As if reading his mind, Jerry studied Micah's face.

"In a hurry to be on your way, aren't you?"

Micah nodded as he chewed a strip of bacon. Jerry shook his head.

"I doubt you'll find an intact bridge anywhere south of Iowa. But I hear some enterprising fellows have set up barge crossing around Hannibal, just gossip, mind you, but they say people are crossing up there."

"I'll keep that in mind."

Sam walked into the kitchen with Rita behind him carrying the breakfast tray. He was holding his cell phone and looking at the screen. Rita put the tray on the counter and hurried to helped Sam to a chair. Sam rolled his one good eye about Rita's fussing over him. He held the phone out to Micah.

"Look at this. I heard what Jerry said about the barges."

Micah scooted his chair back from the table and took Sam's phone. Sam had pulled up a report on river traffic.

At the latest count, only six hundred towboats were operational, which was about half of the usual fleet. A few barges were self-propelled and didn't need a towboat, but the number was uncertain.

There was no accurate count of how many of the more than twenty-six thousand barges were still available. The Mississippi was far out of its banks from southern Iowa all the way to the Gulf. River traffic was sporadic and even more difficult because of how the earthquakes had changed the river's main channel. Everything afloat on the river when the largest quake struck was either broken apart or driven off course. Ports and docks disappeared with the crafts harbored within them. Yet, the barges were more important than before, since bridges and pipelines were gone. Micah handed the phone back to Sam.

"Good news is there might be a way across on a ferry," Sam offered.

Jerry poured another cup of coffee.

"People take the Big Muddy for granted. There's a ton of traffic on that river. Those barges are sometimes lashed forty together. I once heard they move more than sixty tons of grain a year. Not counting all the coal and petroleum."

Micah stood and carried his plate and cup to the kitchen sink.

"If I can't find a bridge, maybe one of those barges will have room for one old pickup."

Micah looked around at the people who had taken him in for the night. "I wish I could do something in return for all your kindness. I'm well rested, and far better fed than usual."

Rita and Mary offered a chorus of protests and Sam shook his head.

"You did plenty getting Rita here."

"I was heading this direction, it wasn't any trouble."

"We thank you anyway," Sam said, settling the matter.

Micah collected his backpack from the bedroom and started for the front door. Jerry, Mary, and Rita followed him. Sam waved from his chair. Rita moved to Micah's side.

"He still gets dizzy standing up too long," she whispered.

Micah nodded. When they were all on the front porch, Jerry went out into the yard and headed for the gate. The large truck with the generators and other supplies stood near the back of the lumberyard. Micah, standing beside Rita, pointed to the truck.

"Can you drive that?"

Rita laughed. "Of course."

Micah stepped off the porch and looked around for Dog. The three dogs came running around the corner of the house. Dog was panting and wagging his tail as he bumped against Micah's legs.

"You ready to travel?" Micah asked, patting Dog's head.

Dog turned and trotted back to his new canine friends. They all three ran to where Jerry was unlocking the compound's gate; Micah looked back at Mary and Rita and shrugged.

"Maybe Dog's found a place he likes better than the truck."

"I doubt that," Rita called.

The Harmons' three daughters were not in sight but he didn't feel it necessary to bid them goodbye. At the pickup, he threw his backpack onto the passenger side floorboard. Dog would ride on the seat now that Rita was no longer with them. Micah would miss her. She was good company. He shook hands with Jerry, held the door open, and called for Dog who ran to the pickup but didn't jump onto the seat. Micah frowned at him. Dog hesitated, then turned away and trotted toward the other dogs. After saying goodbye to the Harmons' dogs, he bounced back to Micah where he jumped into the truck. Everyone laughed. Micah shook his head.

"Thought I'd lost him for a bit."

Once in the truck, Micah started the engine and drove through the security gate He gave a last wave to the family, and turned right. At the east/west street that ran under the interstate, he stopped at a red light, then continued north to the interstate on-ramp. He wished Rita and Sam a good trip home, but wasn't too worried about them. They seemed capable. Maybe if he ever came this way again, he'd visit them. The day was bright, the sky clear, and the early morning breeze was cool. Good traveling weather. If only the earth beneath were as settled and serene as the heavens.

Dog sat tall in his seat near the window and held his nose forward into the wind. His coat needed a good brushing, but it didn't seem to bother him. Physically, Micah felt better than he had in days. When he had reached Forrest City, Missouri, he had been tired from traveling, and after the earthquakes started, he hadn't much rest until last night. In the early morning, there was little traffic even in Kansas City. On the north side of town, he took the Des Moines, Iowa exit. Interstate 35 was heading north, and the middle of Iowa must be away from the chaos behind him. From there, maybe it would be safe to turn east for a river crossing. He reached over and patted Dog's head.

"Just you and me, fellow. What do you think of going to Des Moines?"

Dog ignored him in favor of savoring the morning breeze. However, when they reached Cameron, Missouri, Micah realized a right turn on Highway 36 would take him straight to Hannibal. It was a risk going back to the river this soon. But if Jerry's story of towboats and barges ferrying people across were true, there might be a chance of crossing there. Besides, no one had said the bridge at Hannibal was impassable. It was a gamble, and if the area was in as much trouble as areas to the south, he'd continue north. The loss of four hours, two there and two back, didn't make that much difference. He'd almost lost sight of the original destination. It didn't matter where he ended. Maybe a piece of land this side of the river was better than the rough twenty acres in North Carolina. He'd assumed the cabin was still standing, but it could be gone. It had suffered years of neglect. Storms might have taken off the roof, animals moved in, or perhaps it had burnt to the ground!

If he knew anyone in the area, he could have called ahead to ask about the property. There were real estate agents in town. If he wanted to sell the property, any one of them would drive to it and give him a report on the condition. He should have done that before heading across country; he'd lost all business sense. As he came to the stop sign at the intersection of the off-ramp and Highway 36, he automatically turned right. Something tugged at him to go east. As the sun climbed higher the traffic increased, it was mostly big tractor-trailers and tanker trucks. He glanced at the pickup's gas gauge, it showed a little over half a tank. That meant he should have close to ten gallons, but he wasn't that sure of the gauge. A Shell station was immediately ahead conveniently on the right side of the highway. The gas station was busy, and Micah didn't see any signs limiting the purchase. There might not be many towns along the way, and he was still hording the supply in the truck bed. Twelve gallons of gas could be a lifesaver in certain conditions.

While Micah filled the gas tank, Dog barked to get out of the cab. When the tank was full, he parked at the side of the station and turned Dog out into an open field. With the truck filled and Dog emptied, Micah waited in a line of about five vehicles in order to turn back onto Highway 36. Heading straight east, the morning sun made him reach for his sunglasses. Dog had forsaken his breezy pastime and gone to sleep on the seat. It had been polite of him to let Rita have the seat when she was riding with them. Micah smiled at the thought of her caring for her husband and children. In truth, it was painful, yet hopeful, knowing such goodness still existed. It would be easy to fall into despair and bitterness without such thoughts.

The rolling green countryside seemed strange in comparison to the earthquake-destroyed areas. Here there was nothing to show that a part of the country lay in ruins. The miles clicked by, the tires setting up a sort of rhythm, and Micah's mind wandered. He found a personal connection with the state of the country. His life was as torn apart as the Mississippi River basin. Yet, people carried on as if things were normal while he and part of the country suffered. On the highway outside Cameron, without news reports, no one would know of the destruction to the east and south. Micah's life had taken on an aura of unreality. He suspected those affected by the earthquakes felt the same. It could take them a long time to feel normal. He wondered if he ever would.

The divided highway made the driving easy. When the land flattened out with fewer trees, fields stretching beneath a pure blue sky, Micah fought to keep alert. Dog was no help. He slept soundly, probably worn out from his romp with Jerry's dogs. The miles of wide-open land made him feel like a bug on a plate. There was no place to hide in this type of country. This was far different from what he remembered of his grandfather's cove in the Blue Ridge.

Maybe he was heading there to hide, to burrow down, and try to heal. A few tall, billowing clouds, like giant globs of shaving cream, drifted across the vast sky. Occasionally, a farmhouse appeared in the distance. Once, a faded red barn stood isolated and forgotten beside the highway. Most of the fields were dry, but ponds brimmed, and some roadside ditches glistened with water.

To his relief, the landscape grew more interesting with the return of rolling hills and a few small towns, but the highway bypassed them. With no need of gasoline and Dog an unmoving mound of fur, Micah drove on toward Hannibal. A couple of times he tried the pickup's radio, but there wasn't any news, only a few stations with music. As he neared a river in a forested area, he came to attention. The low concrete bridge over a wide span of water revealed a river far out of its banks. Small waves lapped at the roadside railing, and water stood halfway up the trees. Some shorter trees showed only their top branches. Unless the area had recently had a downpour, this was probably the result of the earthquake. Tributaries couldn't empty into blocked rivers. At least the roadbed was still a foot above the flood line.

Beyond the river, the land flattened out again. A few small towns were visible from the highway; however, he was glad he didn't need to stop for gas. He was anxious to reach the Mississippi and a chance of finally getting across it. Passing the town of Brookfield, he checked the mileage to Hannibal. He was making good time. With no mishaps, the drive from Kansas City to Hannibal should take about three and a half to four hours. The last road sign proved he was over halfway there. He poked Dog's ribs.

"Wake up. Stick your nose out the window."

Dog rolled his tongue over his lips, barely opened one eye, and shifted into a more comfortable mound.

Micah's window was down a few inches and the wind carried a distinctly nasty odor. It smelled like stagnant water and rotting vegetation. It was a preview of the air over the mighty river. Micah imagined dead fish, and miles of submerged land. Even worse would be the broken sewer lines, dead bodies, and piles of debris.

Micah's foot automatically pressed harder on the gas pedal. When the speedometer hit seventy, he backed off. The old truck had run perfectly for nearly two thousand miles, no sense pushing it. Although right then, Micah wished he could go over one hundred miles an hour.

Starting on this journey, time had had no meaning. He'd intended to walk or hitchhike, maybe catch a bus part of the way. His feelings changed from day to day. Part of the time, he couldn't wait to reach North Carolina, at others he didn't care if he ever arrived. The up and down shift was the same with the attacks of sadness and sorrow. When his mind was busy with tasks, the ache in his chest subsided until unexpectedly the pain struck. It hit, heavy, hard, and destructive. Looking toward a time when this would be over, Micah straightened his back, squinted against the midday glare, and pushed on down the highway. As a big Walmart truck roared past him, he pulled closer and let the air slip help carry the pickup along. However, the truck blocked a view of the highway and he soon lost interest in the game. For long distances the westbound lanes were out of sight, making it seem there should be oncoming traffic. Until once again, they merged with only a grassy divider between east and west lanes.

The monotony of driving lessened when there was another flooded river to cross. Here the water spread out across the flat land, but left the raised highway dry. The distant fields shimmered, the wind raised tiny white waves, and it was like driving across an inland sea. Dog finally awoke and decided he needed to stop. Sitting up, he turned in the seat, whined, and nudged Micah with his nose. Micah raised an eyebrow.

"Hope you can wait."

Although he did drive faster, and kept watch for a convenient stop. Shortly, they came across a side road leading to old Highway 36. After turning off onto the old road, he let Dog out of the pickup. It was a short stop and Micah wished he dared take relief as Dog had, but there was a house nearby and other structures across the road. Micah yelled and Dog jumped into the truck and they were again on their way.

The sun was finally high in the sky and Micah removed his sunglasses. He didn't like driving in them. He wanted to see every bright color and to feel life all around; it helped combat the darkness inside him. The miles rolled away and with every one of them, the traffic increased, but not enough to crowd the highway. It was hard to stay within the sixty-five mile an hour speed limit, despite trying to keep to Taylor's rules. The closer he came to his destination, the faster he drove, and the more nervous he became. He tried to remain calm by reasoning that it didn't matter. If there was total destruction and no way across, he would turn around and travel farther north. In reality, time didn't matter. It was the strange urgent, anxious feeling within driving him, and he argued against it. Winter was months away, and fall in the mountains was beautiful. If the cabin was uninhabitable, he'd find a room somewhere. He had no obligation to anyone, and Dog wouldn't object to his decisions. Micah patted Dog's head and Dog responded by licking his hand.

Approximately sixty miles from Hannibal, Micah took a side road to arrive at a small, two-pump Casey's gas and grocery store. The pickup's tank was just under half full, enough to reach Hannibal, but with uncertain conditions ahead it was wise to refill. Besides, Micah badly needed a stop, and Dog was always happy for a quick run. A pickup and a passenger car were using the pumps. Micah pulled in behind the passenger car to wait his turn. Otherwise, the store looked deserted. Several vehicles drove past on the side road. Micah parked the pickup, left Dog inside, and entered the store. A tall, thin young man was behind the counter, and Micah paid him for nine gallons of gas, plus a bag of peanuts and a bottle of water.

"Have you had any gas rationing around here?" he asked.

The attendant counted out Micah's change and shook his head.

"Not right now. We did have for a couple of days, but our supplier comes from the west and we're okay. Course they can't promise anything for later."

"I'm going to Hannibal. What is it like there?"

The fellow shrugged his thin shoulders. "Part is flooded. Television don't say much about that area. It's too busy with the worse parts, and how it's affecting the whole country."

After filling the gas tank and using the restroom, Micah parked near the edge of the lot's pavement and let Dog out into the open field. The stop revived them and they were soon back on the highway. The station's attendant hadn't given much information, but considering the enormity of the disaster, reporting on it was a huge job. The news Micah had watched at Jerry's covered everything from what might have caused the quakes to location of stations for victim aid.

In less than an hour, Micah was on the highway near the north edge of Hannibal. There was nothing to see, only rolling hills and exit signs for the town. The truck traffic in both directions gave an indication of a clear way across the river. On a whim, Micah took the last exit and drove into Hannibal.

The Mississippi seemed a dividing line, and even if he didn't ask much of the future, there was always a chance it might be worse on the river's other side. At first, the town appeared to be okay, until he noticed the cracks and missing chunks in the paved streets. And many of the brick buildings, like the pavement, had cracks and top corners missing. The painted clapboard houses fared better, although who could say the condition of their foundations. Some of the streets had makeshift barriers blocking them, where water lapped at the curbs and steps leading up to houses. Micah took open streets where he found them, weaving through the town. It was plain the town had suffered structural damage. Either shockwaves had traveled nearly two hundred seventy miles, or it was the work of northern faults set off by the large quakes. When he reached streets closest to the river, all the lower areas were under water, while the upper slopes were dry. A Best Western motel sat on a high corner while a block away, shops had water up to the windowsills. The hilly topography saved much of the town, proving that water is opportunistic. Nothing stops its flow, and it easily invades using the path of least resistance.

The river was his journey's final obstacle. Once across it, his destination was a straight shot to the southeast. Yet, he was hesitant. While wandering through the town, he kept to an easterly direction to get a view of the river. He hoped to see the extent of the flooding, and if traffic was crossing the river. One narrow road that angled along the mountainside led to a small park, an overlook atop a high bluff. Micah parked, let Dog out, and walked to the railing at the cliff's edge. He sat on a park bench and stared in wonder at the scene below. The town, the river, and the bridge to the north lay like a diorama. The toy town climbed in stair steps up the sides of the curved hills, the distant bridge spanned the river with a silver truss above the flat deck. Most amazing of all was the vast expanse of water. The riverbanks were invisible. The muddy flood spread far into the distance; it encompassed all the low areas of the town. From this vantage point, it seemed far worse than when driving the streets. Micah's pulse quickened, hoping the bridge was passable. The bridge deck looked at least a few feet above the water, and on Highway 36, there had been no warnings about the bridge.

Micah rested his elbows on his knees and lowered his head into his hands. He'd felt well and strong when he left Kansas City. Now, as another wave of sorrow washed over him, he felt too weak to get off this bench. Something had triggered the despair in him. If he understood the grieving process maybe he could manage it. He expected to grieve for a long time, as he owed it to his little family, for they deserved mourning and remembrance. The suddenness of the attacks was debilitating. The overpowering hopelessness opened up a hole in his chest, and a cold lonely wind whistled through it. He wanted to cry, wishing tears could cleanse him of this pain. Dog came to his side and bumped his knee with his nose, whined and uttered a long, sad howl.

Micah lifted his shoulders, took a deep breath, and looked across the flooded land. The destruction of buildings and lives lay before him. He had no right to pity while others suffered such devastation. It was difficult to comprehend how much loss of life and damage the earthquake had caused. Looking down from the mountainside park, he remembered Helena, Arkansas, how that river town was wiped out, and the not much better condition of the towns farther west. The highways, bridges, pipelines, homes, and businesses...it seemed impossible they could recover. Yet, the people he'd met along the way had not seemed defeated. They took the aftershocks in stride, and they helped those around them. The resilience of some people was amazing, although they claimed help from an Almighty source. This made Micah wonder how a loving deity could inflict such suffering, maybe just to test the strength of humans. Yet, for him none of it mattered. His loss was no worse than what people down through the ages had endured, and for Jena's sake, he would survive. Whether he wanted to or not!

Before leaving the mountainside, Micah called his attorney, Harry Miller. Harry's secretary put Micah on hold for a few minutes. Dog sat at his feet, seeming impatient to be on their way. Micah felt the same, but he needed to keep in touch with Harry, at least until they finished their business. When Harry answered, the first thing he asked was concerning Micah's condition, both physical and mental. Micah laughed.

"Physically I'm fine. Probably better mentally than I deserve. Just wanted to advise you of my progress. I expect to be in Illinois within the hour, depending on traffic and other delays."

Harry wanted to know about Micah's last few days. Micah gave him the short version so he could find out where Harry stood on wrapping up the insurance, and other details of ending Micah's life in California. The insurance had paid the claim. Harry had deposited the money in Micah's account, and he'd checked on the unit where he had stored Micah's possessions. Everything was ready for Micah to establish an account near where he was to settle. Harry would arrange for a mover when Micah called for the items in storage. Micah felt the ties with his old life unraveling. After Harry completed the information concerning Micah's affairs, he spoke about the effects of the earthquake.

"The entire country is disrupted," Harry said. "At first we thought we would escape the gas shortage. Our state has about eighteen refineries, and great oil and natural gas reserves, but you know how people go crazy. They even started rationing here! Good news is we use practically no coal. Looks as if the Gulf Coast is totally out of business."

"I heard that. Hey, Harry, I should go. I'll call in a few days."

They wished each other well, and the call ended. Micah put the phone back into his pocket and took a long look out over the flooded countryside. He abruptly stood, pointed to the pickup, and said, "Come on, Dog."

Dog seemed eager to comply. Making their way back through Hannibal to Highway 36, Micah noticed additional damage. He should have asked Harry if the magnitude of the quakes had been determined. The first tremor he'd felt in Forrest City seemed like a magnitude 4, possibly a 4.5. After that, the continuing tremors felt near the same strength, until the much larger one in Helena, which must have been at least an eight on the scale. The continuing shocks seemed much less, until the one that knocked the pickup into the guardrail in Little Rock. To Micah's knowledge, that was the largest. Reports said the epicenter was a bit south of New Madrid. For the waves to have reached Little Rock with such power, it must have been closer to a magnitude 9. These huge jolts and the continuous rattling tremors had made Micah ignore the shaking he had encountered outside Oklahoma City. It would keep geologists and other experts busy for years determining which fault lines were involved, and which one had triggered the main event.

As Micah neared the highway, the traffic slowed. He made the right-hand turn onto the access road and followed the vehicles onto Interstate 72 which had joined with Highway 36 a few miles west. The first thing he noticed was a huge four by eight plywood sign painted white with black letters. It advised that the bridge crossing was 'AT OWN RISK.' Near the bridge, improvised highway barriers narrowed the four lanes down to two, one lane in each direction. Further precaution was a flagman overseeing the crossing. As Micah pulled even with the worker, he leaned out the truck's window.

"Has the bridge had an official inspection?"

The man stepped a foot closer and yelled, "No, just local engineers took a look, but it was built for seismic stress. We're being careful by limiting the crossing load."

With that, he waved his red flag, urging Micah forward. The news concerning the bridge's construction was encouraging. However, he questioned if limiting the weight was necessary. If the bridge was sound, it should be able to carry four lanes of traffic. Still, under those conditions, it wasn't surprising that people were cautious. The eastbound lane nearest the center concrete divider was the one closed. A thick, yellow braided line, supported by bollards spaced about twenty feet apart, served as traffic control. The barrier to traffic was flimsy, still drivers kept to the right and obeyed the one-lane restriction. They probably didn't want to test the bridge, especially when big tractor-trailers were rumbling in both directions. Micah was grateful the bridge was open, and he gladly crossed at 'his own risk.' From the amount of traffic, others felt the same. It was possibly the only bridge open this far south. It was certain there were no crossings south of St. Louis.

Halfway across the bridge, Micah decided he was in Illinois. The state line ran down the middle of the Mississippi River, but it was almost impossible to say where that middle was. He used the bridge as a guide. The Mississippi River had changed its course in the upheaval. It was easily done, the wide basin with soft soil offered many opportunities to form new channels. He'd heard of the dams and restrictions on the mighty waterway, all constructed to make the river serve mankind. Since the earthquakes had set the river free, it had destroyed all the restraints.

Continuing on Interstate 72 in Illinois, a mile or so from the bridge, traffic slowed even further. There was water covering the pavement to a depth of about four inches. Vehicles seemed cautious when first entering the flooded road, but finding it shallow, they resumed speed. The surrounding countryside was under water, the river spreading through any low ground and filling the fields. Micah was almost accustomed to the stagnant smell of rotting vegetation, and it could be months before the waters receded. If the big river found a new course, and the tributaries washed away the debris blocking them, the great basin could drain and the flooding end. Mapmakers would be busy drawing the new topography.

The sun was a bit lower in the western sky; its slanting rays glistened bronze and copper on the road water, while the spray splashed high by the spinning wheels flashed golden droplets into the air. Due to road conditions, most traffic moved below the speed Taylor had set for his pickup. Micah smiled at the thought of the old man. He wondered what Taylor would think about his pickup traveling this far. Still, he had known where Micah was going. Micah wondered, too, about Charlie Redman, knowing he would never see him again. The two old men were part of the past, just as Harry Miller would probably be once their business was over.

Dog heaved a sigh in his sleep. Micah glanced at him and wondered how long Dog would be with him; he didn't know Dog's age. With every passing day, something or someone fell behind him and became part of the past. Life's journey. Micah puffed his cheeks and blew out a deep breath. If he didn't watch it, he'd become maudlin, thinking of only what could never again be. Such morose thoughts dragged him down, even though he felt kindly and loving toward those memory people. And that was exactly what they were, people who would only and forever live in his memory. Around three in the afternoon, Micah came near Springfield, Illinois where he had planned to turn south, but the highways south ran too close to the river. No reason to chance additional roadblocks or destroyed areas. Indianapolis, Indiana was about another one hundred and eighty miles east. Micah shook Dog.

"What do you say, Dog. Should we go on?"

Dog jerked upright and gave Micah a startled look. Micah laughed.

"I take that for a 'yes.'"

Beyond Decatur, Illinois, Micah was once again on Highway 36, having lost Interstate 72 in a bypass. Traffic hadn't slowed, but farther east on Highway 36 it thinned somewhat. That was good because it was no longer a four-lane divided highway. Somewhere past Raven, he had entered Indiana. Fields stretched in all directions, the flat land lay a gold-brown under the blue sky. Micah glanced at the gas gauge. He'd make it to Indianapolis, where he hoped there was no rationing. It might be far enough from the quake area to escape the shortage. He shrugged; there was no point thinking about it. As his stomach rumbled, he wished he'd stopped to eat. To add to his discomfort, Dog turned restless. He hadn't fed Dog either, and the last rest stop was a long way behind them. Overall, rolling along an unfamiliar highway with no rest stops in sight, they were not in good condition.

Dog fidgeted and whined. Micah searched the road ahead. They passed tiny towns, but none of them looked promising. Micah muttered, "Sorry, Dog," and kept driving, increasing speed with every mile, hoping to reach a place to stop. After a while, Dog gave up. He settled back on the seat, his eyes shining as he stared at Micah. An hour later traffic increased, scattered buildings appeared, and Micah drove faster. He was in a hurry to leave the vast void behind. When more businesses lined the highway, Micah's pulse quickened, and Dog sat up straight to look out the window. Another twenty minutes and the highway widened and became a four-lane with a concrete divider. Ahead to the left stood the Golden Arches. Micah searched for a way to cross the westbound lanes, but the divider carried on to a distant intersection and he edged to the left-hand lane to double back. In the distance, a big Shell Oil sign caught his eye and he swung back into the right lane. When he pulled into the station, he and Dog were both panting.

The station was bright and clean and there was a grassy area for Dog. Micah filled the pickup's tank, as there were no signs stating a limit. When he pulled to the backside of the station, he took the opportunity to feed and water Dog. Micah settled for a couple of candy bars and a bottle of water. After they were refreshed, he turned onto the highway and continued east to the exit for Interstate 465. It took almost an hour to reach the Interstate 65 exit, but when Micah made the turn south and headed toward Louisville, he was encouraged. Dog wasn't that excited. He put his head down on his paws and pretended to sleep, but Micah caught him looking up several times. Hoping to get some news of the country's disaster, Micah turned on the radio. A local station gave news interspersed with music; being near a city the reception was good. Part of the information was on the widespread destruction; it was as bad as Micah had expected. Still, the amount of damage distant from the epicenter was a surprise.

He was glad he'd gone this far east before turning south. Nashville, roughly two hundred air miles from the river, had plenty of damage; Memphis was a total ruin. Part of the news report highlighted warnings about looting and gangs of robbers. They took advantage of displaced persons, killing them if they refused to give up their valuables. The evacuees who gathered their possessions and headed for camps were in danger of becoming prey before they reached the temporary housing. Worse stories came from inside the hastily erected camps: crowding, scarcity of food, and the spread of disease. Micah clicked off the radio. He'd be lucky to take care of himself, and make it to Falls Creek.

He hadn't seen the little town since he was sixteen years old. He and Gramps went into town every Saturday where they bought groceries and, while Micah saw a movie, Gramps sat in the town square to visit with friends. The old man wore overalls all week, but when they went into town he'd put on a pair of khaki pants and a long-sleeved white shirt. He insisted Micah spruce up, too. "Got to have some respect for others," he'd say with a laugh. "After all, they got to look at you." Micah remembered that Granddad Hanson laughed a lot. He never worked up enough nerve to ask Gramps why his own father seemed angry all the time, for he couldn't remember Jack Hanson ever laughing. Micah didn't like to think about his parents. While married to Jena, he rarely gave them a thought. With her gone, and him coming closer to the place where he'd spent part of those growing up years, dark memories descended. Micah shook his head as if that would dislodge them. Maybe coming back was a mistake if it dredged up old troubled times. He turned his attention to the interstate traffic, glad for the distraction. It took concentration to navigate the crowded interstate, and he suspected the earthquake greatly contributed to the packed roadway.

In the late afternoon, south of Indianapolis, he found a rest stop and took the side road to reach it. Signs warned against overnight camping, but the area was packed and he doubted it would clear out after dark. There were no parking spaces, and vehicles were parking on the grass. Only a narrow lane to enter and exit remained open. Long shadows from the trees stretched over people sitting at outdoor tables where women unpacked ice chests to feed hungry children. In corners near the building, people bedded down in sleeping bags, while in the front of the building, some men had gathered to talk. Micah searched for a place to park. As a car pulled onto the pavement, a space near the exit opened. Micah quickly turned into the tight parking space between a small RV and a minivan. He let Dog out, and hooked the chain to his collar. Dog gave him a dirty look, but Micah didn't relent. The rest stop was packed and he could not take chances. He left Dog tied to the back bumper, which caused Dog to crawl under the pickup in humiliation. As Micah took a concrete walkway to the restrooms, a babble of conversations drifted on the air.

When Micah was halfway to the rest stop structure, Dog set up a frenzy of growling, snarling, and barking. Micah whirled around and saw a figure running from the pickup and Dog at the limit of his chain, his teeth bared. His racket set a dozen other dogs to howling and barking. Micah's heart raced and a cold fear caused him to run, his feet pounding the walkway back to the truck. He didn't remember locking the pickup. If his backpack containing the money and pistol was gone—waves of panic washed over him. He had grown sloppy, careless, incompetent...he must be losing his mind. There was something wrong with him. He reached the pickup and rushed to the passenger side door. Jerking it open, he wilted with relief. The bag was there. Dog must have stopped the thief before he reached the door. Micah locked both doors and checked the lock on the pickup's bed cover. Dog came to him on stiff legs, the ruff of fur across his shoulders just starting to relax.

Micah squatted down on his heels and stroked Dog's head. Dog sat, but didn't show any signs of affection; he was still on guard. Micah could feel the quiver in Dog's muscles. Micah bowed his head and closed his eyes. When he looked up, a couple of men were standing near the pickup's back bumper. The taller one, wearing a blue ball cap, a yellow tee shirt, and jeans stepped toward Micah. Micah stood and, holding the chain, put Dog behind him. The man held out his hand, and Micah shook it.

"You okay?" asked the man. He looked younger than Micah. He had a round face, above a tall, lean body.

"I'm fine," Micah answered.

The man pointed to an older man behind him. "I'm Bill Wade, that's my dad, John. What set your dog to barking?"

Micah felt foolish. He wasn't sure the man running from Dog was a thief. Maybe he came too close to the truck and didn't see Dog under it. He tried to smile.

"Sorry for the disturbance. Not sure what happened. I left my dog here, he started barking. I saw someone running, but nothing is gone."

The older man took off a straw hat and ran a gnarled hand through his gray hair.

"Better safe than sorry. Might have been nothing, still you don't know."

Bill Wade nodded. "We've seen some bad things since the earthquakes sent people flying in all directions. I heard there is over a million people without homes, and seems tragedy brings out the worst in some people." The man glanced at the pickup's license plate. "Long way from your home, looks like."

Micah didn't want to be impolite, but Dog wasn't relaxing and he didn't feel like it either.

"Yes, guess I picked the wrong time to see the country."

The older man tugged on his son's shirtsleeve.

"We better get back. Your mother is anxious to be on the road."

Bill nodded. "Okay, Dad." He smiled at Micah. "You take care. We're heading for Cairo. Our kin there is in bad shape. Mom wants to help them come live with us."

Both men waved as they turned and walked away. Micah was still shaking; he wasn't sure he'd been the target of trouble, but he certainly had left the truck unlocked. That unsettled him more than anything else. Dog moved closer and leaned against his legs. After hooking Dog to the back bumper, he decided to try the restroom again and hurried toward the building. The men's restroom was crowded, but after relieving himself, Micah was able to wash his face and hands. It was refreshing after driving eight hours straight. There were no paper towels, so his shirttail served the purpose. He thought about getting something to eat, but the vending machines were empty. He should try to sleep for a few hours, but he was too on edge. As he headed to the truck, his damp shirt began to dry in the warm air.

When he was back on Interstate 65, Micah relaxed a bit. He'd need to cross the Ohio River at Louisville. Then find Interstate 64 going east to Lexington where he'd pick up Interstate 75 heading south. From there Knoxville, Tennessee was about a two or three hour drive, depending upon his and the road's conditions. The pickup seemed to be doing fine. He'd been careful to check the oil and coolant levels, again grateful to Taylor for how he'd kept up the truck. Realizing the journey was nearing an end encouraged him. Despite delays and the greatest earthquake the country had ever known, he could be in Falls Creek in five or six hours. If he'd been able to drive straight through on I-40, he might have been there days ago. With all the delays and switchbacks, he'd started questioning if he would make it. Micah patted Dog.

"You'll like it at the cabin. Lots of rabbits and squirrels to chase."

Dog slumped in the seat, ignoring Micah. It seemed Dog had reached his level of excitement back at the rest stop, and it was downhill from there.

Heavy traffic on the interstate continued. Drawing closer to Louisville, there were more vehicles, all of them speeding. That made it even harder to find the right lane for the exit loop around the city. Along with the normal highway signs, lighted billboards flashed warnings of flooding, and of road closings. The sun was low in the west, sending long shadows streaking across the pavement. Micah leaned over the steering wheel, squinted at the directional signs, and hoped he'd find the right one. At least it wasn't raining; he tried to find consolation in that.

On the north side of Louisville the flooding became evident, and it was a strange sight under the cloudless sky. Rain had not caused the flood. The Ohio, like the other Mississippi tributaries, had nowhere to go and spread into all low areas.

Micah's enthusiasm over having less than four hundred miles to go faded like the afternoon. Coming near the river, the scene was much the same as the one in Hannibal. There were sawhorses and yellow tape blocking half-flooded streets, and detour signs pointing in directions Micah didn't want to go. When he saw an exit for Interstate 64, he did a dangerous swerve through traffic to reach it. He was past the point of choosing which bridge to use. After forty minutes of weaving through interstate loops, he'd take anything that got him to I-64. If he ended heading west on it, that was okay, he'd find a place to turn around and go east. His throat was dry and the back of his shirt was damp. With twilight turning the sky lavender gray, streetlights came on. Where their beams flashed like oil slicks on the floodwaters, the bloated river looked steel-blue. He should have stopped in Indianapolis, but he'd not been this tired and it had felt too early to stop. Besides, all the motels had 'no vacancy' signs. The entire area buzzed in disruption with people fleeing in all directions. He couldn't wait to reach the cabin, and the quiet peace he craved.

There were no tollbooths on the bridge ahead; tractor-trailers and other vehicles had passes for the electronic equipment to read. Micah didn't have a pass, but the sophisticated system recorded the pickup's license plate. The registration address would receive a toll bill. Micah continued across the bridge with no idea how that would work out. Taylor's new address was some place out of this world. The thought made a tiny chuckle bubble in his chest, or perhaps he was mildly hysterical. It had been a long tiring day, and he should have stopped before this. By the time he was following I-64 through Louisville, it was seven o'clock. He considered stopping for the night, but that meant leaving the interstate and there was still an hour or more of fading daylight. He could be in Lexington by eight-thirty, but time wasn't the issue: gas was. The pickup's tank held around nineteen gallons. The last fill up had been in Indianapolis, when reaching Lexington there could be as little as two gallons left.

Above the two right-hand lanes hung a large green sign, the white lettering proclaimed the direction to Lexington. The big white arrows confirmed that Micah was in the correct lane, and he was almost out of Louisville. Micah stopped thinking about time and gas and pressed his foot on the accelerator. He still had the reserve gas, and he'd rather make use of the remaining daylight. However, several miles east of Louisville, there was a service area and without much thought, Micah took the exit. Just beyond the exit was a truck stop with too many big rigs to count. He quickly pulled under the canopy covering eight bays of gas pumps. When the pickup's tank was full, he looked around for a place to let Dog out for a run. There wasn't anything suitable near the travel center, but a few blocks away there was a fast food restaurant with vacant lots on either side. Micah used the restaurant's rest room, bought two hamburgers, a milkshake, a hotdog with no condiments, and a bottle of water. Outside, Dog ate the hotdog and dry bun and lapped up the water. After eating, Micah felt better, and with the interstate in sight, it was easy to continue heading east. Lexington, here we come, he thought.

Eleven

Traffic both east and west remained heavy, and the rest stops on the way to Lexington were as crowded as the one north of Louisville. Gasoline this far from the area of major damage didn't seem to be in short supply, but Micah suspected it soon would be. As the next hour and a half passed so did the daylight, leaving the sky a dusky gray. Outside Lexington, Kentucky moonlight took over, and Micah turned on the headlights. He stayed on I-64 and was pleased when it merged with I-75. The occasional streetlight and the steady stream of vehicle headlights helped dispel the darkness. South of Lexington the interstates parted company. I-64 headed on east and I-75 turned south to Knoxville, Tennessee. The pickup wouldn't make it to Knoxville without another stop for gasoline. Halfway there, Micah found a crowded Love's Travel Stop. After filling the pickup's tank and finding a place to park, he and Dog walked around for a few minutes.

Neon lights from the gas station, motel, and fast food restaurants near the interstate made it almost bright as day. The place had a busy alive feeling with the grinding sound of engines and the underlying susurrus of voices. The area was at least two hundred and fifty air miles from the Mississippi River, and even that wasn't far enough to escape the increased activity. He overheard conversations concerning the earthquakes. People telling one another how they felt the shocks and where they were at the time. As they walked, Micah kept Dog on a chain. When they came to the corner of the station, Micah lingered. There were two men talking, and Micah stopped to listen. One man was eating a sandwich and saying some interesting things between bites.

"Yes, but what you felt might be the fault right under our feet set off by the one to the west."

The second man frowned. "You think?"

"Sure. Why not? It runs from West Virginia on down to Alabama. What I heard, it goes straight through Knoxville! A bunch of faults formed way deep in the earth."

"You might be right. Seems there was something about the Appalachians rising up that created those faults."

The first man finished his sandwich, crumbled the wrapper into a ball, and tossed it into a trashcan. Turning to the other man, he laughed.

"I doubt anyone knows what caused the faults."

Micah moved away, pulling Dog with him. There seemed a chill in the summer's warm night air, and he hurried to the pickup. His knowledge of earthquakes was limited, but it seemed reasonable that the colliding of earth's plates caused mountains to rise. The problem with that theory was that the tectonic plates nearest to this area were in the middle of the Atlantic Ocean and in the Caribbean Sea. Still, the earth forces at work eons ago were a mystery, but it *was* possible the Atlantic plate put enough pressure on the east coast to buckle a mountain chain. He hoped that for now, the earth had finished shaking and that it hadn't damaged his small refuge.

It was about another eighty-five miles to Knoxville. He should be there by eleven o'clock, possibly midnight. If he could, he'd find a motel and have a long sleep. In the morning, if nothing happened, he could take I-40 out of Knoxville and reach the turnoff to Falls Creek in a couple of hours. In Falls Creek, he didn't know how long it would take to find Berryvine Road. Maybe his memory of the area would help. Dog settled on the seat beside Micah, squirmed a bit, uttered a sigh, and seemed to sleep. Micah glanced at him. He never knew when Dog faked sleep just to keep from talking. Beyond the hub of activity, the interstate turned dark, making the road signs almost impossible to read. Even with traffic, the night seemed lonely. The tiny towns near the interstate were as black as the rest of the landscape. As the distance between rest stops increased, the empty darkness seemed never ending.

The night breeze carried the smell of pine trees, while the pickup's engine and tires marked the miles with road music. Micah fought against the darkness and the monotony threatening to put him to sleep...he'd try to avoid nighttime driving in the future. Micah shook Dog's shoulder and Dog reluctantly looked at him.

"The least you can do is stay awake," Micah told him.

Dog sat up, stared out the dark side window, and with nothing to see, turned back to Micah.

"What good are you if you don't keep me awake? You don't want to end up in the ditch, do you?"

Dog scooted closer to him and licked his hand. Micah took his hand off the steering wheel and wiped the back of it against his pant leg.

"You are a sloppy animal, you know that?"

At that minute, he wondered how he'd get along without the stray dog sitting beside him. His life had reached the point of being grateful for a dog. Who knew, maybe Dog was grateful to be with him. After all, he'd saved him from being shot. Then a strange and disturbing question pricked the edge of Micah's mind. Who was of more value, he or Dog? And if one were more valuable than the other, what made the determination? Hidden deep in his thoughts crouched the unwelcome suspicion that perhaps they were of equal worth. Micah pushed Dog away.

"Go back to sleep. One of us might as well be comfortable."

As he reached the north edge of Knoxville, Micah started looking for a motel. Seeing a sign for a Best Western, he left the interstate and followed the signs. His arms ached from holding the steering wheel so tightly. Now that a release was near, he realized how rigid the hours of driving had made his body. Dog sat up, alert and ready to stop. Micah parked and went in to register. The desk clerk gave him the sad news.

"Sorry, sir. We haven't had a vacancy for a week. It's all the disturbance."

"Do you have any recommendations? Know of any nearby vacancies?"

"Sorry. I just called around for a couple before you."

Micah was too tired to discuss it further, and he stumbled out the double doors. When he climbed back into the pickup, Dog tried to push past him to get out, but Micah shoved him back.

"Nope. Can't stop here. We'll find somewhere down the road."

Micah returned to the interstate and drove faster. This was crazy, why didn't people stay home? His head started to pound, his throat felt dry, and he badly needed to rest. It was almost one o'clock in the morning. It had taken nearly an hour to get around Knoxville and head southeast on I-40. The turnoff to Falls Creek was about another one-hundred miles, and probably fifty miles after that to the little town. Micah took a deep breath and exhaled, puffing out his cheeks.

"Okay, mutt."

Dog raised his head and snarled.

"Sorry, Dog. I'm just irritated. Poor planning on my part. I didn't want to reach Falls Creek in the dark, or so early nothing will be open."

Micah rubbed Dog's head. "So what are we going to do?"

Dog sat up straight and stared through the windshield, his ears forward.

"Right," Micah said. "We'll have to push on."

The early morning hours were as dark as midnight. Still heading east on I-40 Micah wished for a place to stop. If he could sleep until daylight, it would be easier to find the state highway leading to Falls Creek. When he'd almost given up hope of finding a place to stop, there appeared a Pilot Travel Center. He took the exit and pulled onto the grounds of a crowded lot. The big rigs scarcely had room to turn around, and many had backed into the available spaces leaving nothing empty. Micah refused to give up and finally found a spot on a nearby property. The Ford pickup bounced across some weedy rutted ground and came to rest beside a cinder block wall behind a restaurant. He turned off the headlights and engine. As he slumped behind the wheel, Dog pawed at his arm. Micah opened the door and swung around in the seat to plant his boots on the ground. He stared down at the desert boots he'd started the trip in and realized they were dusty, dirty, and maybe not the best for the mountains. Behind him, Dog whined and pushed at his back. Micah stood and Dog jumped out and Micah didn't bother tying him to the truck. Dog roamed around a bit, found a place to his liking, and watered it. As if understanding they weren't in a welcoming place, Dog trotted back to stand against Micah's legs.

Too tired to do anything else, Micah put Dog into the pickup, got in beside him and slumped back in the seat. The window was down and a soft night breeze cooled his face. In minutes, Micah was asleep.

~ * ~

A thumping, clattering racket along with a yip and startled bark from Dog jerked Micah from sleep. He sat up and blinked.

"What? What's the matter?"

A heavy-set man in a blue tee shirt was standing beside the pickup's window.

"Can't sleep here, buddy. Come on now, move it out."

Micah was too foggy to argue.

"Okay, okay. I hear you."

Dog had calmed down, but sat alert, staring intently at the man. Micah fumbled at his wrist trying to see his watch, but he couldn't read it in the dim light.

"What time is it?" he asked the man.

"Close to four o'clock."

"Thanks. Give me a minute and I'll be out of here."

The man nodded and stepped away, but didn't leave. He stood swinging a big wooden club at his side; it was probably what he had used to hammer on the roof of the cab. Micah hoped it hadn't left any dents. The poor truck already had a scrape on its side. Micah started the engine, backed away from the cinder block wall, drove across the weedy space, and back onto pavement.

In the rearview mirror, he saw the man watching until Micah was back onto the service road. Interstate 40 was only slightly less busy than before. Micah shook his head and wiped his eyes, trying to come fully awake. He'd probably slept for a couple of hours. If he continued, he'd still be looking for the turnoff in the dark. As he neared a town, still in Tennessee, he took the first exit. The gas stations near the exit were open. Micah pulled in, once again filled the truck's tank, and drove toward the center of town. A few blocks away a sign pointed to a Walmart Super Center. He parked in a space at the edge of the store's lot, took Dog for a short walk, and then left him in the truck, one window down a few inches.

"You wait here," Micah told him.

Dog rolled his eyes and dropped down onto the seat.

Micah wasn't sure what he was doing in the big store, but not knowing what Falls Creek was like after all the years, it wouldn't hurt to buy some supplies. After making a stop in the restroom and having a large cup of coffee at the snack counter, he found a cart and made the rounds. He bought a hammer, a saw, some light bulbs, towels and washcloths, plastic bowls and buckets. Walking the aisles, he took anything that seemed useful. Passing through the clothing, he added shirts, socks, underwear, and jeans to the growing pile. Some sturdy leather boots caught his attention. He took time to try on a pair, and they ended up in the cart. He also hit the personal hygiene section for toothpaste, and other items.

In the middle of the store, the shelves with cleaning supplies and paper goods were almost empty. There was enough toilet paper for him to take two giant packs, and three bottles of dish soap. Close to five o'clock in the morning, there weren't many shoppers, but the ones who were there pushed carts as loaded as his. When he entered the grocery section he stopped, a little stunned at the nearly depleted stock. He headed for canned goods, and picked up any vegetable that vaguely seemed like something he would eat. When he'd taken all the flour, sugar, salt, and coffee he could find, the cart was loaded, top and bottom. Adding two large bags of dry dog food made it almost too heavy to push. When he checked out, the items needed two carts, as the bag boy didn't stack as neatly as Micah did. Trudging across the parking lot, pushing one cart pulling the other, he kept looking around. The lot was well lit and one third full of cars, but as he realized what the destruction could mean, he grew nervous. The country, at least the middle and the east, was in serious trouble. There were going to be shortages, the empty shelves proved that. Up to now, he'd been lucky. Thinking back over the miles he had come and all that had happened, he was surprised he'd made it this far.

At the pickup, in the semi dark the tall security light threw a sickly glow over the area. He unlocked the bed cover and loaded his purchases. Dog barked a welcome. With the bed cover secured, he stepped up into the truck and sat behind the steering wheel. Some instinct had prompted the stop at this store. Staring into the gloom he realized he'd been operating on instinct for months; putting one foot in front of the other, believing he was thinking things through and making decisions, but in reality, it was as if he were on autopilot. Since he didn't believe in divine providence, it had to be some kind of grief response. Sitting there, probably less than a hundred miles from his goal, Micah wondered if he'd lost his mind. He didn't know anyone in Falls Creek, and the cabin might be in ruins. Even if it were still standing, living there could be all wrong. Dog whined, and Micah patted him. The dog seemed the only solid touch of reality. He could take Dog back to California; Dog would like running on the beach.

Micah would hate to sell the pickup, sort of like running out on Taylor, but the old man would understand. Besides, Taylor was dead. The dead didn't need to understand anything, and it was ridiculous to continue thinking about them. It only brought a searing pain. He hadn't heard how many were dead because of the earthquake, but it didn't make any difference how a person died. Under normal conditions many died each day in hospitals, even more in car wrecks.

Micah put his face in his hands and gritted his teeth against a choking sob. Reasoning was of no help, not in his condition. Dog pushed a wet nose against Micah's cheek. Micah took a breath and raised his head. Thinking about the situation made things worse. Going back to California would not help. If he had stayed, he might have sought relief in drugs or alcohol, and probably found it in his own death.

He sat straighter, turned the key in the ignition and listened as the engine purred. Instead of driving away, he hesitated...he'd forgotten to buy motor oil, and coolant. The Ford probably needed an oil filter change, too. He could drive on and take a chance on an automotive store, or garage. Still, he was here, and with the thought of 'no time like the present,' he drove to the front of the store and parked. Dog frowned.

"I'll be right back," Micah told him.

The second shopping trip was fast. Evidently, people were more concerned with food and household supplies than they were with auto parts. Micah found supplies for the truck and was back before Dog could go to sleep. He stored the items in the bed with all the rest, got into the cab, and headed for the interstate on-ramp. Sunrise was still more than an hour away. He'd hoped killing time with the shopping would keep him from driving in the dark. With a break in traffic, he quickly edged onto Interstate 40. Micah almost laughed... he was once again traveling the road he'd started out on, despite all the detours. I-40 was the road across the nation, California to North Carolina, well, not any longer. The earthquake tearing the Mississippi basin apart put a stop to that. As the highway cut through increasingly higher mountains, the dark rock walls topped with thick black trees shut out the lighter horizon. Micah drove for another forty-five minutes until he came to an overlook situated on a mountaintop. A sign proclaimed it the last stop before the North Carolina state line.

There were two vehicles, a minivan, and small car parked at the near end of the graveled turnout. Micah slowed, drove past them, and parked at the far end. Neither he nor Dog needed a rest stop, but Micah thought the highway to Falls Creek wasn't far ahead. He wanted to wait for dawn in order to see the road sign. No point in driving on in the dark; the east-facing overlook showed a faintly brighter sky. Micah opened the cab's door and stepped out with Dog's chain in his hand. Dog wasn't happy with the arrangement, but when Micah walked close to the end of the knee-high rock retaining wall, Dog made the best of it. He edged out into the high weeds, and ventured as far down the slope as the chain allowed. Above him, Micah stood with one foot upon the rock wall and stared out over the dark rolling mountains. The summer air was cooler at this altitude, and Micah remembered it was cooler still in the deep ravines where ferns grew.

Dog came back panting and sat at Micah's feet. Micah didn't move. Staring out over the old, softly rounded mountains wearing their thick coat of hemlock, oak, hickory, and pine, Micah recalled walks with his granddad. Albert knew every type of tree, spring dogwood and fall red maple. He knew where the black walnut and Chinquapin trees grew, where morel mushrooms popped up after the rain, and the best blackberry patches. Dog whined, but Micah paid no attention. He was seeing a field where at the foot of a hill dewberry vines grew in a tangled profusion, and Gramps was frowning because the gooseberry bush he expected to find was gone. "Old Henderson wouldn't know a gooseberry from a pokeberry, just cuts down anything in his way," he'd said with a laugh and a wink. "But I know a spot near the creek where the sweetest little strawberries grow."

Back in a hollow just off Berryvine Road, there had been an area of tall hickory and walnut trees shading the leaf-carpeted ground. Gramps said hogs once ran there, rooted out all the underbrush, but there was left a wide shallow pond in the trees' dark shadows. A thick layer of leaves covered the pond's bottom, and they were visible through the clear amber-colored water, which made the leaves seem a reflection of the overhanging trees. Tadpoles flourished there, easy to catch and carry away in pint jars, and it had seemed a mysterious place. Micah gazed across the lower hills to a high ridge where the first faint tinge of palest pink backlit the treetops. He wondered if the hog pond was still there. If so, would he still find it intriguing. Probably not, he was too old now and without Gramps, ponds and picking berries had lost their charm. He was physically close to his goal, yet a million miles away emotionally.

The turn-off to Falls Creek was about twenty-five miles farther, and another twenty to the town. He could be there within the hour. The plan was to spend the first day in Falls Creek, establish a bank account, see about title to the truck along with a new driver's license, and get a feel for the town. He remembered most of it, but couldn't imagine the changes over the last twenty-four years; maybe it would disappoint him. Dog gave up and wandered away again to investigate along the base of the rock wall. Micah continued to study the panorama, while seeing only the past and an uncertain future. He felt lost beyond help, no good to anyone, and less use to himself. He removed his foot from the rock wall and turned to Dog, who had found a black beetle to push along with his nose.

"Come on, Dog."

Evidently, the beetle wasn't of much interest because he quickly trotted to Micah's side. They settled themselves in the pickup, Dog sitting up tall with an expectant look, while Micah folded his arms across the steering wheel and stared into the distance. The gentle curve of the tree-covered mountaintops seemed like the rolling swells of a mighty sea, almost hypnotic, nothing like the rugged, jagged Rocky Mountains of the west. Maybe this is what made them seem a refuge, a place to rest from the destruction in the outer world. It was difficult to face the truth that he didn't need to rest, but to hide. This showed a lack of courage, a man beaten by life's storms, but it was getting easier to admit, which might be the first step to redemption. Micah sat for a long time gazing through the windshield, while Dog finally slumped into a heap and rested his head on his paws. Dog seemed far more accepting of things he didn't understand than Micah was.

The distant mountain range brightened. Slowly, streaks of dawn reached up into a silken sky. As the sun rose to the rim of the mountains, its rays pierced the ridge-top forest turning it dark green.

With the morning light, the scene below awoke, distant blue-green mountains skirted by ghost-white fog that drifted in the valleys. In the brightening sky, the tops of the clouds glowed pinkish-gold, while their under bellies were lead gray. The swollen clouds could be rainmakers. Micah did a couple rolls of his tight shoulder muscles, leaned forward, and turned the key in the ignition.

Dog perked up and gave a soft "Woof."

In the daylight, the information sign pointing to Falls Creek was plain. Micah didn't know if he wanted to speed up, or hang back. With the feeling of jumping off a high board, he took the turn. The two-lane highway cut across the mountainside, a ditch and rock cliff on the left, a ditch with a steep drop-off on the right. The wide pavement was well cared for with a yellow strip down the middle. Traffic was light but it was still early. Micah studied the countryside. He'd traveled this road with his parents when they had delivered him to his grandfather. He remembered always being excited; it meant three months of stability and peace. As a child, he hadn't recognized what prompted his eagerness, but at sixteen, he knew what he was escaping. Driving along the mountain road, he pushed the memories aside; the past didn't matter. If things didn't work out, he'd put the place up for sale and leave.

Coming around a bend in the highway there was an intersection with a narrow paved road. A couple of cars in front of him had slowed, and he did too, because there was a roadblock ahead. A jacked-up pickup sitting above giant tires blocked the middle of the highway. Vehicles might have been able to edge around it by using part of the side road, but the two men, one at the pickup's front bumper and the other at the tailgate, seemed ready to prevent that. The men looked to be near fifty years old, both wearing jeans, long-sleeved shirts, and bright yellow vests trimmed in red. They carried rifles, yet as they approached the first car, they were smiling. Micah turned to Dog.

"Lie down, keep still, let me handle this."

Dog rolled his eyes, but obeyed. After speaking with the driver of the first car, a small blue Chevy, they moved on to the larger tan

Escape in front of Micah. He leaned out of the window trying to hear the exchange. He only caught a few words. Something about the highway ahead. Micah groaned. He wasn't in the mood for a detour. When they finished with the driver of the Escape, the men parted, one going to the pickup which blocked the road, the other coming toward Micah. As he approached, the smile was still on his face, and Micah hoped the news wasn't as bad as he feared. Micah leaned out the window.

"What's wrong?"

The man stopped about two feet from the pickup. He kept smiling, but his eyes narrowed as he studied Micah.

"Nothing wrong," he said.

"What's the holdup?"

"Sort of a neighborhood watch."

"Out here?"

Ahead, the blocking pickup was pulling to the roadside, and slowly the first two vehicles drove on. The man in the yellow vest nodded.

"Yes. Due to the shift in population because of the earthquake, we have to be protecting our neighborhoods."

"From what?"

"People that don't belong, people who have no business here. From your license plate you're a long way from home."

Micah was tired, his eyes burned from lack of sleep, his first instinct was anger. Beside him, Dog raised his head, a rumble in his throat. Micah patted him and smiled at the neighborhood guard.

"I'm on my way to Falls Creek. It should be a mile or so ahead. I own a piece of ground there where I expect to live."

"You mean to stay."

"Yes."

"Did you just buy this place?"

"No. It belonged to my grandfather. He left it to me. Check the courthouse, you'll see. I used to spend summers here."

"What's your name?"

Micah told him and narrowed his own eyes.

"Look, I'm dead tired. I was in the middle of that earthquake. I nearly didn't find a way across the river, so how about I just drive on? Okay?"

A tiny light brightened the man's eyes.

"Sorry to make things any harder for you, but we haven't had it easy here either. Water's not the only flood. People been pouring east for days now. Hope you have some food where you're going because Falls Creek isn't high on the government's supply list."

Micah nodded. He should have known this place wasn't immune to the calamity. The man stepped closer to the pickup.

"Where is your place?"

"Berryvine Road. Past where the pavement runs out, unless they've paved it by now. I haven't been there in a long time."

Two vehicles had stopped behind Micah. The man looked at them and held up his hand, while turning to Micah.

"That's on the other side of town." He reached into the vest's pocket and pulled out a small piece of paper, like a theatre ticket. "Take this. When you get out of town there's another checkpoint. Show this and they'll get you through quicker."

With that, he strode toward the next car. Micah quickly put the pickup in gear and drove past the big truck that was again moving to block the road. Finding the area in a state of defense dampened the hope of a vacant motel room. When the outskirts of town came into view, Micah's breathing quickened. There was the Exxon gas station, a bit updated, but the old peaked roof was still there with the red trim, and beyond that, an auto repair with the roll-up bay doors closed. But on the left side of the street, a square white building with 'Cafe' painted on the front was open. A neon sign in the window glowed with the news, 'Open 24 hours.' The town wasn't fully awake, but a surprising number of vehicles occupied the diagonal parking spaces. People sat in the cars as if waiting for stores to open. The highway through town was Falls Creek's main street. Down a side street to the right was the town's small square. It was a patch of green, a few trees, a flowerbed, and benches around the edge. Across the street from the park stood the county courthouse, a tall silverstone building. Next,

Cornerstone Bank, a building of red brick trimmed in black wrought iron. The bank and its parking lot took up half the block.

Micah drove slowly and glanced down the side streets where there was a grocery, a hardware store, and other shops. Near the south end of town, an intersection with a larger street marked the entrance to a newer part. Micah slowed at the stop light, and as it turned green, he made a left turn. The town had expanded toward the east...here were the big box stores and fast food restaurants, and more traffic. It was almost a disappointment. Still, to be practical he might need those stores. Here also shoppers were waiting for doors to open. As the street spread out in a web of residential properties, Micah turned around to drive back to Main Street. The bank and the courthouse wouldn't open for hours, so he headed for the south end of town. There he found a Motel 6 and another one called Sleepy Inn. He parked in front of the Inn's office, told Dog to wait, and walked up the three concrete steps to the glass double doors. An old man was behind the counter.

"I don't suppose you have a room?" Micah asked.

The old man straightened his bow tie and slicked back his few strands of white hair.

"You suppose right, young fellow."

"Know of any rooms in town?"

"You might try Iris Fenton's old rooming house."

"Where would that be?"

"On past us about two blocks. Take a right on seventh. She's on the next corner to the left."

"Can we call and ask if she has anything?"

"I imagine so."

"Well, do you have the number?"

"Oh, you want me to call."

"I would appreciate it."

Micah leaned on the counter and waited as the old man made the call.

"Iris? This is Herb over at the motel. Yeah, we're full up. You got anything?"

As he talked, the old man eyed Micah up one side and down the other. "Yep. Just one fellow..." he held the phone away from his ear. "...you are alone, aren't you? What's your name?"

Micah nodded and told him his name. The old man could see the truck through the glass doors. Yes, Micah was alone unless someone was hiding under the bed cover. Dog was lying on the seat out of sight.

"Okay, I'll send him over."

Micah thanked him and went off to find Iris Fenton's place. It was right where Herb had said it would be, but with no off-street parking, just an old two-story white house sitting square on the corner with a wrap-around porch complete with a swing. The white fretwork gingerbread trim's paint was flaking and the wooden steps were warped. Micah almost turned around to leave. Instead, he parked on the street and knocked on the door. A lace curtain in a side window swung back into place, and the heavy old door opened. A short, plump lady with a mass of red curls invited him inside. Micah took off his hat and entered.

"You must be Mr. Hanson."

"Yes."

They were standing in a wide entry hall with a staircase toward the back. To the right was a small room that served as an office. To the left was a large living room with a fireplace. Iris gestured toward her left; the many rings on her fingers glittered in the morning light.

"We can do the paperwork in here."

She stepped behind a huge ornate desk and sat. Micah took a chair across from her and sat holding his hat in his hands.

"I only need a room for a day, two at the most."

Iris frowned, tilted her head, and bit her lower lip between small white teeth.

"I can't offer more than one day. Would you pay one hundred dollars, and promise to be out in the morning no later than six o'clock?"

Micah looked down at the frayed carpet between his boots, not knowing exactly what to do. Maybe one day would be enough.

"I need a place to park, and I have a dog."

Iris frowned and heaved a big sigh.

"Oh, all right. You can park near the garage out back. Make sure you don't block the garage door. I need out to go to the store. You can take the dog up the back stairs. If it barks, out you go! No questions asked!"

Hardly knowing what he was doing, Micah paid with a crisp one hundred dollar bill and left to drive around the corner to a side driveway. The back yard was mostly weeds with a dirt drive down the middle. The white board garage with sagging double doors was as run-down as the house. Micah made sure to park well away from the doors. At the rear of the house there was an outdoor staircase made of untreated lumber, gray and weathered. It went to the second floor where there was a shaky landing with a short set of steps to what must be an attic. When Dog was out of the pickup, he sniffed around the yard, lifted a leg at the corner of the garage. After that he trotted to the bottom of the staircase. He looked up at Micah with sad, sorrowful eyes. Micah slung his backpack over his shoulder and started up the stairs.

"Come on, Dog. This is the best we can do."

The upstairs had four bedrooms, a center hallway, and a large bathroom. It looked as if the bath were once a bedroom. The bathroom had a line of three sinks along one wall, three stalls with stools, and three enclosed showers beneath a high row of windows. The old house in its declining years was obviously destined to be a boarding house. Micah found his room at the end of the hall where a big numeral four was stuck in the middle of the heavily carved wooden door. The furnishings were sparse and worn, but there was a bed. On the side table stood an old alarm clock. Micah set it for two in the afternoon, unpacked a few necessities, and took advantage of the bathroom while Iris's borders were surely all at work. With luck, he'd get some rest, take care of his business in town, and be on his way in the morning.

After a shower and a shave, and dressed in clean underwear, Micah fell onto the bed. The springs squeaked, the overhead fan clattered, and as a bolt of lightning announced a thunderstorm, Micah closed his eyes and passed out.

When the alarm set up a harsh jangle, Dog yipped and jumped off the bed. Micah moaned and rolled over to slap the clock into silence. Dog tried to climb back onto the bed, but Micah pushed him away.

"I doubt the hundred dollars covers dog hairs on the bedspread."

He sat up and looked through the front window above the veranda roof. Huge tree limbs hung heavy with wet dripping leaves and rivulets of water ran down the mossy green shingles. Micah dressed quickly, straightened the bed, and taking the backpack, went down the rear steps. The rain had stopped and left behind a sultry summer afternoon. Micah broke out Dog's water bowl and his food. With Dog's needs satisfied, Micah reloaded the pickup and drove to the twenty-four-hour restaurant he'd found on the way into town. At three in the afternoon it wasn't too crowded; Micah ordered a hearty meal of chicken fried steak, potatoes, gravy, and two side dishes. He topped it off with cherry pie and vanilla ice cream. His waitress, a tall thin woman in a white uniform, was talkative.

"Hope you enjoyed the pie."

"I did."

"Well, just don't expect the same tomorrow."

"No?"

"No. There isn't another can of cherries in town. Least not Ms. Halkins can find. Now, she has a cousin who does a ton of home canning. But I bet she'll ask a dear price for any of her fixings." She gave a loud chuckle and slung a towel over her shoulder as she started to remove the dirty dishes.

Micah paid at the front cash register and took a mint-flavored toothpick. Out on the sidewalk he looked up and down the street. Most of the activity he'd seen in the early morning had slowed. Either people had found what they needed, or the rain had chased them away. The pavement washed clean by the rain, and the blue cloudless sky, made it seem like a trouble-free world. Micah was glad to be near the end of his journey but he had yet to feel any sense of accomplishment. Maybe it would come when he stepped foot on the cabin's porch, if it still had a porch. It had been five years since his grandfather's death. Micah had received a small pamphlet from the church Albert had attended; it was in memory of Albert, giving bits of his life, and the place of his burial. They had buried Albert in the graveyard behind the church, and Micah had sent money for a gravestone. At some point, he'd have to find that grave and look upon it, and he should take some flowers. Standing in front of the restaurant, Micah's day turned dark...going to visit that grave was the last thing he wanted to do. That would make it final, no way to push it aside, or pretend Gramps was just away instead of gone forever.

He shook his head to clear it. What was he thinking? Did he expect to go to the cabin and find Albert there? How he hated death. It made living useless. Micah threw the toothpick in the gutter and climbed into the truck.

Dog greeted him with a "Woof."

The bank was his first stop, where a young man was helpful in setting up two accounts, and providing a debit card. Micah made a call from the bank giving Harry Miller instructions...he was to send some of the money to the new bank accounts and deposit the remainder in a mutual fund they had already discussed. Micah's financial arrangements were simple, and he didn't like thinking about how the money came to be. When finished, he asked directions to the Department of Motor Vehicles. By five o'clock, he'd completed his business, the government offices had closed, and Micah was sitting in the town square watching two old men play checkers. They didn't seem bothered by the destruction, anticipated shortages, or the future of the torn asunder country. If you had lived long enough and faced enough disasters, one more probably wasn't anything exciting.

Micah put Dog on the chain and took a long walk down Main Street. Traffic seemed orderly, but there was an atmosphere of tension. As evening approached so did more men wearing the yellow vests. They stood at intersections and watched each vehicle that passed. Micah wondered if he should take time to put the new North

Carolina license plate on the truck. He'd planned to do that at the cabin. He was going to nail the two California plates up on the barn door, but since North Carolina issued one rear plate, maybe he could turn the old front plate around to cover the bare spot. He reached into his shirt pocket and pulled out the ticket the man at the highway stop had given him. It was red with a yellow stripe on one edge, the word 'checked' in black. He didn't see anything about it that would stop someone from printing fake tickets, or what real purpose they served. Dog pulled on the chain and Micah headed back to the pickup.

It was after six-thirty, still early to Micah, but when he returned to the boarding house, the tenants were all in the living room watching television or reading a newspaper. The television stood beside the fireplace; a long, dark green velveteen sofa was across the room, its back to the entrance. Two armchairs sat on either side of a small round table. The man with a newspaper in front of him sat in a brown lounge chair, and Iris was in a rocking chair in the corner near the front windows. She was busy with some sort of needlework. Two other women were present, both gray-haired, one plump, the other very thin, and they were watching television along with two of the men. One of the men looked of working age, the other was old and fragile, and it was surprising he could sit upright. From the number assembled, Micah guessed Iris had five regular tenants. As he stood in the center hall's wide archway, Iris looked up.

"Oh, Mr. Hanson. Come in." She rose and put the needlework on the chair's cushion. "Ladies and gentlemen, this is Mr. Hanson. He'll be with us just for the night." She narrowed her eyes and gave Micah a hard look. "He's visiting in Mr. Gill's room. Mr. Gill will be back in the morning."

As the five turned to greet Micah, he stepped into the room. The man with a newspaper lowered it for a minute, long enough to give Micah a nod of greeting. The old man sitting in an armchair beside the table pointed a shaky finger to the other chair.

"Have a seat, young fellow. Come look on this television what the Lord has wrought."

The two ladies on the sofa frowned at him.

"Now you quit that, James Harris. You know good and well the Lord never did such a thing!" said the thinner one in a lavender dress.

Iris waved both ring-covered hands. "Now, now. Behave. We're all entitled to our opinions. Do sit down, Mr. Hanson."

The tenants settled back into their previous interests, the younger man on the sofa with the two ladies intently watching television. The aftershocks continued, some strong enough to finish destroying buildings damaged in the major event. Micah took the seat offered by the old man, who returned his pale-eyed gaze to the television screen. He nodded, seemingly to himself.

"The Lord has had enough. Fixing to shake 'em up good." He was sticking to his theory, but spoke too softly for anyone except Micah to hear.

Iris had gone back to her handiwork and there was no real conversation other than the occasional comment by the man on the sofa. Micah was comfortable with the arrangement. As the broadcast continued, even when the man on the sofa with the remote control changed channels, it was clear there was nothing but earthquake coverage.

One of the biggest fears was speculation that this cleaving apart in the near middle of the country would set off great faults in the west. Experts gave details concerning the Cascadia zone, which runs for hundreds of miles off the Pacific Northwest coast. Unlike the Great Mississippi Rift, Cascadia lies along the line where one tectonic place is sliding beneath another. The expert gave a figure of perhaps thirteen thousand deaths if this fault ruptured. To say nothing of the over two million displaced persons who would need food and shelter.

"Huh," said the man on the sofa. "How about the several million we got right here? Be fixing to run us over we don't take care."

No one answered. There was nothing to say. The men in yellow vests were doing what they could to protect their small town. People living in cities seemed to think fleeing to the countryside would provide them with their needs. Farmers always had food; there were edible things in the wild...they'd bring their guns and hunt for food. Micah knew enough about how his grandfather lived to know it was nothing learned in a day. People would starve before they understood what it took to survive in the woods. City people would do better to stay near their homes, shelter in place, provided they had sense enough to be prepared. The station went to another report concerning Yellowstone, the gigantic eruption waiting to happen. That would end it for this country, while the swirling ash cloud could darken the entire world for months. The man controlling the remote clicked and changed the channel again. Micah didn't blame him, for hearing about the disaster at hand was enough. The news stations had introduced a new phrase into their reports, the 'Great Mississippi Rift.' Before, news people had spoken of the Reelfoot Rift, the Marianna about 100 miles east of Little Rock, and they named branches of other nearby faults, some in southern Illinois such as the Wabash Valley Seismic Zone. But because of the vast area affected, they had lumped them all together under this new title.

Strangely, no stations mentioned the fifteen nuclear plants in the danger zone. Earlier, in Arkansas, one report had said the plants were okay, they were shut down, and any minor damage was contained. Now, commentators seemed to ignore that aspect of the quakes. Perhaps the first report was true and there was nothing to talk about, or the problem was too serious to reveal, and the government didn't want the public to know. Micah dismissed the thought. He recalled Gramps saying 'sufficient unto the day is the evil thereof' or something like that. He wasn't positive of the meaning but 'don't borrow trouble' seemed close enough. He turned his attention back to the television where a long list of statistics concerning emergency supplies, deployment of regular Armed Forces and National Guard units, and general instructions scrolled across the screen. As did Federal laws concerning rationing of gasoline, other energy sources, and threats of severe punishment for any lawbreaker.

A click of the remote took the viewers in the boarding house to another station. There, the spokesperson was in a detailed account of the great Cushing Oil Hub in Oklahoma and the Diamond Pipeline, which connected it to the Valero Oil terminal in Memphis. Maps displayed the route of the pipeline across the country and under the Mississippi River, where they had ruptured spewing billions of gallons of oil into the great floodwaters. Now, the once fertile Delta to the south was beneath not only water but also oil. Experts measured recovery in years, if at all. Further destruction of oil supplies centered on the salt domes along the Gulf of Mexico. Those four locations housed the nation's Strategic Petroleum Reserve in Louisiana and Texas.

The man holding the remote handed it to the plump lady on his right.

"That does it for me, Ida. I'm going to bed."

She put it on an end table beside the sofa and stood. One by one, the boarders said goodnight and left the room. Iris arose and clicked off the table lamp near her rocker.

"Stay if you like, Mr. Hanson. Be sure to turn out the lights."

Micah said he'd head for bed, too. Iris and the ladies retired to rooms on the first floor; Micah followed the men up the stairs. Dog was glad to see him, and resumed his place on the foot of the bed. As Micah undressed, he wondered about two things. If this was Mr. Gill's room, he didn't have many personal items, or had taken them with him. The second thing was, under current conditions, if it came to it, how hard would it be to find a horse for sale? With no answers to his pondering Micah set the alarm clock for five o'clock, and climbed onto the creaking bed.

Twelve

The next morning, Micah made a six o'clock stop at the gas station where he found more regulations in place. The gas pumps had locks; a large sign read, *see attendant*. There were several cars in line where a man was dispensing the gasoline. As Micah waited, a tall, thin man wearing a red ball cap came to the pickup.

"Let's see your license," he said.

Micah took the temporary license from his billfold.

"I got this yesterday. The permanent one is coming in the mail."

The man studied it, twisting his mouth to one side, and handed the license back to Micah.

"Where you fixing on going now?"

"Out past Berryvine Road. That's where I'll be living."

"Okay. New rules is residents get ten gallons twice a month. Y'all get a ration card in the mail. Pull on up to the pump for ten gallons, and next time bring the card."

He waved to the pump jockey. "Okay, Dave. Residential allowance."

When Micah left the station, he stopped for a hearty breakfast before heading south out of Falls Creek. The restrictions on gasoline made him consider stopping for additional groceries, but he decided against it. The cabin was a little over ten miles from town, and two gallons would cover a round trip. If rationing of other necessities occurred, there might not be any reason to come into town. He couldn't have imagined such conditions when thinking of living in the cabin, and the shortages would certainly affect the area, although what it might mean to him was uncertain. Dog fidgeted, moving from the window and back to Micah's side. Micah told him to calm down. Dog had been fed, watered, and had had a quick stroll around Iris Fenton's backyard. Dog ignored the command, and Micah couldn't blame him, for he wasn't feeling all that settled either.

He couldn't stop thinking about the television news of the night before. Pictures shot from helicopters gave astonishing views of the ravished land and the destroyed towns and cities. The Gulf had expanded over a great crescent of sunken land and washed away some coastal towns, and others were standing many feet deep in a mix of fresh and salt water. The entire Mississippi Basin was under water, making the path of the river invisible, dams and levees submerged or turned to piles of rubble. It was as if the land and the mighty river were tired of man's control, and had thrown off the constraints. The east and west of the nation looked held together by part of northern Missouri, Iowa, and Minnesota; everything south was like a vast inland sea. Micah had no doubt the country would recover. This was the United States. The country's geography would never be the same, but it would survive. Even having been in the midst of the destruction he'd not realized the magnitude until seeing the television reports, and he was amazed he'd made it to Falls Creek.

The morning was pleasant, but under the clear sky, it was warming up quickly. About a mile out of town, he slowed for the expected roadblock. He had the ticket in his shirt pocket. Three men patrolled this crossroad, and rather than using a vehicle as a barrier, a swing arm was in place. It looked hastily constructed, but surprisingly official, with its bright yellow paint the same color as the men's vests. One man stood at the heavy upright post which held the long pole. He operated the lever controlling it. Even a small car could crash through the lowered arm, but none of the drivers was trying such a thing. The three men carried rifles, and in addition to the long guns, each wore a holster with a sidearm. Waiting in the short line, Micah removed the ticket from his pocket. A stocky young man wearing a straw hat came to the pickup.

"Your driver's license, please," he said.

"Why the change, aren't the tickets being used any longer?"

The man pushed the brim of the hat back from his sweaty forehead, revealing a hank of damp hair.

"We changed. Those was just temporary. Licenses is better."

Micah again pulled out his billfold. He had thought to remain silent and pass the check station quickly, but curiosity prompted a question.

"Have you had much trouble because of people fleeing the earthquake area?"

The man returned the license and shook his head.

"Just a little, but we moved them on quick enough. Most heading east stay on the interstates. Our biggest problem will probably be shortages of stuff. That and fending off the feds if they try to put one of them camps in our county."

Micah didn't like the sound of that, but he drove on. The country, to some extent, was in turmoil and it made him even more inclined to hide away in Gramps' distant cove. He passed several vehicles that were heading toward Falls Creek, and about the same number were going in his direction. The morning sky was bright blue with a few brilliantly white clouds. Tall trees and patches of shorter dark green laurel crowded the roadside, while seen through breaks in the foliage, a small brook flashed copper and silver in the sunlight. The countryside seemed familiar. In places, the highway curved around the foot of a mountain and either headed higher or slid lower and across a rock-walled bridge. The air, heavy with the scent of pine and fresh water, was like breathing in a tonic. Micah glanced at Dog, who had his nose in the breeze.

"Dog, this may turn out fine. Don't you think?"

Dog didn't acknowledge; he was too involved with the odors on the wind.

After five miles, Micah drove slower, keeping watch for Berryvine Road. In some ways, the Blue Ridge remained as the first explorers had found it. In other ways civilization had invaded. There was scarcely a mile between buildings of some sort, with homes that clung to hillsides or lay low in the curve of a creek side. The types of structures were as varied as the number, houses built of cedar or clapboard on the same road as shanties of plywood painted red. Old barns of weathered oak, some traces of paint in the cracks, occasionally stood across the pavement from a white farmhouse on the opposite hill. There were yards with beds of bright-colored flowers and decorative trees, while other dwellings stood on rocky, weed-covered ground. Green street signs marked the roads, the same as the metal ones in town, perhaps in an attempt to tame the wild mountains with manmade markers. If eons of rain, hail, and snow had not destroyed the mighty mountains, only rounded them, perhaps the earth with one more great shrug could throw off mankind's puny efforts to change them. The idea sent a chill to the back of Micah's neck, for he had seen what the earth could do when it decided to move.

A rambling roadside building displayed benches and lawn ornaments outside, and advertised antiques inside. A tin-roofed open shed attached to one end of the building displayed tables holding open boxes of tomatoes, ears of corn, and green beans. Gramps had grown vegetables in the valley in front of the house, and he had watered his garden from a good-sized stream that flowed along the foot of the hill. Would the narrow valley still be cleared, or had brambles and small trees reclaimed it? Micah didn't think it mattered. He wasn't much of a gardener anyway, but if he decided to try it, he could clear the land. He was more interested in getting the electricity turned on once he inspected the cabin. He'd always called it a cabin because it was of log construction, but it was more a conventional house. There were three bedrooms, a living room, a kitchen, and dining room. The one bathroom was large, nearly the size of the one in the boarding house.

As he drove the increasingly narrow pavement, watching the road signs, he wondered about the condition of the house, and the camping equipment in the truck's bed was a comforting thought. The water pump on the well could need servicing and the condition of the septic tank was uncertain. Micah had been a city dweller all his adult life. The summers with Gramps hadn't taught him much about country life. A flick of the switch turned on the lights, a turn of the tap provided water, there was radio and television...he'd never thought about what it took to provide these far from town. For a minute, these things were troubling, but reality set in and none of it mattered. There was no family to care about. He and Dog could live in a cave if necessary. The pickup held all they needed. Besides, there were servicemen in the area who could take care of those things. He'd check the place for damage, get the lay of the land, and call about getting the electricity restored. When he knew what needed repairing, he'd find the right people to do it.

He rounded a curve in the road...it dipped down into a narrow valley, and across a one-lane bridge over a swiftly flowing stream. The clear water tumbled over gravel and larger stones, producing small whitecaps that gleamed in the sunlight. If the stream were wider, it would resemble the one on the Hanson property. Micah had loved the creek. He had rolled up his pant legs and waded in the cold water, the round slippery rocks hard against his feet. There were crawdads hiding in the gravel and strange flat-footed insects that skimmed across the water's surface, and he had named them ski-mosquitoes. After crossing the narrow bridge, the road curved again, running along the edge of the stream. Nearly a mile farther on, the road left the bubbling stream and formed a 'Y' with the pavement heading in two directions. The sign to the left stated Berryvine Road, and as he turned left, Micah's pulse quickened. He topped another hill and saw a white house on a flattened area, a steep driveway leading to it, and a black mailbox stood at the bottom by the road. It looked familiar. Yes, he remembered this house. It didn't look much different than it had years ago.

Micah drove a bit faster. He hadn't seen another car for several miles, but no one other than residents of the area had any reason to travel the back roads. When the pavement stopped, and the road turned to dirt, he knew it wasn't much farther.

"Okay, Dog. This is it."

Dog gave him an intense stare as if trying to determine what would happen next. He'd lived in the country before, and it hadn't ended well. Micah patted him.

"Don't worry, these hills aren't going to shake or fall."

Dog didn't seem convinced, and continued the distrustful stare. Around the next bend, the road came alongside another stream, this one following the foot of the hill beside a small, cleared valley. The dirt road ended in a turnaround in front of a house. Micah pulled to a stop and stared at the scene. This was his granddad's place. It had always been at the end of the road. The mailbox beside the road, and the looping driveway the mailman used to go back the way he'd come. It all looked as if Gramps were still here.

Except the long front porch that had been open was now screened. Micah sat and stared. Of all the things he'd expected, this wasn't one of them. The logs of the house were the same stained red-brown, the slanting roof was still cedar-shingled. The house sat far back at the very edge of the small valley, and the well house was to the right, its corrugated metal roof rust-less and bright in the sun. The old barn still had weathered gray boards and sagging doors, but it didn't look any worse than it ever had. Beside it was the chicken pen with a small house for them to roost. What really made his spirit sink was the vegetable garden neatly laid out beside the stream. There was absolutely no doubt someone was living here! He gripped the top of the steering wheel and lowered his forehead to his fists. Just what should he do now? Dog shivered, and whined.

When he raised his head nothing had changed, and he couldn't find the energy to climb out of the pickup. Dog paced in place; the truck wasn't moving, there was a wide field before them, and it was obvious he should be outside. Micah shook his head.

"Just wait a minute."

There had to be a mistake. Maybe someone had bought the property, but that couldn't be. Micah had paid the property taxes for five years; he'd made sure to do that to keep it off the auction block. All the people fleeing from the quake area, maybe squatters had found the empty house and moved in. No, there wouldn't have been time. That could not account for the garden and the well-maintained condition of the place. Despair nearly overwhelmed him. He foresaw a court battle, an ugly protracted fight, and the words 'sick at heart' floated through his mind. Maybe he should start the pickup, drive the loop like the mailman did, and leave. He could get back on Interstate 40 and drive to the Atlantic, and become a beach bum on the east coast rather than the west. He had not come this far to face a struggle. There was supposed to be rest here, a refuge, a place to learn how to live without Jena and Jordan.

Dog whined and nearly climbed onto Micah's lap; he wanted out. When Micah didn't move, Dog barked, sharply.

"Okay, okay."

Micah pushed Dog away, started the engine, and slowly drove the curve of the driveway taking the turn toward the barn. Gramps had used the center hallway for a garage although he rarely parked there, only in the worst of storms. Near the barn, to the north edge of the garden, Micah killed the engine. He sat studying the house. Without the motor noise, it seemed silent, until the cluck of chickens and the occasional birdsong drifted on the slight breeze. Micah opened the driver's side door and before he was halfway out, Dog pushed by and alighted first. The drive from town hadn't taken long, yet when Micah stepped to the ground, his legs shook. Finding the place occupied was almost one shock too many. Micah remained beside the truck while Dog started exploring.

When there seemed nothing else to do, Micah headed up the slight rise to the house. He'd knock on the door, and see what happened, but if anyone was home, they should have seen him by now. He'd left his hat in the pickup and the sun warmed the top of his head. It brought back a flood of memories of long ago summers that had put blond streaks in his brown hair, and freckles across his nose. Likewise, the smell of fresh water from the stream, along with the odor of old hay in the barn, and dust from the road all seemed familiar. A sun-warmed place rich in quiet peace, where it was easy to take a nap on the porch swing.

He climbed the two steps to the porch and could see through the screened door that a swing was still there. He started to knock, but instead opened the door and entered the veranda that stretched across the front of the house. The new screening made it darker than just the shadow of the roof. Micah went to the heavy oak door with a window in the top, and knocked. He leaned forward and listened, but the house was silent. He knocked once more then turned away and went back outside, where he stood surveying the yard. Dog had found the creek and was helping himself to a drink.

Suddenly a voice behind Micah shouted out, "Hey, what you want here?"

Micah whirled around toward the house. At the corner near the well house, a person, he wasn't sure if they were male or female, came striding forward. The person wasn't very tall. A wide-brimmed straw hat covered most of their face, the denim overalls and long-sleeved blue shirt hid their body, but the voice sounded feminine despite the rough quality. Then he saw it was an old woman, a basket hung from her left arm while she cradled a rifle in the crook of the right.

Micah flushed with anger, nerves, and feelings he couldn't name. This was his property; he held title to the land, and no one had a right to demand answers of him! He was the one due an explanation. His world was upside down and he had counted on finding peace in this place. He'd made one plan after Jena died...it was to bury himself in these hills and endure the remainder of his life. He'd held together long enough to get here only to find this obstacle. Dog raced, barking, to his side.

"Shut that yapping mutt up," the old woman yelled as she waved the rifle at them.

Dog didn't stop...he stood stiff-legged, close to Micah, while the bark lowered to a growl.

"I said, shut him up or I'll shoot the dang thing!"

Micah put his hand on Dog's head. He hated giving in to the rude demand, but he needed to talk to this woman.

"Quiet, Dog. I mean it."

Dog stopped, but stared hard at the woman as she came closer.

She stopped a few feet from Micah and squinted at him from under the brim of her floppy hat. She looked as old as the mountains surrounding the valley.

"Okay, who are you and what'd you want?"

"I'm the one who needs answers. I own this land. What are *you* doing here?"

She turned away and started to the house. She waved the rifle forward, motioning him to follow.

"I spect I almost knew when I seen the California license plate," she said over her shoulder.

There was nothing else to do but follow her. Dog kept to Micah's side even when they went onto the porch. There was a table near the swing and the woman set the basket on it and leaned the rifle against the wall. She took off the big hat, hung it on a peg, ran her hand through her damp gray curls, took a blue handkerchief from her back pocket, and wiped her forehead.

"Hot out there even for this time of morning. I was fixing to weed the garden, but saw you."

"I knocked, didn't you hear?"

She frowned, and looked up at him with eyes as bright blue as the sky.

"How could I hear? I was outside, just coming back from up the hollow. I was cleaning leaves out of a little spring. You know the one I mean?"

Surprise made Micah raise an eyebrow. Yes, he did know the one she meant. There were several springs on the property, but a small one that fed into the creek was deep in a crevasse that always filled up with dead leaves. Gramps used to go up there to clear them away.

"Yeah, I see you remember." She reached into her pocket for a door key and unlocked the door. "Well, come on in."

Dog started to squeeze through, but she stopped him with her knee.

"He stays on the porch."

Micah followed her and shut the door in Dog's face. Again giving in until he knew her story, but when he did, Dog could certainly come inside.

The living room looked different. The slipcover on the couch was bright with big yellow daises and green leaves. It used to be a brown material that seemed like leather, but wasn't. The two front windows had blue curtains where roll-up blinds used to be. Micah had fond memories of the old interior, but he had to admit the improvements were nice. They passed through the dining room and that looked almost the same, the oak table with the high-backed chairs, but the kitchen was entirely different. A new set of white cabinets surrounded a double sink, and the window above the sink had a ledge where pots of herbs stood in the sun. The kitchen table had a white cloth with a green border, and the four chairs around it had green seat and back cushions. What Micah noticed most was the electric stove and new refrigerator, both in stainless steel. Years ago, the refrigerator was white with a rounded door, the stove white enamel with four black metal burners. He'd expected to need new appliances if the old ones were even still there.

The old woman stood at the sink with her sleeves rolled up washing her hands. She glanced back at him.

"Sit on down. I got some tea made."

Micah took a seat at the table. There didn't seem much sense in demanding answers at this point, and she had obviously been living there for a long time. She probably knew Gramps. Maybe Gramps had married her! She obviously knew who he was. A strange lassitude settled over Micah. Nothing seemed real since Jena had died, life moved on and it carried him along. The woman dried her hands on a dishtowel and took two glasses out of the cabinet. She removed a large glass pitcher full of tea from the refrigerator. She glanced at Micah.

"Hope you take it sweet, that's all I got lessen I fix some different."

"What you have is fine."

Sweet tea and Cheerwine both brought back summers with Gramps. He looked at the tall glass she set before him and wondered how he should feel; maybe he should thank her for keeping the place in good shape. Still, part of returning was to make it his by rebuilding if necessary. He'd bought tools, made provision for living in a tent until the house was ready, now all those plans were useless.

Micah sat with his hands in his lap, the tall glass of cold tea sitting on the table before him. The woman across the table lifted her glass, draining nearly half of it, after which she wiped the back of her hand across her lips.

"Thirsty work tramping around out there in the heat. Course, not like it gets in August. Round that time seems all the green stuff starts to simmer and the humidity gets a bit wicked. Still, not near as bad here in the mountains as it is out yonder in the flats."

Micah watched and wondered what his first question should be. *Who are you? What are you doing here? Did you know my Gramps? You surely can't maintain this place alone, does someone live here with you?* Still, he was too tired and dismayed to ask anything. She frowned at him.

"Don't you want your tea? What's the matter with it?"

"There is nothing wrong with the tea. I'm tired. It has been a long trip, interrupted by an earthquake."

"Well, why didn't you say so? Get your things. The guest room is always ready. Rest. I'll fix a nice meal for when you wake up."

"I'm not that kind of tired. I'm tired of things not going as planned. I need you to tell me what you're doing in a house that the courthouse says is mine." Micah bit back sharper words.

She held up both hands. "Nobody is disputing that. Albert left the property to you and that's a fact. He left it to you in a will. I spect you got a letter from Jerry Meyers, the lawyer, telling you that very thing."

"I did. So who are you and what are you doing here?"

"I'm Gwen Turner." She spread her hands out, indicating the space around them. "This is what I'm doing here. You think this place would stay in good shape if it was vacant? More than likely tramps would have moved in." She picked up the glass of tea and finished it.

"So, you took it upon yourself to maintain it for me?"

She pressed her wrinkled lips together and nodded. "Yes, if you want to look at it as purely neighborly." She shrugged her thin shoulders. "Otherwise you can take it from a legal standpoint."

"Meaning what?"

"See, nobody thought you'd come here. Albert hadn't heard from you for years. You didn't even show up when he died."

"Wait a minute! I sent flowers. My wife had just had a baby. I couldn't come."

She patted the air in a calming motion.

"Simmer down. I'm not judging. I'm just saying true things. From how you acted, it didn't seem you'd show up."

"And you just moved in."

She stood and shoved her chair back, picked up her empty glass and pointed at his glass.

"You going to drink that?"

Micah picked it up and took a long drink. He was thirsty, and his throat was dry. When he finished, she got the pitcher from the refrigerator and held it toward him.

"You want more?"

Micah shook his head. Gwen returned the pitcher and took both glasses to the sink where she rinsed them. With her back to him, she continued speaking.

"I lived with Albert for twelve years. We started living together when he was eighty and I was seventy. We was good company. Our kids was all on their own. Well, his was just newly dead. Mine are still around but they pretty well take care of themselves. You know how kids are when they grow up." She turned around to face him. "You said you had a child. Boy or girl?"

"A boy."

She smiled. "Boys is nice. My grandson comes around and helps with the chores here. You got him to thank for that garden. He plows it. I plant and weed, we share the crop."

"That's nice. Now how about getting to the legal reason you are here."

"Albert didn't think you'd come back either. He knew you'd married. He showed me the announcement. Sent you a right nice amount of money, if I remember. We talked about some other kind of gift, but we didn't know anything more useful than money."

"Yes. And I sent...well, Jena sent a thank you note."

"Your family didn't come with you?"

Micah shook his head.

Gwen gave a quick look at the gold band on a finger of his left hand.

"You fixing to send for them? Y'all intend to move here permanent?"

"No. Just me. I mean to live here. Alone."

"Oh, I see. Well, none of my business. Things happen. My girl, Nora, three children and her husband just up and leaves. Found something more to his liking. But she did alright raising them herself."

Micah's throat swelled shut. He couldn't bear to spread his pain and sorrow out for this woman to see. She was right; it wasn't her business. His trouble was private, not for display to be picked over, speculated about, and him to be seen as a *widower*. He hated that word. This was what he had traveled so far to escape. Not to forget Jena and Jason, he'd never forget them, for they'd always hold a special place in his heart. A secret place where they'd be safe. He'd had them too short a time to share their memory with anyone else, certainly not people in this area. The only thing they needed to know was that he was Albert Hanson's grandson and he'd come here to live. From what Gwen had said, she already knew more about him than he liked.

"You still haven't explained the legal aspect of you being here. If there is one."

Gwen sat across the table from him and drummed her fingers on the white tablecloth. The rims of her stubby fingernails were dark with stain, as if she'd been picking berries.

"It's real simple. Albert had me sell my place when I moved in here. Told me to put the money in the bank, something to supplement the social security. When he wrote his will, he left the place to you, but gave me a living right for the rest of my life."

"Why didn't I know this?"

"Like I said, nobody thought you'd ever come back. I'd live here, die, and leave the place empty. What would you have done if you did know, fly back here, and have a big lawsuit over it?"

Micah stared out the kitchen window, thinking. There was no answer to her question, for he didn't know what he might have done, but the attorney should have had a duty to tell him.

"This attorney, Jerry Meyers, he should have told me."

Gwen rolled her bright blue eyes.

"Like I said. What good would that have done? We all just decided it was easier and best to keep still. Albert thought it best too. Besides all that, we figured I'd be dead way before you came from way out yonder."

"So it is legal. I have to let you stay here until you die."

"I can stay if I want." Gwen stood and squared her thin shoulders under the blue cotton shirt. "But I doubt it'd work out to anyone's benefit! I got a place at my grand boy's house. I can help with their two little uns."

The condition of the house and the grounds had made a good impression on him. He couldn't do better if he worked for a year. The barn was the only out building in need of repair, and he doubted he'd have done anything to it either. It would probably stand for another twenty-five years even in its present shape. His grandfather must have cared a great deal for Gwen to have so provided for her. Gwen stood with her hands on the top of the high-backed kitchen chair watching Micah. When he didn't speak, she drew a deep breath, shrugged and started for the back door.

"Well, let me know what you decide. I'll be in the garden...after that I'll be gathering eggs."

Gwen stepped onto the screened-in back porch where she put on another straw hat and picked up a tin bucket. The back porch also served as a sleeping porch in the summer. Micah stood in the kitchen door looking at the old rollaway with a faded pink chenille bedspread on it. He could almost swear it was the same spread from years ago. There was a wooden table in the corner; it had empty canning jars and a square box of old lids on it. Beyond the screen door were three steps down to a stone walkway that curved around the corner of the house and ended near the well house. Grass grew in the yard surrounding the house, but it was field grass. Still, when mowed it served to cover the bare ground. A few tall trees shaded the sides and back of the house, and under the trees grew soft, wide-bladed grass, the kind that put grass stains on the knees of his jeans.

When Gwen rounded the corner of the house, Micah went to the window above the kitchen sink and watched her progress to the garden. She set the bucket at the edge of the garden, went to the barn, and came out with a hoe. It was near noon and while there was a breeze coming down the valley, it had to be hot in the garden. For a while, Gwen scratched out weeds from the middle of the rows; next she took the bucket to the creek and scooped up water in it. She walked past the garden, going toward the front porch, and Micah left the kitchen to meet her there. Dog was resting beside the screen door, but jumped up when Micah entered. Gwen lugged the bucket to a front corner of the house where she dumped the water around the base of a medium sized bush. Micah opened the door and stepped out onto the steps as Dog shot out before him.

Gwen looked up, her face flushed in the shade of her hat.

"That's my Rose-a-Sharon. It's fixing to bloom. Trevor, he's Nora's boy, helped me trim it up. Should be getting a good amount of flowers this year. I don't try to keep much in the way of flowers, but this one is special. Albert planted it for me."

Micah wondered if she was purposely making his decision harder. Gwen left the bucket on the front steps, went inside, and came out with the large straw basket. When she headed back to the garden, Micah sat down on the concrete steps. Dog, his tongue hanging out, ran across the open yard back to the porch where he dropped down at the base of the steps in the shade of the house. Micah leaned over and scratched Dog's ears.

"What are we going to do, Dog?"

Dog didn't answer, but he closed his eyes and held his head higher for more scratching.

The day grew warmer. Micah hadn't paid much attention to the summer heat when traveling as the breeze created by the moving pickup made it cool enough. Now, he'd arrived, and it was July. In thinking of the February tragedy that changed his life, the months between were a blur. The drive across country had taken far longer than it should have, but it didn't matter. The trip seemed as unreal as the previous months. He wondered if the remainder of his life would pass like a faded dream, one day melting into another, the memory of that day dissipating like a morning fog.

When he saw Gwen was coming toward the house carrying the straw basket, he stood. Dog sat up and looked at Micah as if seeking instructions. Micah patted him.

"You better stay on the porch for now," he told Dog.

Micah opened the screen door for Gwen. She glanced down at Dog.

"He can stay on the porch," she said.

Dog raised an eyebrow and gave Micah a bored look.

Micah followed Gwen to the kitchen where she emptied the basket's vegetables into the sink. Some of the tomatoes were bright red, some a rosy pink, but all were plump and ripe. She put string beans into a colander and turned water on them...there were a few handfuls of spinach, and some small green zucchinis. Micah sat at the table and watched. With the vegetables washed and put away, Gwen dried her hands on a dishtowel and filled a glass with water which she drained completely. She turned on an overhead fan in the center of the room.

"Does heat bother you much?" she asked.

"Not really. I don't remember the fans."

Gwen pulled a chair away from the table and sat on it.

"No, don't guess you would. Albert put them in when he got sick. Said the pain was bad enough, didn't need to be hot too."

"What did he die of?"

"Stomach cancer. Not an easy passing."

"Was he in the hospital?"

Gwen shook her head. "I tried to talk him into it. By the time he found out what was wrong, it was too far gone. He knew he was dying and wanted to do it right here."

"I'm sorry."

"Well, no need to be. We all got to go sometime."

They sat in silence, the hum of the fan droning on. Micah wondered if he should leave. He didn't even know what had killed his grandfather; he didn't deserve to live on Albert's land. That made him think of the many things he didn't deserve, such as Taylor's truck and the Coopers who picked him off the roadside when he was hurt, to say nothing of Dog, who he couldn't think of being without. He looked at Gwen, his gaze taking in her wrinkled face and thin body; she looked weathered and worn, but tough as aged oak. The house and grounds were due to her work, all this was his if he wanted it. She had said she'd go, and leave him a place in good condition. He'd never expected help; rather, he'd looked forward to a rough, hard life where each day was a challenge where he'd need to fight to live. He didn't deserve comfort or happiness; he'd had all that and lost it!

Gwen flattened her palms on the tabletop and pushed to her feet.

"You may not have anything to do, but Trevor is coming by to carry me to the store. I best get cleaned up."

She left the kitchen and entered the hallway out of the dining room. Micah knew the hallway led to the three bedrooms and bath; he doubted the layout of the house had changed. For a few minutes, he stayed seated at the table before standing and heading for the front porch. Maybe while Gwen was gone, he'd walk out to the barn, look around, and come to some decision. In the meantime, he'd talk to Dog and see what he thought.

Tall oaks at either end of the house shaded the front porch, and the cushions on the swing were comfortable. Dog lay on the floor near the door and Micah sat in the swing. As the swing moved slowly back and forth, Micah studied the front yard. It occurred to him that there must be a riding mower somewhere; the area seemed too big to do by hand. Maybe Trevor, he thought that was the grandson's name, had a mower he brought over. He tried to remember how Gramps kept the grass down, but that memory was gone. He'd spent every summer between the ages of six and sixteen on this property and he didn't even know the work it took to care for it. All he knew was happiness and fun. A child's life.

Gwen stepped through the front door onto the porch. She was wearing a blue dress with tiny pink and green flowers on it; the sleeves were short, and the collar lace. Her gray hair formed a curly halo above her tan face, and she was carrying a leather purse that matched her sandals.

"I called Nora. Told her about you being here. She thinks we should have supper at her place. I told her I'd leave it up to you."

Micah stood, his heart beating a bit faster. He didn't want to meet Nora, or anyone else, Gwen was quite enough on this first day. His refuge was becoming a hazard.

"That's nice of her, but I'd rather not."

"That's okay. I'll just have them all over here. There is plenty in the freezer, and I'll be back in time to do the cooking. Oh, there's Trevor now."

Gwen hurried out the door; Dog stayed where he was, but Micah followed her. He didn't want a bunch of people coming here, and he didn't want to go to Nora's house.

"Wait," he yelled after her.

A black Ford double cab pickup drew near the top of the circle drive and stopped. The young man behind the wheel opened the door and stepped to the ground. He looked to be somewhere between thirty and forty years old, a blond crew cut above a smiling, blue-eyed face.

"Hey, Grandma," he called as he came toward Gwen.

His gait seemed stilted, one leg not bending as it should and the arm he waved at Gwen was metal; it flashed in the sunlight. Micah stopped, standing back as Gwen and Trevor exchanged a hug. Gwen turned and motioned Micah forward.

"Trevor, this is Micah Hanson. Albert's grandson."

Trevor extended his left hand. "Hi. Mom told me you were here."

Micah tried to smile as he shook Trevor's one good hand.

"Nice to meet you."

Gwen reached up to pat Trevor's shoulder.

"Lost most of two limbs over yonder. But praise God we got him back in one piece."

Both Trevor and Gwen shared a hearty laugh. Trevor nodded at his grandmother.

"You have to excuse Grandma's humor. When I came back minus some parts, she came up with the good news that I was at least whole, not scattered all over the Middle East."

They both laughed again. Gwen started toward the truck, calling back to Micah.

"If you're hungry, help yourself to what's in the frig. We'll be back in a couple of hours."

Trevor helped Gwen onto the passenger's seat and hobbled around the front of the truck to climb in. He started the truck and they both waved as it rounded the rest of the circle and headed down the dirt road. Micah stood silent in the midday sun. The old red Ford pickup sat closer to the house where the shade of one tree almost reached it. In the afternoon, Micah idly thought, the pickup would be in shade. He headed toward the porch with no idea what he should do. When he opened the screened door, Dog rushed out. Micah let him and they both started toward the barn. Passing the chicken coop, Dog made a trip around the enclosure sniffing at the ground and eyeing the clucking, pecking hens. A large white rooster strutted on his side of the fence making head thrusts at Dog, who completely ignored him. Micah patted his leg, whistled, and Dog trotted obediently back to his side.

One of the barn's double doors stood open, the other sagged, and its bottom gouged the dirt. Micah stepped into the dim interior, sunlight striping the wide center hallway. A golden haze misted the air and the smell of dry hay made Micah brush his nose. The underlying scent of mold and damp earth made it seem cool inside the gray old building. Tools hung on the wall to the right; the hoe Gwen had used had a bit of green grass clinging to the blade. A wooden ladder, supported by two wooden arms, stretched horizontally across the opposite wall. The first stall had sacks of chicken feed along with garden fertilizer, and at the end of the hallway, the doors stood open revealing the forest beyond a cleared barn lot. Since there were no large animals on the place, the barn was neat and almost empty. Looking around, Micah thought for a minute how it would be to have a couple of cows and a horse, animals to keep Dog company. Still, Dog might be insulted if lumped with ordinary farm creatures, and besides, Micah didn't know how to milk a cow, or ride a horse if it came to it.

Exiting the barn and walking back to the house, Micah acknowledged the work involved with just the garden and chickens, and he doubted he'd be up to keeping more. When he'd pictured the cabin in ruins and what rebuilding entailed, it had seemed doable. In his version there'd not be chickens or a garden, just a rebuilt cabin stocked with canned goods. He hadn't pictured a home, but more of a hideout. Instead, he'd landed in the middle of active home life, complete with an extended family, which if he didn't drive away he'd have to meet that evening.

Thirteen

Halfway across the yard, Micah stopped and looked at the pickup and back toward the house. All of his possessions were in the pickup; he hadn't taken anything into the house. Until he knew how things stood, the truck was his home. If he unloaded and put tools in the barn, and his backpack into the house, he doubted he'd ever leave. Still, he didn't have any other place to go. He couldn't think straight; he truly did not know what to do. As he pondered, a thought struck him. He shouldn't believe Gwen...she could be lying, hoping he'd decide not to stay. When he had asked why the attorney hadn't told him, she'd brushed it away. Maybe no one told him because he could have decided to sell the property. He wasn't sure why he hadn't sold it. He and Jena could have used the money, but maybe he'd wanted to bring Jordan here someday.

He ran to the pickup, took out his backpack, and dug to the bottom to retrieve the legal papers. There was a letter from the attorney, Jerry Meyers, who had an office in Falls Creek. Micah suspected he'd be stupid to take Gwen's word for anything. How'd he know if she ever lived with Gramps? He shoved everything back into the bag, called to Dog, and held the truck door open. Dog loped to the truck and jumped onto the seat. Micah slammed the door, went to the other side of the pickup, and climbed behind the steering wheel. He pulled out his cell phone, found a signal, and dialed the attorney's office.

A woman answered. "Yes, Mr. Meyers is in."

"Tell him to stay there. I'll be there in half an hour."

"Let me ask if he's intending to stay. Can I give him your name?"

"Micah Hanson."

As he waited, Micah started the pickup.

"I'm sorry, Mr. Hanson. He won't be available. Can I make an appointment for you tomorrow?"

"No, never mind."

The road back into town looked even more familiar this second trip, but traffic was heavier. On the highway, about a mile from the city limit, he again stopped at a checkpoint. It took longer because of the many out of state license plates. People were questioned as to their destinations, and it was surprising how many vehicles were loaded with bags and baggage of all descriptions. It appeared the town's anticipated problems had arrived. Micah questioned the guard that checked him through. The man pushed his ball cap back and wiped sweat off his forehead. He tried to smile, but he looked tired.

"Yeah, we're starting to get more of the overflow now. Nashville is in worse shape than first thought. They tried to set up shelters there, but no water, no electric, and you don't want to know about the sewer plants. I don't know where all these people expect to go, but we're full up."

Near the middle of town, Micah turned left to reach the courthouse. He passed the town square and found a parking place nearby. He was sure the attorney put his grandfather's will through probate, and tax records supported the fact that the property was in his name. One of the things he needed to do was change addresses with the county collector. If he didn't stay in the area, Gwen could forward the bills. Jerry Meyers might not have time or inclination to see him, but there was more than one way to get the information he wanted.

Dog didn't want to stay in the pickup, but Micah wasn't in the mood to argue. Dog laid down, put his chin on his paws and frowned. The front of the courthouse had a set of wide, tall stone steps, and at the top of the stairs stood carved wooden doors. Each of the double doors had a window with gold lettering, and heavy brass handles that looked worn smooth with use. Micah grabbed the curved handle and pulled open the door. A wave of cool air carried the scent of old books and lead pencils. The wide center hall had offices on either side; in the middle a winding staircase with marble steps and a heavy wooden handrail led to the second floor. On the wall to the left of the entrance was a square glass case with information for each office. The clerk of the court was on the first floor, and Micah found the office behind the winding stairs near the courthouse's back entrance.

He stood at the counter and waited while an assistant made copies of Albert Hanson's last will and testament. The office charged two dollars a page, but the will was only three pages and more than a bargain, in Micah's opinion. He thanked the clerk and asked for directions to the collector's office. As he walked along the wide marble-floored hallway, he hesitated...he wasn't ready to give the tax office a new address until he knew exactly what he'd do. Instead, he sat on a hallway bench near the restrooms and read Albert's will. It had been recorded soon after Micah's parents had died. Albert had probably originally left everything to his only son, Jack Hanson. A heaviness settled in Micah's chest. He had tried to erase the memory of what his father had done. He could see someone killing himself, but to kill another person too was beyond understanding. The only reason Micah ever settled on was that his father wasn't brave enough to take his own life. The awful act of killing his wife would leave him no choice but to commit suicide. Behind that dreadful reasoning lurked the question of Micah's character. Maybe the taint had stained him and he wasn't any stronger than his father had been.

He swallowed, squared his shoulders, and read more legal terms. On the last page, he found a codicil dated seven years after the original will, and five years before Albert had died. If Gwen was telling the truth, they'd been living together for those seven years.

Whatever made Albert do this for Gwen, he'd not done it on a whim, and Micah quickly scanned the short two paragraphs. It did give Gwen a right to live on the property, but with certain stipulations: she was the sole person granted this right...if she married it was to be revoked. If she moved away for more than eight months, the privilege ended. She was to pay all utilities and maintenance. She was exempt from paying property tax. Micah wondered at that. Maybe Gramps felt leaving that responsibility to him would keep him tied to the property. Still, as the courts say, no one can read a dead man's mind.

Micah put the will on the bench beside him and lowered his head to his hand. His forehead felt warm, but his entire body was like an overheated engine churning on and on, trying to settle on a proper course. He could be rid of Gwen if she went to live with her grandson, and stayed away longer than eight months. He stared at the marble floor between his boots. The good condition of the place bothered him, that and the fact that she had lived there for seventeen years! She'd lived in the house with Gramps for twelve, plus another five after he died, and some states considered their arrangement a common law marriage. Micah took out his cell phone, but remembered he hadn't arranged for internet access yet. Instead, he went back into the clerk's office and asked his question. Her answer was short; North Carolina didn't recognize common law marriage, so Micah thanked her and went back to his bench.

This might explain Albert's addition to his will. Since they never legally married, it was his way of providing for her, but why hadn't they married? Gwen said they were good company for each other, so it was probably monetary. Micah had heard of seniors living together in order to keep social security payments, and Albert had told Gwen to sell her property and save the money. Maybe that is what she'd been drawing on to replace Albert's social security check. Gramps had made his wishes known the best way he could. It was clear he wanted Micah to have the property, eventually. If he'd willed it to Gwen, her children would have inherited when she died. With his questions about the will answered, he folded the sheets and left the courthouse. Dog perked up and greeted him with a muted bark. He obviously wanted out of the pickup, but Micah pushed him aside and put the will into his backpack. When Dog saw they weren't stopping, he took his place on the seat and waited for Micah to start the engine. When Micah didn't put the key in the ignition, Dog said, "Woof."

"Easy, fellow. I'm thinking."

Dog turned his head toward the side window, and with a low rumble in his throat ignored Micah.

Across the street in the town square, a family was unloading a car. They had backed into the diagonal parking space, the rear bumper toward the square. The trunk was open, a woman and three children were busy taking things out as the man spread a blanket on the grass. In minutes, they had set up camp with two cots, a small folding table, an ice chest, and a folding lawn chair. Micah watched as sandwiches appeared in the children's hands, while the father took a jug to a water faucet near a flowerbed. When it was full, he returned and poured a cupful for each child. There were no wasted motions; this family was in a hurry.

Down the block at the corner of Main Street, several pickups loaded with suitcases, plastic boxes, and even bicycles started to turn toward the square, but a patrolman directed them away. Micah wondered how the family in the town square had made it past the guard. About five minutes later, he saw they hadn't escaped notice. Another man, this one wearing a yellow vest, came to move them along. The family packed up as fast as they had unloaded and joined the traffic on Main Street. They headed north, so maybe they'd find refuge in Knoxville, or farther east. Unsettled. Everything was unsettled. The thought of leaving and joining the mass of displaced persons made Micah moan. This got Dog's attention, and he turned and nudged Micah with his nose.

"Okay, okay, we'll go."

Just as Micah started the truck, the patrolman in the yellow vest reached his window. He tapped on the door with the wooden club.

"Hold it a minute, mister."

Micah turned to face him. "Yes, sir?"

"You plan on stopping, or just passing on through?"

"You must have noticed the license plates. Here," Micah started to reach to the passenger side floorboard for the backpack.

The man took a step back and put his hand on a sidearm.

"Put your hands on the wheel. Right now!"

Micah quickly held both hands at chest level, before slowly lowering them to the top of the steering wheel.

"Take it easy, fellow. I was reaching for papers I just got from the courthouse. They show I belong here." Micah gave a half laugh. "Better still; let me reach for my billfold. I have a driver's license for proof. I'm a bit rattled or I'd have offered that first."

The man stepped back and his face relaxed.

"Okay, but slow."

Micah killed the engine, produced the driver's license, and explained his situation. The man smiled.

"Sorry to be so rough, but things are getting bad around here. The camps are overcrowded so people are spilling out everywhere. We've done taken in all we can!"

Micah told him how he'd started for Falls Creek to live on his grandfather's place. The man's face brightened.

"Hey, I think my dad knew old Albert Hanson. Didn't he marry Nora Gilbert's mom? Nora was way ahead of me in school. I see her sometimes, nice lady. Not so nice what happened to her boy, Trevor."

Micah nodded. "I met him. I admire him for the way he seems to be handling his disability."

"Yeah. He gets around right good. Lot of respect for those who serve. Well, I best get back to work."

"Wait a second. You said the town was full…what happens now? You can't just turn away people with children."

"I don't know what else we can do. We're full up. Lord knows, it's a pitiful situation. If we take in more than we can handle, the town will be as bad off as other places. Right now we're sweating utilities, gasoline, and groceries."

Micah nodded. "I see what you mean."

"We're waiting word from state and federal authorities as to what they'll offer in the way of help."

Micah restarted the engine. "Good luck to you. I'll get the new plate on this old Ford so you fellows won't have to waste time with me."

The man laughed, stepped to the curb, and waved Micah away. As Micah reached Main Street, he decided to turn north. Near the middle of town, he took a right into the newer section. He couldn't think of anything he needed to buy, but he went on, curiosity pushing him. If supplies were short, he wondered how the stores were handling the situation. He passed Best Buy, a grocery called Munson's Market, and finally reached the big parking lot in front of Walmart. Most of the parking spaces were full, and it looked as if people with RVs were staying for a while. Right away, he spotted the system that was in place. People were in line, only a certain number at a time allowed into a store. From the amount of items they carried out, it appeared rationing was in full force. Micah was impressed. He wondered if other small towns were doing this well. He turned around, and as he drove toward Main, he passed a vacant lot with a paved entrance where he quickly turned in.

He parked, jumped out, and went to the rear of the truck where he took out a pair of pliers and a screwdriver. With the new license plate in hand, he made the switch from California to North Carolina. It made sense to make this change, and it would ease his passage through the checkpoint on his way home. Home, the word hit Micah in a strange way. Where was home? Certainly not on the west coast, that was an empty, ruined place. If he had ties to any spot on earth, it was here. Nothing was as he'd expected, or even wanted, but few things were. Micah tossed the two California plates into the truck's bed along with the tools, and got back behind the steering wheel.

When he reached the checkpoint south of town, the new license plate didn't clear him.

"Sorry, bub. Things are tightening up, but we got a plan. You get your gas ration card yet?"

Micah shook his head.

"Well, you might get both cards at the same time. They're making up cardboard passes for residents to put behind the windshield. That'll speed up checks."

"Good idea. I'll try to keep my trips back and forth to a minimum."

The man waved him on, calling after him, "Might not be much to come in for if things don't get better!"

The drive back to the house felt even shorter than the trip into town. It seemed strange how distance and time changed in various situations. While traveling across country, Jena's death seemed like yesterday, an event too fresh to comprehend. Now, it seemed years ago, but no easier to bear. It had been a long journey in many ways.

When he reached the house, he saw Trevor's black pickup parked near the front door, so Micah drove toward the barn and stopped beside the well house. He sat for a minute while Dog whined. When he leaned across the seat and opened the door, Dog jumped out. He seemed happy with the place and ready to treat it like home. Micah wished he could do the same, but he didn't know what to do about Gwen. She hadn't told him her age, but he thought it was around eighty-seven. She couldn't live forever; it didn't seem right to move her from a place where she'd done this much work, and she'd taken care of his grandfather. That should count for something. Although she did have a place to go. Her daughter and at least one grandson were close by and seemed helpful. Maybe he should wait, give it more time, and see what happened. Gwen could decide to go...she might like living with Trevor, she'd said he had two children. Great grandchildren could be a big draw and the work couldn't be as hard as tending this place.

Micah started toward the house. Things could well work out all by themselves. As he reached the front porch, Trevor was coming out the door, and he smiled as he made a stiff-legged descent down the steps.

"Hey there, Micah. Where did you go?"

Micah stopped beside him.

"Into town. I had a couple of things to check on. Did you and Gwen get all you needed?"

Trevor's bright blue eyes darkened.

"Yes, but I wonder about the immediate future. I'm sure in time things will be normal, but could be rough for a while." Trevor stepped away, taking his keys from his pocket. "I have to go pick up my wife from work. She's a nurse for Doc Jenkins over in Grant. Guess I'll see you later this evening."

Trevor swung up onto the truck's seat with surprising ease. As Trevor drove away, a small cloud of dust rose behind the truck. Micah wondered how Trevor felt about his showing up to disrupt Gwen's life, and maybe his, too. Micah needed more information, so the dinner might be a good thing after all. As he opened the screened door, Dog came running, obviously expecting to get into the house. Micah held the door open, but when he crossed the porch and opened the wooden door, he made Dog remain on the porch. No need to create tension.

Gwen was in the kitchen, and two bags of groceries sat on the counter beside the sink. She was putting items into the cabinets. Micah came to her side.

"May I help?" he asked.

"Thanks, but no. I been doing this so long, you'd just be in the way. Why don't you go out and bring your things in? You surely need to stay the night. I doubt you'd get a room in town."

Micah start toward the door to the dining room, but Gwen turned from the sink to stop him.

"Wait. You weren't here when we got back. Where'd you go?"

Micah's shoulders stiffened as he faced her. She might as well know, probably did anyway.

"To the courthouse. I was going to see that attorney, but he wasn't there."

Gwen pushed a white curl back from her forehead.

"I thought so. Oh, not that you'd go to the courthouse, but that Jerry Meyers wouldn't be there if you tried to see him."

"Why would you think that?"

Gwen chuckled and her eyes twinkled.

"Cause he's a smarmy little weasel. I imagine he heard you was here and he didn't want to explain anything."

"You think he's a crook?"

"Not exactly. He just sort of slides around things if there's any room."

"Gramps shouldn't have used him."

Gwen sighed. "Well, you see, he's the only lawyer in town. Albert was a smart man; he read everything real good. If Jerry's done something wrong, Albert would have found it. Jerry might talk to you, once he knows you'll not pound on him."

Micah shook his head and started for the door. Gwen hurried across the kitchen to him.

"Wait! That's not the main thing I needed to tell you. When you was gone, the house was unlocked. Never leave it like that. Nothing was gone that I could see, but we was lucky."

"I'm sorry. I didn't think. I didn't have a key anyway."

Gwen pointed to the door leading to the back porch.

"The cabinet beside the door. Keys is always in there. Keys to front and back doors, one for the well house, and even for a padlock on the henhouse."

For a second Micah was startled. Gramps had never locked things up this much. He frowned and started again to say he was sorry, but Gwen reached up and patted his shoulder.

"Never mind. How was you to know? Besides, they might not be around here right now anyway."

"Who?"

"Dopers. There's a empty house back over the ridge. They moved in there several years ago. I doubt it's even the same ones coming and going. They was making meth. The sheriff run them out once, but them or some others come back. That's why I carry my rifle when I'm a ways from the house." Gwen squinted. "I caught them one time trying to steal eggs. They'd a took a chicken could they catch one!"

She stomped back to the sink and continued putting groceries away. Micah suddenly felt very naive. Big cities were awash in crime, from people cheating to the taking of other lives. Law-abiding citizens learned to live with it, and they locked doors, told children to run from strangers, and kept a careful watch on all business dealings. He had thought to leave this behind. That was a mistake...crime was in proportion to population, and Falls Creek had grown in twenty-four years. The memory of those childhood years belonged to the past. When Micah reached the front porch, he let Dog out for a run while he carried his backpack into the house. Gwen told him which bedroom he could take. It was his old room, and he suspected she knew that.

While Gwen spent the rest of the afternoon in the kitchen making a cobbler and baking a pork roast, Micah went outside to arrange for Dog. He found a piece of rebar in the barn, then got the mallet from the truck bed, and took them along with the length of chain to a spot near the front porch. Dog stood a few feet away watching. Micah pounded the metal stake into the ground, attached the chain to it, and called Dog. Reluctantly, Dog came to him.

"Sorry, but we have to do this for a while. See? There's shade by the steps."

Micah took the mallet back to the truck and returned with Dog's food and water bowls. He put them at the bottom of the steps where he sat and stared out over the valley toward the road. He had accomplished his goal. Thinking about his trip, he remembered Rita and almost laughed. She was so right...he couldn't find peace by changing locations. *He* had to change. His interior was a wild and strange territory, and he didn't know how to tame it. Yes, his parents had made growing up difficult, and his father's final act was awful; however, he thought he'd taken it well enough.

He'd made sure his own life didn't follow that path, but with the loss of his family, the barrier against the past broke. The sorted mess of childhood tension and fear spilled out, that along with the death of everyone he loved, made life useless. He could stay or go; it probably didn't make any difference. At least, judging by the delicious aroma filtering out to the porch, he'd have a good dinner and a safe place to sleep. Maybe tomorrow would bring suitable answers. He stood and Dog jerked his head up, alert for Micah's next move.

"Relax, Dog. I'll not go anywhere without you."

As Micah stepped inside, Dog laid down and pretended to believe Micah. The dining room overhead fan was turning and Gwen was pulling a table leaf from the closet. She looked at Micah.

"Here, help me put this leaf in the table. Seems Nora asked Tom Wiley to eat with us." Gwen talked as they put the leaf in place. "Tom's a widower, lost his wife four years ago. Wanders around like he knows what he is doing, but I doubt it. Poor old man. He lives one street over from Nora; she knew his wife. Most he ever eats is pork n' beans, out of a can!"

The table was as Micah remembered, a big oak plank, but he'd never seen it lengthened with a leaf. There were six chairs; he and Gwen carried two from the kitchen to accommodate eight. Micah silently counted the dinner guests. There were he and Gwen, Trevor with a wife and two children, Nora, and this new fellow, Tom. Gwen returned to the kitchen and Micah followed.

"Do you often make dinner for this many people?"

Gwen had put a navy blue apron over her dress and exchanged her sandals for house slippers. She shook her head.

"No, not any more. Usually around holidays, Nora takes over. Her daughter Cindy comes over from Asheville with her family. Course, Trevor's wife always helps out."

Gwen stopped, turned from the sink, and leveled a potato peeler at him.

"And for your information, we don't hold get-togethers out here. Trevor has a great big house, and any of Nora's kids that visit stay with her."

"Was it that way when Gramps was alive?"

"Not always. Sometimes he and Seth Riley would go catch a mess of fish. Albert would invite everybody he knew out for a fish fry. Course, Seth is gone now. He was a few years older than Albert, but passed on a couple years later. At first, when we was all younger, we'd have family here, but toward the end we left things to others."

Micah asked again if he could help and Gwen refused, so he sat at the kitchen table and waited for Gwen to tell him more about his grandfather. She put potatoes in a pot to boil, and started slicing tomatoes and onions.

"Albert didn't have it easy, you know! Him losing Marylee so soon."

Gwen looked over her shoulder at him.

"You never could have known your grandma. She died of a stroke when your dad was fifteen. I was married to Henry. We knew the Hansons. Went to the same church as Albert and Marylee. She was a pretty girl and turned into a handsome woman. We all missed her, and I tell you, our hearts nearly broke for Albert. He didn't let on how bad he was hurting. He and Jack carried on like nothing had happened."

No one had ever talked about his grandmother, but Micah knew she had died young. He never thought about his grandfather's feelings, how it was to live alone. All he knew or even thought about were those summer months. If his grandmother had lived, maybe his father, Jack, would have been different.

"Did you know my dad?"

Gwen took a deep breath, her thin shoulders rising under the apron's straps; she dried her hands on a dishtowel and came to sit at the table. She studied Micah's face for a second.

"Yes! I knew your dad. Boy and man. Now I don't intend to speak ill of the dead, and I do not believe in any taint in the blood. What a person does is up to them. They make choices. I don't mean to be hard, but he was selfish. Never gave a hoot to how his actions hurt others."

Gwen pressed her wrinkled lips together and clasped her hands on the table. She stared at Micah, her blue eyes like small lasers.

"I swore I'd never let these words pass my lips, but here you are. I'm old, and it may could help you. I'm sorry as sin to say this, but I think Albert catered to the boy. He felt so bad that Jack was without a mother, he just bent over backwards to make it up to him. Jack, being so selfish, never gave a thought to how Albert was suffering. Jack grew up thinking the world owed him something! And he never grew out of it. The last thing he did proved it. But I guess you know that story."

Micah nodded. He remembered how he was so busy tamping down his feelings he had let Gramps handle everything. Maybe Gwen didn't believe in traits passing by blood, but his actions made him wonder. He'd been twenty-three, old enough to think of someone other than himself. Gramps had been eighty; his son had just shot himself and his wife. Gramps must have felt awful, yet he found the courage to carry on. Micah recalled one of their phone conversations. Gramps had asked if he could come for the double funeral, Micah knew there was no excuse for what he had replied. It wasn't a lie, but it came close. His ship *was* leaving port, but he could have gotten a pass. His parents' death was almost a relief. He knew he should feel sad, but he had blocked it and thanked Gramps for taking care of the details. Now, sitting in his grandfather's kitchen, Gwen's bright eyes fixed on him, he wanted to cry. He'd taken all the love his grandfather gave, and never gave it a second thought. He hadn't really tried to understand his parents either. All he'd felt toward them was anger about how bad they'd made his life. Yet, he'd never heard Gramps say one bad word about them. Gwen reached across the table and patted his hand.

"I don't know what's happening that made you show up, but if Albert was here he'd want you to stay long as you needed."

Gwen pushed away from the table and stood. "I best get moving. Trevor and his bunch should be here pretty soon."

Gwen hadn't told him anything new, except for her perception of how Gramps raised his father, Jack. It sounded as if Albert was to blame, yet she didn't blame him because of *his* condition. However, it was clear she held people responsible for their actions. Micah agreed with her, and he was ready to admit his own past failures. He should have been more aware of others, the struggles they faced. Painful as it was to think about it, he knew what Jena and Jordan had given him, but maybe he hadn't given enough back. He had not thought about things from any point of view other than his own. In his relationship with his parents, with Gramps, and with Jena, it all centered on what they brought to his life. Now, they were gone and he was stuck with himself!

He stood, but the lump in his chest felt like lead. He wished he'd done more for his family when he'd had one. Instead of selfish sorrow, he mourned for the years Jena had lost, and Jordan had no life at all. The sadness was still there, but it had a different center. He was sad for the lost ones, not just for himself. Jena's last words were selfless. She'd not been thinking of herself when she wanted his promise that he'd live.

Micah went to sit on the front steps and wait for people who probably knew far more about him than he knew of them. Trevor drove in first. Blond heads bobbed in the back seat of the double cab. When he stopped, a tall, thin young woman got out of the passenger's seat, and helped two boys alight. The boys started to run to the house, but upon seeing Micah and Dog, they stopped short. Trevor was slower getting from behind the steering wheel. Micah wondered at the courage it had taken to adjust to the loss of limbs. The woman waited for Trevor and when they neared the porch, Micah stood. Trevor put his arm around his wife's shoulders.

"This is Ilene," and pointing toward the boys he said, "The wild Indians are John...he's nine, and Billie is six."

The boys stood beside each other paying more attention to Dog than to Micah. Ilene held out her hand and Micah shook it. She was almost as tall as Trevor, her long dark hair in a braid hanging over her shoulder, and she wore green scrubs. Her smile was wide and bright while her brown eyes sparkled.

"I didn't have time to change. I have a dress in the truck. John," she called to her oldest son, "get my things out of the truck."

When she reached the steps, she stopped, patted Dog, and said, "Good dog."

Dog watched with awe as she hurried onto the porch.

Trevor pointed to Dog. "What's he good for?"

Micah shook his head. "I'm not sure."

"Maybe he'll make a watch dog. Be good to have one around here. We have a couple of labs at home, but they mostly just lick everyone to death."

"Gwen said something about meth dealers."

Trevor shrugged. "I think they've mostly cleared out. I was thinking of the influx of strangers. But they'll probably be a bigger problem in town than in the countryside."

As they talked, a blue Ford Escape rounded the curve of the circle drive and parked beside Trevor's truck. Trevor waved.

"There's Mom. Looks like she has Tom with her. Would you believe he's a veteran of the Second World War? Must be nearing one hundred. Still comes over to the VFW some times."

Nora had gray hair cut in a long bob that hung forward, hiding her face as she helped an old man out of the car. She was wearing black pants and a bright flower-patterned shirt. There was a big cloth purse hanging from her left arm. The old man she drew from the car was small, frail, and his hair was a faded pale blond, as if it had turned yellow instead of white. He walked bent over, but when Nora started to help him, he pulled away, and tottered to the steps.

When Nora neared the porch, Micah gestured toward Tom.

"Is he okay?" he asked.

Nora laughed, and she had the same bright blue sparkle in her eyes as Gwen. Nora was short with a sturdy build and a pretty face, even with the deep wrinkles at the corners of her eyes. She reached up and gave Trevor a kiss on the cheek before turning to Micah.

"Hi, I'm Nora."

"I thought as much."

Tom had made it to the top step and was struggling to open the screen door.

"Seriously, is he okay?" Micah asked again.

"He gets upset when people help him too much. I figure when they reach his age it's best to give in."

Trevor nodded. "I agree. He's made it this far, but losing his wife nearly did him in."

Nora took Micah and Trevor each by an arm and started to the steps.

"Come on, boys. Mama will need some help."

Micah looked at her. "I doubt that. She won't let me do anything."

Trevor and his mother both laughed, and the three of them entered the porch. John and Billy had come back from taking Ilene her clothes. They stood together studying Micah. Nora went into the living room and on toward the kitchen while Trevor sat on the porch swing.

"You boys go outside and play. We'll call you when it's time to eat."

The boys were a mix of Trevor and Ilene, dark blond that would probably turn brown, but sun bleached for now. Both of them turned to Micah.

"Can we play with your dog?" John asked.

"I don't see why not. Introduce yourselves first. But go easy... he's had a long trip."

Six-year-old Billy, his greenish eyes wide, looked up at Micah.

"Where'd he come from?"

"I'm not sure. I picked him up in Arkansas."

"Wow," they both said and turned to run out the door.

Micah sat on a rocking chair across the porch from Trevor, and didn't know what to say. Trevor finally spoke.

"So, what do you intend to do? Grandma can move to town and live with Nora or with us. What made you show up now? With the country in an upheaval seems a poor time to be moving around."

"I started quite a while before the earthquake. I expected to find a rundown piece of property. Far as I knew it was empty."

"Now you don't have anything to do. Right?"

Micah nodded. "Right."

"You could probably find plenty of work anywhere when the rebuilding starts. If you're into volunteer work, the Red Cross has put out requests for helpers."

Ilene came to the door wearing a long blue skirt with white flowers on it; the blouse matched in reverse, white with blue flowers. She had combed her hair out and it curled around her shoulders.

"Come on, you two. Dinner is ready." She stepped to the screen door, held it open, and called to her sons. "Get in here and wash up, time to eat."

The boys hadn't gone far. They patted Dog and scurried up the steps as Dog stood at the bottom and hung his head. Micah wondered if Dog had once had a family and children who played with him. He and Dog might be two of a kind. Inside, Ilene herded her boys toward the bathroom.

Tom had already found a seat at the table. Gwen had the table set with large white plates and glasses of water. As Nora carried in a platter with the pork roast, Ilene settled John and Billy beside Tom. When all the side dishes of mashed potatoes, corn, sliced tomatoes with onions and cucumbers, and carrots with peas were in place, Gwen motioned to Micah.

"Come around here to the head of the table. This is where Albert always sat."

To be polite, Micah followed her orders. He didn't feel like heading this table full of strangers, but there was nothing to do about it. Trevor, Ilene, and his mother, Nora, sat across from Tom and the boys. Gwen sat at the end of the table nearest the kitchen door. When they all held hands and bowed their heads, Micah did the same. With a chorus of 'amen,' the clatter of silverware and the clink of china sounded as the dishes moved from hand to hand. With plates filled, and the overhead fan gently stirring the air, the meal started. The roast was delicious, and the vegetables fresh and flavorful, and most of it stuck in Micah's throat. He wanted to put his fork down, scoot back from the table, and run. Ilene wiped her lips with a white napkin and narrowed her brown eyes as she studied him.

"I hope you don't take offense, Micah, but are you well? I see people coming into Doctor Jenkins' office that look better than you do."

Micah nodded and tried to smile.

"I'm fine. I've lost some weight."

Nora fixed her bright gaze on him.

"Some weight? I didn't want to say anything, but you'd do for the garden scarecrow!"

Gwen rapped on the table, calling them to attention.

"Now, now, you two. He's been a traveling. Came through an earthquake and he's not been eating regular. Isn't that right, Micah?"

All faces turned to him; even Tom suspended his fork. Micah felt an emotion rising in him. If he broke down in front of the strangers, his pride would not survive. Gwen came to his rescue. She pushed her chair back and stood, picking up her empty plate.

"Who is for blackberry cobbler? Nora, come start the coffee. Ilene, you and Trevor can clear the table."

Trevor grabbed a last biscuit, buttered it, and ate it before handing Ilene his plate. She smiled at him and turned toward Tom and her sons.

"Y'all stay right where you are. I'll bring your cobbler."

Micah helped by carrying the meat platter to the counter beside the sink. In minutes, dishes of cobbler replaced the dining plates. Gwen explained how she had used berries from the freezer and everyone expressed hope that this year's crop would be plentiful. Despite his emotions, Micah's physical body benefited from the meal. He'd managed to eat more than he realized. As the three ladies finished cleaning the kitchen, Tom, Trevor, and Micah moved to the living room. Trevor started to turn on the television, but Tom shook his finger.

"Nothing but bad news. Tell Nora I want to go home!"

"It's okay, Tom. Mom will be through in a little while."

Micah sympathized with the old man. He wanted to go home, too. Big problem was he didn't have a home. He looked up as Trevor was continuing to speak.

"Mom knew your dad. Did you know that? Well, he was almost ten years older than she was. She was in high school when he got married. I guess they married in the church where everyone went. We go to the Methodist in town; Ilene's folks go there, but Mt. Carmel still has a fair congregation."

"Is that where Gramps is buried?"

Trevor nodded. "Yes. We attended the service. It was small, but very nice. Grandma has certainly missed him. Well, we all have."

"Albert Hanson was a good man," Tom declared. "Raised that boy all by himself. People don't get the credit they deserve for going on alone." Tom wiped at one eye.

"I don't guess they do," Trevor said. "Mom carried on without our dad. Kind of a different way of being left alone." Trevor started laughing. "But instead of being sad, she was mad! Every time we turned around, she was blessing him out. I'm the oldest, Cindy is thirty-three, and Hank is thirty. It got so the three of us would make bets on what she'd call him next time she blew up."

Gwen had mentioned that Nora had raised her children alone. If the other two were anything like Trevor, she'd done a good job.

"Where did your dad go? If you don't mind saying."

"We got a postcard from Chicago. About a year later, another one from New York. They just said he was sorry and we were better off without him. Then, about six or seven years ago, there was a letter from a woman in Oregon. Said Frank Gilbert was in the hospital and might die, wanted us to know. He'd married her and was trying to clear his conscience."

"What did Nora say about that?"

Trevor shrugged. "Not much. She gave the letter to me saying I had a right to know because he was my dad. And I could tell Cindy and Hank if I wanted to."

"Did you tell them?"

"Yeah. Wished I hadn't. Just gives them more bad memories to get rid of. Cindy and her husband have a business in Asheville, two nice little girls. Hank works for an advertising company. He's the good-looking one, having too good a time playing the field to settle down. But he did bring a nice girl home last Christmas."

Nora and Ilene entered the living room together, Nora rolling down the sleeves of her flowered shirt. Tom started to push up out of his seat, and Nora motioned him to stop.

"Wait a bit, Tom. We'll get you home before dark."

Ilene sat on the arm of the sofa next to Trevor.

"You've been talking a blue streak. I heard you giving the family history."

"Well, Micah is the only one that doesn't know the stories. Rest of y'all get bored with me."

Gwen stood in the dining room door and Tom pointed to her.

"Gwen's been all alone, she knows how I feel."

"That I do, Tom. There's nothing to do but go on. Now, I don't want to hear of you eating just pork n' beans. It's not hard to fix something else."

Nora left first, taking Tom with her. The old man looked tired. He clearly hadn't adjusted to the loss of his wife, and maybe it was more difficult the longer a couple had lived together. Micah felt as if he'd lost ten years of life…fifty or sixty years must leave an awesome hole. As Trevor rounded up his boys and Ilene hugged Gwen, Micah slumped with weariness. He hardly had the energy to walk out into the yard to bid everyone good-bye. John and Billy gave Dog a good ear scratching before running to Trevor's truck. Ilene carried two plastic containers with the rest of the pork roast and the remainder of the blackberry cobbler. Gwen waved to the departing family.

"That girl's got plenty to do, working and caring for those three. I'd sent her home more if she'd a took it."

Evening settled a soft lavender glow over the valley, and clouds had turned pink in the sky's fading blue. Micah and Gwen stood in the quiet, the faint gurgle of the rippling creek harmonizing with the lonesome hoot of an owl. Behind them Dog whined and Micah turned back toward the house.

"I should settle Dog in for the night. I'll feed and water him out here. Okay if he sleeps on the front porch? He's used to sleeping with me."

Gwen flapped her arms and started up the steps.

"Oh shoot, take him on into your bedroom. But you're responsible for vacuuming up the hairs!"

Micah finished the chores with Dog and, undecided about taking him into the house proper, left him on the porch. When Dog curled up on a braided rug and seemed happy, Micah let him stay there. Inside, Gwen had taken a key from the cabinet, gone out the back door and headed for the hen house. Micah followed. Most of the chickens had gone to roost; the big white rooster was still strutting around. Gwen entered the pen and after shooing the strays inside, locked the door. When they were back in the kitchen, Gwen returned the key to its peg in the cabinet.

"I'm going to bed," she said. "Might be too early for you. If you turn on the television, keep it low, I'll read a while."

With Gwen in her bedroom, the house settled for the night. It was early for bed, but it was dark outside. Micah checked on Dog, went to the room he'd occupied during the years he'd stayed with Gramps, and turned on the light. The quilt on the bed had a blue star pattern; Gramps had said Grandma had made it. In the corner was the same small pine desk with a lamp that looked like a lighthouse. Micah undressed and climbed into bed. His weariness and the flood of memories put him to sleep almost as soon as he fell into bed.

Fourteen

The next morning Micah awoke to the rooster crowing and Dog barking. He pulled on his pants, shoved his feet into his boots, and hurried to the front porch in his tee shirt. Dog was at the screen door staring at something. Micah told him to hush, and looked out into the morning mist. He didn't see any reason for Dog to be barking, so he let him out hoping he'd have enough sense to keep from running away. When he went inside, his nose led him to the kitchen. Gwen was busy with pancakes and bacon on a griddle set over two of the stove's burners. She turned to him with a big spoon in her hand.

"Get washed up, breakfast is almost done."

Micah did as she said. After a quick shower and shave, he dressed in his last set of clean clothes, and straightened the bedroom. Today was the day of decision. He'd awakened with a determination to settle things one way or the other. He wasn't sure how it would go; he'd talk with Gwen, and that might help him decide. Although something in him had changed. He felt his loss just as keenly, but considering the plight of others left little room for self-pity. It wasn't that he hadn't known that people suffer, for the human condition was common knowledge. He'd given to charities, and done what he could to help, but he hadn't felt it this deeply until his own experience. When he saw families such as Trevor's, and how they bravely coped, he was proud of them. Long ago he'd read something that stated how 'pain cracked the shell of our understanding.' Just another way of saying 'walk in my shoes.' Maybe he should be thinking of what was best for Gwen, what a change at her age might do to her.

He had rejected the idea of them sharing the property. Besides that, there was nothing for him to do here. If he went away, he could keep in touch. After what he hoped would be far in the future, when Gwen was gone, he'd come back. One thing certain, time changed everything. If he left and returned years later, time would have changed even him. His attitudes and ideas would be different. Micah repacked his backpack, putting the copy of Albert's will in the packet with other personal papers. He looked forward to breakfast because he didn't know where he'd have the next meal. Gwen was adding another pancake to the stack warming in the oven. The table was set with butter and syrup, and some type of red jelly. Gwen took a warmed plate from the oven, put three pancakes on it, along with several strips of bacon. She handed it to Micah.

"Here you go. Watch the plate, it might be hot. You want milk, coffee, or both?"

The smell of breakfast filled the kitchen, and morning sunlight came through the window above the sink.

"I'll take both, if you don't mind."

Gwen laughed. "Milk now and coffee later, right?"

"That's right. You didn't have to do all this. I could have made something myself. I may not look it, but I can cook."

Micah took a bite of the pancakes and found them light as air, and with butter and syrup sweet as honey. Yes, he could cook, but doubted he could match Gwen's pancakes. The thick slices of bacon were crisp, with a strong smoky flavor. Gwen filled a plate and joined him at the table. They ate in silence, the morning air wafting through the open back door was refreshing, with just a hint of the warm summer day to come. When they finished, Micah helped clear the table and as Gwen washed the dishes, Micah dried them. Afterward, they returned to the table to drink coffee. Gwen was wearing her overalls and blue cotton shirt. As she sat across the table, she rolled down the long sleeves.

"Are you planning to work outside?" Micah asked.

"I usually do. What are you fixing to do?"

"I'm thinking of moving on. How do you feel about that, would you want to stay on here?"

"I'm satisfied most anywhere. I told you I'd be happy to stay with Trevor. For that matter, I reckon Nora would have me. Just seems it's easier getting along with grandkids." Gwen laughed and took a drink of coffee.

"Look, I don't want to put you out. This place isn't what I thought it would be. Face it. There is nothing for me to do here."

"What do you think there's to do out yonder?"

"I don't know. I'll find something."

"Drifting, is that what you've a mind to do?"

Micah shrugged. "I guess. It isn't that bad. Dog keeps me company. I'll keep going east and see what that ocean looks like."

"You could come back through from time to time. See how I was keeping. See if I was still alive."

Micah stood and went to the counter to pour another cup of coffee.

"You'll live a good long time, Gwen. At least I certainly hope you will."

"But, when I am gone, if you're still alive, you'd come live here. Isn't that so?"

Micah sat down and stared into the steaming dark coffee in the cup. He shook his head.

"I suppose I would, or if I have found somewhere to settle, I might sell this property. Listen, Gwen, I don't know what the future will bring. I'll just go day to day."

"Well, you don't have to go today, do you?"

"I don't have any reason to stay, Gwen. There is no point in hanging around."

Gwen took her empty cup to the sink to rinse it. She turned and spoke over her shoulder.

"Will you help me with something before you go? Won't take more than an hour or so."

Micah carried his cup to the sink, considering what she'd asked. With no set destination, leaving around noon wouldn't matter.

"Okay, what do you need me to do?"

"First, you got any heavier footwear, like a pair of boots?"

Micah looked at his desert boots; they seemed sturdy enough. Still, he did have the new boots in the pickup bed. He held his foot up for her inspection.

"These aren't heavy enough?"

"Not where we're fixing to go. It'll take a tromp through the woods to help me post some no trespassing signs. The fence between this property and the one up over the ridge is near down. I want to nail up some signs. That way, the dope cookers can't say they wasn't warned!"

Micah went out the front door, called Dog who came running from the barn. At the truck, Micah found the boots, and took Dog's food out. After he fed Dog, he went inside to change into the new boots. Gwen was wearing her straw hat. A hammer, some nails and the signs lay on the back porch table. She locked the front door, and they left by the back door, which she also locked. Micah called for Dog and the three started walking north along the stream. Gwen set the pace, not too fast but steady. Dog ranged, but never far. Under the tall trees there wasn't much of a breeze. The water rushing over the streambed gave a cooling effect, but the day was warming. Gwen pointed out the sights as they trudged along. When the land began an upward slope, they left the creek side. As the climb grew a bit steeper, Gwen looked over her shoulder at Micah.

"We could've followed the creek," she said, "but it would've been a long walk. Up and over is fastest. I don't want to keep you any longer than need be."

Micah found it hard to breathe. The effort to keep climbing put an embarrassing strain on him. Yes, he'd lost weight and hadn't been doing any real exercise for several months, but it was surprising to be this out of shape. The long muscles in his calves and thighs quivered, his mouth was dry, and there was even a slight pain in his side. His last clean shirt was damp under the arms. He wanted to ask Gwen how much farther, but it wouldn't make any difference, and just be a waste of energy.

Gwen stopped a few feet ahead, put her boot up on a knee-high rock, turned, and looked back the way they'd come.

"You'd hardly credit it, but there was once a path through here."

Micah stopped and looked behind them. It had seemed they were pushing through woods, but upon seeing the backward slope, it wasn't as overgrown as the rest of the hill, and the trail wasn't as steep as he'd thought. That made him feel worse about his physical condition. Gwen didn't seem to suffer from the trek, and over her arm, she carried the basket with the tools.

"We best be moving on," she said.

They had stopped at the halfway mark; a bit later, the trail flattened, and started a gentle downward slope. When the trees thinned and an area opened to the sun, Micah knew they had arrived. He looked across a shallow valley...at the far lower end a wide stream glistened in the sunlight. He pointed to it.

"Is that the same one flowing by Gramps' place?"

Gwen nodded. "Least I think so. Course, back around the foot of the hill there's a small spring flows in with it."

In the semi-cleared land stood a house. To one side was a long shed, the boards gray with age and the roof missing shingles. An overgrown driveway, faint ruts on either side of tall weeds, led through the valley to a low water bridge crossing the stream. Dog, his tongue hanging out, flopped at Micah's feet. Gwen pointed behind them.

"Look close you'll see part of the barbed wire fence. Most of the posts has rotted out."

Micah walked back several yards and found the cut wire dangling to either side of the pathway.

"This where you want to put the signs?" he asked.

Gwen set the basket down and removed the hammer, nails, and the signs.

"Might as well. But doubt those crooks can read!"

Micah gestured toward the house.

"Looks empty."

Gwen started hammering a sign in place.

"I reckon it is right now. But never know when someone will be back." Gwen pointed with the hammer. "See that creek crossing? Once over it, it's just a little ways to the road."

"The same road I came in on?"

"Almost. That 'Y' where Berryvine Road goes to the left, well the leg to the right winds on around and goes by this place."

Gwen handed him the hammer.

"Here, you fix the other two to them trees. I'm tired."

When he finished, Micah stood surveying the wild, overgrown, deserted property. He turned to Gwen.

"When's the last time someone lived here? Not the drug dealers."

Gwen twisted her lips into a knot, tilted her head, and wrinkled her forehead, the straw hat almost hiding her bright eyes.

"Let's see now. It's been a good long time. Ten years, least that."

"Can we look at the house?"

Gwen shrugged. "I reckon so. Nobody to stop it. I don't see any no trespassing signs on this side of the fence."

When Micah looked, he found her chuckling to herself as they headed into the more open land. Dog regained his curiosity and bounded ahead. Gwen, wading through knee-high weeds, waved at Dog.

"You should ought to call him back, if you don't want him snake bit. Specially round that old shed."

Micah took her advice. Dog wasn't happy staying closer, but he was also a cautious dog, knowing enough to listen to Micah.

The house had a long front porch of poured concrete, as was the foundation. Four large square posts, one at each end and two close to the center steps, held up the porch roof. The house had once been painted white, and the roof shingles had either been green, or moss turned them that color. Gwen kept looking around, watching for snakes, she told him. Micah decided it was wise. They stood on the porch where a row of windows bracketed the front door. Some of the glass was gone in a few of the panes. Micah took hold of the large metal doorknob and glanced at Gwen. She shrugged, and he turned the knob. The door was heavy with big metal hinges. It opened, but dragged on the interior floor. The living room stretched across the entire front of the house. At one end was a brick fireplace with long narrow windows on either side. A dirty yellowish linoleum covered the floor, and a lingering smell of ash, mold, rat droppings, and something chemical hung in the stale air. Gwen held her hand over her nose, while Dog stayed in the open front door.

Two doors exited from the living room. The one to the right led to a large kitchen that could also serve as a dining room. The back door went straight out to a set of steps. Micah closed the back door with its grimy square window in the top. The left-hand door from the living room entered a hallway with two bedrooms and a bathroom. Gwen grimaced, waved her hand in front of her face, and started for the front door.

"Me and Dog will wait out here," she declared.

When Micah had seen enough, he joined them on the front porch. The place was a wreck, in need of either blowing up, or burning to the ground. He doubted anything else could help it. But he hadn't expected Gramps' place to be much better. Micah shaded his eyes and looked to the far edge of the property where the stream ran along the edge of a hill. He could envision the field cleared, a garden spot, and the driveway graveled to the low water bridge. Maybe when he left, he'd take that turn at the 'Y' and come back this way. Find out where that road came out to the main highway. Dog whined, and Gwen put the basket back over her arm.

"We'd best be going on back. Be near noon, and you'll want to rest up before getting on."

Micah nodded and followed her back to where they'd nailed the signs. The pathway back didn't seem that steep, and it would be an even easier climb with a cleared trail. When they came down the side of the hill and joined the streamside, Gramps' house was in sight. As they passed the henhouse, the chickens were pecking at potato peelings and some greens Gwen had thrown to them. They went in the back door where Gwen left the basket and her straw hat. She went into the kitchen.

"You want some sweet tea? I can fix some lemonade if you'd rather."

Micah, passing through to the hallway, said tea was fine. In the bathroom, he washed his face and took a good look in the mirror. His cheeks were red, his eyes had deep, dark circles beneath them, and his jaw line was too sharp. The brown of his eyes looked muddy and was barely distinguishable from the white, and with the bloodshot condition and puffiness of the lids, he wondered how he could see. Ilene had been right...he didn't look well. Examining further, his collarbone made a high ridge under the white tee shirt, and when he ran a hand down his side, the ribs were like fence pickets. He was still tired from the walk, while an eighty-seven-year-old woman was in the kitchen making drinks. Jena would be disappointed. He knew exactly what she'd say. *Take care of yourself!* So far, he'd failed. It was hard to come out of the cloud of sorrow and grief; his body was proof of it. As he combed his hair, he vowed to do better.

When he entered the kitchen, Gwen had rolled up her long sleeves and was sitting at the table with a glass pitcher of tea. When he sat, she poured a tall glass for him. She watched as he drank some.

"Taste alright, does it?"

"Fine. Hits the spot. I was thirsty. That was quite a little hike."

"Well, it's not bad once you get used to it."

"That place is certainly run down. Where are the owners? How can someone abandon property that way?"

"There's reason for everything."

"Did you have a reason for taking me there? Was it to show me how this place might have looked with no one living here?"

Gwen raised her eyebrows. "Why, that place has set for ten years. This one would have been only half as bad, since Albert's been gone just five years!"

Micah caught the sparkle in her eyes and the twitch of her lips. She was teasing him; it was Gwen's way of joking. Still, as she had said 'five years,' a faint shadow darkened the bright blue eyes. When, oh when, would he feel other people's loss as deeply as his own? He clearly needed to rebuild his emotions as well as his body. Maybe he could find a health spa, check in, and let them help him get back into shape. He and the house over the ridge were a pair. He'd been abandoned, too, and he'd let himself slip into ruin.

Gwen poured another glass of tea.

"Yes sir, that place was nice a long time ago. Too bad what's happened to it."

"What did happen?"

"The old man died. A few years later, the wife went into an old folks' home, but her sister took her out. They live in town. Neither of them has got the strength to mess with the property."

"Why don't they sell it?"

"Reckon they tried. It got so run down nobody would even show it. Besides, they got mad at the real estate people and said it could just set there, for all of them!"

Micah finished his tea and took the glass to the sink where he stood staring out the kitchen window. He was tired. If he drove the rest of the day, he might be far enough from the disaster to find an empty motel room. Behind him at the table, Gwen gave a big sigh.

"I don't guess anyone will ever want that old place."

Micah turned around. "Everything sells sometime. The land is worth something."

Gwen narrowed her eyes. "What do *you* think its worth?"

"I don't know. Why would I even care?"

"Well, I swear. This place is too fixed up and that one too torn up. I doubt you'd find any place pleasing."

"Are you thinking I should buy it?"

Gwen smiled. "Why not? I know that old lady. She won't deal with real estate people, but she'd sell to a person. It'd be a job, but once it was put back in shape, that's a good place!"

"I'd have to think about it."

Micah rolled the idea around. He'd had the same thought when he first saw the house, but he didn't need two places. However, from the looks of Gwen, that wouldn't be a problem for many years. As he thought, Gwen studied him.

"The bank would probably take this place for collateral, and make decent terms on a loan. Sara Martin wouldn't ask much for it. I'd talk to her."

Micah tried to decide. He didn't want to kick Gwen out, and he couldn't live here with nothing to do. Gwen would end up taking care of him! He needed work. He had to build something to find a purpose even if it were only repairing an old house. Years from now, if he ended up with both houses, he'd sell one. Probably the one over the ridge.

"You could live here until the new place was fixed up. I'd pack a lunch to carry over there every day. I imagine Trevor would visit you once in a while. He likes building things. Sides that, people round here'd be grateful to have that eyesore repaired! How about it?"

"I don't know."

"If it's money, I know the bank would make a loan. Say! You aren't wanted by the law anyplace are you?"

"No, Gwen. No, I'm not running from the authorities."

"Well, that's a relief. Not that I thought Albert's grandson would, but things do happen. Sometimes not the person's fault."

Micah went to the front porch and let Dog inside. He sat on the porch swing and Dog found a place on the nearby rag rug. The yard was bright in the midday sun...the two big trees either side of the house made pools of deep shade, and at the end of the drive a mail truck made the circle, left mail in the box, and drove away. Micah didn't need a loan. He'd pay any reasonable price. Although, that much cash might arouse Gwen's suspicions. He supposed that one day he'd have to tell his story. However, when he did, he wanted to do it from a healthier position. The wound would heal better if he tended it alone. When he was strong, ready to face people's pity, he'd tell why he'd returned to Falls Creek. He'd made it across the country and over the big river, and found things here not as he had expected, but maybe they were better. He stood and went inside.

"Gwen, can you call that lady and see if she's interested in selling?"

Gwen came to the dining room door, a dishtowel in her hands.

"I surely can. They'll be home. They never go anyplace. We'll get cleaned up and go into town. I'll call and tell her we're coming."

"Could it be she's expecting us?"

Gwen opened her mouth as if she were shocked.

"What a thing to say. Just 'cause I happen to know how glad she'll be to be rid...well, never mind. Let's get going."

Micah wondered what he'd stumbled into, but he'd not made a deal yet. There'd be no closing on any property without inspections and titles searches. He'd hire a good agent to go over everything, and he'd pay a commission for the service. Jerry Meyers might come in handy, and Micah already knew to watch him. Meyers might shave corners, but he couldn't get away with much, if everyone knew. The rundown property was a challenge, maybe one too big, but he had to stop running. He'd set a plan to come here. If he left when there was a way to stay, he truly would be afloat. It could take several years to rebuild the house, doing most of it alone. He'd seen a well, but it certainly needed repair. Maybe he'd call a company and drill a new one. He went back to his bedroom to change the big boots and dust off his pants and shirt. He combed his hair, trying to look like a respectable buyer.

When Gwen met him on the front porch, she was wearing clean slacks and a blue shirt, her purse over her arm. Micah left Dog on the front porch, and hoped the pickup seat wasn't too dirty for Gwen. When they reached the truck, Micah dusted the seat and made apologies for its condition.

"I've seen worse," Gwen said as she laughed.

Micah drove around the circle and onto the road, the pickup bouncing over the ruts. Gwen held her purse in her lap and was too quiet. Micah glanced at her.

"What are you thinking?"

"You haven't mentioned going to see Albert's resting place. Why would that be?"

Micah cleared his throat and still the lump didn't move.

"I meant to, before I leave. If I leave."

"And if you stay?"

"Yes, of course. I do intend to visit the gravesite."

It was hard to say Gramps' grave. There'd be something too final when standing before a plot of ground with a gravestone declaring his grandfather was dead. Micah's eyes burned. They were in poor condition to start with, tears made his vision worse. Gwen tapped the toes of her sandals on the floorboard, and looked out the side window.

"Just past that fork in the road, next turn goes by Mt. Carmel. The church has been there for years. Trevor and Ilene go to the Methodist in town, but we went to Mt. Carmel until Albert was gone. I gave up on driving after that. Nora comes by to carry me out there once in a while." Gwen continued looking out the side window.

"Are you saying you'd like to stop by there now?"

"If it wasn't too much out of the way. Sara and her sister will be having lunch about now."

"What time did you tell them we'd be there?"

Gwen turned to smile at him. "Oh, close on to two, maybe?"

If Gwen had decided to move in with Albert all those years ago, Micah wondered if Albert had had much to say about it.

"How far is the turnoff to the cemetery?"

"Not much farther."

Micah followed instructions and shortly they reached the church. It was larger than Micah had expected. The original church formed the center of a more modern building. The white frame chapel, with a tower topped by a cross, stood on a slight rise. In the middle of the curved driveway was a neatly mowed lawn with a flowerbed in full bloom. Long wings extended to either side of the chapel, more than doubling the size of the church. Gwen pointed to a graveled area used for parking. He parked, helped Gwen step to the ground, and followed her around the church to the back area. The church, the parking, and the front lawn were on a level section, the graveyard behind occupied a gentle slope rimmed by tall trees. Gwen passed by the first five rows before pointing to a spot near the trees.

"Right back there. See the stone, the taller one with the point?"

Micah followed her, his heart beating a bit faster, and not from the short walk. They reached the site and Gwen bent down to remove some dead flowers from a vase at the base of the stone. She shook her head.

"I meant to keep these fresher, but everyone's been pretty busy."

Micah stood staring at the gravestone. It was a good five feet tall, a foot and a half square, with a pyramidal top. He couldn't imagine how heavy the granite monument might be. He turned to Gwen.

"Did you pick this out?"

"No. Albert did. We had it all settled when we knew how bad off he was. He said he wanted something pointing up to heaven, sort of show the direction he'd taken." Gwen stopped because of her laughter.

Micah couldn't find humor in picking out your own gravestone, and he was sure the couple hundred dollars he'd sent didn't come close to paying for this one. He'd thought he knew Gramps, but listening to Gwen talk of him, it seemed he didn't. Micah knew a grandfather who loved and cared for a little boy. It seemed he knew nothing of a young man, widowed at forty-five, left alone to raise a son. For an instant Micah thought, *at least he had a son left*. Instantly, the memory of an old man of eighty taking on the burden of burying a son and daughter-in-law under painful conditions, made Micah cringe with shame. His grandfather had done much for him, while he had done nothing in return; he took the love for granted. Gwen was patting his back.

"Albert knew you loved him. Children grow up and get busy with their own lives."

Micah realized he must have been voicing his thoughts. He wiped at his eyes.

"I shouldn't have left him to bury my parents. I could have gotten leave. Gramps never talked about Grandma."

Gwen nodded. "That's 'cause it hurt him. I doubt he ever forgot his Marylee. Come, look over here." Gwen pointed to a flat stone a few feet away. "He was always going to get an upright marker for her, just never got to it. There wasn't money for more when she died. Medical bills and all just made things worse."

The flat marker was large, shaped like a natural slab of rock, but smooth and inscribed with her name and dates, with a big dogwood blossom carved in one corner. Albert had never taken Micah to see his grandmother's grave.

"He should have brought me here. He should have told me of his sorrow."

"Albert wouldn't have wanted to burden a child. If grown children don't feel enough love to do for the old ones, well, shame on them. Some I've known grudgingly do their duty, but that's just a misery for both. For my part, anyone don't enjoy my company, they don't need come around."

Gwen wandered away. As she stopped at various gravesites, she pointed and called to Micah.

"My Henry is buried over yonder. There's a space for me beside him."

He watched as Gwen made her way to her husband's grave. A whole community of the dead rested on the sunny slope. A sharp pain shot through Micah's chest. It broke a hard glass globe of sorrow and regret. Sorrow for all he'd lost, loved ones and opportunities. Regret for lacking understanding and willingness to do more. There were things he wished he'd done, and things he was sorry he had done. Gwen and Gramps had shared their sorrows; maybe grief should not be private. He was on one knee beside his grandfather's grave when Gwen returned. He quickly wiped the tears and stood. Gwen motioned him toward the parking lot.

"Come on, we better get to Sara's before she has time to decide on a high price for that old place." Gwen spoke over her shoulder as she trudged along. "Let it set there for ages, someone comes along willing to even consider it, and she'll start getting big ideas!"

Micah hurried to open the pickup's door and help Gwen inside. Gravel crunched beneath the tires as he drove out of the parking lot. They were quickly to the turnoff, and back on the highway to town. Micah had no idea what Sara Martin might ask for the property. He wondered what he'd do if they couldn't reach an agreement. The idea of staying in the area was more appealing than traveling on with no place in mind. The image of Gramps' grave and thinking of the life he'd lived sobered Micah. His grandfather hadn't complained, and he'd never asked Micah for anything. Gwen's life had handed her a few hard knocks. Still, she had one child that had stayed close. Nora, along with Trevor and his family, seemed to care a great deal for her. Micah wondered if they all knew how blessed they were, but remembering Trevor's disability and the way he handled it, they probably did know. Maybe sharing made the load lighter. Gwen folded her hands in her lap.

"One day at a time," she said.

Micah looked at her. "What are you talking about?"

"How to live. Don't matter what happened yesterday, we got to face today. Can't change the past, just have to make the best of today."

"Yes, but what happened yesterday affects today!"

"Sure it does." Gwen nodded. "I don't know why you came back here, it don't matter. What's done from this day on does."

When they reached the checkpoint, Gwen waved at one of the men. He smiled and waved back. They passed through quickly. Gwen directed Micah to the house where Sara Martin lived. The elderly sisters were spry enough and evidently enjoyed haggling. It took two glasses of lemonade and half a plate of sugar cookies before Sara settled on a firm price. Micah thought they should make the sale legal before Sara changed her mind. However, Gwen assured him she would not.

"She's tickled to death to unload that place!"

The sisters followed Micah and Gwen to the courthouse in their old white Lincoln. Gwen arranged for the local real estate broker to meet them. When earnest money was paid, and a contract signed,

Gwen and Micah drove home. All ten miles back to the house, Micah questioned the purchase, but couldn't find any problem with it. Everyone had to be somewhere, and this place seemed good as any. One thing tugged at him: Jena and Jordan, their graves were too far away. It had been his decision to leave, run as far as possible. That was yesterday's decision; he'd need to live with it. How to live tomorrow was today's decision.

When Micah parked near the henhouse and got out of the pickup, he heard Dog barking. Gwen climbed out and started to the house. Micah ran ahead, hoping nothing was wrong. He was relieved to find Dog only wanted out, yet when Micah opened the door, Dog stayed at his side, leaning against his leg and whining. Micah stooped down and hugged him. He could feel the quiver in Dog's body.

"Hey, buddy. Take it easy. I'm not leaving you. We're going to live here. You'll like it."

Dog licked Micah's face, and with his confidence restored and eager to be outside, he ran to the door. There were a million odors to smell and thousands of bugs to chase, but Dog stopped at the foot of the steps and looked back at Micah. When Micah waved him away, Dog took off. Dog was the companion Micah never knew he needed and now didn't want to do without. Maybe if he gave Gwen and her family a chance, they'd be the same.

Gwen crossed the porch to sit on the swing. Leaning back, she drew a deep breath and sighed, a satisfied look on her face. Micah supposed the day had gone just as she had planned. After a bit, she leaned forward and pointed toward Micah's pickup.

"Albert used the barn for a garage. Least it kept his old truck out of the weather, but I swear that pickup out yonder looks a sight older than his was. How'd you come to have such an old piece of transportation?"

Micah sat in the rocking chair on the other side of the porch and told Gwen about Taylor's red Ford pickup, the dry barren cemetery in the west, and he told her about the sandstorm in the desert that caused the terrible wrecks. A soft warm breeze drifted across the porch as Micah stared into the distance, lost in the telling of his story.

Even now, he couldn't believe what he'd done to reclaim the stolen pickup. Although, memory of the tremors in Oklahoma and thinking he'd hit something in the road remained vivid. Gwen sat entranced, and when he would pause, she urged him on. His experiences during the earthquakes took a long while to tell. He spoke of Rita and the rest of the Coopers, and the many detours before finding a way across the river. As Micah shared with Gwen, a peace settled over him. He had reached his goal; it was time to rest. It was late afternoon...shadows of the trees beside the house were stretching far to the east, when Micah finally told Gwen why he had left California.

Meet H. L. Chandler

This author writes in several genre: thrillers, paranormal, adventure, and mysteries. H. L. Chandler has also written stories for children. She has lived across the U.S. and for a short time in Canada.

Other Works From The Pen Of H. L. Chandler

The Keepers - A story of a family torn apart by an insidious force intent on using each member for its own evil purpose.

Evil Intent - Gary married for money. When the money ran out, it was time to collect Janet's life insurance. Yet, *something* at the mountain cabin where Janet takes refuge has other plans.

Lost in Fear –In childhood, Julie Taylor survived a family massacre. As an educated young woman, she strives to live a normal life. She might succeed if it were not for the evil which plagues her.

Song of the Sparrow - Living with a cruel stepfather, Lugene and Harley grow up fast. But not fast enough to escape the dangers that face them as runaway teens in New Orleans.

Legion's Land – In a post holocaustic world, Nora lived a comfortable life. She never questioned the system until it threatened her children. How far will she go to save them?

Hoodoo Murder – A murder and kidnapping put Private Investigator Ladonna Rose in the middle of a case that merges with a tragedy from her past.

Mystery at Sunset Ridge – Is the missing real estate developer a murderer, or a victim? When P. I. Billie Ross gets too close to an answer, she disappears as well.

Murder Bayou – Was Ross Delroque worth more dead than alive? Or was he about to report a toxic waste dump? To arrive at the truth, P.I. Ladonna Rose searches for answers among his sadly dysfunctional family.

Sure and Certain Shadows – Ingrid grew up on rough Kansas City streets, proud to have survived. Thrown into an alien world, she fights to stay alive and return to her own planet.

Letter to Our Readers

Enjoy this book?

You can make a difference

As an independent publisher, Wings ePress, Inc. does not have the financial clout of the large New York Publishers. We can't afford large magazine spreads or subway posters to tell people about our quality books.

But, we do have something much more effective and powerful than ads. We have a large base of loyal readers.

Honest Reviews help bring the attention of new readers to our books.

If you enjoyed this book, we would appreciate it if you would spend a few minutes posting a review on the site where you purchased this book or on the Wings ePress, Inc. webpages at:

https://wingsepress.com/

Thank You

Visit Our Website

For The Full Inventory
Of Quality Books:

Wings ePress.Inc
https://wingsepress.com/

Quality trade paperbacks and downloads
in multiple formats,
in genres ranging from light romantic comedy
to general fiction and horror.
Wings has something for every reader's taste.
Visit the website, then bookmark it.
We add new titles each month!

Wings ePress Inc.
3000 N. Rock Road
Newton, KS 67114

www.ingramcontent.com/pod-product-compliance
Lightning Source LLC
Chambersburg PA
CBHW070621100726